A
Simple Winter

BALLANTINE BOOKS

NEW YORK

A *Simple Winter*

A SEASONS OF
LANCASTER NOVEL

Rosalind Lauer

C

Copyright © 2011 by Rosalind Lauer
Excerpt from *A Simple Spring* by Rosalind Lauer
copyright © 2011 by Rosalind Lauer

Published in the United States by Ballantine Books,
an imprint of The Random House Publishing Group,
a division of Random House, Inc., New York.

BALLANTINE and colophon are registered
trademarks of Random House, Inc.

This book contains an excerpt of the forthcoming title *A Simple Spring*
by Rosalind Lauer. The excerpt has been set for this edition only and
may not reflect final content of the forthcoming book.

All scripture taken from *The Zondervan KJV Study Bible*.
Copyright © 2002 by Zondervan. Used by permission
of Zondervan Publishing House.

Library of Congress Cataloging-in-Publication Data
Lauer, Rosalind.
A simple winter: a seasons of Lancaster novel / Rosalind Lauer. —
p. cm. — (Seasons of Lancaster ; 1)
ISBN 978-0-345-52671-7 (pbk.) — ISBN 978-0-345-52672-4 (eBook)
1. Amish—Fiction. 2. Women journalists—Fiction. 3. Lancaster County
(Pa.)—Fiction. I. Title.
PS3612.A94276S56 2011
813'.6—dc23
2011028875

Printed in the United States of America on acid-free paper

www.ballantinebooks.com

2   4   6   8   9   7   5   3   1

First Edition

Book design and title page photo by Karin Batten

For my Aunt Roz,
the first Rosalind Lauer,
who taught me how to turn lemons into lemonade

A
Simple Winter

February

All the seats were taken.

Remy McCallister held on to the straps of her backpack and inched through the train, wobbling around boots and elbows protruding in the aisle. Her father had told her to hop on a plane, but she preferred to keep her feet on the ground and maintain a low profile.

Slithering home after four and a half years of failure.

Weighed down by her heavy backpack, she did a monster walk to the end of the aisle and paused to hold on as the train gathered speed. In all her dreams and plans for the future, Remy had never considered returning to Philadelphia to live with her father. College had seemed so promising when she'd checked in to her dorm for freshman year, and for a while she had succeeded in school, juggling exams and papers and jogs through Washington Square Park.

Granted, she wasn't one of the university's top scholars, but she was on a steady track toward graduation. Until the seizures.

Disappointment was a sour taste in her throat as she thought of how her body had betrayed her. It wasn't fair. It wasn't her fault.

It just was.

Clamping her lips together, she popped the connecting door open and marched into the next car, another full house. Halfway through the car she noticed an empty window seat, a spot beside a guy around her age who seemed to be hiding beneath a beanie and a flannel shirt.

"That seat taken?" She nodded toward the window seat.

He'd been zoning out, but her question snapped him back to reality. He stood up and stepped into the aisle. "It's yours." He didn't smile, but his body language was friendly enough. "Let me help you with that."

"Thanks," Remy said as she eased off her overstuffed backpack, grateful for his help hoisting it into the overhead bin.

"You carry this around?" he asked. "Is it loaded with bricks?"

"That's what happens when you have to pack your life into one backpack." She'd spent the last few days stuffing the rest of her stuff in boxes that would be shipped home. Well . . . shipped back to Philadelphia. It was Herb's home, not hers.

She slid into the seat with her newspaper and iPod, figuring that between the two, she could create a look of preoccupation that would give off the signal that she wanted to be left alone. A chance to mull over her failure to launch.

He sat down beside her with liquid grace and an aura heavy with thought.

She suspected he had an interesting story. Fumbling with the earbuds of her iPod, Remy had second thoughts about trying to ward off conversation.

"Mind if I have a look at your paper?" he asked.

"It's the *Post*." She had frequented a newsstand in the Village that carried the Philadelphia newspaper, one jewel in the crown of her father's media holdings.

"Good. I'm looking for news from the Philadelphia area."

"Knock yourself out." She caught a look at him as she handed it over. Strong jaw, a little scruffy on the shave issue, and bold brown eyes so intense they could burn a hole in your heart. Rock star handsome.

With her tunes plugged in, Remy settled back against the window and slid her gaze back to him. He was staring at the front page of her newspaper, just staring. On closer inspection, he looked a little sick, his lips dry, his eyes tinged red. Remy patted the pockets of her ski jacket, then reached in the left one for two snack bars.

"Want one?" she offered.

Weariness shadowed his face as he began to shake his head in refusal, then paused. "Nancy's Nutty Muesli Bars?"

"They're really delicious." She handed him one.

"They are. Nancy is a friend. An old family friend." He tore open the wrapper and bit into the bar. "So why are you headed to Philadelphia? If you don't mind my asking."

"My father is there. I went to college in New York, and I'd stay there if I could." She didn't want to go into detail about how she had watched her friends graduate and move on, while she was left to struggle with classes that she had considered cake courses two years ago. Herb's voice blared in her head: *I'm not paying for the six-year plan. If you can't make the grade, you're done.* Trying to shut down the noise in her head, she said, "I'm finished with school. Until I can make other plans, I'm stuck in Philly."

"Is it that bad?"

"The city is fine. My father is the problem. Herb is a control freak. If he has his way, he'll turn me into an automated doll that does his bidding twenty-four/seven."

"You call your father Herb . . . ?"

"Everyone does. He's not very paternal." She stopped herself, not wanting to reveal too much about her father. Over the years, she'd seen the way people's expressions had changed when they learned she was Herb McCallister's daughter: the hollow smiles, the hungry glaze in the eyes, looking as if Remy could lead them to a pot of gold.

"So it's independence you want," he said, tucking the snack bar wrapper into the pocket of the seat back in front of him. Remy did the same.

"Well, yeah," Remy said, though that wasn't entirely true.

What did she want?

She thought of her college roommates, who were off pursuing careers and relationships. These days she got only a few rushed emails from Dakota Ferris, who was attending grad school in Boston. At least once a week she talked with Kiara, who had moved to Chicago to be near her boyfriend, Jayson. Remy knew they'd be announcing a wedding soon. Although Remy had never articulated it before, the relationship thing seemed like the answer to everything else. To fall in love, to connect with a person she could laugh with and talk with and work with . . . someone to build a home with . . .

Her heart ached at the realization that love was really what she wanted out of life. A boyfriend. A soul mate. And love was not in sight right now. She hadn't even dated in months.

"And you don't want to be dependent on your father," he said, bringing her back to the conversation. "Is that why you don't want to return to Philadelphia?"

"Pretty much. But Herb is offering one thing I can't afford to turn down right now: a job." The position at the *Post* was a great opportunity, even if it did put her under Herb's thumb for a while.

"Where I come from, family is the thing that holds us up. Our foundation," he said.

He made it sound so much better than the reality. "I've never seen it work that way."

"No?" He cocked his head, his dark eyes penetrating. "Wasn't your father your greatest teacher?"

She winced. "Not really." She glanced away, breaking the spell of his dark eyes. "But I've had some great teachers. My mom taught me the most, but she died when I was little. I've met some awesome teachers in school. Maybe that's why it's so upsetting to leave college. I felt like I was getting somewhere. In the process of metamorphosis. You know, a squishy caterpillar about to transform to a butterfly? Some good things were happening, but then . . . I just started getting these seizures." It wasn't something she normally told people about, but he seemed genuinely interested. "The first one was during finals week, last winter. My friends were a big help, but they graduated in the spring. I thought, with the medication I'm on, I'd be able to finish this spring, but . . . that's not going to happen now."

"Because of your father?"

She pressed her palms to her cheeks, admitting defeat. "Yeah, Herb pulled the plug. He doesn't think I can manage my life." And maybe she couldn't. She'd had a seizure two weeks ago . . . thank God she'd made it to the couch before she went out. "And now I'm headed to Philly. Going backwards."

"You want to stay away longer," he said. "And I should have returned years ago."

"You think so?" She turned to him, curious about his story. "What's your name, anyway?"

"Adam." He removed the cap and raked back thick, dark hair. "Adam King."

Remy tried not to stare, though Adam was getting better look-ing by the minute. "I'm Remy McCallister," she said, holding for a second to see if he responded to the McCallister name. When nothing seemed to register, she let out her breath and plunged ahead. "So anyway, I'm headed home to the cranky father who wants to run my life. And you? Sounds like you've stayed away too long."

He stared at the newspaper, his lips twisting. "I need to get home."

"So you live in Philly?"

"West of the city. Lancaster County. I have been living in Provi-dence." He leaned back, staring off in the distance. "But not any-more."

Remy sensed his resistance, so she took a lighter tack. "Dude . . . toss me some details," she teased.

"Maybe later." He looked down the aisle, stood up. "I'm going to the snack car. Want something?"

As she shook her head, Adam crumpled up the empty wrappers from the seat backs in front of them and headed down the aisle.

Definitely avoiding the topic. Remy wondered at the forces driving Adam's turmoil. Or maybe he was just one of those natu-rally intense guys. She supposed everyone had a personal burden to bear. Every person on this train was dragging something around, the proverbial baggage. It was kind of shallow to think that her issues were any worse than anyone else's. She leaned against the window and closed her eyes. Within minutes the rocking motion of the train lulled her to sleep.

Somewhere at the edge of her consciousness she felt his return: his weight in the seat beside her, his warmth. When Remy shifted and opened her eyes, Adam sat beside her, staring at the front page of her newspaper once again.

There was something warm and intimate about this proximity. Another inch and she would be leaning on his shoulder, nuzzling up to the soft, warm flannel of his shirt. She studied him through the twilight slits of her eyes. This was a thoughtful guy, a man with a profound, heavy aura. Was it caused by some sort of pain? A broken heart, maybe? She was dying to know if he had a girlfriend.

No ring on his finger.

Could she get his email or phone number without making a complete jerk of herself?

He turned to her.

Caught, she hugged her arms close and yawned.

"I brought you hot chocolate." He touched one of the paper cups on the tray in front of him and nodded. "Still warm. It can't pay back the Nancy's bar you gave me, but I tried."

"That's awfully nice of you. Thanks." In a world of fancy latte drinks, Remy couldn't remember the last time she'd had a cup of cocoa. Warmth soaked through her palms as she took a sip. "And you're still glued to the front page of the newspaper."

His lips mashed together as he folded the newspaper. "Caught me."

"So you owe me a story," Remy said, daring to push the issue. "You never did tell me what brings you back home to Philadelphia."

"It's my family. They need me now."

"Need you, like . . . for a weekend or a hundred years?"

"For good. I'm heading home to run the family farm and take care of my younger siblings." He looked away, his jaw clenched. "My parents died this week."

Remy felt her mouth drop open. That explained a lot. "Oh, Adam, I am so sorry." Instinctively she squeezed his arm, solid bone and muscle beneath the flannel of his shirt. Ordinarily it would have been taboo to touch a stranger, but she sensed that they had already moved past the bounds of etiquette to a place where two people could reach out to each other. "I had no idea."

The emotion in his dark eyes was hard to decipher as he nodded.

"What happened? I mean, if you don't mind me asking."

He rubbed his jaw, his eyes flashing on a point in the distance. "I'm not really sure. The details are not clear yet. But the important thing is to move ahead and take care of the little ones. I'm the oldest of eleven."

"Eleven kids? Wow." She swallowed back a swell of emotion, imagining the pain of eleven children who had lost their parents. Remy had been just seven when her mother died, and some days she still felt a tug of loss. "Your brothers and sisters must really need you now. Do you have any other family close by?"

He nodded. "Lots of aunts and uncles and cousins. The Amish stay close to their families."

Remy tilted her head, trying not to stare at him as images of horse and buggy, broad-brimmed hats, and Pennsylvania Dutch pretzels swam through her mind. "Not to perpetuate a stereotype, but you don't look Amish."

"I've been away for years." He rubbed his chin. "But I'll be shaving this off when I get home. I'll be back to my black pants and suspenders."

"Were you away for that trial period?" Growing up in Philly, Remy knew some of the customs from nearby Lancaster County. "When young people are allowed to check out the rest of the world?"

"*Rumspringa,* yes. But that's over now. I'm sorry I didn't end it much sooner. I was planning to return earlier, but I made a business. I build furniture from wood."

"Handmade furniture . . ." She nodded. "People must have loved that."

"It was successful. But I got stuck in my own ... *Hochmut*. Pride, you call it."

"Caught in your own success," she said.

"Like a fish on a hook." He rubbed his jaw, his face pale with sadness. "It took this terrible thing to cut me loose."

"But you're so honest about it all," Remy said. "That's an unusual quality these days."

He shook his head. "I know no other way to be."

"What were your parents like?" Remy asked. In her experience, talking was the thing that helped you work through the bad times.

They talked for the rest of the trip, details about their parents spilling forth as the train sped through the night. Occasionally the conversation lapsed into a comfortable silence, a resting place they both respected before illuminating other anecdotes from the past. Adam painted a picture of his father, Levi, as a man of peace, an easygoing farmer who plowed his fields to the symphony of birdsong, a man who maintained his farm as a sanctuary for all living things. He recalled his mother, Esther, as a steady beacon of faith and joy within their home, an apt teacher and a good listener who never seemed to tire of maintaining a home for her family. And his brothers and sisters! Remy couldn't keep track of them all, though Adam pulled out some anecdotes worthy of a TV sitcom.

Adam's reveries prompted Remy to share some pieces of her own past, snippets of her mother that seemed too thin and hard to catch, like ribbons in the wind. Her mom had loved games, everything from duck-duck-goose to board games. And bedtime stories. And lullabies about barges floating on water or stars shining in the sky. And baking ... Remy recalled trays of buttery shortbread and racks of homemade cookies cooling on the kitchen counter. Peanut butter and chocolate chip and cinnamon snickerdoodles. Sometimes when Remy passed a bakery on the street, she closed her eyes and reached for a snippet from the past.

When there was a silent pause, Remy pursued the conversation, posing other questions about Adam's parents. In talking, Adam could recall the good times and lay his burdens down. Their quiet words still burned with genuine intensity when the conductor came down the aisle to announce the train's arrival in Philadelphia.

"We're here," she said, "and I feel like I just sat down. I wish we could continue our conversation." Passengers filled the aisles, pulling down bags and pressing toward the exits. They had to get moving.

"It was good to talk." He nodded, then rose.

Before Remy was even out of her seat, Adam had her backpack down and ready for her to loop the straps over her shoulders.

"Thanks." She turned around and allowed herself a blatant study of his face now, eyes smoky as obsidian, a broad brow and high cheekbones. "Adam, I'm so sorry about your parents. I wish there was something I could say. . . ."

"You've already said a lot." A crooked smile frayed his lips, defying the sadness burning in his eyes, and she wanted to cry and laugh at his jab at humor in the midst of pain.

He hitched his own duffel bag over his shoulder. "I'm grateful to you, Remy. You've been very kind," he told her as he made room for her in the crowded aisle.

She stepped into the space beside him, wanting to say so much, but unable to find the right words.

"Maybe Philadelphia won't be so bad for you this time, yes?"

"Oh, that . . ." She waved it off as insignificant compared to what Adam would be facing. "It'll be fine. You take care." She touched the flannel of his sleeve again, but she could tell he was already thinking ahead, already gone. Biting her lips together, she withdrew her hand from his warmth and retreated to the loneliness of her solitary world once again.

Adam insisted that she go first, and though she appreciated his old-world manners she missed the chance to watch him for one last moment and soak up his steely grace, his quiet strength.

The train clamped to a stop and Remy followed the line, traipsing out the door onto the platform. Joining the queue for the escalator she noticed a flash of blue flannel scaling the stairs two at a time, quick and agile.

Watching him, she wondered at the unrealized heroes in the world, people who sacrificed everything for their families.

The next step was connecting with Herb. He had promised her a ride, and after hearing of Adam's loss, Remy felt a tug of anticipation over seeing her father. She made her way through the station, following signs for the main exit. Beyond the taxi stand a few cars idled, drivers waiting. She searched for Herb's Mercedes . . . and was disappointed.

Strolling past the cars, she came upon a black limo with a sign stuck in the window. REMY McCALLISTER.

Thanks, Herb. At least he had remembered to send someone.

The driver jumped out, stowed her pack, and they were on their way.

The leather of the seat was buttery smooth under Remy's fingers as she leaned back and faced the tinted window. People outside the terminal noticed as the limo passed. Heads turned, eyes narrowed. Stung by the attention, Remy wanted to lower the glass and wave them off, telling them that this was not the posh life they were imagining, that good fortune could fill a bank but not a heart.

Once they hit the highway Remy unfolded her newspaper and checked the headlines. When her eyes lit on the story, she felt a stab of raw sympathy for Adam.

Roadside Killing of Amish Man, Wife

Oh, no. This was the story he'd been staring at during their train
ride. Could it be *his* story . . . his parents?

The article said that the couple had been found shot, their
buggy pulled off to the side of a country road in Lancaster County.
Their eight-year-old son was found in the buggy, unharmed. The
horse, also not injured, had remained at the roadside until one of
the couple's sons had come upon the scene after his parents had
not arrived home for dinner. The couple, Levi and Esther King,
had eleven kids ranging in age from nine months to twenty-three.

Nine months old? Adam would be taking care of a little baby . . .
as well as nine others. And a farm. She couldn't begin to imagine
the responsibility he would be shouldering, not to mention the
heartache of having lost his parents so suddenly and violently.

Dusk had fallen over the city, and the lights of shops were a blur
as Remy dashed away the tears in her eyes. She wished she could
do something to help Adam and his family. She remembered the
fruit baskets and flowers that had arrived when her mother died. At
first there had been a swirl of excitement when the doorbell rang
and a fragrant burst of white blossoms was ushered in the door. But
the smooth white petals browned and dried, their fragrance growing cloyingly sweet.

Besides, she didn't think flowers were part of the protocol for an
Amish funeral. But what could she do to help?

She wasn't sure about God, and she'd never been a churchgoer.
But she thought it couldn't hurt to say a small prayer for Adam and
his family. She rolled down the window to the rush of blustery cold.

"God . . . if you're out there, please help this family."

Her words traveled on the wind, and she imagined the prayer
circling the city's glimmering skyline before rising to the navy blue
night sky.

Rolling up the window, she resolved to make the most of her
own situation. Which meant trying to connect with Herb. Granted,

he was mercurial and boisterous, controlling and demanding, but he was the only father she would ever have. She had happily kept her distance these past few years, remembering how Herb tried to control her when she was within reach. Summer internships at the paper had been nightmarish, with Herb expecting her to prove herself as the "crowned heir to the McCallister fortune," and editors sticking her with menial tasks that had required her to work into the late night hours.

Remy would need to show everyone that she had grown some backbone and was able to strike a balance. She would have to make it clear to Herb that she would not play prima donna. That she wanted to learn the workings of a successful newspaper. That she wanted to learn how to spend ten minutes in the same room with her father without gritting her teeth.

It was time to meet Herb halfway. And maybe, with persistence and patience, she would have a chance to get to know her father.

PART ONE

Look Homeward

One generation passeth away,
And another generation cometh:
But the earth abideth forever.

—ECCLESIASTES 1:4

ONE

January, eleven months later

Adam King hoisted the wooden bench from the wagon and lowered it to his younger brother's reach. "Go on and grab the end there, Simon. Think we can carry this in together?"

"Ya." Simon's face lit at the prospect of an adult task as he gripped the end of the bench. The boy's crooked smile shone like a break in the clouds.

At last, Simon was coming around. As Adam navigated into the living room of his uncle's house, which had been emptied of furniture for the benches, he considered the boy's recently renewed interest in family events. Nearly one year since the murders, and at last his brother was showing signs of progress.

Simon had been silent for months after the deaths of their parents, a tragedy that had hit him particularly hard as he'd been the only witness. Last summer when the boy finally started speaking, there'd been only basic words—yes, no, *denki*. Over time, Simon had volunteered more conversation, but the boy rarely mentioned the traumatic episode. When he did he seemed confused about details, saying that a bear was to blame. Sometimes it worried Adam, who felt sure that one day Simon's memories would overflow like a bucket of milk, and memories from that terrible night would spill forth. So far that had not been the case. So Adam contented himself with the occasional string of words from his kid brother, and the sure knowledge that Simon would be shadowing him when he wasn't off at school or doing other chores.

Inside the house the rugs had been pulled up from the floor of the large room, and from the gleaming wood floorboards and shiny windows it was evident that the women had been hard at work cleaning the space for tomorrow's preaching service. Come the morning, dozens of buggies would line the lane, along with men and women dressed in their Sunday garb for the service, which was held in members' homes or barns, weather permitting. Although this was not Adam's home, he and his siblings were happy to help his uncle and aunt, Nate and Betsy King. In the future, Adam hoped to hold a preaching service at his own house, but right now the preparation would bog down his sister Mary, who would be responsible for cleaning, cooking, and baking for more than a hundred members.

"This is the last of the benches from the wagon," Adam told Uncle Nate, who was supervising the setup.

"Right over here." Nate motioned Adam to a space near the windows, and they lined up the bench with the others, completing the last row of one section. "That should be enough seating for the women. Good work." Nate clapped Simon on the shoulder.

Simon straightened and brushed his hands together, such an adult gesture for a small boy.

"And look, you've been growing, ya?" Nate's eyes twinkled as he assessed the boy. "How old are you now?"

Simon steeled himself, his lips tensing as he pronounced the word: "Nine."

"So I thought." Nate's voice was gentle, as if he understood how difficult it was for Simon to participate in conversation. "Have you started going in with the boys on Sundays?"

"Not yet," Simon said, meeting his uncle's gaze. "Mamm wanted me to learn the *Loblied* first."

Adam touched his brother's shoulder, pleased that the boy had responded so well. "Mamm made us all learn the hymn before we could walk with the boys."

"Ah, a family tradition." Nate nodded.

In their congregation, going in with the boys was a rite of passage boys experienced after their ninth birthday. At Sunday worship services men and women sat on opposite sides of the room, and members entered in a specific order, with ministers first, married men next, followed by women with the little ones. Then boys and young men entered as a group, as did girls and young women. Age nine was the time when a boy got to leave his mamm's side and walk in with the group. It was considered a privilege for a boy like Simon to walk in with the boys—a rite of passage—though their mother had required that they first learn to recite the Loblied, a hymn sung in High German during every service.

"So . . ." Nate clapped his hands together. "You are learning the hymn?"

"Ya," Simon said solemnly.

"We've been practicing," Adam said. With Simon's reluctance to speak, it was hard to tell how much of the hymn the boy had learned.

"*Gut.* You keep working, Simon," Nate advised. "Practice until you hear the song in your heart, ya?"

Simon nodded, his shiny hair bobbing.

Nate lifted his bearded chin, his dark eyes scanning the room. "Our work here is done, though I can't say as much for the women in the kitchen. Last I heard, Betsy was making another chocolate cake."

"You can never have too much chocolate cake," Adam said.

"Speak for yourself." Nate patted his round belly, his ruddy face relaxed with a gentle smile. "Mary will probably be a while yet in the kitchen. Before you go, I have a problem in the barn I could use your help with. One of the doors is rotting, I think."

"Let's have a look," Adam said with a nod, noticing that Simon, too, was nodding with interest. *My shadow,* he thought as Uncle Nate uttered *"Kumm,"* and led the way out to the barn.

When Nate pointed out the wobbly door, Adam extracted his pocketknife and pressed it to the wood. The blade sank right in, like a knife in butter. "Dry rot."

Simon's eyes grew round with interest. "Can I try?"

"As long as you're careful." Adam handed him the knife, and both men watched as Simon pressed it easily into the soft wood.

"Ya, it's rotten," the boy agreed.

Adam tapped the door, then the strip of wood overhead. "The door is fine, but the frame must be changed. The hinges and hardware can probably be saved. If you want, I'll measure now and cut the wood in my shop."

"When you have time," Nate said, tipping his hat back as he watched Simon poke the wood once more. "You've got a list of chores as long as the day, and you're still a young man, Adam. I hear you've barely attended one singing since you returned to us. You must give these young women a fair chance to win you over, ya?"

The smile froze on Adam's face, his jaw aching with regret as he sensed where this conversation was heading. "I can handle the door repair, Nate. You don't need to worry about my social life."

"But what of the singings? Will you be attending tomorrow night?" He nodded over at the corner of the barn, where Adam's teenaged cousins cleaned the stalls. "Ben and Abe are in charge of preparation. You wouldn't want to disappoint them, ya?"

"Of course not," Adam agreed, nodding at his cousins, who seemed to be making a game of hockey with a cow-patty puck. At seventeen and nineteen, Ben and Abe were at the prime age for singings, casual youth events intended to give young people a chance to socialize with other Amish their age. *Their age.* If Adam attended tomorrow night, he would no doubt be the only person there in his mid-twenties. "But the singings . . . they're not for me, Uncle."

Nate's mouth puckered. "How else will you find a wife?"

It's hard to find something when you're not looking for it, Adam thought as he rubbed his clean-shaven jaw. He didn't want to be disrespectful to his uncle, who had kept their farm running for the past year. Hardy, genial Nate King was a gifted farmer who could turn a handful of soil into a bag of beans, seemingly in the blink of an eye. Whenever Adam had a question about the farm, Nate had the answers and explanations as to why potatoes were too labor-intensive to grow or when it was safe to put tomato plants in the ground. Nate's support was a blessing. But pressure like this . . . this Adam could live without.

"Was denkscht?" Nate prodded in the language used in conversation among Amish. "What are you thinking? Perhaps you already have someone in mind . . . a courtship I'm not aware of? I know, it's none of my business, but in some ways it is. If your father were alive, he would have had this talk with you long ago, ya?"

"Uncle Nate . . ." Adam paused when he glanced down and saw that his younger brother was hanging on their every word. "Simon, do you want to see if Ruthie is still out by the pond with the others? I'm sure you could borrow a pair of ice skates."

Simon shook his head. The boy was staying right here.

"Adam?" Nate prodded. "Are you trying to change the subject?"

"That would be great." When his uncle squinted critically, Adam added, "Just trying to be honest."

Nate's low chuckle was full of mirth. "I appreciate that, but I do worry about you, Adam. Gott will provide, but we must have our eyes open to see His gifts. What you're doing, trying to manage a family without a wife, it's like trying to plow your fields without a horse. Everything is one hundred times more difficult."

Adam grinned at his uncle's inadvertent comparison between wives and plow horses. *"Ich vershteh,"* Adam said. "I understand what you're saying. But right now, I'm not interested in going through courtship."

Besides the fact that he felt far too old to participate in courtship rituals involving girls as young as fourteen, courtship reminded Adam of his past pursuit of a girl outside the community, a relationship that had led him far from his family and faith. At the age of nineteen he had fallen for Jane, a college student he'd met in Philadelphia. He had followed her to her home in Providence, where things had fizzled between them in the first few months. But while working odd jobs he'd nurtured a skill for building furniture by hand under the guidance of a salty old artist who took a liking to him. Cap Sawicki had taught Adam how to design around the natural elements in the wood, allowing the grain or color or slight imperfections to stand out. The handmade furniture had brought in more than enough money to pay the bills, but the real satisfaction was in rubbing oil into the wood or making dovetailed joinery by hand.

Before his baptism last fall, Adam had tried to deal with his issues. He had made the commitment to live the Amish way here with his family, and he knew that the skills learned during his rumspringa amounted to a craft that might one day help support his family . . . if he ever found time to return to the wood shop. He could not undo those years away from home, but on more than one occasion he wanted to kick himself for leaving. His departure had brought his parents distress, and that was a wrong he would never have the chance to right.

A burden he would have to live with.

"Come to the singing tomorrow," Nate said.

Adam shook his head. "I'm too old for those gatherings."

"I hear your brother Jonah attends, and he is what? Only two years younger than you."

"I'm sure he'll attend," Adam replied, dodging the question. Even as kids, Adam and Jonah had kept company while knowing that God had made them from two very different molds. Adam was intrigued that his quiet brother seemed to enjoy the organized social events, but he didn't probe. Jonah was a private person.

"It looks like the women have finished," Uncle Nate said.

The three of them looked toward the kitchen door where women filed out, their arms laden with blankets and warming bricks. Adam's oldest sister, Mary, tipped her head toward her best friend, Annie Stoltzfus, and the two shared a laugh. Fourteen-year-old twins Leah and Susie, two dark bells bundled in winter coats, stood out beside their grandmother. Except for Sadie, who had stayed back at the house to mind the little ones, all the women of his family had pitched in with the baking, which was quite an undertaking when there would be more than a hundred mouths to feed after tomorrow's worship service.

"Thank you for your good help." Nate touched the brim of his hat and winked at Simon. "I'd best set to milking the cows."

Adam nodded good-bye to Nate, grateful to end this conversation with his uncle before Nate delved too deep into Adam's personal life. Ordinarily, the older generation left the younger ones to their own devices when it came to courtship, but there was nothing ordinary about Adam's situation, a single man left to lead his siblings after their parents' deaths.

He turned to Simon. "Go find Ruthie. Tell her it's time to go," Adam instructed, and the boy scurried off as Adam went to the back of the barn to fetch his horse.

In the steely gray light of dusk he led Thunder to the line of buggies parked in a row at the front of the house. The horse nickered as Adam hitched him up to the covered carriage, Dat's finest, with glass windows and nearly enough seats for the entire family.

"Think we'll be getting more snow?" The question came from behind Adam, and he turned to find his cousin Jacob checking his horse's harness. Jacob King was still in his rumspringa, and from the stereo speakers and spoiler installed in his buggy, Adam could see he was enjoying it.

"Not today," Adam said, "but it's only January. I'd say we're in for some more winter storms."

"I'm thinking of getting rubber tires for my buggy," Jacob said with a grin. "That would be good in the snow, ya?"

"Probably better than steel." Adam didn't mention the fact that sleighs were more functional in heavy snow. Rumspringa was the time for a boy to enjoy customizing his buggy.

Studying the row of buggies, he saw that Gabriel and Jonah had taken the smaller one home when they'd left an hour ago to start the afternoon milking. Eager to return and help with the chores, he climbed into his carriage, clicked his tongue, and eased Thunder toward the main house.

The King women approached the carriage, Susie and Leah first, followed by their grandmother.

"It's cold out here." Susie blew out a puff of air and jabbed at the small cloud with her finger. "I can see my breath."

Adam came around the carriage just in time to notice that her fingertips were red. "What's that on your hands, Susie?"

With a grin, she slipped her hands out from under her shawl, revealing red-tinged palms. "Beet juice," she said with a smile. "Did you know that's the secret ingredient in Aunt Betsy's chocolate cake?"

"A healthy ingredient," Adam said, "though we'll have to check and make sure it's on your diet." Susie suffered from glutaric acid-uria, an inherited metabolic condition that required a low-protein diet. Adam pretended to scowl over Susie's stained hands, though he couldn't keep it up. Susie's smile was quick to melt the sternest disposition.

"Oh, Aunt Betsy's chocolate cake is wonderful good and I've had it plenty of times," Susie said. "But beets! Imagine a vegetable in cake. It's no wonder she keeps it a secret."

"But not a secret anymore, ya?" There was a twinkle in Mammi's dark eyes as she proceeded toward the carriage. When she placed a hand on Adam's shoulder, he felt a swell of love for the grandmother who had showered them with strength, wisdom, and love this past year. As bookkeeper for the farm, Mammi Nell was a solid mathematician and a practical planner. She kept a steady eye on the farm budget for the family.

He helped her into the back of the carriage, then turned to his twin sisters. "I hope you watched the baking carefully so that you can make us something delicious at home."

Leah pressed two fingers to the side of her white prayer *Kapp*. "It's all up here, and you know I have a good memory."

"That you do," Adam said.

"Careful to make way." Mary trudged out of the house bearing a bundle of old towels covering hot bricks from the fire. More than anyone, Mary had taken over Mamm's duties in the past year, and sometimes Adam worried that it was too much for a girl of twenty. Granted, most Amish girls that age had families and babes of their own, but to inherit an instant family of eleven in a cloud of such heartbreak and grief . . . that was too much.

"You've a fine head for books, Leah, but sometimes I think you'd forget to wear your kapp if it wasn't sitting by your bedside," Mary said as she used a folded blanket to deposit the hot bricks in the back of Adam's carriage. "How about fetching the other warming bricks from the fire?"

As Susie and Leah hustled back into the house, Simon appeared with Ruthie, her cheeks pink from the cold, ice skates dangling from her mittened hand.

"You remembered to warm the bricks! Denki, Mary." She plopped her skates into the back of the carriage and climbed in. "I was just about to turn into a snowman!"

"Now share this, and mind it doesn't slip away," Mary said, tucking a blanket around Simon and Ruth.

When everyone was settled in at last, Mary climbed onto the seat beside Adam, and they were off, following a handful of carriages bumping along the dirt drive. Nightfall came early this time of year, and Adam was eager to get home and help his brothers with the cows, their udders swollen with milk by now.

As he steered his horse toward home, the horizon unfolded before him: frozen winter fields and western sky. A ribbon of peace. The sun, a golden glow bleeding to the purple of night, was a reminder that nothing of consequence could be rushed. They would get home soon enough to tend the livestock.

They passed a flock of women who turned at the fork in the road—neighbors who had come to help ready the house for tomorrow's church meeting.

"Bye, Hannah . . . Miriam!" Mary called, waving from the carriage.

"You'll see them tomorrow at preaching service," Adam said, pulling the reins in the opposite direction.

"There's nothing wrong with being social." Mary shifted in the leather seat beside him. "A lesson you seem to have forgotten."

"I didn't forget. I just don't have a spare minute for socializing, what with the cows to milk and the winter repairs." *Not to mention eleven of us to keep fed, clothed, safe, and happy.* More than anything the idea of leadership weighed on his mind, but he didn't want to sound like he was complaining. Especially to Mary, who tackled so many chores every day, and cheerfully at that. "The work doesn't scare me, but many times I don't know what to do first. When the cows bellow to be milked and the stalls have to be mucked and the chickens are waiting to be fed, I don't know where to start."

"We all have our chores, Adam, but still Jonah and I find time for singings and courtships." Mary rarely missed the chance to slip out on a Saturday night or attend a Sunday singing with her beau, John Beiler. Nicknamed Five because, when he was twelve, his hand-me-down overcoat was so large, five boys fit inside it, John Beiler had won over Mary soon after she began her rumspringa. Adam was surprised they did not marry last December, during wedding season. "You ought to join us tomorrow night," Mary went on. "Annie was just saying she's hoping you'll be there."

Adam kept his eyes on the road. "Are you setting me up with Annie? That's where this is going?"

Mary heaved a sigh thick with frustration. "Do I have to spell everything out for you? Three years you spent with the English and you lost the ability to see the most obvious things."

"My eyesight is fine, denki." Though he hadn't seen the plug for Annie coming. Was that the source of the giggles and whispers between Annie and his sister whenever he saw them together?

"I don't know if you've noticed, but Annie is very good with Katie and Sam. Ruthie, too. The children like her."

"I see that."

"I'm just saying. You might want to pay Annie some attention."

"It's not that way between Annie and me," Adam said quietly. When he thought of Annie Stoltzfus, he could see those naturally red lips that always brought him back to that summer day more than a decade ago when she had been picking berries with Mary. The girls were ten or so, and a bee in the strawberry patch had stung Annie on the back of her hand. Although Adam had been detasseling corn in a field nearly half a mile away, he had heard her wail as it echoed through the rows of corn. He ran to help, only to find Annie collapsed in the brambles, her mouth stained with red from strawberries that didn't make it into the pail.

Adam helped her back to the house that day, and ever since, Annie had marked him as her hero. She made it clear that she looked up to him. She enjoyed being with him. Life would have been simpler if Adam felt the same way, but every time he looked at her, he saw a whimpering ten-year-old with a face stained by berries.

"There you go again, getting lost under your own personal storm cloud." Mary poked him in the ribs.

"Ouch," he complained, though it didn't really hurt.

"I wonder how you would know what it's like to spend time with Annie, since you've never really tried it?" Mary's words were puffs of steam in the cold air.

"Sometimes you just know. The way you know that you and Five belong together?"

"Oh, now you're turning the topic to me?" Despite the light trill in her voice, she turned away and stared down at the road.

Personal relationships were just that—personal, and not something to be discussed, even with a sibling. Adam knew that, but it wasn't often he could tease his sister.

"Are you blushing?" He leaned toward her for a closer look at her face. "You are!"

"I'm just red from the cold." Mary unfolded a blanket over her lap. "I'm chilled to the bone. Do you want some of this?"

"The warming brick will do me fine." The heat threading up his legs from the hot stone reminded him of the many winters when Mamm wouldn't let them leave home until there was a warming brick in the carriage. He turned to his sister, who looked so like their mother, cheeks pink from cold, her dark hair scraped back neatly, her face framed by her black winter bonnet. "Good thinking, Mary. You take excellent care of us."

"Everything I know, I learned from Mamm." She wrapped the blanket closer, tugging it over her shoulders. "I still miss them. Sometimes in the middle of my chores, hanging laundry or rolling out dough, I hear Mamm's voice and it's as if she's right behind me, telling me not to knead the dough too much, reminding me to go easy on the seasonings. 'Just a pinch of salt,' she used to say. 'Mind you don't add too much salt.'" Her voice caught, and she pressed a hand to her mouth.

Adam felt a tug of pain at the wound Mary was probing, but he kept his eyes on the frozen road. He would have liked to take his sister in his arms and hug her, try to console her . . . but it was not the Amish way.

She pressed the edge of her shawl to her wet eyes. "Bishop Samuel preaches absolute forgiveness. We must forgive the man who killed our parents, and truly, I have no hatred in my heart. But still, I do miss Mamm and Dat. I do."

"I miss them, too," Adam admitted, at a loss as to what to say to ease her pain. He wasn't sure what had prompted his sister's tears. Perhaps it was the fact that they were approaching the anniversary of their parents' deaths, which, as a rule, they didn't discuss. Or was it simply Mary's own feelings that had been pent up all year? "There's nothing I wouldn't give to have them here with us, heading home on a winter's day. We all miss them, Mary. It's part of the healing."

"And Simon . . ." She glanced behind her. "He's nodded off, God bless him. I don't think he spoke but a dozen words for months after it happened, but he's gotten so much better lately. Have you noticed?"

"Ya."

"And the way he follows you around, trailing you from barn to wood shop like a duckling chasing his mama duck. He's grown so attached to you, Adam. I thank the good Lord that you traveled home to us when you did, when Simon needed you most."

He nodded. "I always knew I'd come back."

"Is that so? With you being gone for nearly three years, some of us weren't so sure."

"Oh, ye of little faith." Having left during his rumspringa, he had not broken any rules of the Ordnung. However, his father and the bishop were not happy with his absence, his departure from the Amish way of life. Had he returned before the murders, he would not have been so quickly welcomed back, but the terrible circumstances that brought him home had folded him back into the congregation quickly.

In a flash he recalled the panic . . . that overwhelming anxiety at being too far from home, unable to act fast enough when he got news of his parents' murders. Looking back, he realized there was no way he could have saved his parents. God's will was not to be changed. But the miles he had to cross in the journey home had added to his grief, and he'd arrived here to find more questions than answers about his parents' killer.

Since then he had given up hoping for some sort of justice—a concept that did not exist here in the Amish world, a notion he had vowed to turn his back on with his baptism. Still, at times he tried to piece together the events of that day. It was the only way to calm the questions burning in his mind like a firebrand: What were Mamm and Dat and Simon doing out on that wooded road, Juniper Lane? It was an out-of-the-way road beyond the edge of their farmstead, not a well-traveled route. The police had found the family rifle in the buggy, but for what purpose? And why had the killer spared Simon?

Just the memory of those panicked days set fear burning through his body like a fever. Dark, dismal days laden with sadness, guilt, and anguish.

"I had to come back," he said as the steel wheels of the carriage thumped over a frozen bump in the road, and they both bobbed in the front seat.

"Well, it's been good for Simon, having you here." She pulled the blanket tight around her and seemed to retreat into its cocoon, her hazel eyes focused on the slope of frozen white fields.

Her tender mood kept Adam from any more teasing. Instead he let his eyes fall on the silhouette of their farmhouse, the two barns set apart in an L-shape, domed silos rising beyond the stand of bare beech trees. Like a scattered set of building blocks, the smaller out-buildings sat awash in golden sunset.

When he closed his eyes and thought of home, these were the pictures he saw. None of the majestic mansions of Newport, with their views overlooking the water, could bring him the peace he found in this land; none of the relationships with the Englishers he'd met could hold a candle to the bonds in his family. Despite his journeys and worldly success during his rumspringa, Adam had always known he would return here to his Amish home.

Whenever he passed the wood shop in the maintenance shed, he thought of the hours he'd spent there shaping furniture from raw wood, learning how to fit things together and go with the grain. As a boy, even as a teen, he'd been happy, working alone in there, but his arrogance, his hochmut, had driven him to make more of his carpentry skills. In the headstrong path of youth he had indulged himself, overlooking the importance of home and family. If only his father could have known that his oldest son would one day come back to the Plain way of life . . .

The brick glowed near his feet, warming his legs and easing his heart. A quick glance behind him told him that most of the passengers were fast asleep, lulled by the motion of the carriage. Mammi Nell had nodded off with Ruthie asleep on her lap, and the twins snuggled with their heads together. They would rest well tonight, tired by a day of conversation, activity, and brisk winter weather. The clip-clop of horses' hooves was the music to a melody he'd been born to, a straightforward life on the earth but not of it.

Adam had always known he would come back to Halfway. His greatest regret was that he had not come home sooner, before his parents were lost to him. Just a week earlier . . . that would have made all the difference.

TWO

Floodlights splashed silver over the frozen lawn of the brick Colonial. Remy McCallister parked her car along the sidewalk and killed the engine, wondering if the family who now lived in this suburban Philadelphia house was asleep inside. She didn't want to disturb them. Although the residents might be alarmed if they realized a stranger was outside, Remy could not resist stopping by to soak up old memories from the brick and mortar of their home.

Sometimes she needed to reconnect with the only true home she'd ever had—even if that meant gazing from the curbside.

Turning in the driver's seat, Remy hugged herself at the notion that the old house was grinning at her, its two porch columns goofy white fangs hanging over the grin of the wide double doors. This was the home of her youth, the house where her mother had sung her to sleep with lullabies, served her hot corn bread dripping with honey, helped her capture fireflies on summer nights. Just sitting here, staring at the brick façade, brought her back to those days, a halcyon period when she'd thrived in her mother's embrace, wrapped in boundless love.

At the time she had not thought it possible that those sweet days could end so abruptly. How could she have known...a seven-year-old girl who'd lost her mother overnight from heart failure? In her grief and confusion Remy could not imagine how her life would change after her mom's death. She had not expected to lose her father to another woman, her home to a larger mansion in a tonier neighborhood, a cold box of high ceilings and wrought-iron grillwork that reminded her of prison bars.

A house where loneliness echoed in the spacious corridors.

Pulling the collar of her jacket up to cover her neck, Remy shook her head at the idea that Herb's second wife, Sonja Allen, had chosen the house in Wynnewood over this. Maybe it was about helping Herb move on. More likely Sonja had been looking for a home that would boost their social status. Either way, the house and the marriage had been history before the year's end.

Remy's search for a home had almost been fulfilled during her time in New York, when she and her friends had set up housekeeping in a Greenwich Village apartment. During college Kiara and Dakota had become the sisters she'd always longed for. The arrangement had been so copacetic that, despite the fact that Remy knew the end was inevitable, she had been crestfallen when her friends finished their degrees and moved on.

Although Remy had moved back to Herb's Drexel Hill townhouse, which was walking distance from the newspaper offices, the arrangement had lasted less than a month. Remy had felt like she was imposing on strangers, and Herb's third wife had done nothing to allay her discomfort. It was no surprise that Loretta did not object when Remy asked Herb to fund a small apartment for her until she got on solid financial footing.

The apartment, Remy's current home, was small and sleek, a lonely island in a fabulous location near the Museum District. Was it home? She shook her head as she let her eyes blur over the brick house that seemed to be wrapped in a halo of light. No, the apartment wasn't home. More like a safe resting place.

She wondered if Herb ever missed this house, this place chock-full of heart and memories. Having lasted more than ten years now, wife number three—and the townhouse—seemed to be working out for her father. Herb had his family, though it didn't really include Remy. Having just come from dinner at Herb's, she felt her outsider status acutely. Loretta and her teenaged daughter, Heather, had been conspicuously absent from the meal of gourmet take-out food.

"They're at the nail salon," Herb had explained, "doing that mother-daughter thing."

Although Remy had shrugged it off as if it didn't matter, it hurt to be ignored. Would it have killed Loretta and Heather to join them, sit at the dinner table and pretend for just one night that they cared? She knew Loretta didn't like her. Did Loretta think of her as Herb's grown daughter who occasionally came around to hit up her father for rent money?

In the year that she'd been back in Philadelphia, things between Remy and her father had improved. She had learned how to express herself without making him angry, and Herb had figured out that, occasionally, he needed to shut up and listen to his daughter. They had taken baby steps, but Herb still had a long way to go, and Remy sensed that Loretta felt threatened by any hint of a relationship between father and daughter.

Herb's gift twinkled on the passenger seat, and Remy picked up the cellophane-wrapped treat that her father had given her—a glazed marzipan heart for Valentine's Day. An early gift, he'd said. It was a nice gesture, a concoction pretty as an ornament or brooch, but she knew it would be a ball of sugar in her mouth, cloying and overly sweet.

Okay, Herb was trying. She had to give him that. Still . . .

She dropped the cellophane bag on the floor and leaned toward the friendly house framed by her car window. How she longed to wrap her arms around those porch columns, check the back-yard for the tree swing, and peer between the balusters along the stairs for lingering traces of the love and joy that once blossomed there. Her heart ached for the lilac bushes that once hid her in hide-and-seek, the lawn where she'd made snowmen and snow angels, the room beyond that second-story window on the left that had once held her bed and books and stuffed animals. Stretched out on the bed, Mom by her side, she had traveled to story lands of friendly monsters and bulls, purple crayons and green eggs.

How her heart ached to visit that world one last time.

If only she could go home . . .

Her eyes were fixed on her old bedroom window when she caught a flicker of movement that made her pulse quicken. Was it just the reflection of a wavering tree branch? Or was someone watching from the window?

She would have to leave soon. She wasn't exactly trespassing, but she didn't want to disturb anyone in the neighborhood.

Wind whipped around the car, bringing down the temperature inside. Barren branches danced in front of her old bedroom win-dow, like fingers wagging away the past.

You can't go back.

You cannot return to the past.

You can't go home again.

THREE

*B*ears were everywhere.

Round black bears walking two by two. They meandered down the road in small packs. They forged ahead, flattening winter grass under their heavy paws.

They didn't seem angry now, but he knew that could change in a heartbeat. With one flash of anger, he could be dead.

On his knees so that he could peer out of their moving carriage, Simon shivered. "The bears are following us," he said aloud. When one of the bears nodded its black head at him, he ducked down, his heart hammering in his chest.

Simon squeezed his eyes shut and waited for the pounding in his chest to stop. He shouldn't have told Mammi what he saw. The grown-ups didn't like to hear about bears. Whenever he talked about it, they got mad. So he tried not to talk about it.

"Sit down on the seat, right and proper," his grandmother said. "You've nothing to fear out there." Mammi turned her head, casting a look at the country road. "See that? Just folk making their way to Sunday worship."

A quick peek told him Mammi was right. No bears. Just Amish families walking to the service, two by two and in groups of three, kids straggling behind their mamms and dats.

Still, his heart drummed in his chest. Sometimes the rattling fear lingered there. "They looked like bears for a minute," he said, trying to explain so his grandmother wouldn't be cross. In their dress-up clothes, women bundled in dark shawls and kapps, men in black broadfall trousers, coats, and hats, they could have been bears. Dark figures against the pale glaze of snow.

Ruthless creatures who killed without warning.

You had to watch for bears. He knew because he'd seen it. He knew. Mammi knew a lot of things. She was a wise woman. But she didn't have much experience with bears.

"You'd be better served practicing your prayers than staring out at the road." His grandmother's dark eyes were as shiny as glass, and the lines formed by the crinkles at the edge of each eye forked and spread like the veins of a leaf. "Have you learned the Lord's Prayer yet?"

"Ya, Mammi."

"And the Loblied?"

"I've been practicing," he said.

"Gut." Mammi Nell patted his arm, her touch firm but loving. "Keep practicing so you can walk into preaching service with the boys. Your mamm wanted all her boys to know the Loblied first."

He nodded, knowing that Mammi was right. His mother had started him learning the hymn when he was seven. Sunday was an important day for his mamm. On days when they had church service the buzz of activity started right after the morning milking. Breakfast would be quick—scrapple with some raisin bread or sweet rolls. Then Mamm shooed them to their rooms, where their special Sunday clothes were laid out on their beds.

Simon still wore the Sunday trousers Mamm had sewn. They were now too tight, but he wasn't ready to give them up to be put away for Sam to wear one day. Simon shifted on the leather seat of the carriage, wincing at the way the pants gripped his waist. Surely Mary would sew him a new pair if he told her they were too small. Just like she'd replaced his work clothes when he'd grown out of 'em. But he hadn't gotten around to saying anything just yet. These were the clothes Mamm had made with her own hands. These were the trousers she washed and ironed for him. Preacher David had warned against becoming attached to material things, but Simon didn't think a pair of pants could matter to God. It wasn't so much the trousers themselves as the love that went into them. All those times Mamm washed 'em and fed 'em through the wringer . . .

That was a lot of love.

And it helped to think of the love instead of the terrible thing that had happened to Mamm and Dat. Just thinking about it brought night to his insides.

So what if his Sunday pants were snug?

Ruthie had told him he was *verhuddelt,* that Mamm and Dat were in heaven with God and it was a sin to pretend any other way. "When God calls someone to heaven, they go," she'd told him, her amber eyes stern as Mammi Nell's.

Maybe Ruthie was right. He ought to tell Mary he needed a new pair of Sunday pants. One of these days.

"Whoa, there," Adam called from the front, and the carriage rolled to a stop. "Let's lighten Thunder's load on this last hill. Who's going to walk?"

Before Adam finished the question, Simon's brothers and sisters were disembarking from the seats in front of him. Jonah and Gabriel were the first ones out. They turned to help the girls disembark.

No, don't get out. It's not safe to stop. . . .

Simon felt frozen with panic as he watched the girls drop down to the road . . . Leah, Susie, and Sadie. Mary's hands went up to check her dark bonnet as Ruthie called to Simon.

"What are you waiting for?" She stood, hands on her hips, at the far end of the rear seat. "It's time to walk."

"I'm going to stay in the carriage," he muttered.

"Oh, Simon, you do this every time." Ruthie glared at him, looking stern for her eleven years as she climbed down from the carriage.

His eyes darted to Katie and Sam, who sat like little dolls bundled next to Mammi. "I'll help with the little ones."

"I can manage," Mammi insisted. "Go on now, Simon."

Stay here, his mother's voice entreated. *You'll be safe in the buggy.*

"But I can help," Simon pleaded. "I'll help Adam unhitch the horses."

"Your brother wants you to walk." Mammi's brows lifted in disapproval. "It's too much for the horse to take all of us."

Just then Jonah poked his head into the backseat of the carriage. "What's the holdup here?"

Mammi said with gentle reproof, "'Tis Simon, wanting to ride with the little ones again."

"Kumm." With pursed lips, Jonah reached in and lifted Simon to the ground. He signaled to Adam, and the carriage rolled off.

Crestfallen, Simon buried his face in his hands and sucked the insides of his cheeks, trying to keep from crying at the injustice of it all. Mamm had told him to stay with the buggy. She had promised to hide him there, and he'd stayed safe.

But no one else understood that.

They listened, but they didn't understand.

They didn't know what bears could do.

"Simon? Are you sick?" Jonah's voice was gentle.

Through the slits in his fingers Simon saw another carriage roll to a stop to discharge passengers.

No bears. Just the Zook family.

Sniffing back tears, Simon stepped into Jonah's shadow. "If Eli Zook sees me crying, he'll tell everyone and all the boys will think I'm a baby."

"We can't have that." Jonah produced a handkerchief, and Simon quickly wiped his eyes. "There you go. Want to join the boys?"

With a deep breath of resolve, Simon gave back the handkerchief. "Let's just start walking. I'll be happy if they stay ahead of us." They were really not friends to Simon, but since they were his age, people expected Simon to spend time with them.

Jonah touched Simon on the shoulder, and they headed up the hill. It was getting close to the time when the service would be starting, and now plenty of Amish people climbed the hill. If Simon squinted they were rectangles of dark color, blue or purple or green. He felt foolish for thinking they were bears before. How could he think that of Marian Yoder or Abe Zook or the Lapp family?

Up ahead, he noticed Eli and John Zook waiting along the road, tossing pebbles at something on the side.

Waiting to tease me for crying, Simon thought. Steeling himself, he straightened his hat and walked right up to them.

"Good morning," he said in Pennsylvania Dutch.

To Simon's surprise, they had no criticism for his tears. Maybe he'd hidden himself well behind Jonah's tall silhouette.

"Target practice," Eli said, casting a pebble. "I've hit that fallen branch four times. John only got it once."

"You try," John said.

Simon stared at the fallen branch, but didn't answer. Mamm used to say that contests were arranged to make the winner look better. "It's best not to participate in competitions," she once told him.

"Kumm," Jonah said, beckoning the three boys. "No time for dawdling."

Simon felt relieved when John dropped his handful of pebbles and brushed the dirt from his hands. They continued up the hill while Eli took a few more shots.

"Wait for me!" Eli ran to catch up. By the time he reached the boys, he was breathing heavy. "Simon, I forgot to ask you. Will you be going in with the boys today?"

One of the many questions Simon dreaded. Eli had been hounding him with it ever since Simon's ninth birthday had approached. He glanced over at Eli, the boy's mouth a pink slash against his pale, round face. Did Eli Zook know how much his question bothered Simon?

Simon shook his head no, letting his eyes meet the harsh question in Eli's eyes.

"No? What is going on?" Eli spread his arms wide, as if dumbfounded. "Don't tell me you still haven't learned the words to the Loblied, like your mamm wanted."

Simon didn't answer, but waited for the sting of guilt and embarrassment to fade. He wanted to tell Eli how much he sounded like an old man. He wanted Eli and John and all the boys his age to leave him alone and stop talking about his mamm.

"He just turned nine," John pointed out. "And the Loblied is hard to memorize. Twenty-eight lines!" He clapped a hand to the top of his hat, leaving a pale dust print. "I'm still learning it."

"But you walk in with the boys," Eli told his brother. "Come on, Simon. Today you walk in with us. You can't be sitting with the women and babies forever."

Ach, but that's what I want to do, Simon thought. He liked walking into worship services hidden between his sisters' skirts. He felt safe coming in with Mary and Sadie and the little ones. Why did that have to change?

Simon's boots dragged up the dirt hill as he watched Adam's carriage disappear around a bend up ahead. Next time, he would stay inside, all the way to the Sunday service. He would talk to Adam about it. His oldest brother would understand.

From his pocket Eli took a few stray pebbles and made a game of bouncing them over the iced pond at the edge of Nate and Betsy's farm. John began searching for scattered stones to give it a try, and Simon retreated to his own thoughts, glad that the boys were distracted.

Overhead the winter clouds broke, and sunlight gleamed on the windows of the house, which had been thoroughly cleaned yesterday in preparation for the Sunday meeting. Simon himself had helped haul wash water so that the floors could be wiped down before the benches were set up in rows, one side for men, the other for women.

Squinting at the sunburst, he sighed quietly as the tightness drained from his chest. The preaching service would begin soon, and once the first hymn started he usually found some peace, lulled by the familiar Hochdeutsch language of the service.

His step lightened as the words to the hymn rose in his heart.

O Gott Vater, wir loben Dich und deine Güte preisen; Dass du uns O Herr gnädichlich . . .

Ya, he knew the Loblied. All twenty-eight lines. Sometimes he ran the song through his head when he needed to quiet the fear in his racing heart. But he wasn't ready to admit that he knew the hymn. For now, it was a secret he shared only with God, a secret to hold in his heart.

FOUR

"*P*urple carrots. Are they not beautiful?" Dakota Ferris said as she dropped a bunch of heirloom carrots into a canvas shopping sack. "Love the Reading Terminal Market. Love these beets." Her lips pursed in an air kiss as she lifted the bag of crimson root vegetables. "I can't wait for you to taste my vegetarian stew. Did you get the cranberries?"

"Got them." As Remy added the bag of ruby red berries to their collection she couldn't help but smile. Dakota's excitement was always contagious, and her friend was right; Philly's indoor market was a splash of color and warmth on a gray winter day. She would have to remember this after Dakota went home, how just walking past the bins of bright red, orange, and green produce lifted her spirits. The chatter, the flurry of activity, and the mouthwatering scents of coffee and vanilla and fresh flowers all made her smile.

Many of the vendors at the market were Amish, easily distinguished by their clothes: modest dresses, aprons, and bonnets for women, dark suits and hats for men. Although Remy tried not to stare, she couldn't help but check the face of each Amish man she passed, searching for soulful brown eyes and the angular jawline of the man she'd met a year ago on that train. Perhaps it seemed like a stereotype, thinking that Adam King might be here, but since their first meeting she had looked for him whenever she'd happened upon a group of Plain folk. She had lain awake plenty of nights thinking about how an act of violence had impacted his life. She'd worried about the toll something like that would take on his youngest siblings, and she'd tried to imagine him as an Amish man, clean-shaven, which was an indication of being single.

Or not.

What if he had a beard, a growth of thick, dark hair below his chin line? That would mean he was married, as Amish men let their beards grow after they got married. It was one of the cultural details she'd picked up in her research of Amish customs. Disappointment cast a shadow over her mood at that possibility. Somehow, the idea of Adam with a wife bothered her. It seemed wrong that he might marry so soon after his parents' deaths. It just felt wrong.

"You know what I'm thinking?" Dakota asked.

Remy blinked back to the moment. She had no clue, but at least her friend didn't seem to have noticed that she'd zoned out.

"This place is newsworthy." Dakota tucked her blond hair behind one ear and did a quick scan of the marketplace. "You should do a story on the Reading Market. People here need to know what a great resource they have, right in the downtown area."

"Really? I'd love to." They had spent a good part of the afternoon in a café trying to come up with stories Remy could pitch. After nearly a year with the *Post*, she still hadn't come up with a newsworthy angle. "But it's probably been done to death. This place has been here for a hundred years."

"So you put a new spin on it." Dakota cocked her head, the gold streaks in her hair catching the light. "You'll think of something. But I'm getting hungry. Let's grab the rest of our ingredients and run so I can get this on the stove. All the flavors need time to intermingle." As Dakota sorted through the satchel, taking inventory of their groceries, Remy was reminded of the good times they had shared in college, along with Kiara, pooling resources and talents in their New York apartment. Having Dakota here for the weekend was like a trip back in time to their college home.

"We'll probably need a forklift to get this stuff to your apartment, but we're not done yet. I'm going to get some almonds for the stew, while you head over and pick up some homemade cheese to go with the Tuscan bread." Dakota hitched the handle of the tote bag up on her shoulder. "See if you can get cheddar or Havarti. Dairy is thataway." She pointed past the flower stand.

"Got it. I'll meet you back by the roses." Remy dodged the wide berth of a double stroller and headed toward the aisle of refrigerated cases, where signs boasted of homemade ice cream, farm-fresh milk, and handmade cheeses from the King Family Dairy.

The King family? Her radar flared. King was among the most common Amish names in Lancaster County, but still . . .

A handful of people were lined up along the cheese stand, where an Amish man and woman waited on customers. She shot a quick glance at the man, but he was short and solidly built, with dark glasses; definitely not Adam.

Shaking off disappointment, Remy moved forward to look over the selections of orange and white cheeses behind the glass.

She recognized the cheddars, but Havarti? There were half a dozen varieties; choices beyond her expectations. She stared at the rectangular prisms and wheels of cheese as the young woman leaned into the case, her hair tucked neatly into a starched white bonnet.

"Did you have a question?" The voice came from behind her.

An Amish man was her first thought as she turned and fell under the spell of penetrating dark eyes and a face engraved in her memory.

Her heart skipped a beat as the improbable suddenly became reality. It was him. Adam King.

"I could help you with the cheeses."

Her breath caught in her throat as she dared to face him. Under the brim of that black hat his dark eyes, soft but alert, had a warming effect.

"Oh. Hi." She struggled to diffuse the intense buzz of energy in the air between them, struggled not to stare at him. His face—clean-shaven, thank the Lord—was still a handsome blend of sharp angles and smooth jawline.

She forced herself to breathe, hoped that he would not hear the nervous tension in her voice as she said, "Not to sound weird, but have we met before?"

He touched his chin, his dark eyes level and cool. "I was thinking the same thing. You remind me of a girl I met on a train last year."

"That's it!" She snapped her fingers and grinned. "Amtrak to Philly. We were both headed home. You're Adam King, right?"

He nodded. "How are you, Remy?"

"You remembered my name. . . ." Something about that warmed her. Really, with all the people he had encountered in the past year, to have remembered her . . . "That's amazing."

"Well, you remembered mine."

"Your name was in the newspaper. It was on every channel." She almost regretted the words the minute they were out, but there was no getting around the horrible tragedy he'd returned home to.

"It was. But you made an impression." He moved behind the

counter to replace the plastic carton on a stack. When he stepped out again he seemed taller than she remembered, with the strength of a man who was no stranger to hard work. "I don't meet many girls with hair that color. Like a bright copper penny."

Self-consciously, she grabbed at the curls springing over one shoulder. As a kid, she'd hated being teased about her hair, but coming from Adam, the comment seemed like a compliment.

"You made quite an impression, too," she admitted. "Though I felt awful when I learned the details about your parents. When you walked off the train that night I had no idea just how terrible . . ." She shook her head. "I couldn't imagine what you were going through. You know, I really worried about you. I prayed for you and your family . . . that you'd heal."

"Thank you." He stared at her lips, as if watching words form there. "That was very kind of you."

"How is everything going?" She glanced toward the sign over the cheese stand. "The King Family Dairy . . . so these are your products? Is that your brother at the register?"

"My cousin. Market Joe, we call him. He's in charge of sales here. The family pools resources so that we can bring our products to various markets."

"And your siblings? You said you had ten brothers and sisters. How's everyone doing? Are they here with you?"

"Not today, but they are doing well. They move ahead with each day, trying to follow God's plan for them. It's been difficult at times, especially for the younger ones, but they have faith and they're surrounded by love. Plenty of love."

He made it sound so simple, she thought. As if love was the magic cure for a broken heart, a broken life. To have lost their parents in such a violent way, those children had suffered major trauma. Had they gotten professional help?

Adam, too. She couldn't imagine how hard this year must've been for him. "Well, you look like you're doing well." He looked healthy and solid in a dark, *American Gothic* way, but she didn't want to gush.

"I'm grateful for all the good things in my life. Blessings, big and small," he said. "And how about you? You were coming home to live with your father, right?"

His eyes, when they caught hers, took her breath away. "I was," she managed. "But I'm not living with Herb anymore. Long story. Sort of boring. Bottom line, he has a new family that really doesn't include me. But I'm doing okay. I'm happy to have a job and my own place and . . ." She was babbling; she knew she was babbling, and she had to stop herself before she revealed the bare truth. *I have an empty apartment, an empty life, an empty heart.* Funny how it would be easier to make that admission to a near stranger like Adam than to a close friend.

"But you're still not overjoyed to be in Philadelphia," he said.

So . . . he remembered how she'd felt that day on the train. Remy had no quick answer, and she couldn't help but wonder how he could extract her current attitude from the past two minutes. "I haven't found what I was looking for here. My job, the work, it keeps me busy, but—"

She was interrupted by Dakota, who trundled over with grocery bags in both hands. "Time to make the stew, sweetie," she called, not realizing Remy was engaged in conversation. "You ready?"

"Dakota . . ." Remy took one of the shopping bags from her friend. "This is Adam. We met last year, sort of by accident. And this is my friend Dakota." Remy's free hand balled into a fist as she watched Dakota take in the situation and hoped that her friend wouldn't reveal that Remy had talked about her meeting with Adam for months last year.

Dakota's hazel eyes went wide as she gave Remy a look that clearly said, "I get it." She turned to Adam. "Nice to meet you. Are you part of the King cheese dynasty?"

He laughed. "Dynasty? That's not us. But our family has been running dairy farms for many generations."

Cheese . . . suddenly Remy remembered her mission. "So, Adam, what kind of Havarti do you recommend?"

"Well, it depends on what you're looking for." He shifted from one foot to the other, and she was struck by the width of his shoulders and broad back. In her memory he'd been a smaller man, but perhaps that was because he'd been huddled under a wool cap and baggy shirt when she'd met him, hiding from the world. "Havarti is a creamy, semisoft cheese. Everyone seems to like the plain cream, but there's dill or caraway if you like those flavors."

Remy and Dakota decided on the plain cream Havarti, and Adam kindly ushered them to the side so that he could handle the transaction himself. As she watched him wrap the cheese in paper, Remy wondered if he worked the market every day. In a surge of courage, she asked him.

"I'm here every few weeks," he explained. "My cousin Joe and his wife handle the sales here. The rest of us alternate delivery duties, as we've all got responsibilities on our farms."

When he handed her the wrapped package, Remy held out a ten-dollar bill. But Adam shook his head. "Consider it a gift. I never got a chance to thank you for feeding me on that train ride."

"I seem to remember some hot cocoa. Really, what do I owe you?"

"Take it, please." He dropped it into the canvas bag at her feet. "We don't always understand what God has in store for us, but even through our sadness, He is in control."

She squinted at him. "Are you saying God wants me to have that cheese?"

He laughed. "I didn't say that, but I do."

She smiled and looked down at the cheese, realizing that it was time to go, though she wanted to stay. She couldn't remember the last time she'd enjoyed talking with a guy her age. The air between them was both easy and intense, like the undertow of an ocean that pushed and pulled at the same time. If only she could stay in the water awhile longer.

"Well, thank you," she said, trying to be gracious. "We appreciate it."

He nodded, the slow burn in his eyes steady and intense. "Have a good evening."

"Thanks! You, too!" Dakota called, waggling her fingers as they headed off.

It was difficult to move away from him, as if they were stepping from a halo of light into darkness. "Did you notice his eyes?" Remy asked, steeling herself to keep from looking back at him.

"His eyes?" Dakota let out a snort. "Honey, I could barely see with the glare off that dazzling puffy heart around the two of you."

"What are you talking about?"

"It's obvious that he likes you, and you like him."

"You mean, like like?"

"To put it in fifth-grade terminology, yeah. Uh-huh."

"Really?" Remy hitched the canvas bag higher on her shoulder, bolstered by her friend's observation.

"Definitely. If he wasn't Amish, I'd be picking out my bridesmaid dress right now."

If he wasn't Amish . . .

Dakota's words were a cold wind of reality blowing through her daydream paradise. They lived in different worlds. Adam King was not going to be her boyfriend, no matter how she felt about him.

But wading through the disappointment, she wondered if he could be her friend. There was no denying the connection between them. In the two times they'd met, she and Adam had shared some very personal thoughts and feelings, and she liked his attitude of respect and caring. This was a guy she could trust.

My Amish friend . . .

Remy felt warmed, knowing he was out there, knowing he cared even a little bit for her.

My friend. It was enough. More than enough.

FIVE

*D*rawing her shawl closer for warmth, Mary gazed back at the roaring bonfire as Five clicked his tongue and the horse drew the buggy away from the gathering. Groups of young Amish men and women sat on benches and blankets around the fire, sipping hot chocolate and singing fast songs. Their high-pitched young voices carried merriment into the stillness of night.

A joyous event, and now a buggy ride beside the one person who made her feel alive and special and loved. On nights like this her heart danced with expectation and happiness—the sheer joy of being beside this solid young man, whom she'd known since they both were children. If only they could be together, just the two of them, more than once every two weeks.

Reins in one hand, Five stretched his arms wide and took a deep breath. "Such a beautiful night."

"Who calls it a beautiful night in the deep freeze of January?" Although Mary teased her beau, she secretly appreciated his never-ending enthusiasm. Five could make a thunderstorm into a chance to huddle together under cover, a broken buggy wheel into an excuse to enjoy a slower pace. "You have a crooked way of looking at life, John Beiler."

"Can't a man admire the Creator's handiwork?"

Five's father, also named John Beiler, had instilled a strong love of God in his children. Mary was ever inspired by Five's faith, that quiet strength he possessed deep within. Sometimes, when she dreamed of the children they would have together, the Lord willing, she imagined their sons and daughters echoing Five's faith through kindness and good works.

"The winds have died down, there's not a cloud to be seen, and look at the stars overhead. Sparkling gems in the sky. Mary, have you ever seen stars so magnificent?"

His enthusiasm never ceased to amaze her. "Can't say that I have."

Holding the reins in one hand, he reached back with another and handed her a blanket. "There you go. You can tuck this over your legs. Or simply move a bit closer to me and I'll keep you warm."

"The blanket will be fine," she said, laying it over their legs. Immediately it began to capture the heat from the warm brick Five had placed on the floor of the buggy. "But I'll not get too close. We can't have people talking about us before we have a chance to wed. It would break my heart if people thought we were doing the wrong thing."

"Sweet Mary. Always concerned about doing the right thing." Even in the soft darkness she caught the light in his blue eyes as he reached toward her. How wondrous it was to see that glimmer of love there just for her.

She felt the warmth of his hand on hers and she linked her fingers with his, encouraged by the privacy of darkness. "And don't you share the same concerns? We're both baptized members of the church. Our time for rumspringa is over. Of course I feel responsible for making the right choices."

"That's one of the many reasons why I love you."

Delight bubbled inside her upon hearing his words. "And I love you. Truly, I can't wait to be your wife."

How many days and nights had she dreamed of a life with Five? So many times when she was changing Katie's diaper, wringing laundry, or preparing a stew, she had imagined herself doing these tasks in a home she shared with Five. Diapering their own baby . . . tending to Five's britches and shirts . . . cooking a meal to share with her husband and their family. She would bake for her new family . . . shoofly pies and butterscotch brownies and dilly bread. And oh, the quilts she would sew with other Amish women, her sisters and aunts and friends. And someday, God willing, her own daughters would join in and sit across from her in the quilting circle, soaking up the wisdom and tales of their elders as their fingers deftly moved a needle.

"We don't have too much longer to wait, Mary." Five's voice drew her back from her fantasies. "I'm ready to go to the bishop and declare my intentions. We could publish in the end of October and marry at the beginning of wedding season in November."

The effervescent joy in her heart suddenly went flat. "Oh, I don't know about that, John." She tried, but she couldn't even muster a smile when she thought of the year ahead.

"Hmm . . ." His voice was a low rumble. "When you call me John, I know we're in trouble."

"God willing, the worst trouble is behind us, losing Mamm and Dat."

"And I'm not making light of that, Mary. You know I'd never—"

"Of course, Five. You've been nothing but wonderful through it all. Sticking beside me and putting off our wedding plans." When it became clear that Mary's family needed her after her parents' deaths, Five was the first to suggest they delay their wedding. He'd understood that it wasn't only the little ones who needed care, but also the middle ones who required Mary's nurturing. Ruthie and the twins were responsible children, but they needed guidance, especially Susie, who had her health issues. Then there was Sadie, sneaking off with Englishers every chance she got. That girl had always had a defiant streak. Gabriel had talked with Bishop Samuel about the anger burning in his soul at the loss of their parents. Jonah, always a quiet one, had receded into himself, and though he was a grown man now, Mary still felt concern that he would ever find happiness. And Simon, deeply traumatized by what he'd seen . . . how she prayed that the healing would save Simon from his constant fear.

"I know it's a sin to worry, but here I am like a tangled ball of yarn and I don't know what we're going to do. When Adam arrived, we were all so relieved to have him back and in charge of things. And it was wonderful gut when he went for *die Gemee,* his instruction, and got baptized last fall. My brother is doing the best he can, but as time goes on it's become more and more clear that he can't handle the family alone."

"Of course he can't," Five agreed. "Everyone needs the support of the community."

"Ya. That and a wife. And that, I've come to think, is the thing that's holding the family back. Adam can't handle the family without a woman at his side. And right now, I happen to be that woman."

"But you're to be *my* wife." Five squeezed her arm against his, sending warmth radiating up her arm. When he lifted their joined hands to his lips and kissed the back of her hand, she felt his love, a bird's wings beating in her chest. "The time is approaching for us to be man and wife, Mary. This is what God wants for us."

"Ya? God has told you that?" she teased.

"I know it as surely as there's a moon and stars shining on us tonight. It's time for us to be together, day and night, Mary. Time for us to start a family, God willing. Isn't that what you want, too?"

"I want it with all my heart," she vowed, and she felt the truth in her words. Being with Five, even sitting here beside him on the worn leather seat of the buggy bench, it felt just right. She knew this was where she wanted to be, and she had a strong sense of God's approval for their life together.

And yet, the endless sense of duty to her siblings tugged at her, like an insistent goat pulling laundry from the clothesline. They needed her every day, nearly every minute of every day. At times the burden seemed overwhelming, but Mary set to one task at a time with faith that the good Lord would not give her more than she could bear.

"I keep waiting and praying for God to make it easier for me to part with my family so that we can start our life together," Mary said. "Unfortunately, He hasn't moved any mountains yet."

"Maybe you need to take the first step. Have you told Adam about our plans to marry come autumn?"

"He's hinted around about it. But how could I tell him that? He'd think I'm about to abandon him and the little ones."

"But he needs to know. To start with, just because you wouldn't live under the same roof doesn't mean you wouldn't continue helping with the cooking and cleaning there." He tipped his hat back and moonlight washed over his angular face, illuminating his pale golden hair. "And another thing: If Adam knows of your intention to marry, it might start him thinking of finding a wife."

Mary shook her head. "Oh, he seems so far from considering marriage. You know Annie favors him, and I've tried so many times to get Adam to pay her some attention, all without success. I can't even get him to talk of courtship."

"But it's time for him to find someone to spend his life with. Maybe he's waiting for a little push. And you can give him the kick in the pants he needs, good sister that you are." Five squeezed her hand again. "I've found the love of my life, and I want Adam to know the same happiness."

She sighed. "How wonderful that would be." Although her relationship with Five was no secret to close members of their families, no one else knew that they had planned to marry in the wedding season that had just passed. To hear Five talk of their marrying this year brought such joy to her heart, and yet she feared it was not a realistic goal, much as they both wanted it.

And if she was unable to extract herself from the complicated web of family commitment this year, how would Five react? He'd been supportive and patient for so many years, and now, for the first time, he was steering her strongly toward marriage.

She understood that Five's patience was wearing thin. She felt the same way, so tired of waiting for things to change, so eager to spend her days and nights beside this man she loved. But her brother Adam was no closer to taking a wife than he was a year ago when he returned to the family. And if Adam refused to marry, then who would manage the women's work in their household? All the cooking and cleaning, sewing and washing . . . not to mention helping with the milking.

Oh, what would she do if she were forced to choose between this man she loved and her commitment to her family? Mary huddled under the blanket and bit her lips together in frustration; she'd considered the dilemma many times before, never able to puzzle out an answer.

"What's the matter?" Five said as he turned the buggy from the highway to a country lane. "You look like you've got the weight of the world on your shoulders."

The moment Mary saw the spark of concern in his blue eyes she tossed her worries away, casting them up to scatter with the stars and moon. "It's nothing." She glanced up at the three-quarter moon in the sky, so amused by the silly grin she could make out. "The man on the moon is smiling down on us. Do you see his face up there?" she asked, eager to change the subject.

"I hate to break it to you, but there's no man up there. Only dark patches on the surface. Craters and rocks."

She laughed. "I knew that."

"Of course, you can think that it's a symbol of God's face shining down on us, because that, I know, is a reality."

Warmed by the love in his eyes, Mary squeezed his hand. How blessed she was to have Five in her life. They would find a way to take care of her family so that they could wed. God would help them do the right and proper thing.

"I never tire of looking at the stars with you," she said. "How many years have we been courting now? Three?"

"Soon to be four," he said. "Though it feels like a thousand years."

"Why, John Beiler . . ." She pulled a hand out from under the blanket to tap the brim of his hat. "You make it sound as if we've been together so long that you're beginning to think of me as a familiar old shoe."

As he held on to his hat, his deep, soulful laugh filled the night. "I didn't say that. Though I do appreciate having comfortable boots on my feet. Never underestimate the value of a familiar old shoe, Mary."

SIX

When Adam stepped outside to connect the hot water hose to the porch tub, he was struck by two things: the deep silence of the winter night, and the brilliant diamonds in the sky overhead.

Such a clear night. He could make out Ursa Minor, the pattern of stars known as the Little Dipper. Dat had taught them how to spot Polaris in the night sky, the tip of the ladle's handle. "If you can find your way north, you'll never be lost," he used to say.

Now, watching the North Star throb like his own pulse, Adam wished his father were here to point up at the sky. Stars like this were meant to be shared, but everyone in the house was asleep.

Past the crisscross of roads beyond frozen pastures, Mary and Jonah were off at a youth get-together, a bonfire for single Amish men and women. And beyond that, Remy McCallister's green eyes and curly copper hair shone under these same stars in the city of Philadelphia. Since he'd run into her at the market today, her image had been emblazoned in his mind. Her smile. Her sympathetic eyes.

Even the smattering of freckles across her nose. Goodness swirled behind those green eyes, though he sensed she hadn't found a way to express that. Chances were he'd never see her again, but somehow it lightened his heart to think of her spending Saturday night under the same starry sky.

He almost laughed as he attached the hose to the rig outside the mudroom. His big Saturday night plans—a bath—and he was looking forward to it. Although the house had plenty of space, the indoor plumbing was limited—something Adam planned to change. On a night like tonight, when his body was weary to the marrow of his bones, it would be very nice to have a hot water line that ran to an upstairs bathroom. A tub room with more privacy than this passageway between the barn and main house. When he was a boy, Mamm had thought the tub was perfect on this closed porch. She could scrub her children down, wiping the muck and mud of the farm from their little bodies before they even stepped foot inside the kitchen door.

He grinned at the memory. Mamm's clean kitchen floor was family legend.

But these days, a tub in the entryway was not practical. He stripped down to his undershorts, knowing he wasn't guaranteed privacy, and stepped into the steamy water with a groan.

The pain at the back of his neck had nothing to do with work, and everything to do with stress. Since he'd returned here, Adam hadn't slept a single night without first lying awake with worried prayers for his brothers and sisters.

Tonight he'd had to look the other way when, as soon as she finished wiping the dinner dishes, his sister Sadie had headed down the dark road on her scooter, no doubt to meet her Englisher boy, as was her habit recently. Sadie had fallen for pop music and a boy from the outside, and since she was seventeen and in her rumspringa, she was entitled to some freedom.

As hot water covered his knees and sent warmth up his spine, he thought of Mary and Jonah off at the bonfire. Mary had pestered him about going along, insisting that Mammi could keep watch over the little ones. Even teased him that he'd wind up an old, lonely man if he didn't start taking an interest in the local Amish girls. She didn't mention Annie Stoltzfus's name, but he knew if his oldest sister had her way, she'd have Adam marrying her best friend come wedding season.

With a groan, Adam rose from the tub and, dripping, reached over to turn off the spigot. Not a good setup, this tub. He'd work on the hot water situation.

He sank back into the hot water, thinking of Simon, his little shadow. The boy had been coming out of his shell, but something had been bothering him of late, set him talking about bears at bedtime when Adam spent some time alone with him.

"Bears kill people. Did you know that?" Simon's amber eyes were shiny with fear. "I read it in a book. They attack. Sometimes people get murdered by bears."

"That's true," Adam said. "But actually, I don't think they call it murder when a bear kills. They don't mean to kill the person."

"I know, but it's still scary."

Thinking back over the conversation, Adam realized that he and Simon had discussed the topic of deadly bears half a dozen times, though today had been the first time Simon had used the word "murder" in connection with bears.

The social workers, police psychologists, and doctors who had interviewed Simon after their parents' deaths had come away with the same opinion: The healing would take time. They believed that eventually Simon would begin to sort through the things he'd seen at the crime scene in the moments before he'd been hidden under the skirt of Mamm's dress.

At the time, what little Simon said sounded like one of Grimm's fairy tales—a bear had attacked their parents but missed seeing Simon hidden under Mamm's skirts. A bear, Simon insisted. But bears were rare in this part of Pennsylvania. And from what Adam had read, bears had an acute sense of smell, even stronger than bloodhounds. Wouldn't a bear have sniffed Simon out of hiding?

Besides, a bear could not have pulled the trigger on the handgun that killed their parents.

Adam sighed over the wedge of frustration that stuck in his gut. Simon had been doing so well, but now, with this talk of bears again, Adam didn't know what to think.

He ducked his head under the water, slicked his hair back, and worked in some shampoo as he considered the best way to help Simon. His brother seemed a bit afraid of the bishop. Maybe a talk with Uncle Nate? Simon had been warming up to him yesterday.

After he rinsed his hair, he looked around for the soap. Nothing in sight, but then it was the mudroom. He lathered some shampoo onto his arms and chest, resolving to make some improvements in the stone farmhouse. Nothing that would violate the Ordnung, of course, but there were many acceptable changes that would make their lives easier. They could install a gas water-heater with a gasoline engine to keep up the water pressure. Then he and Jonah could work with one of the Amish plumbers from the community to build a bathroom upstairs. Hot and cold running water. No more chamber pots upstairs. No more public baths in the mudroom.

Adam's lips puffed as he let out a long breath, sending steam scurrying along the surface of the water. Could they afford to build a bathroom upstairs? He didn't know what it would cost, but he would find out. And he would talk to Mammi Nell, who took care of all the family bookkeeping.

And if they had the money to change the house, did he dare do it? Change was a hard row to hoe. So far he hadn't even found the nerve to move into Mamm and Dat's bedroom. That room . . . it just didn't feel right to take it over. With just one double bed, it was meant for a couple, man and wife, and Adam had no plans to marry any time in the near future.

Instead, he slept upstairs in a small bedroom under the eaves, which Gabe had been eyeing since he began his rumspringa. Amish teens were usually allowed to move from the bedrooms shared with siblings to their own rooms, but with five of the Kings now older, there was a shortage of single rooms. That left Sadie bunking with the younger girls and Gabe with Simon. But that empty room downstairs weighed on Adam.

The *clip-clop* of a horse's hooves beyond the mudroom windows alerted him to someone's arrival. Most likely Jonah, as Mary would probably stay out later with Five. Adam knew the Amish courting practices well. Years ago he had spent some time with Lizzy Mast, an Amish girl who was now married. That chunk of time was very much a part of his boyhood; before the fall.

Before he had skipped off to court an Englisher woman.

Memories clenched, a fist in his belly, and he worried that his interest in Remy was part of a pattern, a flaw in his character. Was he a man who could not fall in love with his own kind?

He had once thought he was in love. He had left home for Jane, an exotic, striking woman he still likened to one of the rare orchids sold at the Reading Terminal Market, where they'd met. He'd been selling family-made quilts; she'd been peddling jewelry that she made from polished rocks and melted metals. He had followed her to Rhode Island, where it became clear that their relationship was not going to work out.

Although he'd been swept away by her at first, by the time she broke it off he'd felt only relief. In his heart, he knew Jane wasn't the one for him.

The one . . .

Adam had always believed God had a strong hand in bringing people together. For every man of faith, there was a special woman out there, a woman who would be his partner, his wife. Adam's faith was strong, but he was beginning to wonder if marrying was part of the Lord's plan for him. There weren't enough hours in the day for proper courtship, and now the Amish girls in Halfway seemed like children. He was a lot older than most of the young girls starting their rumspringa. Looking for a bride in the traditional Amish way just did not feel right these days.

Still, he prayed for a good woman. He wanted that close bond he'd witnessed between his parents. And he'd felt that solid connection today, with Remy. Another Englisher girl. *Dear God, please don't let me stray down that path again.* Something about her earnestness, her goodness, appealed to him, but he had to remind himself that there were plenty of good people in the world.

His task was to find a good Amish woman, a partner, a friend. Although he was always surrounded by people here at the farm, loneliness sometimes clung to him like a panicked cat, its claws gripping deeper with each passing month.

As if to give voice to the proverbial cat, the door opened with a yawning screech, and Jonah strode in.

"Adam." Jonah removed his hat and hung it on the peg. "That's a good idea on a cold night. Sorry to barge in."

Sitting up in the tub, Adam waved off the apology. "Actually, you're the person I wanted to talk to. What do you think about installing some cold and hot plumbing up on the second story?" He outlined the plans for his brother, who mulled them over, hands in his pockets.

Jonah's dark brows rose. "I think it's a very good idea. We could do a lot of that work ourselves, and you know Zed Mast, the bishop's brother? He's a plumber. We can hire him. I'm sure he'll teach us how to lay pipe, and weld it, too."

"Welding pipe." Adam grinned. "Is there no challenge you won't take on?"

Jonah shrugged.

As they discussed ways to improve plumbing and use solar panels to heat their water, Adam was relieved at Jonah's receptiveness. Although Adam as the oldest son had been called upon to lead the family, Jonah knew this land. He was good with building and growing. It was Jonah's practical experience and knack for innovation that had carried the operations of the dairy farm this past year. From tending to a sick calf to operating the harvester, Jonah was a natural-born farmer.

As the water cooled, Adam realized he hadn't asked about the singing. "So how did your evening go? You never mention anyone, Jonah. Is there a girl you're secretly keeping company with?"

Jonah shook his head. "I always leave with an empty buggy. But you should come next time. Annie Stoltzfus asked about you."

Annie and her mouthful of berries. Adam groaned. "Mmm. Between the two of us? I wish she would leave me alone."

"Annie's a sweet girl," Jonah said, methodically coiling the hot water hose as he spoke. "And you seem to have won her heart. Would it be such a terrible thing to take her for a buggy ride one night and see how you two get on?"

Rising to sit on the edge of the tub, Adam realized what a grump he was being. "You're right," he told his brother. "She's a kind person, a good friend to Mary." It was wrong to complain about a young woman when Jonah had not found a special girl, despite attending every singing.

Jonah scraped one side of his dark hair back, his eyelids heavy with weariness.

"You look tired."

"A good tired," Jonah said. "But then, I'm not the one carrying this family on his back."

"Excuse me?"

"I can read it on your face, Adam. You've taken on more than any one person can handle."

Adam gripped the edges of the tub. "But Dat carried the burden on his own."

"Dat knew how to delegate chores and even things out."

"I'm just trying to do the right thing for everyone."

"No one's questioning your commitment, Adam. But you're trying to do it all alone, and that's not going to work."

"Are you telling me to get a wife?"

"No. I'm telling you to lean on me. And Gabe and Uncle Nate and the rest of the congregation. You're trying to deny a need, and the more you do it, the worse it will get. The quilting that Mary's organizing for the Troyer family . . . the house that burned to the ground in Paradise. Do you see the Troyers telling people not to sew clothes for their children or rebuild their home?"

"That's different—"

"Is it? Is it really?" When Jonah's brows rose in a scowl, he resembled Dat. "You know, every day I pray to God that you'll find it in your heart to let Him help you. I figure if you let Him in, the rest of us won't be too far behind."

Adam stared into the bathwater. It wasn't pleasant, being called a control freak, and it bothered him to know Jonah was right.

"I hear you, brother. I get it."

When Adam looked up, Jonah was kicking off his boots, one by one. He lined them up beside the kitchen doorway. "And I'm not the only one who's tired," Jonah said. "You sound like an old man."

"I feel like an old man."

Jonah poked him in the shoulder. "Get some rest, old man, and think about what I said. God gave you ten siblings for a reason." With that he went into the kitchen, leaving Adam to stew, his feet beginning to prune in the cooling bathwater.

SEVEN

*I*t was Sunday night, and Remy couldn't sleep. She flipped over and faced the numbers that glowed blue on the nightstand beside her bed: 1:37.

Monday morning, actually.

She was tired, having stayed up late last night talking with Dakota about anything and everything, and yet sleep eluded her.

She threw back the covers, grabbed her laptop, and burrowed into the corner of the sofa. No stranger to insomnia, she knew that it was better to get up and do something than to beat yourself up in bed. She logged on to the Internet, skimmed the headlines, then closed her eyes with a groan.

She was in no mood to be sucked into the Internet vortex, the array of articles built on varying degrees of truth and writing skill. The nasty comments from readers, the meaningless postings from friends she barely knew—it was a cold, impersonal lifeline after her weekend with Dakota, chock-full of shopping and cooking and animated conversation. Not to mention running into Adam King at the Saturday market.

What a pleasure it had been to see him, looking healthy and whole less than a year after his family tragedy. In his dark Amish attire, he had been attractive in that *American Gothic* way. With his long dark hair and old-fashioned clothes, Adam reminded her of Heathcliff in *Wuthering Heights,* although unlike the hero of the Brontë classic, Adam's deep brown eyes held compassion and insight. She'd been touched that he remembered small details about her. Yes, Adam King was a man with backbone, someone who cared about people.

With a small burst of interest, she did a search for King Family Dairy and found that the only reference was to their booth at the Reading Terminal Market. Hmm.

Next she tried to find information about how his family was doing—especially the little boy, Simon, who had witnessed his parents' murders. There had been plenty of coverage in the weeks after the tragic event, but the story had been dropped eight months ago, with a brief report from a Lancaster TV affiliate saying that the murders were still unsolved.

How had the King family recovered over the last year? Remy tried to imagine a line of Amish boys and girls who resembled Adam as she set her laptop on the table and walked purposefully to the window. Despite the cultural differences, grief and sorrow were a universal response to losing someone you loved, and it must have rocked their world to lose both parents. Did they know who had committed the heinous crime? What if someone in the community had murdered Mr. and Mrs. King? What if it was someone Adam knew?

Outside, wind stirred the bare branches of the trees that lined the street. These were the dreary days of winter, the merry twinkle of Christmas lights stripped away to reveal skeletons of trees and walkways riddled with ice hazards. Looking down toward Logan Square, she saw a slice of the lit fountain, and only two cars moving slowly through the traffic circle. Street lamps cast pools of light along the pavements, pin dots of loneliness. It was small comfort to live in a majestic, sophisticated place when you had no one to share it with.

In that, she envied Adam King, with his ten siblings. His life was probably crazy-hectic at times, but with so much family around, loneliness was an impossibility.

She pressed her forehead to the cool glass, stretching to look west, toward the river. Somewhere, fifty or so miles beyond Philadelphia's buildings and lights, Adam's family was at home in Lancaster County. Probably asleep. Probably bundled under blankets in this cold.

If only she knew more about them. And she wasn't the only person who was curious; she suspected a lot of people would like to know how the King family was doing.

The idea glimmered in her mind like a twinkling gem.

A follow-up on the King family would make a good story . . . a great story for the *Post*. A look at how the family was faring a year after the eleven siblings had lost their parents. Considering the thorough coverage the paper had done on the tragic incident, Remy suspected that the editors would love her idea. She opened a file on her computer and started copying in scattered information about last winter's murders.

She glanced at the time on the computer screen. The weekly editorial meeting was just hours away. If she pulled together some quick facts now, she could pitch the story today.

It was hard to sit still and listen while the other editors discussed the status of their current articles. Remy wiggled her toes inside her boots, eager to share her pitch, impatient with Ed Green, who seemed to be rambling on about the unscrupulous heating contractor he'd been trying to expose.

"A timely story, with these freezing temperatures," Arlene said, arching a dark brow. "Do we have enough to run it this week?"

When Ed shrugged, Miles Wister jumped in. "We have to run with it now, Ed, not in the spring. And we need to wrap up this meeting, as we all have places to be," Miles said without looking up from his notepad. As managing editor, Miles's job was to keep things moving, and Remy appreciated his taut but judicious demeanor.

"I have a few more leads," Ed said.

"Great. Do it," Arlene said brusquely. The paper's editor in chief did not waste words. Rumor had it her early colleagues had dubbed her "Ms. Brevity."

"Next item . . ." Miles glanced up at the editors. "New stories."

Yasmina nudged her, and Remy's hand slid across her folder. Yasmina, the only other junior assistant in the office, had "adored" Remy's idea when they'd discussed it this morning, and though Remy was determined to make her pitch, she didn't want to go first.

"There's been a sighting of Evan Canby, the boy who went missing six months ago," Carla Willis suggested. "He was spotted at Disney World with a woman who resembled his birth mother."

Arlene folded her arms over the sizable bulk of her midriff. "See what you can find out."

"Preferably without a trip to Orlando," added Miles.

Remy's palm flattened on the folder as she waited a moment, then sprang to the attack.

"How about a look at the aftermath of the Amish murders? Esther and Levi King, the Lancaster County couple killed while riding in their buggy." Remy worked to keep her voice steady. She didn't want to sound like a novice, and yet she felt the power in her words. This was a solid story pitch. "I'd like to follow up on the family—the eleven children left behind—and check on the progress of the homicide investigation."

"The Amish murders . . ." Arlene's dark brows pulled together. "Tell me more."

As if in unison, the other reporters bowed their heads to consult their BlackBerrys. This was a good sign.

Remy pushed her typed pitch across the table to Arlene, who lifted the bejeweled reading glasses that hung around her neck.

"Was that case ever solved?" Miles asked.

"No. They never found the killer. The *Post* followed the story for a few months, until the investigation fizzled without any strong leads."

"I covered that story." Alfonzo Nunez stroked the soul patch on his chin as he squinted at the small screen in his palm. "There was some talk of a bear attack. Also rumors that the little boy in the buggy went berserk. And the Amish don't make the best witnesses. Apparently they don't believe in the justice system."

"Hmm." Arlene tugged on one earlobe. "I like that one, too. See what you can find on it," she told Remy. "And make sure your sources are solid. It would be nice to include an interview with the family."

Everyone in the room knew that in Arlene-speak, "nice" meant "necessary" and "Don't come back until you've at least tried it." But that didn't frighten Remy. She had an "in" with the family. And now, she had a professional reason to see Adam King again. The logic may have been as twisted as a pretzel, and yet she had a good feeling about this story. Finally, she had something to work toward, something to look forward to.

"I'll start working on it today," Remy said. She pretended to jot a note in her folder, but the tactic was really a diversion to keep herself from jumping up and bursting into a happy dance.

As the meeting broke up, Yasmina grabbed Remy's wrist and shook it. "Look at you, pitching a first-rate story. This is going to be amazing, girl!"

"I hope so," Remy said, shooting a glance over to be sure that Arlene and Miles had left the conference room. "I think so. It has the making of a good article, right?"

"A great article. Pulitzer material."

"Well, let's not go too crazy," Remy said as they moved into the newsroom together. The room, dubbed the "ice cube tray" because of the configurations of work spaces, eight cubicles in two rows, thrummed with chatter and ringing phones.

Back in her cubicle, she immediately spotted a pink phone message slip placed squarely atop the proofs on her desk.

"Your father wants to see you . . . before noon." The message was inked in his secretary Viola's reliable penmanship.

Remy crumbled the note into one hand, wishing she could find a job that didn't put her under her father's thumb. Although everyone at the paper knew she was Herb's daughter, she tried to be discreet about it and stayed away from his office during business hours. But today, the big boss had summoned her. She turned down the hallway containing the executive offices. Here the carpeting was plusher, the air colder. The brass nameplates on the doors were polished to a shine.

Viola looked up from her desk. "What took you so long? I thought he was going to have a cow."

"I was in a meeting."

"Oh, don't tell him that." Viola rolled her eyes. "You can't top your father."

No one knew that as well as Remy.

"He's on with Mr. Gefeller in sales, but you can go in."

Remy felt that strange mixture of intimidation and longing as she entered the office. A male retreat designed to resemble a cross between a cigar bar and a paneled library, Herb's office sat empty much of the time, as the demands of his work required him to be elsewhere.

Phone pressed to his ear, Herb shot her a look, then nodded for her to sit.

Remy sank onto the leather sofa as he rolled an unlit cigar between his fingers and argued about numbers with the man on the phone. Was it any wonder that she felt as if he didn't have time for her in his life?

Glancing down at the design of the sculpted carpet, she recalled a time when she had rolled on the rug of her father's office, and once or twice Herb had gotten down on the rug beside her. In the months just after her mother died, Herb had indulged her, letting her miss school to be with him. The huge, dark area under his keyhole desk was her playhouse, a place to curl up and read a book, nap, or create stories about what the families of paper clips did together after the lights went out in the office each night.

How precious that time was.

No one had seemed in a hurry for her to grow up. Grades were never mentioned, and for that interlude she had been the only family her father needed.

As Herb prattled on, she imagined herself under his desk, holed up with a doll or favorite stuffed animal—Bunny. The white rabbit was actually a hand puppet, so its body was slim and very huggable. She had slept with her every night, and though her fake fur had worn thin and the ribbon around her neck faded from blue to a pale gray, Remy had loved Bunny unconditionally.

Every night, before falling asleep, she and Bunny recited the prayer her mother had taught her. "Now I lay me down to sleep, I pray the Lord my soul to keep . . ."

She grabbed at the lapels of her blazer, equally pleased and disarmed by the memory.

"Herb, what happened to Bunny?" she asked the minute he was off the phone.

"Bunny." He frowned, his lips thinning as he tucked the cigar between them. "Who in the world is that? I can't keep track of all your friends."

"Don't you remember? Bunny was my favorite stuffed animal, the one I slept with every night."

"A stuffed animal? How could I forget that?" His voice was thick with his usual sarcasm. "Would you look at the time?" He rose from his chair and went to the closet behind the door.

But Remy wasn't backing down. "Seriously, what do you think happened to Bunny?"

He slid his suit jacket from its hanger. "I don't know. Maybe the housekeeper got rid of it. Or was it Sonja? She was such a clean freak. I know she put it through the wash at least once."

Herb's second wife Sonja had purged their lives of so many things, though Remy liked to think the woman had pushed forward with good intentions.

"Anyway, I have a new business associate I'd like you to meet: Max Menkowitz. He's putting up some money for a new enterprise of mine, bringing his son to Philadelphia to handle the whole thing, and the son is about your age."

Remy fell back on the sofa. "Herb, tell me you're not setting me up on a blind date."

"Who said anything about a date? Max and Stuart are going to be partners with McCallister Inc., and I'd like you to be on their radar. You weren't planning to fritter your time away on the newspaper forever, were you?"

"I figured I'd stay until I mastered it, and there's still a lot to learn in editorial," Remy said. "I haven't even gotten a byline yet."

Herb's laugh came out as half roar, half bark. "Don't worry about that. You know you'll be well taken care of."

"I know you've got the money thing covered, Herb," she said. If only her father could be half as attentive in other areas. When she tried to picture his heart, she imagined a small, shriveled organ. The heart of a Grinch.

"So we'll go to dinner one night next week," he said, smoothing the lapels of his well-tailored jacket. "Just the four of us."

"Sure. It'll be like one of those 'date with Daddy' dances. Only Stu won't be dancing with his dad."

Herb laughed again as they stepped into the reception area. "Attagirl. I'm thrilled that you've inherited my cutting sarcasm. But maybe you should do something with your hair first. . . ."

Remy shot a look at Viola, who shrugged.

"What's wrong with my hair?" Self-consciously Remy reached behind one ear for the thick reddish locks she wore long to keep them from curling into little-girl ringlets.

"When was the last time you cut it? You could go to one of those salons . . . get a total makeover, like on TV. My treat."

"Herb!" Remy rolled her eyes.

"In fact, a few phone calls and I might get you on that makeover show. Wouldn't that be—"

"Mr. McCallister, excuse me?" Viola reached for him, as if directing traffic from behind her desk. "I don't butt in much, but I gotta say you are over the line."

"Really?" Herb shrugged then stuffed the cigar back into the corner of his mouth. "Fine. Leave your hair long, then. Just wear something nice, will you? No jeans."

The idea of a night out with Herb and his two cronies had as much appeal as a root canal, but if business was the way to her father's heart, Remy was willing to give it her best shot.

EIGHT

"Two dozen more Holsteins would nearly double our herd. . . ."
Jonah shook his head, his dark eyes round with awe as he scanned the barn from end to end. Gray afternoon light seeped in through the open doors of the old wooden structure. "Where would we put them all?"

"That's a good point," Adam said. "We would probably need to pour cement and build some new stanchions. From what I read we need more than sixty cows to turn a profit. It's just an idea right now, nothing definite yet, but I wanted to see what you both thought."

"It sounds crazy to me." Gabriel rested the shovel beside the bucket and looked from Jonah to Adam in disbelief. "How would we ever milk a herd like that?"

"Milking machines, like the one at Uncle Nate's farm. And Mark Zook's. Plenty of Amish dairy farmers use them now. It would save us lots of time."

Gabe notched his hands over the top of the shovel's handle and leaned on it. "I can hear Dat's voice in my head, saying: 'Just because all your friends jump from the roof of the barn doesn't mean you should do it, too.'"

"It's a way for the farm to grow," Adam said, trying to keep his voice level. He had expected resistance from his brothers—logical objections—but he could not fight the memory of their father, who had clung to the old ways, even when certain types of change were permitted. "I'm still not sure about the cost, and there are other considerations."

"Like mucking out twenty-four more stalls." Gabe adjusted his work gloves. At sixteen, Gabriel was the member of the King family who seemed to be most in tune with the cows. Although everyone save Sam and Katie helped with the milking, Gabe knew the names and personalities of all the cows, and he had a handle on who could be the most stubborn and who tended to wander off to the back fields. "And don't forget, we'd have twenty-four more to feed," Gabe added.

"Right," Adam agreed, realizing Gabriel, who had been close to Dat, was going to be a tough sell. "I've been wanting to go over the numbers with Mammi, see if we grow enough hay and alfalfa to sustain a larger herd."

"I know that last year we had a surplus of alfalfa, more than our cows could eat. We ended up selling it off." Jonah tipped his hat back and scratched his chin thoughtfully. "It might just work."

"Nay." Gabe's face was sullen, his jaw set as he scraped at a clod of hay with the shovel. "The old ways are best. Dat wouldn't want us turning into a fancy dairy farm."

"It's not about being fancy," Adam said, concerned that his younger brother misunderstood his motives for changing things. He was about to argue that they wouldn't be violating the old ways, that the Ordnung permitted use of milking machines powered by diesel, when a soft noise outside the barn alerted him that a horse was approaching.

"Must be the women arriving for the quilting," he said. "We'll talk about all this later, and the whole family will have a voice in the decision making." That wasn't the Amish way; usually the man of the house made important decisions, which the rest of the family were bound to accept. But Adam didn't have Dat's experience, and he didn't think it right to hand decisions down to his siblings so close in age. Without a parent at the helm, they were an unusual family. Most Amish family traditions did not apply to a household run by the oldest son.

Gabriel continued mucking the stalls as Jonah and Adam headed out to greet the guests.

"That didn't go so well," Jonah said under his breath.

"He'll come around," Adam said. "As soon as he figures out that I'm not trying to undo Dat's lifetime of hard work."

Two buggies sat in front of the house, and a group of women, Aunt Betsy and her daughters, Rose and Rachel, among them, were following Mary into the house. Sadie was nearly finished unhitching one carriage. Inside the other, Annie Stoltzfus wrapped the reins around the resting post and climbed out.

"Hello, Adam," Annie called, her berry-red lips curved in a grin. "Do you think the rain will hold off till evening?"

"It looks that way." His stomach curled at the unwanted attention, and he wondered if she'd bothered to say hello to his sister and brother, too. "Annie . . . I know Mary's grateful you could join in the quilting."

"Oh, I'm happy to do it. The Troyers lost everything in that fire." She reached into the carriage and lifted out a fat hamper covered with cloth. "I brought strawberry muffins—still warm from the oven. Mary said you like muffins."

"Strawberry . . ." He was struck by the irony, but then he'd heard that she thought fondly of her rescue from the strawberry patch. "I'm sure they're delicious," Adam said, trying to keep his voice level. He didn't want to give Annie false encouragement, but he couldn't be rude.

"That basket looks heavy," Jonah said. "Would you like me to carry it for you?"

"Oh, I think I can manage. But would you mind unhitching the carriage for me?" The weight of the hamper on one arm had Annie nearly waddling toward the house, her dark green skirts swaying as she walked.

"No problem," Jonah said, guiding the horse ahead a few feet so that the buggies were neatly lined up.

"And Adam, would you mind getting the door for me?" Annie called. "This hamper is heavy."

Adam shot a look at his siblings. Though Jonah's head was concealed behind the horse, he did see Sadie hiding a smile behind one hand. They were enjoying his discomfort with Annie's affections, were they? Of course, they all had a match in mind for him.

He followed Annie to the door, thinking how his life would be simple if he could just take an interest in the right person, an Old Order Amish girl. Dear God, it would be so simple. . . .

An hour later, school was out and four children appeared at the end of the lane. Leah and Susie walked arm in arm. Simon circled the beech trees, dragging a very long stick, about which Ruthie appeared to be scolding him.

Adam took a break from chopping to watch the amusing tableau in the distance. This was what it was about. Whenever he had doubts or faced obstacles, he needed to think of their faces. His most important job was to raise these children the right way, teaching them to love God and live a Plain life. That was what really mattered.

Just then Jonah came around the corner of the house, pausing at the sight of Adam wielding the ax on the old stump. "You're a step ahead of me," he said. "Mary just asked for more wood."

"This should be enough for a while. Would you mind taking a stack inside?" Adam buried the hatchet in the stump and picked up three split logs. "I'm trying to make myself scarce in there."

"I'm happy to take credit for your work," Jonah said with his usual stoic grimace.

From the way Jonah had been hovering near the house, Adam suspected his brother was interested in one of the young women at the quilting. The idea of shy Jonah closing in on a lady friend after years of patient observation made him smile.

"This is ready to go." Adam stacked wood high in his brother's arms. "You can be the hero who feeds the potbellied stove."

"I can do that," Jonah said, lugging the wood toward the door.

When Adam turned back toward the driveway, Simon waved as he raced down the rutted lane, swinging his plastic lunch cooler in one hand. But something emerged over the rise behind the children. A dark vehicle rolled slowly toward the house.

The sheriff's cruiser.

Fear twisted through Adam, a sharp stone in his belly. The last time Hank Hallinan had come out this way, he'd been trying to gather evidence for the homicide investigation.

Was he back with more questions? Or had something else happened?

Quickly calculating, Adam knew Sadie was safe at home today, not working at the hotel. The little ones were inside, and the schoolkids were now in sight. It had to be old news. That was some consolation.

Leaving his hat and coat on the woodpile, Adam strode down the lane to meet the sheriff. The children paused at the sight of the passing cruiser, then broke into a run, curious to see what was going on.

The vehicle pulled right up to the house, meeting Adam beside the two parked buggies. Sheriff Hank emerged from the driver's side.

"Adam. How's it going?" Even with his slight paunch, Hank cut a fine appearance in his dark uniform. Black stripes ran down the sides of his creased navy pants, and the front of his parka was decorated with his sheriff's star as well as three rows of medals. He reached into the car for a hat to cover his snow-white hair before closing the door.

"Can't say I'm happy to see you, Hank," Adam admitted. "There's still a lot of heartache here, and you know the Amish attitude toward the punishment aspect of law enforcement."

"I respect both points." Hank moved away from the car, motioning for Adam to walk along with him. "You know I would have called, but . . ." He shrugged. "The phone shanty doesn't work well for incoming."

"True," Adam said, thinking of the phone shanty down the road that they shared with Uncle Nate's family. Mostly it was there to call out in an emergency.

The four children raced to a breathless stop behind the sheriff's vehicle, mesmerized by the flashing red and white turret lights. Simon's mouth hung open in awe and a shade of fear as he looked past the vehicle to stare at Hank. Of course. Simon would always remember Hank as the man who questioned him about his parents' murders.

If he'd been on top of the situation, Adam would have asked

Hank to wait while he walked Simon into the house, out of sight, but it was too late for that. The damage had been done.

"Listen, the last thing I want to do is cause your family any more grief over your folks," the sheriff was saying. "I'm sorry we hit a dead end with that investigation. But I was starting to think the worst of it was over when, just last week, I started getting calls and visits from media people."

"Really?" Adam shook his head, rubbing at the sweat cooling on the back of his neck. "Why now, Hank? Has something changed? Did you come across some new evidence?"

"No progress there. Seems to be because the anniversary of their deaths is coming up," the sheriff said. "The reporters want an update on the case. They're asking where the family lives and how to get in touch."

"You know we don't want publicity." Adam frowned at the prospect of someone from his family being photographed. Everyone in Lancaster County knew the Amish avoided the graven image, based on biblical teachings and the notion that such things led to personal vanity. "And I need to protect the younger kids. We can't have a media frenzy."

"Which is why I sent them packing." Hank pinched his upper lip, stroking the white mustache that grew there. "But just as soon as I send one of them away, another three call or email the station house. They're coming out of the woodwork."

Lord, help us. Adam looked up to the cold blue heavens and let out a sigh. "We don't want them here, Hank."

"Believe me, I know what a nuisance they can be. Of course, I'd never give them information about anyone in Halfway, but I felt the need to warn you about what was going on. Thing is . . ." The sheriff glanced back at the children, then leaned closer, lowering his voice. "I thought you might want to take some precautions, limit the children's trips into town for a while. Not that they're in danger, but there's a chance they'll be approached by reporters. Not everyone respects Amish customs, and I know you don't want photos of the family on TV or, God forbid, reeling out over the Internet."

"That's a good point." Adam thought of Simon, who would be one of the main targets of the media. Maybe he should homeschool for a while. "The children know they're not to appear in graven images, but they could be taken advantage of easily."

"Just thought you should know."

Adam met the sheriff's pale gray eyes. "Thanks for the warning."

"No problem." Hank turned to take in the children behind him. The three girls stared, their eyes round as whoopie pies. Simon was nowhere in sight. "Ladies . . . aren't you getting cold standing out here?"

"Ya, but we don't want to miss anything," Ruthie said. The voice of honesty.

"You're not missing anything," Hank said wryly. "The best part of this show is the flashing light on the cruiser. Did you girls have a good day at school today?"

The twins nodded politely.

Ruthie stepped right up to the big man and folded her arms across her chest. "Are you going to put someone in the jailhouse?"

Straightening to his full height, Hank dwarfed Ruthie, but his voice was gentle when he spoke. "We save the jailhouse for the really bad guys. So far today, it's empty."

She sucked in her lower lip and nodded, satisfied for now.

Pebbles crunched underfoot as Adam walked Hank back to the cruiser.

"You let me know if any unwanted visitors come knocking on your door. There are laws against trespassing."

"My father used to say that God gave us plenty of farm to shield us from Englishers."

"He had a point there. And in my experience, the reporters seem to know where they don't belong. I don't think they'll invade your privacy here."

"Thank you, Hank." Adam extended his hand for a handshake, an inadvertent slip back into the gestures of the English.

The sheriff shook his hand firmly, then climbed into the vehicle.

Watching the cruiser disappear beyond the bare beech trees, Adam realized he was getting cold. He'd left his coat and hat by the woodpile.

"Did you see his gun?" Leah asked, her face a small pale patch beneath her kapp and scarf.

"I wonder if he's ever used it." Susie's voice was breathless with high drama. "You know, it's for hunting people, not animals."

"Why was he here?" Ruthie demanded.

"Sheriff Hank wanted to warn us that there might be some reporters around for the next few weeks," Adam explained, looking around for Simon. "He says they've called him, asking questions about Mamm and Dat. We'll talk more about it later, but in general, we're to watch out for photographers and reporters."

"Kinder!" Mary called from the door. "Kumm."

"I hate when she calls us children," Ruthie said, her forehead creased with concern. "I am eleven years old, not a baby anymore."

"You all need to go inside," Adam said. "But where's Simon?"

"Die Scheune," Ruthie answered. The barn. "He got scared of the flashing light, I think."

Adam split away from the girls and jogged to the horse barn, glad for the movement, which warmed his freezing body. Inside the barn a deep voice lingered on a few notes and Adam recognized one of the hymns from the Ausbund, the songbook used in preaching services. He followed the source of the song to a stall, where Gabriel was spreading fresh hay with a pitchfork.

"Have you seen Simon?" he asked.

Although Gabe kept singing, he paused from his chore and jabbed the handle of the pitchfork toward the loft overhead.

"Denki," Adam said quietly, moving toward the ladder. "Simon?" he called, not wanting to startle the already frightened boy. "Are you up there?"

He paused on the second-to-the-top rung and listened. The only sounds were Gabe's voice and the scrape of the pitchfork as he shoveled in time with the hymn.

"Simon?" he tried again. *"Was ist letz?"*

When he said the phrase, in his mind he heard his mamm's voice and thought of the countless times she had come to console him when he was a boy Simon's age. "What's wrong, dear Adam?" she would say, folding him into her arms. "What's the matter?"

Gripping the worn wood of the ladder, he felt a surge of anger that Simon didn't have Mamm to comfort him. Instead, he was stuck with Adam, who knew next to nothing about children. A man so pitifully prepared for fatherhood, he doubted he would ever have children of his own.

But Simon needed him now.

Climbing the last rung, his head rose into the loft. Simon sat huddled beside a bale of hay, his hat crooked, his face wet with tears.

"Ach, Simon." Adam crouched beside his brother, their faces inches apart. "Tell me what's wrong."

Simon shook his head. His eyes and nose were red, and tears matted the dark hair against his cheeks.

"You were scared by something," Adam said. "What? Because you don't have to be afraid of Sheriff Hallinan."

"Not him. It's the bear," Simon said, his voice breaking with a sob. "The bear wore those pants. Pants with a stripe."

Adam held back a groan of frustration at the mention of bears once again. How could he help his brother when he kept reverting to a fairy story? A bear with striped pants.

"I know you don't believe me, but the bear killed them." Simon's shoulders shook as a new tear spilled down his cheek. "It was the bear."

When a pathetic moan escaped Simon's lips, Adam felt his throat grow thick. His job was to help, not to judge. "Simon . . ." Sitting beside him, he scooped the boy into his arms and held on tight. "Okay, it was the bear. The bear killed them."

As if Adam's words fueled the fire, a sob burst from Simon. A swell of emotion overcame Adam as he closed his eyes and rocked the boy gently.

And Mamm's words came to mind again.

"*Was ist letz, Liewi?* What's wrong?" she would coo, her voice deep and rich with the confidence of a grown-up able to lessen the pain of a childhood hurt. It was up to Adam to be the wise one now; the older, wiser voice capable of easing a young one's mind.

"I want you to know that you're safe, Simon," he whispered. "We will take care of you. You must know how Mary and I work and plan so that you have good food and a good life on this farm."

"But Mary wants to leave." Simon's voice came out as a tortured squeak. "I heard her talking with Sadie. She wants to go away and marry Five."

Anxiety flared at the thought of losing their oldest sister, though it shouldn't have been news at all. Of course, Mary had to be eager to start a family of her own with John Beiler. Was the idea of losing her adding to Simon's anxiety?

"We won't truly lose Mary when she weds Five. She will always be your sister who loves you. And you can count on your family to take care of you, with God's blessing. Do you hear me? *Verstehst?*"

A whimpered breath indicated that Simon understood.

"And there is no bear out there now, Simon. That's the truth."

"I know." Simon sniffed. "But it hurts, Adam. It hurts me to talk about it."

Adam released his brother so that he could see his face. "Where does it hurt?" he asked, thinking it might help to be more specific.

Simon pressed the fingertips of one hand to his chest. "In my heart. It hurts in my heart."

"Then we'll pray to God for healing," Adam said. "We'll ask Him to make our hearts new again. Can you do that with me?"

"Ya." Simon let out the stiff breath he'd been holding. "I pray to God all the time, but I don't think He's been listening."

"He listens." Even as Adam said the words, he realized he had better start believing them. Lately he'd been praying out of a sense of duty, a sense that God needed His chunk of Adam's time, just like everyone else. How foolish he'd been, not to share his burdens with God. Jonah had been right about his desire to sacrifice himself; he'd been trying to shoulder a burden alone, when help had been there all along. If he was going to convince Simon to trust in God's love, he had better know that truth in his own heart. "God listens, all right," he told his younger brother. "But if we want help, we need to lay our burdens down."

Simon nodded, a new light in his eyes. A light of promise. A glimmer of hope.

NINE

*F*ear and excitement warred within her heart as Remy copied the last detail of the Halfway map, then tossed the pen down and rubbed the crick in her neck. What time was it? Almost two A.M., and there were still so many details she hadn't been able to find over the past few days.

Information about the King family was sparse; however, she'd found a site sponsored by the town of Halfway. The site included a map that detailed the town's retail establishments, including quaint tourist stops that might prove to be good sources of information, so she'd copied the basic map into her journal.

She rubbed her eyes, feeling tired but afraid to stop working. If she wasn't prepared, this might all blow up in her face. A phone call to the King family stand at Reading Terminal Market had steered her toward Halfway, as the woman who answered the phone, Adam's cousin, had told her she didn't expect to see him in Philadelphia for a few more weeks. "They'll stay local for the winter months," the woman had assured her. So tomorrow morning,

Remy was off to Halfway to get her interview, despite the trepidation rumbling in the pit of her stomach.

She was afraid of failing. Afraid she wouldn't be able to find Adam King or his family. Afraid they would refuse to talk with her. Afraid she wouldn't even make it to the town of Halfway, as she was not a confident driver for long-distance travel. And then what would she tell Arlene? After the buildup, she wouldn't be able to show her face in the office without some sort of article. If she failed, Herb would use her misstep as leverage to pull her into his new venture with Stu and Max Menkowitz. Just the thought of them made her palms sweat. The memory of dinner with the men was still fresh in her mind; it had been a boring event, full of jokes that weren't funny and tales of gambling in Vegas. She rubbed her hands on her pajamas, realizing Herb's big plans added to the pressure to make this story work.

But when she considered all the things that might go wrong, Remy was most worried about offending Adam. She considered him a friend. Well, she liked to think of him as a friend, and didn't want to wrong him. After the phone calls she had made this week, it appeared that Adam would be a key source for the story, unless she could gain information from the community. When she had called the sheriff's office in Halfway, she was told, in a kind but firm way, to take a hike.

"The investigation has not turned up any new information that wasn't reported last March," Sheriff Hank Hallinan had told her. "It would be much appreciated if you media people would just leave this family alone. Haven't they been through enough?"

When she reported the sheriff's statement to Arlene, her boss had glared at her over her bejeweled reading glasses. "Are you telling me there's no story here?"

"There's definitely a story," Remy had insisted. "It's just a matter of talking with the family."

"But they're insulated. They're Amish. It's a different culture. They're not starstruck like the rest of America. They don't want to make headlines."

"I'll get the interview with Adam King," Remy had said over the nervous thrumming of her pulse. "I know him. He's . . . he's a friend of mine."

In retrospect, she realized that "know" may have been a bit presumptuous, but they had met more than once, chatted, and he'd remembered her. In this age of technology, she figured there was something special about a personal connection. Especially when it came to the Amish.

When Arlene had questioned her further, Remy had tossed out some details she'd learned from her research on the Amish. "When I met Adam King, he was coming back from his rumspringa, the 'running around' period when teens are given freedom from the confines of their culture."

"A custom that's garnered a lot of interest lately. People seem to think it's like college frat boys at spring break." Arlene rested her chin in the V of her thumb and pointing finger, as if settling in to hear more.

"That's a misconception, but we can clear that up in the article. Of course, we won't be able to run any family photographs with the piece," Remy had warned the big boss. "The Amish avoid being photographed. They believe it's wrong to get caught up in 'graven images.'"

"Right." Arlene had seemed impressed. "As I remember, we ran last year's reports with photos of a Lancaster County farm, and shots of a horse and buggy. Anonymous Amish people were photographed from behind or from a distance."

"I suppose that would work," Remy had said, amazed that she was suddenly discussing photo layout with the editor in chief.

Now, leafing through the pages of her journal, she reviewed

the names of the King children—all eleven of them—and tried to picture them in her mind. Adam, Jonah, and Mary were closest to her in age, though Gabe and Sadie weren't far behind. She wondered if the teenaged twin girls were identical, and how they get along with Ruthie. The little baby, Katie, would have to be walking by now, and Sam was almost old enough for kindergarten. And the little boy who had been with his parents that deadly night—Simon. How had he coped with grief and trauma?

Glancing over the driving directions to Halfway, she hoped to find these answers tomorrow. She would drive out to Lancaster County in the morning and chat up the locals. The trip wouldn't take but an hour or two, especially with Saturday's lighter traffic. From the town's website, she thought that Molly's Roadside Restaurant might be a good place to start. There was also the Sweet 'N' Simple Bakery, Kraybill's Fish and Game, and Ye Olde Tea Shop. Behind the town hall was an area designated for a farmers market, but Remy couldn't tell if it was open year-round.

She plunked a painted stone paperweight on her open journal, then moved into the kitchen area, her stomach growling at the thought of food. Dinner had been popcorn and a diet Coke. Inside the fridge, there was only ketchup, a wax container of moo shu pork, pickle relish, and two diet sodas. She closed the fridge, resolving to get some sleep and grab a good breakfast in the morning.

With the lights out, moonlight shone from the wide window. She hitched up her flannel pajamas and nestled on the wide sill, soaking up the night for a moment.

Although her studio apartment was small, its location in the Museum District was excellent, and she never tired of the illumination and color and activity that transpired ten stories down. The orderly line of car lights gliding along the Benjamin Franklin Parkway made her feel as if life were moving on in an orderly fashion, and the pillared façade of the Rodin Museum, awash with light, seemed to connect wandering souls like her to the earth.

But tonight it was the moon that drew her eye. Like a wedge of cheese, it sat in the upper corner of the window, as if it were swinging from a hook.

A cheese moon. *Tell me that's not your subconscious reminding you of Adam King's dairy farm.*

That same moon was shining over Halfway right now, shining over Adam King and his family. What was Adam doing right now?

Yawning, she pressed one palm to the cool glass. Adam was probably sleeping, unless he was already up milking cows. But tomorrow she would close the distance between them. She tried to tamp down her nervous excitement about seeing him again.

Of course, she would maintain a professional distance. She was a journalist, researching a story. Her interest in Adam was purely altruistic.

"Keep telling yourself that, and maybe you'll believe it," she muttered as she hopped down from the windowsill and shuffled off to bed.

TEN

The weight of darkness echoed with footsteps, the sound of bare feet brushing wood.

Adam pushed at the thick walls of sleep, trying to open his eyes. Focusing in the blackness, he could tell it wasn't near dawn yet; the air was still heavy and thick. But the small feet pacing beside his bed pedaled with energy.

"I'm worried. Just so worried about the bear . . ."

Adam sat up, sliding from the warmth of the blankets as he recognized the young voice. "Simon?" He scrambled, feeling along the bedside table to light a lantern.

In the flare of the match, Simon's eyes glimmered, glassy and hollow. "What if it comes again? Bears have a very good sense of smell. He might be smelling us right now!"

The floor was like ice under Adam's feet, but he barely noticed as he fell into step behind Simon, who was pacing the room, ranting.

"It's okay, Simon. Shh!" Adam's voice was soft but firm as he stood by the door, blocking his brother's exit from the bedroom.

He had seen this panic in his little brother before. He'd even talked to a doctor, who had explained it as night terrors. But having a name for the behavior didn't make it any less horrifying. Especially when Simon lifted his chin and gazed straight into Adam's eyes as if he were wide awake and rational.

"He could find us. What if he finds out that we are here?" Simon seemed to notice the window. "What if he sees me?" Gasping in panic, he dropped down beside the bed and curled into a ball, shivering. "Oh, no! Oh, no!"

The creak of floorboards in the hall made Adam look up. Mary appeared in the doorway, her dark hair pulled back in one long braid, the hem of her nightgown balled in her fists so that she could run without tripping. Adam did not remember the last time he'd seen his sister without a prayer kapp. She must have heard their voices from her room next door.

"Oh, *liewe* Simon, is it happening again?" She stepped forward, then paused as Simon cast an eerie stare in her direction.

"He will find the farm. The bear will come. He'll come with his gun!" The boy clapped his hands to his bare head.

Mary shot a look at Adam. "He's afraid of this bear again?"

Adam nodded, edging closer to his brother. "It's okay, Simon. You're safe here. There are no bears."

"Oh, no! He has a gun! Did you see that?" Simon pointed across the room, his face awash with panic. "He has a gun!"

Mary pressed her hands to the bodice of her nightgown. "Oh, dear God, please help this child."

"It's my fault!" Simon panted. "Why did I ever like guns? I told Dat I wanted to shoot, that I would shoot real gut. And he listened to me and then it happened."

"He's talking about Mamm and Dat." Mary's hands were pressed to the collar of her nightgown as if she were having trouble breathing. "Do you think there's any truth to what he's saying?"

"It's like a dream," Adam explained. "Part story telling, part reality."

Huddled beside the bed, Simon rocked back and forth, knocking his head into the bedpost. "It's my fault. It's my fault he killed them. . . ."

Immediately Adam was on his knees, holding his brother's shoulders so that he wouldn't hit the bed. "Can't have you hurting yourself, buddy. Can you wake up and calm down?"

"It's so cold." The boy shivered as a pathetic sob slipped out.

"I'll build a fire." As Adam scooped the boy into his arms and headed down the stairs, he felt slightly reassured, as this was the way Simon's previous spell of terror had ended a few weeks ago. If they could warm his small body by the potbellied stove, he would probably relax enough to go back to sleep.

As he worked he thanked the Lord that Simon always seemed to come to his room whenever he had such a spell. It wouldn't do to have Simon wandering in his panic. So far none of the other sleepyheads in the house had witnessed the night terrors except for Jonah and Mary, who used the small room next to the nursery and seemed to sleep with one eye open for the children.

Mary held a whimpering Simon in the big hickory rocking chair while Adam got a fire going. Wrapped in a quilt, the boy looked small and helpless. That such innocence had been marred by the violent hand of another man . . . it tore at Adam's heart.

Soon, Adam had a fire blazing. He sank into a chair beside them, relieved that the worst of Simon's episode seemed to be over. For a few minutes they sat in the growing warmth of the fire's glow; the only sound was the ebb and flow of the boy's steady breathing. He seemed to be finding sleep once again, his head resting in the crook of Mary's arm.

"Are your arms getting tired?" Adam asked.

"It's fine." She touched the back of one hand to Simon's pale cheek. "Such a sweet boy. But he scares me so."

"It's a difficult thing to watch." Adam always felt a tug of panic over these night terrors.

"I know the doctor said it's normal, considering the trauma he suffered. But Adam, it gives me such a fright. I look in his eyes and . . ." She pressed a fist to her mouth. "It's like the devil is staring back!"

"It's not Satan, Mary. And please, don't let anyone hear you say that. Our boy has been through enough trauma. The last thing he needs is folks saying he's possessed by the devil."

"Of course, I would never tell it to anyone else," she said defensively.

"Then don't say it now. He needs rest, and our support." Adam poked at a log in the stove, his own patience as volatile as the hot coals. At times like this, it seemed that Simon was getting worse instead of better, and Adam felt responsible for that. The doctor had said the bouts of terror were usually touched off on nights when the child was overly exhausted or had suffered a recent reminder of a trauma.

"It must have been seeing the sheriff that caused this," Adam said. "After he left, I found Simon crying in the barn. He was definitely spooked."

"We were all frightened by the flashing lights of the sheriff's car." She lovingly tucked the quilt under Simon's chin. "Will it always remind us of that awful night when we learned what had happened to Mamm and Dat? I don't know. Maybe."

"Maybe," he agreed, taking a calming breath.

In his single-minded focus to keep the farm functioning and the family together, he often forgot the toll they all paid from their parents' untimely deaths. The feeling of loss was complicated by the terrible murders, which the bishop forbade them from delving into. Out of obedience to the bishop, Adam had made it a house rule that no one would speak of their parents' murders. That seemed the safest way to play it. But was it the best way to heal the wounds? Maybe it was wrong to silence their sorrow.

"Do you think I'm too hard on everyone?" he asked his sister.

"You?" Mary snorted, her face softening with a smile. "If you ask Sadie, she'll give you an earful. But I don't think you're any tougher on us than Dat and Mamm were. It's just hard, sometimes, paying obedience to a brother."

"That makes sense. Well, you won't be following my ways much longer, will you? Aren't you and Five going to be wed soon as the season begins?"

Her smile faded. "Who told you that?"

"Simon mentioned something about it, but I've been expecting it all along. It's about time. You two have been courting for an eternity."

"And we'll still be courting come this time next year," Mary said stoically. "I do so want to marry Five, but the two of you have no sense of the practicality of it. Who will manage this household if I go off and start a life with Five? Katie and Sam need someone to take care of them, full time, and you can't expect Sadie to be doing that in her rumspringa."

"Susie and Leah will be around," Adam pointed out. "This is their last year in school."

"Which is breaking Leah's heart, little bookworm that she is. And remember that Dr. Trueherz warned us we need to keep on top of Susie's health issues, and really, can you trust those two to cook a decent meal? They're just learning how to bake, and they've never even looked at Mamm's recipe cards for stews or roasts. They don't know the first thing about putting up fruits and vegetables for the winter, and . . ." She broke off in a sigh. "Those girls have much to learn."

"So you'll teach them," Adam said. "We both will."

One corner of Mary's mouth lifted in a scowl. "You? In the kitchen."

"I managed to feed myself when I lived on my own. And we can teach the other girls. That's the point of growing up, isn't it? They need to learn how to take care of themselves and others."

"Of course they do. But no amount of learning is going to prepare them to manage this household in a matter of months, Adam." Mary tucked a strand of hair behind one ear, and for the first time Adam noticed the puffiness of exhaustion around her eyes. "You need a woman to help you lead this family, and if it's not going to be me, Annie Stoltzfus is more prepared than anyone I know to run a household."

At the mention of Annie's name, Adam sank back in his chair. Mary's friend was a fine baker and a good person. Some men would consider her to be the ideal bride. But Adam knew she was not right for him.

"I know you never thought of Annie that way, but feelings can change."

"Mary, I wish that were true—"

"I'm done speaking for Annie." She held up one hand. "It's up to you to take a wife. No way around that, Adam. And until that happens, I'll be here to make sure the household keeps running smoothly. That's what Mamm and Dat would have wanted. The reality is, you can't manage without me now. So it's up to you to find my replacement."

He let out a groan. "You make it sound as if I'll find a wife on sale at the bulk dry-goods store."

Mary laughed. "Now that would be a sight. The thing is, you know where to look. Open your eyes, Adam. Just open your eyes."

ELEVEN

*P*retending interest in the map of Halfway that she'd gotten from the counter here at Ye Olde Tea Shop, Remy was all ears as the proprietor paused behind her.

"Did you ever hear how the town of Halfway got started?" asked the woman pouring tea at the next table.

"No," said the customer, a middle-aged man wearing a navy fleece with Penn State's lion emblem. "We never heard of it before today."

She'd stopped in for a few clues and a caffeine boost after a night of insomnia, but so far she'd gotten so much more from the shop owner, Lovina Stoltzfus, who was chock-full of information. While she wielded heavy trays of tea as if they were Frisbees, the solid Amish woman entertained and worked the crowd. She drew information out of the locals, some Amish and some "English," who stopped in for what appeared to be their regular cup. And she graciously shared stories with travelers, many of whom seemed to be in Halfway for the first time.

So far Remy had learned that, though deer hunting season was ending, Kraybill's shop was doing well booking groups for pheasant shooting. The Amish man sitting at the counter, a gentleman with a dark beard and a bald head fringed in dark hair, had just had a grandchild. And this week's quilting, hosted by Mary King, had yielded a child's quilt for the family of Eli Troyer, whose house had burned to the ground outside Paradise.

One of the waitresses passed by with a plate of cinnamon buns that made Remy question her decision to stick with tea. She was about to ask for a menu when she caught the mention of Mary King. Could it be the King family she was looking for? One of the books she'd read had explained that with such a closed community, it was not unusual to find many people with the same name.

Still . . . she had made it to Halfway on just a few hours' sleep. And she had a strong sense that Lovina Stoltzfus would know where to find Adam and his family. Whether or not she'd be willing to share it with an outsider like Remy was another story.

"There are many theories on how Halfway got its name," Lovina said as she set a porcelain teapot and cream pitcher down on the couple's table. "I don't know about the others, but this story is a legend in my husband's family. One of his great-great-grandfathers, Jeremiah Stoltzfus, had a small family farm in the Christiana settlement. Now this man Jeremiah had many brothers in Strasburg, and he often traveled by buggy to visit them. But it was such a long trip. So one day, this Jeremiah purchased land smack in the middle and built a farm there. He called the place Halfway, and as a town grew up around it, the name stuck. That's Joseph Zook's old barn here in Halfway."

Most of the patrons seemed to be watching Lovina as she finished her story with a satisfied nod. Remy met her gaze with a smile, then jotted a few notes in her journal so that she'd remember the details later.

"Lovina, that story sounds better and better each time you tell it," Mr. Kraybill said without looking up from his newspaper.

"Practice makes perfect," said one of the Amish girls working behind the counter. She looked young, barely a teenager, but she moved adeptly through the shop, carrying trays of tea things and dishing out pastries from the glass display case.

"I heard it got its name because it was halfway between Phila-delphia and Harrisburg," said the bald man, the new grandfather.

"Oh, I don't know anything about that story," Lovina said, wav-ing him off with a grin, and the customers at the counter laughed.

Such a friendly, homey atmosphere. Remy wished she knew of a shop like this in Philadelphia where she could be one of the regulars. As Remy sipped the last of her tea, one of the waitresses placed the check on the small round table.

"Take as long as you like," the young woman said.

Remy turned over the check, which the waitress had signed: "Thanks! Hannah." A nice personal touch. Remy summoned her nerve.

"Actually, I have a question," Remy said. Glancing up at the girl, who wore no makeup, her honey blond hair scraped back and tucked under a white bonnet, Remy had to force herself to look the girl in the eyes. It would be rude to stare at the unusual clothing—the crisp white bonnets, the dark dresses in rich hues of blue, green, and purple, pinned with black aprons. And yet, Remy wanted to soak up every detail of this new world. "About the farm-ers market." Remy had read that although the Kings' main source of income was their dairy farm, they also sold homemade quilts and cheese at various farmers markets. "I know it's too cold for the outdoor market at the square."

The young woman nodded. "Oh, yes. Far too cold. You won't see the market at the square open up until March or April, usually around Easter."

Remy's heart sank with disappointment. "So Halfway doesn't have a farmers market during the winter?"

"Oh, there's markets here and there. Some go into Philadelphia to the Reading Terminal Market. But on weekends, you'll find most of Halfway at the Saturday market in Joseph Zook's barn. It's just down the road a ways."

Worth a shot, Remy thought as she thanked the waitress and left a hefty tip, grateful for her help.

It didn't take long to navigate through the town of Halfway, a combination of quaint shops with wooden porches and hand-painted signs mixed with the neon of newer stores and asphalt parking lots. Her progress was slowed for a time by an Amish carriage, its steel wheels rumbling on the paved road. The orange reflective triangle on the rear of the vehicle seemed to be a stark contrast to the old-fashioned carriage, but then she supposed safety was a priority.

As it turned out, the carriage turned into the parking lot of the old red barn Hannah had mentioned. Remy pulled past an impressive line of buggies, all without horses, parked in a tidy row, and found a spot for her car in the side parking lot. She decided to leave her recorder and journal in the car, not wanting to appear too aggressive. A blustery wind kicked up just as she got out of the car's warmth, and she quickly tugged on her leather jacket, hitched her bag onto her shoulder, and hurried to the barn door, where plastic sheets blocked the cold.

Inside the market was a surprising array of wares. There were hand-painted signs for sorghum, apple butter, honey, cider, and popcorn. Remy passed tables of ceramics and stained glass, braided breads and jams. There was a long line in front of the Sweet 'N' Simple Bakery table, and Remy stepped aside to let a graying man make his way through the crowd with a pie in each hand. One vendor sold lavender soaps and candles right next to a taxidermist, who had a real deer head on display to demonstrate the quality of his work.

Remy's stomach churned at the sight of the deer's realistic, beseeching eyes. It was yet another reminder that Remy had entered a different world.

Wishing she'd had a pastry at Ye Olde Tea Shop, she turned her back on the deer and scanned the vendors on this end of the barn.

Immediately a display of quilts drew her attention; the deep emerald green provided the background for a vibrant royal purple diamond framed by lipstick red. Although Remy had just started researching quilts, she recognized the Diamond in the Square pattern that was unique to Lancaster County. While the pattern was simple, the bold, vivid colors hardly brought to mind the traditional lifestyle of the Amish. Another quilt pattern of a simple square outlined by alternating light and dark patches of orange and brown gave her the feeling of looking through an open window to a pumpkin patch.

Could those be quilts made by the King women? One article had mentioned that while the family lived from their dairy farming, quilting was the business focus of the women in the family. Remy focused on the people working at the quilt table, searching for Adam's face. At the moment, there were no men there, no little children either, but the vendors seemed to be quite fluid, with some working the crowd in front of the tables or chatting with other sellers. *Hmm. Would families bring little kids to these things?* The lavender vendor had held an infant in her arms, but what about toddlers? She knew Amish families prided themselves on working together, but would it require all eleven of the Kings to sell goods at a market?

Moving with the crowd, she passed by an Amish popcorn vendor and two elderly women who sold rag dolls. At another table boasting GENUINE AMISH QUILTS she counted three girls, a teenager, and an elderly woman. The older woman, with silver hair and glasses to match, was talking with a fashionable shopper in black suede boots, tights, and a fake fur jacket. They seemed to be discussing how to customize a quilt to match the décor in her house.

One of the girls, the only one to wear glasses, was lost in a book, but the other girls, who looked to be her sisters, seemed to be adept salespeople, chatting up passersby, pointing out stitching details on the quilts.

Could they be part of the King family?

Remy thought she could pick out two of the girls as twins. The others . . . yes, the older teen might be Sadie . . . too young for Mary. And the girl with the knowing manner, the attitude of an adult with the body of a child, that might be Ruth.

But if this was the King family, where was Adam? She needed to connect with him today. She was counting on him. She needed this interview.

With the women at the table all engaged in conversation, Remy paused before the dancing patterns of form and color in the sample quilts. From far away the hues drew her in with fiery reds, royal purples, spring lavender, bold blues, and the brown of creamy chocolate.

"Hello." The teenage girl appeared beside the quilt, her smile revealing dimples and clear amber eyes. "Can we help you find something? You look a little lost."

Remy started to open her mouth, but hesitated when she lost her balance and swayed to one side. What a time to start feeling sick. "I'm actually looking for someone . . . a friend." Steadying herself against the table, Remy got a closer view of the quilt, with its stitches forming small flowers and star patterns. So lovely. "His name is Adam King."

"That's my brother." The young woman cocked her head, her

eyes curious. "But he doesn't have Englisher friends. At least, not anymore."

"We met last year. . . ." Like a fizzling television screen, Remy's vision began to blur. "Wow. I'm sorry." She steadied herself against their table.

"You okay?" the teenage girl asked.

"Just a little dizzy," Remy managed to say as the buzz of noise closed around her. "Sometimes I get these seizures, but . . . I don't think this is one of them."

"Kumm. Let her sit," barked an older woman's voice.

With her hands pressed to her temples, Remy wasn't quite sure how it all transpired, but a moment later she sat in a folding chair, shielded from the crowd by the lovely hanging quilt. One of the girls was handing her a paper cup of water, while the smallest one patted her shoulder.

"I think you'll be okay," she said, her lips pursed in an expression of concern.

"Thank you. I . . . I didn't eat breakfast and . . ." When was the last time she'd gotten a good night's sleep? Or a decent meal? Remy pinched the bridge of her nose. It was her own fault. She was responsible for taking care of herself.

"She needs something to eat."

"I think she's sick. Adam's friend is sick." The youngest one put her face close to Remy's. "Do you want some cheese?" she asked, her eyes alight with concern.

Remy knew she needed something. "That sounds good."

"Get the samples." The oldest girl waved someone over to her, and a paper plate stacked with cheddar cubes loomed before Remy's face. "Give her some space, Ruthie," the teenaged girl said.

Even in her daze, Remy heard the name Ruthie. Adam's little sister. At least she'd landed in the right place, but where was Adam?

Remy stabbed some cheese with a toothpick and popped it in her mouth. "Delicious," she said. It was smooth and buttery-tasting.

"It's made with milk from our cows, but they turn it into cheese at Uncle Nate's farm," said one of the twins.

Ruthie was back in her face. "What's your name?"

"Remy. Remy McCallister."

Ruth squinted. "I don't know that name."

"Well, my real name is Rebecca. . . ."

"Oh, we know lots of Rebeccas," one of the girls said.

"But my parents called me Remy," she explained, head in her hands. "After a place in France. A place that's famous for its cognac."

Ruthie nodded, then asked, "What's a cone yak?"

The girl at the end of the table put her book down to explain. "A yak is a bovine animal found in the Himalayan Mountains of Asia."

Hiding a smile, Remy focused on breathing as their conversation washed over her. At the end of the table, the older woman seemed to be in charge of taking orders, while the other girls spoke in Pennsylvania Dutch, their words a soothing background for Remy to relax.

"How are you feeling?" Ruthie asked, patting Remy's shoulder.

"Ruthie, leave the poor girl alone." Referring a customer to the old woman, the teenaged girl hurried over. "Don't feel rushed. Can we get you something else?"

"I'm feeling much better." Remy sighed and pulled herself up straight in the chair. "That was a little scary, but it's passed. I'm thinking I should get some lunch before I eat all your samples up."

"But we don't mind," one of the twins said. "The cows just make more milk. Twice a day, every day!"

Remy smiled. "I appreciate your help. You didn't tell me your names."

"I'm Sadie," the oldest girl volunteered. "That bookworm down at the end is Leah, and over there is her twin, Susie. Ruthie's the one in your face. And that's our grandmother, Nell King, down at the end. That's probably more names than you ever want to know."

"I'll be sure to remember the names of the girls who saved my skin," Remy said, darting a glance at the stuffed deer that had started the whole episode. "I'm really grateful. Thank you." She smiled, glad for their help. "But I was hoping to speak with Adam. Is he here?"

"He's around here somewhere," Ruthie said.

"I can help you find him," Sadie volunteered. "And didn't you want to get some food?"

"Right." Food first, then Adam.

As Remy and Sadie strolled through the market, Sadie seemed relieved to have time away from the other girls, and she talked nonstop about shoes, music, and her rumspringa, which had given her time to explore shoes and music. Sadie had a job at a local motel and a boyfriend. "An Englisher," Sadie announced proudly. "He loves my long hair. Frank thinks I'm beautiful. He helped me get a little cell phone that I charge when I'm at work. And an iPod. Do you have one? It means I can have music in my ear, whenever I'm alone."

So many personal details in a short burst of time. "Sounds like Frank is a nice guy." Remy sensed that Sadie craved attention outside the Amish community. "Has your family met him?" Remy asked.

"Oh, no! They don't want to know about Frank. I'm supposed to be dating Amish boys, looking for a suitable husband, but that's all so boring."

When Remy was seventeen, most of the things her father wanted her to do were equally "boring." She supposed it was a rite of passage.

As Sadie rambled on, an open book, Remy considered asking her for an interview. The girl would probably say yes. But then would she think Remy was just being nice to get her story? That would be awful. Already Remy could tell that the teenaged girl looked up to her, and Remy didn't want to do anything that would violate her trust.

Discouraged by the long line for sandwiches, Remy perked up when she spotted a sign for Nancy's Nutty Muesli Bars. "I can't believe they have Nancy's bars here. Have you ever had them?"

"Sure. Nancy Briggs is the mayor of Halfway, and she always gives out samples. She says word of mouth makes the best advertising."

Now that Sadie mentioned it, Remy remembered Adam saying that he knew Nancy. . . . The topic came up when she gave him a muesli bar. If she were a better reporter, she would have remembered a detail like that. From now on, she was going to collect notes in her journal at the end of each day.

Over at Nancy's stand they helped themselves to samples of a peanut bar and a new one made from almonds and dates. Remy filled a box with a dozen assorted bars, then joined Sadie, who was holding a place in line.

"That's Nancy." Sadie nodded to the petite woman who was working the cash box. Nancy Briggs's salt-and-pepper hair was styled to swirl around her face, yet she wore the clothes of a hiker: black boots, brown pants with plenty of pockets, a flannel shirt, and a down vest. Except for her coiffed hair, she looked as if she could have hiked the Adirondacks that morning.

"What can I do for you today?" Nancy squinted. "Sadie King? I haven't seen Simon in the shop since the weather turned nasty. How's he doing?"

"Better. Denki for asking."

Wide-eyed, Remy waited to see if any more information about

Simon was forthcoming, but the conversation seemed to be over. "I'd like to buy these, please." She handed over the box. "And I just wanted to tell you how many times Nancy's Nutty Bars have saved my life."

"A satisfied customer!" Nancy clapped her hands together. "That's what I like to hear."

"I've eaten them for breakfast, lunch, and dinner," she told the older woman.

"Well, that's a little excessive. Wholesome and delicious is one thing, but you need to vary your diet." Nancy's eyes twinkled as she looked Remy over. "Especially a twig of a thing like you."

With her twinkling eyes and direct manner, Nancy Briggs was very likable. Remy wondered what it was like to be the mayor of a town where the majority of the residents were Amish, and therefore not involved in politics. And would the mayor give her a statement regarding last year's murders and the impact on the town? Remy thought it was worth pursuing later, in a more private setting.

For now, she needed to find Adam.

TWELVE

Adam was talking with Ben Lapp, the two of them catching a breath of fresh air in the wide doorway, away from the smells of popcorn and buttered pretzels, when he saw the van move through the parking lot. Streaked with bright blue and green stripes and emblazoned with the giant letters WPHL, the van obviously belonged to a news station.

He rubbed his chin, hoping that he was wrong. Just because journalists were calling the sheriff about his family didn't mean that the Kings were the only people of interest in the town of Halfway. Turning back to Ben, he motioned the older man away from the door and got back to the conversation.

"You can tell Nell and Mary we'll be needing two double-sized quilts come the spring," Ben Lapp was saying. Since Ben and Debbie Lapp had opened the Halfway Inn five years ago, they had ordered all their quilts from Mamm, and Adam had been grateful when Ben called him over to let him know he'd be wanting more.

"I'll tell my grandmother. The girls will want to start right away, since there's more time to quilt during winter months." As he spoke, Adam led Ben farther from the door. "Is there a pattern or color you want?"

"Debbie would be the one to speak with on design. I steer clear of choices like that, especially with the inn. She likes things just so for the customers."

"A wise man, you are," Adam said.

"Debbie will speak with Nell to work out the details."

"Very good." When Adam turned back to nod at the man, he saw them.

A camera crew.

Adam froze at the sight of them: a man in blue jeans and a puffy vest with a fat camera balanced on his shoulder, and a second man in a bright blue sweater, with tanned skin and eyes that seemed to be circled in dark crayon.

They were being escorted by Chris Mueller, an Englisher neighbor who worked security for Halfway's farmers markets. Chris was responsible for keeping order and peace, but he didn't have the authority to turn these guys away. Too bad.

"*Was ist los?* What's wrong?" The lines at the outer edges of Ben's eyes deepened. "You look like you just saw the devil himself."

"A camera crew just walked in. Television reporters. I hope I'm wrong, but they might be wanting to ask me about all the troubles we've tried to put behind us since . . . since last year."

Casting a look over his shoulder, Ben scowled. "*Aussenseiter.*" Although the literal meaning was "outsiders," the single word alluded to the fact that these men came from another world, a culture with rules and ethics alien to the Amish community.

In that moment Adam knew he was home again. Although in the past year he'd sometimes felt that people in the Amish community perceived him as a man sitting on the fence, one foot in this world and one planted among the Englishers, the balance had shifted. He was back among the Plain folk.

"There he is . . ." Chris Mueller's voice crept their way. "Adam, do you have a minute?" Chris paused, one hand on the nightstick looped through his belt, the other pressed to the silver star-shaped badge that signified he was a security guard. Rent-a-Cop, his friend Jane used to call them. Security people who wore the uniform of a police officer.

"Actually, I've got some things to take care of." Adam looked from Chris to the two men, suddenly feeling like a deer caught in headlights.

"Adam King?" The man in the bright blue sweater and golden tan makeup extended his hand. "I'm Steel Winfield, WPHL news in Philadelphia. How's it going?"

His jaw tense, Adam shook the man's hand, but he didn't speak. Let them read from his silence; he didn't want to talk with them.

"This is my cameraman, Chuck Trotti, and we were wondering if you'd take a moment to talk with us about how your family is doing?"

"Not interested."

"Mr. King." Winfield's voice was smooth as sanded wood. Pearly white teeth and unusual blue eyes completed the package. "We understand your reticence, the pain you've had to endure this last year. We don't have to put you on camera, and we wouldn't have to show anyone in your family. We don't mean to be invasive, but people are inquisitive. They want to know how your family is doing."

"The family wants to be left alone," growled Ben Lapp. "Go away." With his black hat pulled down to his beady eyes and his beard a mass of dark fur beneath his chin, Ben looked every inch the grumpy old man.

Whom Adam was happy to have in his corner.

Steel Winfield focused on Adam, as if they were the only two people in the room. "The thing is, people are curious. They care about you. They want to know how little Simon is faring."

With his personable demeanor, Adam could see how this man won the confidence of his subjects. However, the Kings would not cooperate. "I have nothing to say," Adam said. "And I would appreciate you leaving my family alone." Adam walked away, but the reporter fell into step beside him.

"Mr. King, I understand your desire to play down media attention, but if you don't make some sort of statement, you're going to have a media blitz raining down on you in the next few weeks."

Adam kept walking, kept his eyes straight ahead on the booths and curious faces, the signs for homemade jams and peach preserves.

"An interview with me is the best way to ward off the curious," Steel insisted. "And trust me, we'll make it tasteful. No close-ups or tears on camera. That's not how I work."

For a moment, Adam softened. Would that really be possible . . . to chase the media away with one short interview?

No. In his experience, the curiosity would not abate. One taste of a story would draw other reporters here, like bees to honey. Adam had nothing new to say about the murders, and the bishop had consistently warned them to remain separate from the fancy world of reporters and TV cameras. While the Kings were to cooperate with law enforcement, the Ordnung forbade their involvement in the Englisher media.

"Mr. King . . . Adam . . ." Steel Winfield strode alongside. "Let's help each other out here."

"Go away, Mr. Winfield."

"It'll only take a minute, maybe two."

"No."

"Then we'll shoot what we can, do you want that? I'm free to shoot video, right? Some shots of your family . . . the children on their way to school. Little Simon, one year later . . . Whether or not the Amish like it, this is America."

Adam paused as the other man hoisted the camera onto his shoulder, poised to begin recording. Vultures, preying on people who'd already suffered so much. Preying on children . . .

It was a struggle to keep his jaw from clamping tight as Adam stepped into the reporter's path. "I think you'd better leave now."

Steel's broad smile was cloying. "Freedom of the press."

Adam's fists balled at his sides. He had to control the surge of anger, control the desire to wipe that smug expression from the reporter's face. With gritted teeth, he sucked in a breath. Control, man. Peaceful ways.

"This is a private market." Conviction clanged like steel in Ben Lapp's craggy voice as he pointed to the doorway. "This barn is owned by Joseph Zook, and he'll have you banned from here if you cannot respect the rules of our community."

The reporter frowned. "You're going to throw us out?"

"That's exactly what I'm doing." Ben motioned to the security guard, who was watching from the door. "Chris, can you help these men?"

Adam tucked his thumbs under his suspenders, impressed at old Ben's fortitude. The quick action spared Adam from unleashing his temper, a fit he knew he would later regret.

Chris scurried over, keys and equipment jangling from his belt. "Is there a problem?" he asked.

"These men are leaving," Adam said.

"Yeah, okay." The reporter motioned his cameraman toward the door. "But if you change your mind, call me." He walked toward the exit, then turned back to add, "You can reach me through the station."

Watching them go, Adam gritted his teeth. This wasn't going to subside. Hank's warning about the media had been right on target; they were coming after his family for a story. They were merciless and mercenary.

And he had promised to protect the family. The little ones, Katie and Sam and Simon, who could barely find a peaceful night's sleep.

And protect them he would.

Within the bounds of peace, he would find a way.

THIRTEEN

Remy's heart lifted when she spotted him.

Adam King.

Even with the dozens of Amish men here at the market, Remy would have recognized those dark, smoky eyes anywhere. In his black trousers and cornflower blue shirt, and that black-brimmed hat over his dark, wavy hair, Adam was a strikingly handsome man. A handsome man with the fire of fury burning in his eyes.

That made it all the more intimidating for Remy to approach him, but she couldn't back down now. Sadie was going full steam ahead.

He seemed to be watching the main exit, where people were milling in and out. Watching it like a hawk.

"What's wrong?" Sadie called to him as they approached.

He shot a look back at them. When he saw Remy, his face registered surprise and disbelief. "Remy? What are you doing here?"

"Hi, Adam." She raised one hand and waggled the fingers. She had hoped he'd be happy to see her, but she sensed that she was walking into the middle of a bad situation.

"Remy came all the way from Philadelphia to talk to you," Sadie said. "So you'd better get yourself into a better mood."

"That'll be hard to do, after dealing with these vultures." Adam rubbed his chin, as if trying to slow things down. "I just had heated words with some reporters. Two Englishers with a camera. They want to put our family on television."

Reporters . . . Disappointment stabbed through Remy. Other reporters had gotten to Adam first. She should have thought of that possibility. And now they'd churned things up, muddied the waters for her.

"Really?" Sadie's bright tone drew a scowl from her brother. "Well, it *is* kind of exciting, but why us?"

"Mamm and Dat. We're coming up on the one-year anniversary."

"Oh." Sadie's voice fell an octave as the reality settled in.

Remy bit her lower lip, sharing Sadie's pain. Even the allure of the fancy world with its televisions and celebrity reporters could not diminish the grief of losing one's parents. She knew firsthand; she would always feel the loss of her mother. Time might have healed the surface of the wound, but occasionally the scar still ached.

"I know they've got a job to do," Adam said. "They need to get their story. Sell papers and get viewers and so on. But to push their way in like that. Pushing into personal matters . . . They threatened to start filming us, the children, Simon. . . ." He shook his head in disgust. "I'm going to keep our family safe from them, Sadie. We have to watch out in the coming weeks, especially with Simon. Maybe he should stay home from school . . . I don't know. Whatever it takes to keep everyone safe."

Sadie nodded, her lips pursed, her eyes glistening with unshed tears.

So much pain here. Remy swallowed, her throat thick with emotion. *So much heartache.* And she was planning to drive another arrow through their hearts by taking their story to *Post* readers?

"I'm sorry, Remy." Adam raked back his hair with one hand, then replaced his hat. "Not a very kind greeting after you've come all this way."

"Don't be sorry! I understand." She pressed a palm to her heart. "It's scary to think of those guys pursuing your brothers and sisters."

And here I am, in line right behind them.

Her eyes began to sting, the warning of tears, and she pressed a hand to her face and pursed her lips to keep it all in.

"Don't worry." He bent his head closer, as if trying to read her expression. When she looked up, his dark eyes were warm with concern. "We'll be okay."

His tenderness was more than she could bear. She stepped away, removing herself from the halo of his presence, searching to escape the trap she'd set with such precision. "I need some . . . something to drink. Excuse me." She hurried away, as if she really had a chance of escaping her conscience.

Regret weighed heavy on her shoulders as Remy listlessly followed Sadie to the food court at the back of the barn. She told herself she didn't have to feel so guilty if she was backing away from the story . . . if that was what she was doing. At the moment, she only knew that now was not the time to make a pitch.

But the bad feeling clung to her like a cold, wet blanket as she and Sadie purchased hot pretzels and cider and found a spot at a nearby picnic bench. They were joined by Emma Lapp, the young woman who taught at the Amish school. Sadie explained that she and Emma had been in the same grade when they attended school.

"And now I teach Sadie's sisters and brother," Emma said. The thick line of her eyebrows gave her a serious demeanor that Remy imagined would work well in a classroom of children.

When Remy learned that Emma was responsible for teaching grades one through eight single-handedly, her admiration for the young woman tripled. "Isn't that difficult, teaching all those different grades at once?" she asked.

"Oh, it's a joy to watch the children learn and grow, year after year." Emma had a habit of squinting when she smiled, which was often. "Actually, that's one of the mottos we teach—JOY. It stands for Jesus first, You are last, and Others are in between." Emma tied off a bag of popcorn. "The King girls are some of my best students. I'll be sorry to lose Leah this year. And Simon—" She paused and glanced over her shoulder. "You can tell Adam that Simon is much improved. He's even been talking in the last month or so."

Remy's heart lifted at the news; Simon was doing better. She had read that he'd been rendered nearly speechless after witnessing his parents' murders, so this was certainly a positive development. Part of her couldn't believe how engrossed she'd become with this family . . . and so quickly. It was probably unprofessional, if she was going to write an objective article about them.

"Did he show you the bear book I got for him?" Emma asked.

Sadie twisted off a piece of pretzel. "I haven't seen it, but I'm not the one he turns to. He's become very close with Adam and Mary."

As they chatted they were joined by Nancy Briggs, who took the seat beside Emma with a sigh.

"My body could go on, but my feet are protesting," Nancy said as she stirred a cup of coffee.

"But Nancy, who's minding your table?" Sadie asked.

"I corralled your twin sisters to do it. Leah's so good with making change, and Susie has the gift of gab. They make a great team."

"It's good you put them to work," Sadie said.

"Your grandmother agreed, though Adam seemed a bit perturbed by your lack of interest in quilt sales." Nancy sipped her coffee, her eyes resting on Sadie. "And word of warning, he's looking for you."

"Ach! Adam is always perturbed." Sadie dismissed any worry with a wave of her hand. "He forgets that it's my rumspringa."

"He may forget, but you, my dear Sadie, need to cut him some slack. Adam has quite a lot to handle, trying to run the farm and manage the family with your parents gone. It's got to be hard on him . . . hard on all of us." Nancy sighed. "Not a day goes by that I don't miss Esther. She was a good friend."

Remy stiffened at the sudden turn of conversation. "You know, that was when I first met your brother," she told Sadie. "Adam was on a train, heading home."

Emma bowed her head, as if in prayer, but Sadie's amber eyes sparked with interest. "I think he mentioned you. He used to talk about the angel that lit his path home."

Remy winced. "Oh, I don't know if that was me."

"And why wouldn't it be, dear?" Nancy rolled the paper coffee cup between her palms. "Adam deserved to have an angel sitting beside him. Those were dark times. An unsolved murder that crushed this town for a good while. We were all devastated. One of my greatest regrets as mayor is that our justice system failed us. The police never did find the killer, even though Simon witnessed the dreadful incident."

"But he didn't see anything," Sadie said quickly. "He was hiding under Mamm's skirts the whole time. And Bishop Samuel says we're not to speak of this killer."

"But don't you want the police to find this . . . this murderer?" Remy asked.

Sadie shook her head slowly, gazing down at the table.

"It's not our place to judge," Emma said softly. "We know that God is the only one who can mete out punishment for man's sins."

"Any talk of justice is forbidden," Sadie added.

"That's the Amish way. I know that, my dears, and yet I'm deeply sorry that the killer was not apprehended." Nancy's hand, speckled with sun spots, patted Sadie's arm. "There's a reason we Englishers put monsters like that behind bars. We can't have a murderer on the loose. Let me tell you, lots of people in this town—even most of Lancaster County—would rest easier knowing that killer was locked up."

Remy pretended interest in her pretzel as she sorted through the information. Hearing the details spill out from the view of the Amish versus the town mayor brought a new perspective to the murders. Maybe this was enough information to write a piece without having to interview Adam King, which was out of the question today.

Suddenly, the pretzel and cider held little interest for Remy. These people seemed so kind and genuine, and she was here under false pretenses.

"Anyhoo . . ." Nancy put her coffee down on the table. "Through all the adversity, it was good that you and your siblings could stay together. I know Esther and Levi would have wanted it that way. And I have marveled at the way the Amish community pulls together in a crisis."

"People have been so very generous," Sadie said. "We received many grocery showers, boxes of food. And Emma sent over some of her wonderful good peanut butter cakes."

Emma's smile lit her eyes. "The children love peanut butter."

As they talked of favorite recipes, their sense of community and their enjoyment of each other touched Remy's heart. There was nothing like this in her life, no support system beyond her two college roommates who now lived in distant parts of the country. In fact, she didn't even know the names of the couple who lived across the hall in her apartment building or the older gentleman who lived in the corner unit. How ironic that she lived in a much bigger community but knew far fewer people.

Their conversation was interrupted when a middle-aged man in a police officer's uniform paused by their table.

"Good afternoon, ladies." He nodded casually, a plastic tray of empty cups in one arm. "How's your day going?"

"Fine, just fine, Chris. How was the crowd today?" Nancy asked. "Not too much congestion in the parking lot?"

Glancing up at the man, Remy noticed a gold patch on his jacket that said SECURITY. Unlike the married Amish men who wore beards only under their chins, this man's face was covered in a groomed beard and mustache that, with his round physique, re- minded Remy of a walrus.

"It's been quiet," he said, tugging on the edge of his beard.

Sadie introduced Remy to her neighbor, Chris Mueller.

"Chris is in charge of security at our Saturday markets," Nancy explained. "Don't know what we'd do without him. The outdoor markets get crazy busy in the summer."

"I'm looking forward to checking that out." When Remy met Chris's eyes, he glanced away awkwardly, and she sensed that he was shy. A man in his thirties hiding behind a full beard and mustache. There was something sweet about it.

"Sorry to bother you gals," he said, "but I didn't want to pass by without inquiring about your brother, Miss King. How is Simon doing?"

"He's better." Sadie's voice was smooth as cream. "And how's your mamm? Is her knee all healed?"

"She's able to walk on her own now. And thanks for bringing that stew over. We got quite a few dinners out of it."

"Give Gina my best," Nancy said. "Tell her I'll expect to see her square-dancing again come the spring."

"Will do. Ladies . . . I'm back to work." Chris Mueller tipped the visor of his hat, like an old-fashioned gentleman.

As the security guard headed off, Remy was once again struck by the warmth and charm of this world in which neighbors helped neighbors and everyone, Amish and non-Amish, nurtured a strong sense of community. Sadie had taken her under her wing today, allowing her an inside look at an afternoon in Halfway, and what was Remy about to do?

Write it all up and publish it. Steal their personal thoughts, their hopes and fears, and post them in bold headlines.

The air in the room had become dense, thick with betrayal. It was after three and already some of the vendors were packing up their wares. The lavender lady passed by, her baby in a sling, as she pulled a little red wagon loaded with boxes toward the door.

"People are packing up." Remy glanced toward the large end of the barn, wanting to be reassured by a flurry of activity. "It's ending."

"Some of these vendors have been here since eight o'clock, setting things up," Sadie said. "It's a long day for not much profit."

Remy didn't know how to explain that she didn't want anyone to leave, because that meant she would need to pull herself together and say good-bye to Sadie and Nancy and Emma and all of Sadie's sisters. Say good-bye to these nice people and drive back to Philadelphia, to her empty apartment and the prospect of disappointing her boss come Monday morning.

Somehow the thought of pulling herself up from this picnic bench overwhelmed her.

She was tired . . . so tired and thirsty. But the apple cider in the cup before her seemed cloying and sweet. She pushed it away and rested her head on the table as the edges of her vision grew furry and gray.

Sleep . . . she could never find it, but when she wanted it least, it chased her down, painting over the view.

With a whisper of a sigh, she felt her muscles tense then go slack as she slipped straight down the hole.

FOURTEEN

*T*ucking his hands under his arms for warmth, Adam scanned the parking lot. The news van was gone. They were safe, for now, but plans would have to be made, the children warned how to respond in case other vultures swooped down from the sky.

With that task in hand, he ducked back into the wind shield of the barn and headed toward their table. Mammi Nell would have to be told about the reporters. It was time for the girls to start packing up the quilts, and while they loaded the carriage, maybe he'd have a free moment to talk with Remy. Something had spooked her back there; he had seen the wounded look on her face, and he had to make sure she was okay.

What amazed Adam was how a woman could leave such a brand when he'd seen her just twice in his life. But one look in her emerald eyes and he felt the spark of recognition, as if he had known her forever. Haunting, that one. He didn't usually "notice" women, but there was something about Remy that demanded his attention.

Speaking in Pennsylvania Dutch, he told his grandmother about his confrontation with the reporters.

"Good that you thought to leave Simon back at home," she told him, her eyes stony with resolve. "A wise choice, Adam. And we'll pray on it for these next few weeks. The Heavenly Father will help us through this. You'll see."

He nodded, glad for her staunch faith.

Telling Mammi Nell he'd be right back to help load the carriage, he strode away from their table to look for Sadie and Remy.

Remy . . . the first time he met her, he was left wondering if God had sent her. An angel. A circle of light on a very dark day, in those dark times . . .

That period in his life, when he'd been rushing home to Halfway, quietly frantic to pick up the pieces, was still a sore spot. He'd been at a crossroads, passing from one world to another, choked by a cloud of guilt, hating himself for being gone when his family needed him. He'd been afraid that the bishop and other church leaders would not give him permission to be the caretaker of the family, and without someone at the helm he had no doubt they would have been split up and sent to live with different aunts and uncles. And he'd been afraid of failing the people who needed him. Susie with her medical condition. The little ones, their whole lives ahead of them. Simon, with the tight kernel of trauma buried deep inside. Everyone needed something. Even strong, hardworking Mary needed the confidence to move on and start her own family.

Some of those fears still lingered, but he was working on them, with God's help. These days when he prayed, he gave up his burdens and trusted in the Lord's blessings. He'd realized that his strength and wisdom and patience were not nearly enough to get the family through. He needed to allow God to take over.

As he passed Bob Miller's makeshift village of sheds, he noticed flashing lights blinking through the market exit, spilling over the eating area where a small cluster of people were gathered. The light swirled and washed over everything in a circular motion: the turret lights of an emergency vehicle that had been backed in through the wide barn door.

He recognized Nancy Briggs, the town mayor and a family friend in the group. And was that Sadie, bending down as if to help someone?

Something was wrong.

His pulse quickening, he ran toward them.

Dodging bystanders, he wove his way to Nancy, who was talking with Mike Trueherz, a volunteer in Halfway's fire department. Mike's father was Susie's doctor, a man who Adam believed had saved his sister's life.

"What's going on?" Adam's heart thumped with panic.

"A young woman passed out," Mike said, not looking away from the open bay of the ambulance that had backed into the wide doors of the barn. Two other attendants were working with a red-headed girl who sat in a portable canvas wheelchair.

Remy . . .

Adam's heart thumped as he recognized her, surrounded by medical equipment. A clear mask covered her mouth and nose and a sleeve was clamped on her arm.

"It's Sadie's friend, Remy." Nancy gave Adam's arm a good, hard squeeze. "You should be proud of your sister. She remained calm throughout."

"Sadie did a great job. One of the most dangerous parts about having a seizure is the possibility of injuring the head on the way down." As he spoke, Mike hooked a cable into a small machine as if there was not a minute to waste. So much like his father. "Sounds like Sadie caught Remy as she collapsed. A lucky thing. There are no apparent injuries from the seizure, and it looks like she's going to be okay."

"We can all be thankful for that," Adam said, though he was wondering what would happen next. How would Remy get home to Philadelphia? It seemed that she'd come here alone, probably in a car, he suspected.

As Adam moved toward the ambulance, Sadie straightened and caught sight of him.

"I'm going to collect her things." Her brow was creased with concern, and some of her light brown hair fell in her face, giving her a harried look. "It all happened so fast, I think we left everything at the table."

"Is she okay?" he asked.

"She's getting better, but it was really scary." Sadie's voice was choppy. She was so rattled, he felt sorry for her, too.

"Okay," Adam said. "Get her things, and then we really have to go. It's getting late, and Gabe and Jonah need help with the milking."

With Ruthie, Leah, Susie, Sadie, and him here, more than half the workforce was away from the dairy farm, and he really hadn't meant to stay this late in the day.

He glanced over at Remy, her eyes wide and doelike as people moved around her. She had a glassy stare, not unlike Simon's confused look when he was trapped in a night terror. He drew in a deep breath, infused with compassion.

She looked lonely.

One of the Amish volunteers, David Yoder, was reassuring her, though Remy didn't seem to realize he was talking to her. She seemed to be watching the world around her from a faraway place, as if trying to figure out why everyone was gathered around her.

Adam moved closer and lowered his head so that he'd be in her line of vision. "How are you doing, Remy?"

"I'm fine," she said, her eyes blank as a doll's glass orbs. "I need to go home."

That was going to be a tough one, considering that she lived back in Philadelphia. Adam turned to David, his voice lowered so as not to panic Remy. "Will she be okay to drive back to Philadelphia?" he asked.

"Ach, she can't do that." David shook his head. "No driving. Even a bath is risky after such a spell. She could have another seizure."

"So how will she get back to the city? Or are you taking her to the hospital in Lancaster?"

Before David could answer, Mike was back to work one of the portable monitors. He pressed some buttons and the machine spit out a narrow strip of paper. The volunteer tore it off, took a quick look at it, then handed it to Remy. "This is a copy of your EEG. Everything looks okay now, so you can keep this."

When he handed her the slip of paper, she clutched it in her fist, like a child grabbing at a flower.

"I'll bet you never expected to end your day this way," Adam said in an attempt to relax her.

She handed the paper to him. "Can you sign this? I need your permission."

Adam took the slip of paper, a chart of jagged lines. "What do you want me to do?"

"It's my permission slip. For school." She looked forlorn in the wheelchair, an edge of alarm in her shiny eyes.

Adam exchanged a look with Mike. "What's she saying?"

"She's still a little fuzzy, which is normal for someone who had a seizure." Mike nodded at the slip of paper. "From what she told one of your sisters, sounds like she may have a seizure disorder. Just keep that for her. It's her EEG, which she might want to give to her neurologist back in Philly."

Adam tipped the brim of his hat back. "Why would I keep it for her? Isn't she going with you to the hospital?"

"She doesn't want to go. Sadie says you're taking her back to your place to get some rest, which is what she needs. After a seizure, a patient is usually exhausted. Sleep is the best thing for her." Mike closed up a metal box and turned away to load it in the truck.

Adam winced. He couldn't take this English girl back to the farm. It wouldn't be right. What would the bishop say?

"Mike, hold on a minute. We can't take her home with us." As Adam swept past Remy, she grabbed his sleeve.

"I want to go home. Please." Her doleful plea tore at him even before he saw her face pucker like a child on the verge of tears.

Sadie cut in, plucking Remy's hand from his sleeve and cradling it in her own hands. "Of course you're going home with us." She wheeled on Adam. "What did you tell her?"

"It's not right, Sadie. It won't look right."

Sadie's eyes flared with resolve. "Stop thinking people are so interested in what you're doing, Adam, and think of someone else. For once."

Behind her, Remy began to break down. "I'm just so tired. So tired and . . ." Remy's shoulders shook as a sob broke her voice. "I need to go home."

"There, now. Don't you worry about a thing." Sadie tucked the handbag on Remy's lap and patted the girl's shoulder. "Don't you worry, now. We'll take good care of you." She pressed her cheek to Remy's and gave her a squeeze.

The sight of his sister hugging Remy, a virtual stranger, was a dagger through Adam's heart. Had he forgotten the meaning of his baptismal vow? Was he so caught up with gaining approval from his uncle and church leaders that he was going to abandon someone in need? Especially when that someone was Remy—his angel.

Of course they had to help.

How could he have even considered turning her away, just because a few idle tongues might wag over what looked like an impropriety?

He met Sadie's determined gaze with a nod. "I'll go hitch up the carriage."

FIFTEEN

The screech of an animal made Remy roll over.

A rooster?

She must be having some whopping dream. When a second squeal nudged her from sleep again, she stretched and realized she was not in her apartment. The air was cool and it smelled of brewing coffee. Her hand moved under the sheets, brushing against a soft flannel nightgown. The bed beneath her was firm and a little lumpy, and the pearly light of a winter morning permeated the small, tidy room.

Although her mouth was dry and her brain felt a little like it was stuffed with cotton, she could piece together parts of yesterday's scenario.

The spell at the Amish market.

Just thinking of it made her feel overwhelmed. One minute she was sitting at the table, and the next strange men were peering in her face, asking her questions that didn't make any sense to her.

Had someone called 911? She thought she remembered being

on a stretcher, an oxygen mask strapped to her face. And she remembered telling people she had to get home.

Opening her eyes, she was certain that she had not driven back to Philadelphia. Judging by the colorful quilts and the sparse furnishings in the room, she had spent the night in Amish country. She propped herself on her elbows for a look. The walls were painted a dusky pink hue that gave the room a cozy feel, despite the fact that nothing hung on the wall but hooks with white bonnets and solid-colored jumpers. And the beds . . . there were six single beds, three on each side of the room, reminding Remy of a cabin at summer camp.

Thinking back to yesterday, she recalled the oh-so-important thing that had driven her . . . the interview? It didn't seem quite as crucial right now.

Because . . . the other reporters. Now she remembered. Adam had been furious with them. Angry and worried that they might come after his younger siblings, that they might frighten Simon.

She flopped back onto the bed, a vision of Adam floating in her mind, and she could almost see his dark, intense eyes and feel the powerful energy that sometimes robbed her of breath. Seeing him had been bittersweet, the joy of being with him diminished by her own self-loathing because she was one of the predatory reporters.

She was the enemy.

A girl's smiling face came to mind, dimples and amber eyes. *Sadie.* She had made a friend yesterday in Adam King's younger sister. Somehow, that was what seemed to matter most right now.

So . . . was this the Kings' house? She sat up to take in the room. It reminded her of an old-fashioned dormitory. All the other beds were empty, the covers of a few of them tossed back. At least they hadn't been made yet.

Although it seemed early, she felt well rested, despite the garbled details of yesterday.

She rubbed sleep from her eyes as memories from last night gelled in her mind. She remembered someone asking her if she could climb the stairs, and then suddenly being lifted off her feet. Gentle hands had helped with her clothes. Sadie was there . . . probably another woman, too.

And then, during the night, she had gotten up looking for a bathroom. That memory was more vivid. Had Sadie really shown her to a chamber pot? She tossed back the covers and moved around the edge of the bed to see the corner of the room. There it was, a huge porcelain pot.

Oh, how embarrassing!

Not just the chamber pot, but all of it. She sat back on the edge of the modest bed. To have a seizure in front of total strangers, who, through their incredible generosity, took her in for the night. From the blank spots in her memory, she knew she hadn't just passed out from hunger or exhaustion.

Another seizure. Remy had been down this path before, but she had thought she'd outgrown the seizures. Her last seizure had hit back in New York, when she was in college—more than a year ago. She had thought the lightning jolt of tremors and the blanked-out memories were behind her.

She would have to return to the neurologist, who would probably suggest a new medication, which meant new side effects to deal with. The thought of sitting in Dr. Healy's office filled her with dread . . . especially when she considered the time leading up to the seizure. No sleep, no food save for some cheese and a pot of tea. Days of diet soft drinks and snacks. The doctor had warned the seizures might be triggered by sleep deprivation, poor diet, and stress. Now more than ever it seemed obvious that she needed to start taking care of herself.

The colorful patches of the quilt on her bed were a stark contrast to her bitter disappointment. Her toes curled against the floor, the wood so cold it made the arches of her feet contract. There didn't seem to be any direct heat up here in this bedroom, though the room seemed cheerful enough with its rose-painted walls and white curtains. The quilt on the bed she'd slept in, a random pattern dancing with multicolored patches, had kept her warm and comfortable through the night.

When a quick search of the dresser top did not reveal her clothes, she pulled the quilt from the bed, hitched it over her shoulders, and pushed aside the curtains. Night lingered, the purple darkness of first light. Moving lights drew her eyes to the activity in front of the nearest barn. Closer inspection revealed that the lights were small headlamps, attached with a wide band. Adam and another young man stood by the wide-open doors as cows trotted inside.

Was Adam always up this early? Watching from beyond the cold glass, she savored the moment, filing it away to remember on cold, dark mornings when sleep eluded her. Like a portrait, this stolen view of Adam's life was a memento worth keeping.

After Adam disappeared into the building, Remy shifted her focus and spotted Ruthie, with flashlight in one hand, basket in the other, on the other side of the lane. She seemed to be corralling two small children, the littlest one still waddling like a toddler.

Crack of dawn, and already the farm seemed to be in full swing. Feeling as if she were a step behind, she bunched up the quilt and nightgown so that she wouldn't trip and headed down the stairs. The mingled aromas of wood smoke and coffee drew Remy to a wide-open kitchen, where a young Amish woman was setting dishes on a huge table. The walls and ceiling, painted a dark shade of green, gave the room a cozy aura.

"Good morning." The young woman looked neat as a pin, her dark hair pulled back, the crown of her head covered with the white bonnet Remy had grown accustomed to seeing yesterday.

A prayer kapp, she corrected herself. "I'm Mary," the woman said as she finished doling out the plates. "Would you like some coffee?"

"Please. It smells wonderful." Remy followed as Mary took a percolator from the stovetop and poured coffee into a mug. "I'm Remy."

"So I heard. Adam and Sadie were worried about you, after the seizure and all. But you look much better today." Mary handed her the mug. "Milk and sugar?"

"Just a little milk."

As Mary retrieved a small pitcher from the refrigerator, Remy was curious as to how it ran, if the Amish did not allow electricity in their homes. She wanted to ask, but she didn't want Mary to think she was rude. She also wondered when Adam would be heading back in from whatever was going on out in the barn. She didn't want him to see her like this, with bed head and smudged makeup, wrapped in a quilt. Judging by Mary's neat appearance, she suspected that most Amish did not spend mornings hanging out in their jammies.

"Maybe you should be sitting, after your fainting spell yesterday." Mary nodded toward the corner of the kitchen, where a daybed was set up, well used but comfortable, covered by a clean blue blanket. "A seat by the potbellied stove is probably the warmest spot right now."

Remy added some milk to the mug, returned the pitcher to the refrigerator, and turned to take in the large but inviting room that seemed to serve as a combined kitchen and family room. The only decorations on the bright green walls were an old clock, a pinned-up calendar, and a small piece of embroidery that advised "Let God be your guide in an uncertain world." A desk cluttered with papers sat in one corner, typical of any home. The furniture, an eclectic mix of styles, was plentiful and functional.

Sinking into the daybed, Remy imagined that most of the family's activities took place in this big, cozy kitchen, which she must have passed through while in her altered state last night. "Thank you for taking me in, Mary. I hope it didn't put you out too much, having me here last night."

"We have plenty of beds, and you were sorely in need of a place to sleep." Although Mary seemed friendly enough, Remy could tell that she didn't share Sadie's curiosity about and interest in the fancy life. With an efficiency of movement born from experience, Mary placed a cast-iron pan on the stove and added a slab of bacon. "So you've had seizures before?"

"Yes, and sometimes I zone out for a day or two. But—it's only Sunday?"

"Sunday morning."

Remy was reassured. At least she didn't miss an entire day, which had happened to her with some previous seizures. "That's a relief. I'm just a little confused after collapsing like that."

"And it's no wonder. Sadie said it was an awful spell." Mary stepped away from the sizzling bacon.

"So will everyone be going to church?"

Mary turned back to tend the bacon. "It's a day of rest, but we have our services every other week. Today is the in-between Sunday, a visiting day."

A visiting day? Who would come to visit? For a second Remy wondered who would visit her at home if Sunday were visiting day for her. Would Herb stop by? Wow, she would have to fly in one of her college friends.

But that seemed like a silly comparison. Time to corral her thoughts. Sitting on the daybed in the heat radiating from the stove shaped like a pepper mill, Remy tucked her icy feet under her to warm and tried to work out the logistics of getting home. She could get a ride to her car, but then there was the matter of the long drive home. If yesterday's collapse was a seizure, she knew she shouldn't be driving.

Remy adjusted the blanket on her shoulders and rubbed her temples. What a mess.

"Are you all right?" Mary had turned away from the stove to face her.

"I'm just trying to figure out a way home."

"Such a worry! And with you collapsing like that." Mary waved a hand, as if swatting away Remy's concerns. "Don't be weighed down by such details now. We'll be eating within the hour. If you're feeling up to it, you can help out in the barn. Time is better spent working than worrying a hole in your heart."

"I'd like to help." Remy rose, her feet planted firmly on the ground. Losing herself in some work was exactly what she needed.

"You can fetch your clothes from the next room. They're folded by the fire. I tried to warm them, but I didn't want that fancy coat to burn."

Remy thanked her and hurried to fetch her clothes. She ducked into the downstairs bathroom, splashed some water onto her face, and pulled on her jeans and sweater. As there was only a scratched shaving mirror to the side of the sink, she finger-combed her hair and hoped she didn't scare the cows with the impromptu look.

As she returned to the kitchen, the porch door popped open and Ruthie ushered in two children. The small boy in a baggy jacket whose round face was framed by his hat stomped in bearing a silver pail.

"Sammy, no!" Ruthie called from the porch room. "Your boots stay out here."

"Oh." With wide eyes he crept back out the door, returning in blue-stockinged feet. "It's a beautiful morning for eggs," he said, holding up the bucket. "Lots of eggs, Mary."

"Eggs!" cried the red-cheeked girl who waddled in behind him.

She tripped on the threshold, and her small bucket crashed to the ground.

Remy winced at the sight of the falling toddler, who was quickly helped up by Mary. As the bucket began to roll to the side, Remy realized it was empty.

"Yes, Katie has eggs, but it's a good thing I'm carrying them," Ruthie said as she placed a basket on the counter beside the sink.

"Thank you, Samuel." Mary accepted the bucket from the boy. "Now be a good boy and get the broom. You must sweep up the bits of dirt and hay you tracked in here. After that, the mudroom."

"Not sweeping." He hung his head. "I did that yesterday."

"You must do as you're told, and no whining."

With his lower lip protruding, he trudged to the mudroom.

"What a good kid," Remy remarked. "How old is he?"

"Remy!" Ruthie clapped her hands together as she hurried to Remy's side. "I didn't see you there. How are you feeling this morning?" Ruthie's question ended with her face almost nose to nose with Remy's, a manner that Remy found endearing.

"I got some good sleep, and I'm ready to be put to work. Mary, do you need some help here?"

"I suppose they could use some help with the milking. Ruthie, why don't you take her out to the barn." Mary turned away from the counter, where she was cutting round biscuits from a sheet of dough. "And mind, you can borrow a pair of muck boots out on the porch. Mine should fit you, the ones by the door. We can't have you ruining your Englisher shoes."

Out on the closed-in porch, the rubber boots held a chill as Remy slipped her feet into them. The cold was compounded by the brisk wind that greeted the girls when they stepped outside.

"Whoa. I'm not sure how long I can last out here." Remy hugged herself, rubbing her arms as she slogged behind the younger girl. Nervous excitement fluttered inside her as she considered the prospect of seeing Adam here, in his territory. She longed to talk with him, just for a few minutes alone, though she doubted that would be a possibility until after the milking. Whether or not she wrote about his family, she wanted to convince herself that she wasn't part of the enemy.

"Are you terribly cold?" Ruthie's voice was laced with concern. "It won't be too long. The barn is warmer."

"I'm okay. But about the barn . . ." Remy peered down at the girl. "I just want to warn you, I've never milked a cow before."

Ruthie giggled. "We'll find something for you to do. When it's milking time, we need every hand we can get. We got twelve cows that don't like to wait!"

SIXTEEN

"Ruthie, please go upstairs and find the Englisher girl. Tell her breakfast is almost ready." Adam kicked off his boots, imagining that Remy McCallister might want to sleep through breakfast, but that was not something he could allow. The children were quite observant of the world on their farm, and he couldn't have her setting a bad example.

Not even a visitor was free to indulge in the sin of laziness.

"I'll go to the stables and tell her," Ruthie offered.

"The stables?" Adam removed his hat, raking back his hair with one hand. "What is she doing there?"

"Helping with the milking."

"But Sadie was to finish the milking. . . ." After Jonah had come galloping in on Jigsaw to report a hole in the fence, Adam had left the barn to help with repairs, leaving Sadie in charge. Now disapproval cloyed at him, a sour taste in the back of his throat. He couldn't allow Remy to pull his sister from her duties.

"The milking's done. They're just sending the last of the cows out to pasture. Remy tried to milk Daisy, and you should have seen it. Remy bellowed, worse than a cow!" The hand she pressed to her mouth to suppress a giggle did nothing to mask the amusement in her eyes. "She tried and tried, but couldn't get a drop from Daisy. Sadie and I laughed so hard, it made my belly sore."

Adam felt himself smile, despite his sense of caution. It was good to see his younger sister caught up in fun. "Just let the girls know it's time to get cleaned up for breakfast."

"I will, and I'll be back in a wink." Ruthie pulled a cloak over her shoulders before heading out the door. "Mary made biscuits!"

"Everything is absolutely delicious, Mary," Remy said as she broke off a small crumble of biscuit. "I don't remember the last time I had this many carbs, but it's worth it."

"Please, help yourself to whatever you like." Mary turned to Adam, one eyebrow slightly cocked. "How are your carbs?"

He nearly choked on a mouthful of crumbs. "Just fine." Did Mary even know what a carb was? He picked up a crisp slice of bacon, trying to think of a way to close the gap between English and Amish. "Once I returned home, I stopped counting carbs and calories. With the chores we do, we burn it all up."

"That's great." Remy's green eyes were thoughtful. "And I'll bet you don't have to work out at the gym, either."

"Not necessary," Adam agreed. Shifting in his seat, he was reminded of how he'd grown lean again in the past year. Working the land, so close to God and His creations, honed the strength in a body. He was thankful for the newfound strength in his body . . . and a little self-conscious to think that Remy had noticed the changes in his appearance.

Jonah shared his story about finding the broken fence in the back fields.

"Were you able to mend it?" Mary asked.

"We're working on something to hold it until tomorrow," Gabe explained. "A solid fix is a full day's work, not something we want to start on a Sunday."

"I'm glad you found that before one of the animals wandered off," Adam told Jonah, passing him the bread basket. "Here, brother Jonah. Extra biscuits for you."

Laughter broke out around the table as Jonah rubbed his flat belly. "Gee, thanks."

Beside him, Remy's laugh seemed as natural as the shimmer of summer leaves. Despite her flowing coppery hair and her form-fitting sweater, she seemed to belong here at the table, at his right hand. It wasn't about the way she looked, but about the overall feeling surrounding her. He could not remember seeing an Englisher fit so well at an Amish table.

"I heard you had some fun milking the cows today, Remy," Adam said.

There were more giggles as Ruthie and Sadie exchanged a look.

"I've never heard anyone moo to a cow before," Ruthie said, her eyes shining with mirth.

"Daisy will certainly never forget it," Sadie said, recounting how Remy mooed to the cow, begging for milk.

Remy pressed a napkin to her mouth, covering a smile. "Come on, guys. I tried my best."

The story of the obstinate Daisy led Jonah to recall how he'd once nearly been kicked by a cow who didn't want to be milked. Sadie recalled how a swatting cow tail once drove a fly into her mouth. Soon everyone was contributing anecdotes of unfortunate incidents, how Gabe fell from the hayloft, and how Simon landed in a cow patty.

Even Gabe was smiling as laughter swelled round the table. Remy's presence changed the dynamic of their family breakfast, much for the better. Adam was surprised at how things had turned out; the air seemed lighter with Remy here.

And she had been a very polite guest. He'd been surprised to learn she'd gotten out of bed to help with the milking, and she had bowed her head respectfully when they'd paused for silent thanks before the meal. Although he would not admit it aloud, Adam liked having her here at the table. He saw the way her eyes lit with tenderness when the children spoke. And from the family's warm response, they seemed to appreciate her good humor, as well as her ability to listen.

Too bad, but it was time for her visit to come to an end. Adam didn't want to offend her, but he had to broach the topic of getting her a ride back to Philadelphia. Soon word would get out about her overnight visit, and he wanted to have it all in the past before the bishop or Preacher Dave approached him.

"You know, last night it occurred to me that someone must have missed you when you didn't return home last night," Adam said. "I know you were a little out of it, but we could have made that call for you."

"No worries." Remy broke off a piece of biscuit. "I'm a fairly independent person, and you couldn't do much without a phone or cell service."

"But we do have a phone, down the road in the shanty," Ruthie said. "We share it with the Zooks and Uncle Nate's family."

"Oh. That must be good for emergencies," Remy said, smiling at the young girl.

They loved her. His younger sisters all smiled up at Remy with stars in their eyes. It would be hard to let her go, but it was his duty to keep the conversation on track. "Is there someone we can call today? Someone who can come and pick you up? The paramedics didn't think it would be a good idea for you to drive yesterday, but . . ."

"They were right." She nodded. "You're not supposed to drive after a seizure."

"Maybe your parents would like to take a ride out to Halfway," Adam pressed. "They're welcome to pick you up here."

"My mother is gone," she said quickly. "She died when I was little . . . around Simon's age."

Adam bit his lower lip. Did he know that? Maybe she had mentioned it when they'd met on that train. Although that had been barely a year ago, it seemed like he'd lived a hundred lifetimes in these past few months.

"And Herb, my father, he . . . he doesn't have the time to drive out here." Her green eyes darkened with a hint of trouble as she looked down at the cinnamon apples on her plate. "But he's sending a car for me. I got through on my cell. Do you know you have a lot of dead spots around here?"

Adam nodded. "That doesn't surprise me."

"A driver should be here by noon." Remy nudged Sadie. "That'll give me time to help you in the barn, as promised. Then I'll have to go."

"So soon? And here I thought you'd spend the afternoon with us," Mary said brightly. "It's our day for visitors, and while we're expecting our Uncle Nate and Aunt Betsy and some of their family, there's always room for more, and plenty of food. I spent most of yesterday afternoon baking those shoofly pies over there."

"Samuel baked pies, too." Sam perked up, his chin barely clearing his plate as he held a fork in one tight fist. "And Katie used the ruler pin."

"The *rolling* pin, and yes, you were a wonderful good helper," Mary said, patting the boy on the back.

"Do you have to go?" Sadie turned from Remy to Adam, as if asking permission from him. "I mean, can't you stay a little longer?"

"I . . . I'd really like to stay." Remy's green eyes resembled exotic gems . . . full of light and hope.

Adam blinked. Was he losing his mind? Seeing special qualities in a woman's eyes. An Englisher woman, at that.

"You've all been so kind and generous. I can't thank you enough for having me here," Remy went on. "But I do have work in the morning. And I'll have to see a doctor this week about . . . well, you know. There won't always be someone nearby to catch me when I fall." She gave Sadie a bump on the elbow, and to Adam's surprise, Sadie bumped her back.

Maybe this Englisher girl had been a good influence on Sadie, who had been drifting away in her rumspringa. Sometimes he worried about losing her, the way his parents had lost him.

Still, it was good that Remy's ride was on the way. Watching Remy talk with Mary about a recipe, he swallowed a mouthful of scrambled eggs as an old Amish saying came to mind. *You can't keep trouble from coming, but you don't have to give her a room to stay in.*

SEVENTEEN

The assembly line worked like a charm.

Leah cleared. Susie scraped. Sadie washed. Remy dried. And Ruthie returned dishes to the lodestone green cupboards, gently replacing each cup and saucer as if it were the queen's china.

As Sadie immersed herself in the scrubbing, she launched into a hymn, and the other girls joined in, their young voices following the same notes with precise measure.

Not knowing the German words, Remy couldn't join in, but she was happy just to let their voices fall over her like a waterfall cascading over stones. Sadie's voice was husky and rich, while the other girls sang with heartfelt emotion. Was it love for God she heard, or simply the warm comfort of being in a family that fit like a glove? Whatever the reason, Remy felt privileged to be a part of their work crew, if only for this once.

When the song ended, Remy thrust her arms up, dish towel in one hand. "Bravo! You sound wonderful together."

"Sadie always makes us sing," Leah said as she covered the biscuit basket with a checkered cloth. "And it's permitted, as long as we sing hymns from the Ausbund."

Remy moved next to Sadie. "And you, Miss Sadie, have an amazing voice. Where did you learn to sing like that?"

Sadie beamed, her high cheeks suddenly tinged with pale pink. "I got my start in church services, of course. But I've learned a lot in the last few years. Frank has taken me to places in the city. Have you ever heard of open mike night? And something like Okey-dokey . . ."

Remy nodded. "You've done karaoke?"

"Oops! I keep forgetting what they call it. But yes. I've done it a few times. Frank and his friends say I'm very good at it." She pulled a plate from the rinse basin and handed it to Remy, looking over her shoulder. "I don't know if they're just being kind, but the truth of it is that I enjoy it so. To sing songs from the heart, it just feels like a real and true expression of God's love."

"It sounds like you have a gift. A real talent." Remy ran the towel around the rim and handed the plate to Ruthie.

"Well . . ." Sadie let out a gust of a breath. "That kind of singing is not the Amish way. I'm allowed to try some new things, being on my rumspringa and all, but it's not something I'd ever be allowed to pursue. Not really."

Remy understood her disappointment; it seemed a shame to see such talent wasted.

"And please . . ." Sadie turned to make eye contact with her sisters. "Don't tell Adam about Philadelphia or the clubs or any of it. Do you hear me?"

Ruthie sucked her lips in, nodding, as the twins agreed.

"Adam forgets what he did during his own rumspringa." Sadie scrubbed viciously at a spot on the baking sheet. "And now he's acting like my father. Which is not a good thing."

"I know how that is." Remy felt the need to defend Adam, sensing that he had the best of intentions.

Right now he was out in the back fields, helping his brothers rig a temporary fix on the fence. As Sadie spouted a list of complaints against her brother, Remy glanced out the window over the sink and wondered if Adam would be back before she left. Sitting at his right hand during breakfast, she had felt a strong sense of grace and belonging. Maybe she was mistaking attraction for the love at the family table, the sweet energy that swirled amid the banter and thoughtful conversation.

Maybe . . . but she didn't think so. Something kept tugging her to Adam's side, a real force, like that magnetic pull that kids studied in science class.

"I hate the way he tries to control my life," Sadie said bluntly, drawing Remy back to the moment.

The other girls moved silently, though their round eyes suggested their alarm over Sadie's outburst.

"Sometimes men confuse control with love," Remy said. "My father tries to reel me in when he pretends to care. He either tries to tell me what to do, or else he acts like I don't belong in his family. He can drive me nuts. He made me go to dinner with some business partner's son. A date. He's trying to use me to grease the pan."

From the squinty eyes of Leah, Susie, and Ruth, she could see that she'd lost them.

"But he's your dat, Remy." Standing on the bench so that she could reach into the cabinet, Ruthie was at eye level with Remy. "You must respect his wishes. Your dat wants what is best for you."

"Oh, Ruthie . . ." Remy wanted to think that was true. But how could she explain to this girl who had lost her father that dads did not always do right by their daughters?

Looking away for a moment, Remy pretended to concentrate on the mug she was drying. "That sounds like very good advice," Remy said. "I'm going to file it away and remember it in the future."

"Trust me." Ruthie accepted the mug, her gaze steady with the wisdom of youth. "Dats are one thing I know all about."

"This is much easier than trying to milk a cow." Remy scraped the shovel along the ground and dropped the clods of manure into the large bucket. "Smellier, but easier. Is that it? I'm doing it right?"

"Perfect. Are you sure you haven't done this before?" Sadie teased. "Because it looks like you have a real talent."

"Very funny." Remy recognized her own words from an hour ago in the kitchen. "Actually, I come from a long line of muckrakers."

Sadie paused, leaning on the handle of her shovel. "Tell me, what does that mean?"

"Never mind. The point is, I bow to your superior milking skills. And I now have a new respect for milk." She took a breath, a halting breath. "Do you ever get used to this smell?"

"What smell?"

Remy shot a look at Sadie.

"Gotcha." Sadie's grin revealed those merry dimples. "Actually, it's not that bad when you connect the smell to the animals that are part of our farm. The horses that plow our fields and pull our buggies, the cows and chickens that provide milk and eggs."

"I see what you mean. There are lots of people out there willing to throw money at things just because they're organic. I wonder what they'd think about this organic odor."

"Manure cologne. Please, tell me I don't smell like this all the time."

"You don't," Remy assured her.

"You have no idea how hard it is to hold on to an English boyfriend when you're Amish." Sadie sighed. "This has not been an easy year."

Remy hesitated, seeing a chance to steer the conversation toward the difficult topic of Esther and Levi King. It wasn't just that Sadie's memories might help her write a story about the King family. Remy suspected that Sadie would feel better if she had a chance to open up about her parents.

"You've gone through a lot this year, Sadie. Losing your parents that way, it'd be tough on anyone."

"It's hard, especially when there's always someone around, whether you like it or not. Lots of cousins and aunts and uncles."

"It sounds like privacy might be an issue."

"Sometimes I just want to get away from everyone watching what I do." Sadie scraped at a tough patch on the ground. "And sometimes I get really annoyed with Adam. I know he's trying to be the man of the house, but he's a bit stern sometimes, especially with the little ones. Mammi Nell does her best to cheer us all up, but we all miss Mamm and Dat." Sadie's nose was red, and she paused to wipe it with the back of one hand. "It's like a pain that never goes away. Sometimes it throbs, sometimes it fades to a dull ache, but it never completely goes away."

Remy stopped working as she searched her mind for something reassuring to say. But since Sadie kept her shovel moving, as if in time to some silent song, Remy just kept working alongside her.

"At first, after they died, I think we all just wanted to prove that we could hold together. That our family ties and our trust in God were strong enough to get us through. At first, we were full of faith. But as time goes on, I think we're all starting to look back and wonder. What really happened to Mamm and Dat that night, and why would a person do that to two so very good human beings?"

A knot of thick emotion formed in Remy's throat, but she pushed herself to ask the question that had haunted her since she'd first learned of the senseless murders. "What happened out there that night? I mean, why do you think your parents were killed?"

"I still wonder about that. The bishop has rules—we're not supposed to talk about it—but sometimes things just slip out. When it first happened, poor Simon took the blame from some. Because he was there, because he couldn't bear to talk about it, rumors started. People said Simon went crazy, all verhuddelt, but I never believed that."

"Why would people say such a thing?" Remy asked. "He's a child. How old was he at the time . . . seven or eight? And he wasn't a difficult kid, right?" Remy wanted to ask if the family had a history of mental illness or violent behavior, but she didn't want to sound too clinical.

"Simon was always a good boy . . . Mamm's little angel. I think Dat worried that she babied him, and that was one of the reasons our father took the time to go out that day with Simon, to teach him to shoot a gun. Target practice."

Remy remembered mention of a gun in the early coverage. A rifle. "Was that how your parents were killed? Shot by their own rifle?"

"Shot, but by a handgun. The police could tell from the way the bullets looked. Our rifle had been discharged, too, but the thinking was . . . well, *my* thinking is that Dat and Simon used the rifle for target practice out in the back fields. Neither Dat nor Mamm would have shot at a person. Ever. It's not the Amish way."

"And so the police never found out who did it," Remy said, thinking out loud. "But people are frustrated because Simon saw it all unfold but couldn't say what happened. Was he able to give any clues? Even one-word answers?"

Sadie shook her head. "He closed up tight, like an old wooden door swollen shut."

"He must have been traumatized," Remy said as her shovel

scraped against the ground. Poor Simon had been scared into silence.

"He just started talking to us in the last month or so. I think he's been communicating with Adam longer than that. But really, I can't imagine how frightened he must have been. The police found him hiding under Mamm's legs, under the lap blanket. Mamm had been shot dead sitting in the front seat of the buggy, but Dat had climbed out. They found him near a ditch at the roadside." Sadie's voice cracked with emotion. "The police said they might have been there for an hour or more. They were over on Juniper Lane, and it's not a busy road. They were just left there. Like it didn't matter. As if no one cared . . ."

"I'm sorry. If you don't want to talk about it, I—"

"But I do want to talk. The bishop wants us to put it all behind us and Adam is afraid we'll break his rules. They want us to cover up our emotions, bury our fears like we buried Mamm and Dat in their coffins. But I can't do that. I want to know who did it." She pressed a fist to her mouth, as if to stop the pain from flowing. "God help me, I want to know. I want the killer to be found out. I want him stopped."

"And that's how most non-Amish feel." Resting her chin on the tip of the shovel handle, Remy pictured it all.

A buggy parked on the side of the road.

Levi King's body prone on the frozen ground near one wheel.

Esther King slumped over in her seat, bleeding from the bullet in her chest.

And beneath the blanket at Esther's feet, a small boy whimpering from the sharp fear slicing through his chest.

EIGHTEEN

*S*imon didn't think much of it when he heard the girls talk-ing in the stables. He came here every day around this time to groom and turn out Shadow, the piebald mare Dat had bought from the Muellers.

Although Simon helped with all the horses, Shadow was his favorite. Partly because Shadow had been there that night. She had cried out at the sound of the shots, but she didn't go verhuddelt and take off running. She was a good horse for him.

But even before that night, Simon had known she was a good horse. Dat had told him Shadow would need special attention.

"Did you ever notice how Shadow tries to stay in the stables when all the other horses go out?" Dat had pointed out to Simon. "And when we drive her out, she walks the fence or keeps to herself. Look at her over there. All hunched up and nervous." Dat had stood, hands in his pockets, talking to Simon as if he were a grown-up.

Simon still remembered the sights and sounds of that day when

Dat had talked about the horses. The smell of clover and the mists rising from the dew-covered pastures. Dat had spoken his mind, man to man. Simon would never forget the important things about horses that Dat shared with him. Thinking about it now, Simon was sure God wanted him to take care of Shadow, and that was why He guided Dat to explain these important matters that summer day.

"You got a couple of reasons why a horse might shy away from the others," Dat had said. He raised one finger. "Maybe it's being bullied out in the field. That's possible with Shadow, but I don't think so. Thunder is our leader, and he doesn't waste his energy on the shy ones."

Dat had been right about Thunder. Simon had watched the two horses together, and the herd's most aggressive horse did not bother with Shadow. So it had to be something else.

"Sometimes horses walk the fence because they miss their bosom buddy," Dat had said. "But since Shadow was the Muellers' only horse, that doesn't seem right. So then we go to the third thing. Shadow never had a chance to learn the signals of the herd. She missed some important lessons and now she's afraid of the other horses."

Climbing the stepladder to comb Shadow's mane, Simon thought of the other possibility, the one Dat didn't want to mention. "You don't have to worry about anyone hurting you here, girl," Simon whispered as he ran the comb through the soft, dark threads. "Don't be scared."

He told her that every day, and every day she went to the fence, avoiding the group of horses out in the pastures. If Dat were here, he would know what to do. But maybe Shadow was just meant to be on her own.

"Creating a happy herd is not an easy task," Dat used to say. "You need space, food, and the Lord's blessing. And that goes for horses as well as people." That last part had brought a twinkle to his eyes.

"How did he know so much?" Simon asked the horse as he peered up into her black eyes. He reached up with a damp sponge to wipe one of Shadow's eyes. When Simon was just five, Dat had taught him the basics of grooming a horse, a lesson Simon used every day of his life. Dat knew so many things; if Simon lived to be a hundred he didn't think he could fill his mind with that much knowledge.

"There you go." Simon put the sponge down and looked up at the mare. "You look wonderful good today. Now. Are you ready to go make friends with the other horses?" When Shadow didn't answer, Simon opened the door to her stall and shrugged. "I didn't think so, but you have to try."

He hopped to the ground and looked over her fine spotted coat. Sometimes he saw objects in the white spots that curled in jagged shapes against the chestnut brown. The white marking that reached down from her withers was sometimes a ladle, sometimes a letter b. And the crescent on her rear end, that was always a sliver of moon.

If it were up to Simon, he would have named her Moonshadow.

As he led the mare through the stables, the voice of the Englisher girl carried through the cool air. Remy's words were so round, like a rubber ball in the schoolyard. And always speaking English. He wondered if she spoke a different language when she went home to her family.

He didn't mean to eavesdrop, but clear words crackled in the air. He heard them say "police" and "Mamm and Dat" and "Juniper Lane." Hearing those words made him feel sick inside. He moved the horse faster, wanting to escape the bad feeling and the dark barn.

"Come on, Shadow."

Once the mare was turned out, he turned toward the house. Mary would give him some chores to prepare for the visitors. That would take away the sick feeling.

But as he passed the barn door, he felt the pull of curiosity. Why were Sadie and the Englisher girl talking about that awful night?

Two steps more, and he was in the barn, facing the two girls who were both leaning on their shovels, looking sad.

"I heard you talking," he said, "about the unspeakable."

"So. You caught us." Sadie cocked her head to one side. "I know we're not to speak of it, but I confess, I think of it every day."

Simon tipped his head down. He hadn't expected such honesty from his sister.

Sadie rested her shovel against a rail. "Do you ever think about that terrible night? About what happened?"

He didn't want to answer, but a word slipped out. "Ya."

That was easier than he'd expected. "Sometimes I see it in my head," he admitted. "I hear the shots." His mouth puckered, confusion pulsing through his body. There . . . he'd said it. Was that a sin?

"Does it still scare you to think about it?" Remy asked.

He nodded. "Especially the bear. He was so very big and furry."

"You saw a bear?" Remy's brows went up, and he noticed her eyes were a soft green. Like the moss that grew on the side of trees. He wondered if those green eyes had ever seen a real bear.

"'Twas a bear, all right," he said.

"Some people think the bear is all made-up. That you got mixed up about what happened. That you thought you saw a bear." Sadie sank down onto a bale of hay so that her face was level with his. "They think it's not real."

"He's real, all right. And I'm not the one that's verhuddelt. It was that bear who killed Mamm and Dat. He's the crazy one. Growling at our dat. And Mamm wasn't afraid to talk to him. She spoke firm and gentle, like when she gives us chores. . . ." He had to stop talking because his lower lip was quivering. He wiped his nose with one fist, and a sob bubbled out.

"Ach, Simon . . ." Sadie folded him in her arms and pulled him against her.

For a moment he stiffened.

Mamm had pulled him close that night.

"Get down!" she whispered, pushing him to the floor.

Her legs clamped over his back, and she spread the blanket over his feet and head.

"Now stay put, liewi." Her voice held the gentle warning of a gray sky swollen with a coming storm.

Simon curled around the blanket that insulated the warming brick and clung to its lingering heat. The blanket blocked out the night, darkness muffled by darkness. It would have been cozy if not for the fear that swirled around them.

"You must stop," Mamm ordered the bear. Her voice was thick with authority, as if ordering one of the children to sweep the porch or fetch something from the pantry.

"It will be all right, if you stop. Let me go to him," she said. "Put that down. Please, put the gun away and let me—"

Simon jerked as the shots rang out.

Above him, her body shifted. More weight on his shoulders and back, but not too heavy. Comforting weight. He could hold her up, his mamm.

But then the awful sound started . . . a whistling breath, like a dry leaf rolling in the wind. A dead, dry leaf . . .

"Simon?" Sadie gasped, holding him by the shoulders.

His sudden movement had knocked his hat to the ground.

"The bear killed her." He pressed his lips together, trying not to break down. He didn't want to cry anymore. He just wanted people to believe him. "Why doesn't anyone believe me? It was the bear."

NINETEEN

"Kumm! You must kumm!" Ruthie called.

Remy swung toward the door of the stables, wishing the young girl hadn't interrupted just when Simon was beginning to open up. This was the first time he'd even looked her in the eye since she'd arrived, but because he trusted Sadie he'd talked about that night. . . .

Of the bear that killed his parents.

As Ruthie called again, Remy's mind quickly went back to the accounts she'd read—the brief mention of a bear or wild animal attack—though none of that added up to two people who'd been found murdered by handguns. And yet, Simon was set on what he'd seen.

How could a bear be involved and still add up with the facts of the murders?

Remy had been hoping he'd say more, but that window was closed now as Simon pulled away from Sadie and tugged his hat on so that the brim covered his face.

"You must see this with your own eyes!" Ruth raced to a halt before them, the grin on her face belying the urgency in her voice.

Sadie lifted her chin, her annoyance apparent. "What's wrong?"

"Remy's car is here, and you must come see it!"

"Why such excitement?" Sadie rose and brushed off her skirt. "You've seen cars before, haven't you?"

"But this one is stretched out so very long." Ruthie's arms spread wide. "Like a piece of taffy that's been pulled and pulled."

"Oh, dear. Sounds like a limo," Remy muttered as she moved to the barn door and looked at the sleek white vehicle parked in front of the house. "Yeah. Herb sent a stretch limo. That's embarrassing."

"Ah. It is a very long car. Is there something wrong with a limo?" Sadie asked as everyone gathered at the stable door, blinking from the winter sunlight.

"It's just so showy, like my father."

"We have all ridden in cars before, but none quite like a long noodle!" Sadie's comment spurred laughter from the group.

"I think it was kind of your father to send you this long noodle car." Ruthie took Remy's hand and pulled her toward it. "Let's go look at it together."

"I'm glad you find it amusing," Remy said.

"What she's really saying is that she wants a ride," Sadie said as they all scampered toward the car.

"Me too?" Simon's voice was hopeful now, without a trace of the grief that had ravaged him moments ago.

"Oh, I would love a ride!" Ruthie exclaimed.

"Are we going for a ride?" Susie called from the front door of the house, where she and her twin spilled out to examine the vehicle.

The door opened again and Adam stepped out, a black silhouette against the white of the house.

He was back . . . back in time to say good-bye. Remy's heart hitched at the prospect of stealing a moment alone with him.

"What's going on?" he asked.

"Look!" Simon pointed down the lane. "Remy's big white car is here."

Leah clapped her hands together. "And we want to go for a ride."

"Just down the lane?" Ruthie begged. "Could we, Remy? Please?"

Gravel crunched under Remy's muck boots as she crossed the driveway. "I think that would be fine, if Sarge doesn't mind."

Seeing Remy, the driver killed the engine and emerged in his white shirt and tie. A graying, dark-skinned gentleman, Sarge was one of Remy's favorite drivers. His brusque, perceptive manner was refreshing, and she believed he was one of the few people who would tell Herb exactly what he thought when asked.

"Good afternoon, Remy. My stars in heaven, aren't we a mess." He eyed her from head to toe, taking in her rubber boots, apron, and mud-splattered dress.

When they were heading out to muck the stables, Sadie had insisted that Remy borrow one of the boxy dresses. "Or else you'll ruin your fancy jeans." Remy felt a little odd, being pinned into the gown by Sadie and Ruth, but she figured they knew what they were talking about. As it turned out, they were right.

But Sarge liked to run a tight ship. "What in the world happened to you?" he asked Remy.

"I've been doing chores, Sarge." She smiled, despite the blisters that had formed under the borrowed gloves. "But I have a favor to ask. You've got some interested customers here, hoping for a short ride through the countryside."

"I could handle that." Sarge squinted as he scrutinized the group. "As long as we can shed the muddy boots."

"Of course." Sadie pulled off her oilcloth apron and turned to the house. "Anyone who wants to come for a ride must first find clean shoes."

Susie gave a little leap, clasping her hands together. "Can I go?"

"I want to ride in the very long car, too!" Leah said. "May I come along?"

"Hold on." Adam held his hands up, effectively stopping the moment. "There's nothing sinful about riding in a car, but let's remember that it's the Sabbath, and—"

"That's right!" Susie's hands flew to her cheeks. "We should wear our Sunday bonnets."

"I'll get shawls and bonnets," Leah said as she rushed back toward the house. "And what about a warming brick?"

"The limo is heated." Sadie shot a glance at Sarge. "Isn't that right?"

"A comfortable seventy-one degrees."

"I'll need a hat," Simon said. "My Sunday hat. And shoes without mud."

Sadie shooed them on, and the children raced back to the side porch to change. "We'll just be a moment, finding proper shoes and all," Sadie explained, backing away.

Sarge nodded, then turned sharply and marched toward Remy, who shivered in the cold, arms crossed in an attempt to hold some warmth in her body.

If Sarge felt the cold, he didn't show it; he stood with his shoulders back, his head high. "That goes for you, too," he said, staring down at Remy's mucky boots. "I'm not in the business of importing cow patties into Philadelphia."

"I might need a little more time to get cleaned up, but I'll be ready when you get back. I'll wait for you in the house," she said, walking past the shiny white stretch limo. "And what's with the stretch? Is the Lincoln in the shop?"

"Your father got tired of the underwhelming. His new mantra appears to be 'Spend it like I got it.'"

"Sounds like Herb." She headed up to the mudroom to get cleaned up. "Thanks for giving my friends the ride, Sarge."

"No problem."

On her way to the house, Remy noticed that Adam had vanished. Great. Throughout the morning she had wanted to talk with him, and now that there was a moment, he didn't seem too receptive. Was he mad at her? Not that she'd defied his authority, but she had stirred up the kids' enthusiasm. But really, they were so excited, and how often did they get to ride in a limousine?

Something told her he would not be going for a ride.

It didn't take Remy long to wash up in the water closet downstairs, though she bristled under the spigot of icy water that never seemed to warm up. When she found that someone—probably Mary—had piled her clothes neatly on a chair in the kitchen, she went in search of a place to change. Just beyond the small room with the toilet was a modest bedroom with a double bed and dresser. Since it seemed not only empty but somewhat abandoned, she went inside and closed the door behind her.

Although the sky blue curtains had been pulled closed, enough sunlight filtered in so that she could find her way around. With her clothes on the bed quilt and her shoes on the floor, she quickly unpinned the dirty dress. As she dropped it to the floor and finished dressing, the dresser against the wall caught her eye.

The dark wood had been polished to a smooth luster. She ran her hand over the top and slid open a drawer, just half an inch, to get a sense of the craftsmanship. It was definitely handmade, a treasure in this dark room. She pulled on her boots, wondering why this room was not being used.

One of many mysteries here at the Kings' dairy farm. She would have to file that one away behind Simon's insistence that bears had killed his parents, as well as the actual question of who would commit such a heinous crime.

When she picked up the dress and opened the door, she was startled to find Adam King waiting outside. "Oh, hi. I was hoping for a chance to talk to you before I left." An understatement, if there ever was one.

"What were you doing in there?" he asked, as if she'd violated sacred ground.

She shrugged. "Changing my clothes. Is that not okay?"

"It's ... it's not a room we use right now. It was my parents' bedroom."

Of course ... the double bed, the sense of emptiness. "Oh, Adam, I'm sorry. Is that part of Amish tradition, to preserve someone's room after they're gone?"

"No, it's just a room. I'm the one who has the issues with it." He raked his hair back with one hand, his face taut with strain. "It's my problem. You just do what you need to do." He turned and disappeared down the dark hall.

Remy stared into the shadows. "Wait ... I didn't mean to be disrespectful."

He didn't answer. The only sound was the receding thud of his footsteps.

Remy wasn't going to let him off the hook that easily. She followed him into the kitchen, where Mary sat on the daybed in the corner, reading a children's book with Katie and Sam. Adam and Mary spoke to each other in Pennsylvania Dutch, and Adam disappeared into the mudroom without looking back.

"Is he always this testy?" Remy asked.

"Every day is a new challenge." Mary tried to bite back a grin, but quickly changed the subject. "I don't think they're back from their car ride yet. Would you like some more coffee?"

"I'm good." Remy held up the borrowed dress. "Does this go out by the washing machine?" She had seen an old-fashioned contraption in the mudroom, complete with a washboard and wringer, that she assumed was used for laundering clothes.

"Yes. You can put it in the bundle for laundry day."

Hearing a noise outside, Remy realized Adam was probably stomping off to the barn, where her fancy boots could not tread. "I gotta go. Thank you for everything," Remy said. "Denki."

The sound of the Pennsylvania Dutch word stole Sam's attention away from the book, and he smiled up at her. *"Willkomm,"* he said in a voice cute as a chipmunk.

Mary laughed. "That's right, Sam. You are welcome, Remy."

Out on the porch Remy tossed the dress into a basket of clothes and hurried out the door as fast as her boots would carry her. The sun had broken through clouds, and with the morning frost gone and the wind died down, the day actually showed some promise.

She imagined Adam already off at the farthest reaches of the farm, pretending to mend a fence or move bales from the hayloft— anything to avoid her. But as she jogged around the corner of the house she saw him sitting on a fence near the stables. A spotted brown and white horse stood there as Adam patted its neck.

"You can stop running," he called without turning away from the horse.

"I need to talk to you, and you were trying to get away."

"It's a big farm. If I were trying to hide, I'd be out in the back acres now."

He had a point, but it didn't defuse her agitation. *Calm down. Don't attack him.* Remy tried to pull her emotions in line as she closed the distance between them. Thoughts of an interview had given way to much more specific concerns about Simon and Sadie, two people suffocating in this culture. She wanted to help them—she wished she could—but how could she, when she could not even keep her own life on track?

And then, there was the pull between Adam and her, as inexorable as the force of a wave knocking them onto the beach. Didn't he want to talk about it? Did he not feel it?

She decided to start on neutral ground.

"That is one gigantic beast," she said, eyeing the tall horse—a mighty creature with bulging muscles and clumpy hooves. It was chocolate-colored with splashes of white here and there, as if someone had dropped a bucket of white paint on a brown horse.

"Shadow is a draft horse who doesn't think she belongs on the team yet," he said. The horse tolerated Adam for a moment, then turned and moved away. "She's a good horse. Gentle, great feet, but we still can't rely on her to work with the others. See how she's wandered over here, away from the other horses?"

"She wants to be alone."

He turned to her, his dark eyes hooded, that sleepy look she always found attractive. "No one is ever really alone on an Amish farm. Have you not noticed that this morning?"

"Maybe Shadow hasn't accepted that she's an Amish horse yet."

He jumped down to the ground. "Maybe."

Remy swallowed hard. This was her chance to segue to the issue of Sadie. "Maybe Shadow just needs some time to find herself. You know . . . explore her own identity. Her rumspringa."

"And now I'm getting advice about horses and rumspringa from an *Auswendiger*."

When she squinted, he translated. "An auswendiger is an outsider."

"That would be me." She gripped the split-rail fence for courage, the wood worn silvery smooth beneath her fingers. "And I guess you've also figured out that I'm not just talking about your horse. You know, Sadie and I have gotten close in the short time since we met."

He nodded.

"Well, I guess I just wanted to remind you what a good kid she is . . . even if she's questioning some of the Amish ways right now."

"Questioning is one thing. But sneaking off on her scooter to be with her Englisher friends? And those trips to the city . . ."

"You know about that?"

"Of course. I'm not her father, but when Sadie pushes the limits that way, it puts me in a very bad position."

"I thought she was supposed to be sowing her wild oats. Isn't rumspringa the time to try new things? Meet new people? She's following her heart right now, experiencing how things work in the outside world. I give her a lot of credit. Sadie's got an adventurous spirit."

"You see? This is what I'm talking about. Your definition of rumspringa is exactly the sort of thing that makes outsiders misunderstand the Amish. Rumspringa is a time when parents occasionally look the other way to give their teenage kids the freedom to date people and find a mate. An Amish mate. It's not an excuse to run wild, without conscience."

"Didn't you leave Halfway for your rumspringa?" Remy knew the answer to that, but she couldn't resist prodding a bit. "You moved to Connecticut . . . for a few years. . . ."

"It was Rhode Island, and just because I made a mistake doesn't mean I want my sister to repeat it."

"Of course you don't. But shouldn't Sadie be allowed the freedom to make her own decisions? Think about it. She's not going to decide to get baptized and stay in the Amish community just because her big brother wants it that way."

"It's not that simple." Adam scratched his head under the brim of his hat. "You're only seeing a small part of the picture."

"You said I'm an outsider. Wouldn't that make my observations fairly objective? And I see Sadie on a quest, searching for her identity and for a place where her talents are accepted."

"And that is exactly what I worry about. She's too young to understand the cost of pursuing her identity. There are consequences in life . . . always consequences, and Sadie doesn't see that."

"Doesn't Sadie deserve a chance to learn that on her own?"

He turned back toward the paddock, leaning forward on the fence. "She's had plenty of chances," he said darkly.

"Cut that out." She turned and poked at him with her elbow. "You can't dismiss her like that. She's your sister, and she's just trying to figure out her place in this world."

"Don't you think I know that?" His eyes were a dark storm as he wheeled on her, taking her hands in his, pulling her round so that she faced him.

"What . . . what are you doing?" She resisted the tug but he won, pulling her arms so that they were face-to-face, their arms stretched wide. Only a sliver of air separated their bodies, and despite the fact that they were standing, fully clothed, beside the paddock, Remy felt exposed and vulnerable.

"Look at you." His voice was steeped in wonder and frustration. "Just look at you, a tiny lamb who charges into our midst like an angry bull."

Swallowing back a gasp, Remy dared to look, but Adam was the only thing looming before her eyes. Adam, with his smoky brown eyes and broad shoulders and a clean-shaven jaw of smooth angles. Her fingers ached to touch the thick brown hair that cascaded to his shoulders, to smooth it from his brow and sink her hand into its dark silk. The line of his body swayed just inches away from hers, and for one dazzling second she imagined leaning forward and falling into his arms, into his strong embrace, into his complicated, tortured, solid world.

Would he kiss her?

She lifted her chin and rose on tiptoes, reaching for him as a flower grows toward the sun. When their eyes met, she sensed the pain he was holding back, the subtle ache burning slow like embers that glowed red when you blew away the white ash. How she longed to kiss away the pain, even as she doubted that any human possessed that power. She knew; she bore her own emotional scars.

With a tenderness that stole her breath away he tipped his head down and kissed her forehead. A sweet gesture, almost chaste, except that it closed the space between them and brought her into the heat of his body.

He released her hands and their arms twined around each other, as if by rote, some ancient memory shared by every man and every woman.

Remy closed her eyes. It felt so good to be in his arms.

That was when the horn sounded its boisterous melody—the custom horn of the limousine.

"They're coming back." Regret swirled on the sudden wind as arms dropped away and space was restored between them.

Beyond the bare branches of the roadside trees, the limo paused with its turn signal on. Two figures emerged through the open moon roof, and as a car passed, they waved giddily. Although the road was at least a quarter mile away, Remy could tell that was Sadie standing with one of the twins.

"Look at that." Remy rubbed her arms, suddenly vulnerable to the wind. "She's having the time of her life. They all are."

"But it's not real." He tipped his hat back, his lips strained as he stared toward the road. "Real happiness doesn't center on a fancy car."

He had a point, though it rankled. Her one small gift to them was actually a hollow temptation.

The limousine turned off the paved road, onto the Kings' lane. Another head popped up through the moon roof, and the three girls waved when they caught sight of Adam and Remy. A low, steady melody rolled up the hill.

"Sadie's singing," Remy observed. "She has a wonderful voice."

Adam nodded. "It's a hymn."

As the limo slowly rolled along the curving lane, a gray carriage came into view on the main road.

"Looks like your visitors have arrived," Remy said.

"That's my aunt and uncle." As Adam ran his knuckles over the hard line of his jaw, she sensed his mounting tension. "They'll have some questions about why my siblings are joyriding on a Sunday afternoon."

"It's not a joyride." She bumped him on the shoulder, but instead of the grin she expected he just took a step away from her.

A second gray carriage paused to turn onto the Kings' lane . . . then a third.

"Wow, your aunt and uncle must have a large family," Remy said.

"They do . . . but those aren't their buggies." Strain tightened his face as he studied the vehicles.

One of the girls standing in the moon roof noticed the buggies behind them. Sadie's song stopped abruptly as she turned to look, then quickly popped back down into the car. A moment later, the other girls ducked back in, too.

"Do you recognize those rigs?" Remy asked Adam.

"One belongs to our bishop. The other belongs to Preacher David. The leaders of our *Gemeinde* have come to pay us a visit."

"Is that a good thing?"

"It won't be, now that they've seen the children cavorting in a stretch limo."

"But you can just explain the circumstances. It's not like you hired the limo. They just went for a quick ride. By the time your guests get settled, the limo and I will be out of your hair."

"It's not that simple."

Remy's lips grew taut. Why was he suddenly so cranky? "It could be, if you'd stop glaring at me and calm down."

"I'm through taking advice from an auswendiger. Especially one named after a brandy." He turned and strode toward the house, his long legs closing the distance in seconds.

Leaving Remy alone with her regrets.

It would be hard to return to the incubator of her life without a story.

And it would be hard to leave the King family behind. She had no idea what sort of trouble the family might get into over the limo ride, her conversation with Adam would probably backfire on Sadie, and she hadn't even asked Adam about Simon. But in a short time, this family had gotten under her skin.

Negotiating the frozen path to the parked limousine, she decided she would not say good-bye, but see you later. From her high school German, she recalled that *"Auf wiedersehen"* meant "until I see you again."

That would be her promise to Sadie and Simon and the rest of the family.

Auf wiedersehen.

TWENTY

*A*dam kept his cool by checking off the hosting tasks in his head, one by one.

Start the second coffeepot simmering.

Load up the wood bin by the potbellied stove.

Greet the guests, being sure not to waver under the scrutiny of the older men's eyes.

Unhitch the horses and secure them in the paddock.

By the time Adam made it back to the kitchen, Mary and Sadie had the coffee poured for the men seated around the table. Aunt Betsy stood at the counter slicing up shoofly pie. Judging by the fact that the cousins and other wives had been sent to the living room, this was to be a serious meeting. Not business exactly, since the Sabbath was no time for that. But a minor matter that required a candid talk with the bishop and preachers ... that would be acceptable Sabbath activity.

"Adam, you need a slice." Betsy held the plate aloft, and he quickly accepted.

"Denki." He'd always considered the pie to be dry, with its sticky molasses base and topping of crumbled sugar. But since his return he'd learned to add a splash of cream, and now he found the sweet dessert irresistible.

"Adam, kumm. Sit right here." Seated at the head of the table, Bishop Samuel patted the back of the adjacent wooden chair.

"Thank you for visiting, Samuel." Adam placed his pie and coffee on the table and took a seat. He knew the limo was on their minds, but he decided to do his best to sidestep it. "And you, David. I appreciate the support you've given our family in the past year. We couldn't have kept the farm running and the children healthy without your help."

"Ach! 'Tis the way it should be. Lydia and I know the name and face of every child who heads down that road to the schoolhouse, and that's our blessing." Dave Zook's blue eyes twinkled over his mug of coffee. "This family is the responsibility we all must share. Granted, you and Mary and Jonah are baptized members now, but there are still the children, your family's strength and perpetuity."

"The children and two toddlers." Samuel's eyeglasses rested on the tip of his nose, though he rarely looked through them. With his silvered hair and pale skin, he seemed frail, but Dat used to say Samuel had no color because he worked inside all day, managing the harness shop. "With the little ones, you've taken on quite a responsibility, Adam. It's understandable if you lose sight of it at times."

Lose sight? Adam stabbed at a piece of pie and shoved it in his mouth. Dry, but he'd forgotten the cream. Still, it was better to chew a mouthful of sandy crumbs if it kept him from answering the bishop in a rash manner.

"I think Adam takes his responsibilities to heart," Uncle Nate said in his defense. "The problem is he has no wife to help him care for this family. We all know Mary is a wonderful good cook and a hard worker, but a sister cannot wear a wife's boots."

Bishop Samuel peered over his glasses. "Is that a proverb, Nate?"

"It could be." Nate chuckled, then repeated: "A sister cannot wear a wife's boots."

"Good one, Nate." Adam reached for the cream, trying to ignore the sinking realization that the men had come to offer guidance not about Sadie or Simon, or Susie with her medical condition, but regarding him. *He* was to be in the hot seat this sunny Sunday afternoon.

"It's a good and true saying," Preacher Dave agreed. "And it points to the truth you can't avoid much longer, Adam. You're going to need a wife if you're to continue taking care of this family. Those little ones inside, they need a mamm."

Samuel placed his mug on the table with a thoughtful expression. "And how will you find an Amish wife if you don't get out to the frolics and singings?"

"We've spoken of this before, Adam," Uncle Nate said. "Now, I know you feel like you're too old to be playing a young person's game, and, ya, your rumspringa is over for good. But have you considered that we have a few single women in our district who are close to you in age?"

Adam swallowed, hesitation sticking in his throat. Annie Stoltzfus was the woman they were thinking of. They might as well have come right out and said her name.

"I have considered that." Adam rubbed the wood grain of the old table. "But I'm a confirmed member of the faith, as are Mary and Jonah. If you want conformity, then the three of us should be married. We're all in our twenties."

Samuel winced, rubbing the lines on his forehead. "Two in rumspringa, three old enough to marry . . . what are you all waiting for?"

Preacher Dave swallowed, nodding. "Not to overstep bounds, but there's Verena Miller and Emma Lapp."

"The schoolteacher?" Adam thought of Sadie's friend. "She's barely seventeen."

"I know that Annie Stoltzfus's parents are hopeful about a match for their daughter." Dave squinted at Adam, gauging his reaction.

Not Annie again . . . Adam felt his toes curl in his boots at the thought. He had never formally courted her, but everyone seemed to think it was God's plan for them to be husband and wife.

"Annie is a very kind person." Adam gestured toward the other room, where his sister had tactfully disappeared. "She's Mary's best friend. But I . . . Annie has always been like a sister to me."

Samuel shrugged. "This could change."

Not in a million years, Adam wanted to say, but held his tongue in the interest of being respectful to Annie and the church elders.

"It doesn't have to be Annie." Preacher Dave, always a perceptive man, held a forkful of pie aloft. "But you do need a wife. Sooner than later. You see, you, Adam, are the head of this family. But it's missing a heart. The true heart of every Amish family is the mother. And who can live without a heart?"

"It's time for you to get on with fulfilling God's plan for you," Bishop Samuel agreed.

"That's what I've been praying for," Adam said, glad that he could be honest about that much. "I appreciate your guidance, and I will do whatever you think is right. If that means going to the singings . . ." He paused, swallowing back his resistance. "I'll follow your instructions."

"Good." Bishop Samuel clapped him on the shoulder. "Don't be so glum. Courtship is not difficult work when you get down to it. You'll be fine . . . just fine."

Adam nodded respectfully, though the tightness in his chest wouldn't allow him to smile. His future was going to be miserable, punctuated by bonfires and volleyball games with giddy youths.

There'd be fast singing, reckless boys, and giggly girls. Although that might have seemed exciting when he was sixteen, at the age of twenty-four it would be a trial.

When Uncle Nate rose from the table, Adam sat back with a sense of relief. The inquisition was over.

"And then there's the matter of the big white car taking the children around today," the bishop continued.

"The noodle car," Dave said. "Is that what I heard Ruthie call it?"

"The stretch limousine." A newly sharpened blade jabbed at Adam. "I can explain that, though the circumstances were unusual." Making his story as concise as possible, he explained that Remy, the Englisher girl, had fainted at the market yesterday. Since the girl was all alone and Sadie had befriended her, they had thought the best thing to do was bring her home and offer her safe shelter for the night.

"So she took sick?" Samuel scratched his silver beard with two fingers.

"The paramedics think she had a seizure," Adam said. "It wasn't safe for her to drive, and she couldn't really take care of herself."

The bishop nodded. "Then bringing her here was the right thing to do."

"Like the Good Samaritan," Nate added.

"Although some might question having a young woman in a home with two single men, you and Jonah. Not to mention young Gabriel coming up right behind you." Dave took a sip from his coffee and put his mug down. "But what could you do?"

"What could you do?" Nate agreed as he served himself another slice of shoofly.

"But watch out for Sadie, getting attached to this Englisher," Bishop Samuel said. "An act of kindness is one thing. But youth in their rumspringa sometimes make the wrong friends. If this goes too far, we'll have to take measures to control the youth in our district."

Adam's mouth went dry as he caught the underlying meaning in Samuel's words. Adam had made bad choices during his rumspringa, and to this day he suffered the consequences.

"We wouldn't want them to get involved with fancy folk who pull them away from their families." The bishop's watery eyes glimmered with warning. "Fancy folk with noodle cars. It's a path that leads away from God, away from all we value as Plain folk."

It was exactly what Adam had been thinking.

TWENTY-ONE

*M*onday blues . . . Remy had a bad case of them.

Sinking against the rail of the paneled elevator, she tried to formulate a strategy to save face with the editor in chief.

It wasn't simply her failure to get the story Arlene wanted; her personal involvement with the Kings had taken things to a new level. Last night she'd lain awake staring at the ceiling and second-guessing herself, wondering if she could have done or said something differently to address Simon's overwhelming sense of fear or Sadie's need for freedom.

Her worries had kept her up till after three A.M., when she'd glanced over and seen the digital numbers blaring blue light. Consequently, she must have turned off the seven o'clock alarm in her daze. Now she was late for work, too late to get into Arlene's office to update her on the story in private, but just in time to attend the editorial meeting.

After snagging a notepad and a cup of coffee, Remy passed the mostly empty cubicles on her dash to the conference room. She slipped through the door, determined to join the meeting without interrupting, but heads turned in her direction.

"Sorry I'm late." Remy dared a glance to the head of the table, where Arlene was discussing something with Miles Wister. At least the big bosses didn't seem to care. She leaned into her friend and whispered: "What did I miss?"

"Prince Harry is coming to Philadelphia," Yasmina whispered without looking up from her notepad. "Arlene doesn't know if we have the juice to land an interview with him."

Remy sipped her coffee, expecting the meeting to proceed with the usual agenda, senior editors presenting first.

But as soon as Arlene finished her discussion with Miles, she barked: "Remy McCallister."

Remy twitched, sloshing coffee over her fingers. "Hi . . . good morning . . ."

Yasmina slid a napkin over to her as all eyes were on the editor in chief.

"It'll be a good morning if you're making progress on that Amish story." Arlene glanced at Remy over the top of her jeweled glasses. "Did you get the interview?"

"Not exactly, but over the weekend I did catch up with Adam King in Lancaster County and—"

"Ketchup?" Arlene interrupted. "Ketchup is a condiment. I'm talking about an interview. Did you get it or not?"

"Not." The room was so silent Remy could hear the blood drumming through her ears. "Not exactly."

Arlene threw up her hands in disgust, but Miles extended a sliver of patience. "Explain," he said.

"While I didn't get a formal interview with Adam King, I did meet the family. I even got to talk with the little boy—Simon King—who was in the buggy with his parents the night they were killed."

"Ooh. How old is this kid?" Arlene asked.

"He's nine now, but he was only eight when it happened."

"A nine-year-old boy." Miles's forehead was pleated with creases. "Did you get a signed release from his guardian?"

"No, it wasn't like that. We were just talking, and I didn't introduce myself as a journalist. I don't think they knew I was a writer." Remy struggled to make her point. "The family opened up to me, and I'm not sure I feel comfortable going public with everything I've learned."

"So you were undercover, so to speak?" Arlene squinted. "Slimy, but I could deal with it if you got your information from Adam King or someone else over twenty-one. But the kid . . ."

"Out of the question." Miles wiped the idea away with one arm. "We can't have our reporters preying on minors, no matter how interesting your notes or recordings."

Remy bit her lower lip, afraid to tell them she didn't have actual quotes or notes. In fact, her journal had been locked in her car; it was still there, as far as she knew. Herb had hired a driver to bring the car back from Lancaster County today.

"But I do like this story." Arlene's red-lacquered fingers waggled over her chin as she considered the ultimate prize. "We could do something with this, as long as you go on the record with Adam King."

"Definitely on the record," Miles agreed.

"Can you do that?" Arlene prodded.

Remy opened her mouth, then bit her lips together. After everything that had happened this weekend, the idea of actually pursuing an interview for the sake of a story seemed wrong, especially in the face of Simon's post-traumatic stress, Sadie's battle for independence, and Adam's worry that media exposure might threaten the safety of his family. Remy would not do anything to hurt the family that had stolen her heart.

Still . . . their story was compelling. She couldn't stop worrying about Simon's recovery from the trauma and wondering about the murder investigation itself. And she couldn't keep her thoughts from returning to Adam. Those dark eyes haunted her as if he were part of her conscience.

Remy looked from the table and realized the seven editors facing her were waiting for an answer.

"Feel free to jump in anytime," Arlene said. "But whatever you decide, I'm not giving up this story."

Did that mean she would put another writer on it? Someone swift and ruthless?

Remy couldn't give up the Kings. She couldn't walk away and leave them prey to a reporter who didn't care.

"I'll talk to Adam King again," Remy said. "I'll give the story my best shot."

"Please!" Arlene rolled her eyes. "When are you going to learn to answer yes or no? No one ever conquered a kingdom saying 'maybe' or 'I'll try.'"

TWENTY-TWO

For the first time ever, Adam was glad to have market duty in Philadelphia. In his mind, he equated Philadelphia with Remy McCallister, the girl who had dogged his thoughts for the past few days, and though he didn't understand why, he needed to be here. She had haunted his dreams, her voice a low glaze over images of her sitting at their kitchen table, watching the horses in the paddock, and stomping around in Mary's rubber boots.

Things had ended badly between them, and he kicked himself mostly for losing control and letting himself get close. Just the touch of her hands, the proximity . . . It had been too much to fight.

He would never forget the sight of her wild red hair being tossed by the wind as they stood out by the corral. Her coppery hair and radiant green eyes had burned a brand on Adam's heart. Because of her, he couldn't think straight. Because of her, he lay awake at night. Because of her, he'd looked forward to coming to the city with its honking horns and sirens, its exploding lights and colorful signs, and its food scents mingled with exhaust fumes. Just being in her city, knowing she was near, settled his mind for the moment.

For most of the last hundred years, the King family had been leasing a stall at the Reading Terminal Market in Philadelphia. Founded in 1892, the market had gone through some dismal periods and major renovations to become the current bustling marketplace of colorful wares and fresh produce.

Today was Adam's turn to make deliveries for the King Family Dairy, a weekly duty that rotated through the family. The task entailed hiring a driver, packing a van with cheese from the dairy and quilts recently sewn by the women, many based on special orders, and transporting it all into Philadelphia, where Adam's cousin and his wife managed the stand six days a week. Joseph King, known as Market Joe, had run the market stall with his father since he'd graduated from eighth grade. When Joe and Lizzy wed, Joe's father, Perry, bowed out of the marketplace to focus more on his harness business back in Halfway.

"You have four new quilts for us?" Market Joe hitched his black-framed glasses up his nose and hoisted a box of cheese from the cart. "The women have been working hard."

"They get a lot more quilting done when the weather is cold," Lizzy observed as she unfolded a Basket quilt in bold navy blue, yellow, and red. Five rows of five small basket patches made up the cheerful pattern. "Such nice warm tones for winter. Perfect for curling up by the fire."

"If the person who buys it even uses it," Adam said. "The last two quilts I sold went to collectors, who said they were going to frame the quilts and put them under glass."

"Funny, isn't it?" Lizzy hung the quilt over a wire strung behind the booth, and then smoothed it out to show off the craftsmanship and colors. "An item as basic as a blanket to keep you warm in the winter, and it becomes a showpiece, never to be touched."

Adam loaded the last of the cheese into the refrigerator as Market Joe greeted a customer at the counter.

"How's your sister Mary faring with those little ones?" Lizzie asked as she handed him a plastic carton.

"She's fine. Sam has started doing small chores and Katie is talking more and more."

"Your mamm taught Mary well. It won't be long until all of us have young ones of our own. Of course, you will have to wed first. And from what I've been hearing, that won't come easily."

"I've been reminded of that lately." The meeting with his bishop, preacher, and uncle was still fresh in Adam's mind, though when it came to finding a wife, he really didn't know where to begin. The idea of attending a singing always brought Annie Stoltzfus's berry-red smile to mind. And now there was talk of interest from Emma Lapp, the schoolteacher. A nice girl, but a girl, a child really.

God, I know you've got someone in mind for me, he prayed. *And I'm hoping she's not ten years younger than I am.* As he prayed that God would lead him to a suitable wife, his thoughts returned to Remy, and he pictured her sitting at his right hand during breakfast. He could hear her laughing over the milking story, and he imagined her learning to milk a cow, easy as one, two, three. . . . What crazy thinking. Verhuddelt thoughts.

He was stacking crates when she caught his eye from across the marketplace. A flash of coppery hair, shining like a new penny against her stark black leather jacket.

Remy . . . as if she had materialized from his thoughts, there she was.

He froze in his tracks, surprised to see her and shocked by his reaction, the way his heart lifted at the sight of her, as if God had shown him the path to heaven.

Adam lifted his black hat to rake back his hair.

An Englisher girl. This could not be.

He had fallen for an Englisher girl once, and though the relationship had ended amicably, his time in the fancy world had turned him inside out. Although Jane had stayed with him for less than a year, during that time he had met other people who shared his interests: a greengrocer interested in building a city garden, a carpenter who designed and built crates for shipping artwork, a retired sea merchant who built precision chests.

The Englishers had admired Adam's skills with a hammer and nail, as well as his honesty and determination to get a job done. In his second year he had started a business with Cap, the retired seaman, designing and building furniture by hand. Old Cap, cranky with people, patient with wood. Cap Sawicki had taught Adam how to make woodworking a craft. In turn Adam organized Cap's shop and worked with his clients, building up the business.

Thinking of Cap, Adam wheeled the cart of crates from behind the counter. Although some might call his pride in the old carpentry business hochmut, Adam had felt good about leaving the profitable business in the hands of a man who'd once been destitute. Sometimes he wondered how Cap was doing, though the old man had promised him he would absolutely not be writing any letters, and Adam had told Cap that it was highly unlikely he'd be calling.

Strange, saying good-bye to a friend, realizing you would probably never see him again on this earth.

But when he'd been visited by a police officer with the sickening news about his parents, Adam had known that his time in the Englisher world was over.

In a flash of youthful independence he had left home, left the Amish community and his family behind.

A foolish move.

But never again.

He was a baptized member of the community now. He made

his choice, and there was no room for a girl like Remy in the life he had chosen.

Across the marketplace, she seemed to sense him. In the light of the terminal, her hair looked redder than he remembered. Red and vibrant like the coals of the fire after they've been stoked.

She caught him looking and a sunny smile lit her face as she waved from beyond a spray of flowers. How did she know he was watching her?

He nodded and turned back to Lizzy, who followed his gaze.

"What's the matter?" Lizzy asked, squinting into the distance. "Oh, there's Remy."

"Wait. Do you know her?"

"Joe and I met her earlier this week. She stopped by looking for you, and I told her to come back today, as you happened to have the delivery."

"Really?" She'd come looking for him. . . . Why did the thought of her seeking him out make his day?

"She said you knew each other, but there was something about business." Lizzy spoke quickly as a customer stopped at the counter. "Can I help you, sir?"

Adam was glad to have Lizzy and Joe busy when Remy approached.

"Hi. I bet you didn't expect to see me again so soon." She looked like a healthier version of herself, with a blush of pink on her cheeks that reminded him of a sun-warmed peach.

"You look good . . . healthy," he corrected, annoyed with himself. Why was he so happy to see her? It was as if the energy in the cavernous market was buzzing now, its warm center a halo around the two of them. "Are you feeling better?"

"Much better. But I really appreciate everything your family did for me. You guys were there for me when I needed it most."

"It was nothing."

"I am planning a trip back to Halfway. I promised Sadie we would hang out again." She stepped over to the side table where the new quilts hung, diamonds and zigzags of color. "But I wanted to talk with you first."

Again, he felt a mixture of excitement and alarm. "Why me?"

"You're the head of the family, right? It's about getting permission from you."

"Permission? My sister doesn't need permission to have a fancy friend. It's not encouraged, but . . . she's in her rumspringa."

"I know, but I wanted to ask you about something else."

He could barely decipher her language for the distraction of her emerald eyes; every time he looked her way, he lost track of the conversation.

"What was your question?" he asked, realizing his short responses probably seemed cold.

"Did I tell you I worked for my father? I wanted to—"

"Is he an antiques dealer?"

She shook her head.

"A designer?"

"No, he's . . . Herb McCallister. Do you know the name?"

"It doesn't ring a bell. Is he interested in the quilts?"

"Oh, no, not Herb. But I'm interested. I love this Sunshine and Shadow quilt. But that's not why I wanted to talk to you. I . . ." As if she'd run out of breath, she let her gaze drop to the quilt. Her fingers ran over the small patches of turquoise surrounded by navy, then orange, then peach.

Was she talking about buying quilts or was something else going on here?

Sometimes women made no sense. He often felt this way around Mary and Sadie; that they were not saying what they meant, or that there was some special meaning to be coaxed from their words. As if they were speaking in their own language, a strange dialect.

He noticed the pink gleam of her fingernails. Her hands seemed smooth and delicate, not the hands of a woman who ran clothes through a wringer or tended a garden.

And she seemed nervous.

Afraid of him?

That was ridiculous.

But something gave her pause.

"Not to be rude," he said, "but what is it you're looking for?"

Her eyes grew round, as if she'd been caught stealing an apple. "I'm going to come visit you in Halfway . . . away from the distractions and all the noise here." She nodded, as if convincing herself. "That'll work better."

"You mean, you want to visit Sadie," he said.

She was digging in her purse. "Of course. And the twins and Simon and Mary, too. And Ruthie . . ." Remy smiled as she jotted something down on a slip of paper. "Ruthie is a pip. I really love your family."

"That's good." Again, Adam felt as if he were missing the meaning of the conversation.

She handed him the slip of paper. "This is my phone number, if you need to reach me for any reason. And tell Sadie I said hi, and I'll be heading out your way soon."

He accepted the paper, nodding. "Okay."

"Okay, then. See you soon." One last flash of stormy green eyes, and she was leaving, weaving past the flower vendors.

Adam stared down at the phone number—not too useful for someone who shared a phone shanty along the road with two other neighbors.

Remy was a mystery, and he was not a man who liked unanswered questions in the air. But whatever her association with Sadie, he knew that his feelings for Remy could not be based on anything real. This was proof that the church leaders were right; he had been away from the courtship ritual so long that now his mind was dreaming up feelings for an Englisher girl.

He needed to get back on track.

This weekend, Sunday night, he would hitch a buggy to Thunder and head down the road to the singing.

TWENTY-THREE

The troubled words spilled into his sleep.

The voice was small and helpless, the voice of a child. "Please, Dat! Don't go."

Adam opened his eyes to darkness, the velvety blackness of a safe space. It was still night, but the voice wasn't coming from a dream.

"Don't go down there, Dat! He's a bad man."

"Simon . . ." In an instant Adam was out of bed, fumbling on the bedside table for a match. The flare illuminated Simon pacing at the foot of the bed, arguing in his sleep. Another night terror, though this time the tone was different and Simon had spilled a new detail. He had mentioned a man, not a bear, and Adam wanted to hear more.

The kerosene lamp burst into light, but Simon didn't seem to notice as he continued his rant.

"Dat, no! Please don't go talk to him. Didn't you hear what he said?" Simon's eyes were wild, his cheeks wet with tears. "He's got a gun!"

"Who?" Adam moved closer to his brother, trying to get through to him. He knew the boy was sleepwalking, but maybe in this subconscious state Simon would give him some detail . . . a description or a name. "Who has a gun? Who do you see, Simon?"

"I don't want you to talk to him." Terror pulled Simon's features taut, making his eyes seem huge in the shadows. "Kumm . . ." He tugged on Adam's arm. "Let's go home. We need to get away from the man."

Fear was a bitter taste on the back of his tongue as he faced the boy, leaned down, and put his hands on Simon's shoulder. "Who, Simon? Who do we need to get away from?"

"No, no, don't!" Simon pushed him away and paced to the corner. "Please! Don't go down there! Stay with Mamm and me."

His shrill plea cracked open the nightmare, and Adam saw the scene of their parents' murders, the episode Simon kept reliving in these night terrors. Although Adam had been hundreds of miles away, he could picture it.

A winter's eve, just after sunset. The family buggy sitting on the side of Juniper Lane. And a man on the side of the road . . . someone beckoning their father to leave the buggy.

Had light from the moon washed over the landscape?

Had headlights cast watery beams from the killer's vehicle? If the man had one.

And, judging by what Simon was saying now, there had been a man at the roadside, someone Simon feared. Had he been afraid because he knew the man, or because the man had a gun?

"I'm so afraid, Dat! So afraid of what he'll do to us!" Simon brushed past Adam with his hands clapped over his ears. "You heard what he called us!"

"What?" Adam asked. Watching his little brother go through

this again was like having a knife twisted in his gut, but Simon seemed to have broken through to a new memory this time, and Adam wanted answers before his brother's visit to the past faded. "What did he call us?"

"You know I can't say the terrible words," Simon said as footsteps shuffled in the hall, "but he thinks you've cheated him!"

Someone Dat cheated . . . It might be a telling clue, though Adam couldn't imagine his father cheating another man. It was not the Amish way, not in Dat's nature.

When Jonah appeared in the doorway, raking back the sides of his dark hair, it occurred to Adam that Mary was probably still out with Five on their Saturday evening buggy ride. There was no telling what time Mary's beau would return her to the house, but Adam had handled this before.

"Simon, what's wrong, boy?" Jonah reached out to Simon's shoulder, but the boy darted out of his grasp.

"We've got to get away!" Simon shrieked.

"A bad dream?" Jonah asked.

Adam nodded as he crouched down to his brother's level.

"But this seems worse than usual." Jonah's voice held a jagged edge of panic.

"Because he's remembering." The horror gleaming in Simon's eyes cut deep to the marrow of Adam's conscience, and he wished he could protect this boy, protect not just his body but his mind, too. "Who do you see by the side of the road, Simon? Who do you see?"

"I can't see his face! I can't!" A keening wail came from Simon's throat as he blinked through his tears and made eye contact with Adam. "I'm cold . . . so cold. . . ." He crossed his arms, his teeth chattering.

"Wake him up," Jonah insisted. "Help him!"

"Okay, we'll warm you up." Adam hugged him close and

rubbed his back. "You're all right now. You're safe." Lifting Simon in his arms, he headed downstairs, explaining to Jonah that they needed to get a fire going in the potbellied stove.

While Jonah added wood to the embers, Adam settled down in the rocking chair with Simon in his lap and tried to calm the whimpering boy. Soon the room began to warm in the glow from the stove, and Simon's body relaxed in Adam's arms.

The whimpering stopped, and his chest began to rise and fall with steady baby breaths. *Still on the sweet side of boyhood,* Adam thought. Although he felt glad when Simon's body went slack in his arms, he knew it was a temporary release. The night terrors seemed to be getting worse, coming more frequently, and he didn't know what to do about it.

"That's a terrible place he goes to with that nightmare." Jonah's face was turned away as he fanned the coals with the bellows. "A boy his age shouldn't have to suffer that way."

"You're right," Adam said. "And maybe my reaction was wrong. Maybe I shouldn't have pressed him for details."

Jonah's mouth stretched in a grimace as he closed the latch on the stove. "I was wondering about that. Why did you ask? It seems to prolong his misery."

"I think it could help Simon."

"By finding the killer?" Jonah shook his head. "You can't go there, Adam."

"It's not about solving the murders." In his heart Adam believed that would give them all closure, and yet they could not seek justice. Punishment was something the Amish left up to God. "I want to help Simon work through his pain and fear, and the only way to do that is by helping him separate fact from the stories his mind has created out of fear."

Jonah rubbed his eyes. "That will be hard to do, when we're not to speak of it."

Adam frowned as he cradled Simon, caught in the web of rules that sometimes made life difficult in an Amish community. "I still can't piece together why they were out there that day. Hunting, some of the papers said, though Dat didn't believe in the killing of animals. At least, not in my lifetime. Do you remember what he told us about the annual butchering day when he was a boy? It upset him so much that he chose to stop the killing of animals on this farm."

"And that's why Mamm started bartering milk, cheese, and eggs for meat," Jonah said. "It was that way for as long as I can remember. Dat used to say that no creature would be harmed on this property."

"Remember when the three of us made that bird feeder together?"

The taut, brittle quality seemed to drain from Jonah's body as he sat down in a chair. "Dat was always excited to see birds coming around to share the land."

The memory of their father, his eyes narrowed to observe the birds flitting at the edge of a field, helped to ease the tightness in Adam's chest. "He got a kick out of that birding book. And when he found that vividly blue bird . . . what was it?"

"The indigo bunting," Jonah said.

"Right. The indigo bunting convinced him that God meant for our land to be a safe haven." Adam shook his head. "Dat loved the notion that the farm was a haven for all living things. I guess that's why I can't reconcile the idea of him heading out with a rifle that day."

"I think it was because this one had an interest in weapons," Jonah said, nodding toward the boy sleeping in Adam's arms. "It was Dat's idea to quench the fire of curiosity by teaching Simon some gun safety and letting him do some target practice way out in the back fields."

"Is that where Juniper Road is? At the back of our property?" The location of the murder scene was not familiar to Adam, who didn't recall all the back roads in the area.

Jonah nodded. "Near the plot of land Dat bought from the Muellers years ago. I think they went out there with some rusty cans. Not sure what Mamm was doing . . . maybe visiting someone, though I guess we'll never know for sure."

Adam felt a pang as Simon turned his head and burrowed his face against his chest. "He's a good boy. It's tough to watch him go through these night terrors."

"In the beginning, when he was so sick with grief that he couldn't speak, I feared that we had lost him." Jonah rubbed his eyes. "It was good to hear him talking again, good to see him getting involved in things, playing in the haymow."

"He's come a long way," Adam agreed, "but he still does not feel safe. He's got all this fear pent up inside, and it just bursts out when he's asleep."

"The night terrors seem to be getting worse. Maybe this problem is too big for us to handle. I pray that he'll recover, but he still clamps up with fear."

"I pray for him, too." Adam's voice was hushed, not wanting to wake Simon. "God is the only one who can heal him."

"True, but we are God's instruments. That's why I think you need to talk to Bishop Samuel. Maybe have Simon talk with him."

"Simon is afraid of him."

"Simon is afraid of many things right now. But he needs help. You've seen it with your own eyes. These nightmares are torture."

"The doctor said they should stop eventually," Adam said.

Jonah shook his head. "I know you, Adam. You think you can handle this alone. You think you can counsel him, but you're making it worse. By forbidding Simon, forbidding all of us, to talk about our parents' murders, you are covering wounds that need tending to. It's like bandaging the hoof of a horse when all you really need to do is get in there and pick out the dirt, manure, and rocks."

"But I'm taking direction from Bishop Samuel." Adam let his tired eyes close a minute. "We must move ahead. Leave the pain and sorrow behind."

"And do you think Simon is able to do that? Is he able to forget that someone or something killed our parents? Even left Mamm dead atop him?"

At the graphic image, Adam's eyes opened and fixed on Jonah. "What can I do?"

"Go to the bishop." Jonah stood and brushed off his hands. "Do it for Simon. And tell everyone in the family they are free to talk about this. A bandaged wound is slow to heal."

"Don't you understand? As it is I'm on shaky ground with our church leaders. After the murders, I don't think they really wanted to allow us to stay together. Although I returned, no one was happy about my time away."

"But you did return, Adam. You got back here as fast as you could. You and I made coffins for Mamm and Dat with our own hands. You took your solemn vow, and since then you've been living in submission to the Ordnung. You can't live your life looking over your shoulder, expecting to be chastised for every misstep."

"You weren't around when they came to see me last Sunday."

"Gabe and I had to finish the fence, but I heard you held your own." Jonah folded his arms across his broad chest, his head dipping wearily. "The time for shame is over, Adam. Whatever happened on your rumspringa is past, and I don't think the bishop is going to take the little ones away from you for a few small mistakes. Talk to the bishop about Simon's nightmares and the things he's remembering. Samuel is a wise man. He will counsel you."

Adam rubbed the bridge of his nose. "Isn't this an expanded version of advice you gave me recently?"

"So you *have* been listening. It's hard to tell, with the way you move ahead without looking behind you."

"But I do value your opinion. Jonah, this place wouldn't run without you. You inherited Dat's skills and patience. Me . . . I got all the good intentions without the experience."

"So if we combine our efforts, things will work." Jonah touched Adam's shoulder. "That's the Amish way."

PART TWO

Home Is Where the Heart Is

Keep me as the apple of the eye,
Hide me under the shadow of thy wings.

—PSALM 17:8

TWENTY-FOUR

*T*he morning sun painted a swath of pale yellow over the winter grass as Remy drove slowly behind a gray carriage drawn by a trotting horse. She could see how Amish life forced a person to slow down—literally. But she didn't mind the slower pace, now that she was close. And she hoped the cloud break was a sign for the day ahead.

A meeting with Adam. It sounded so formal for two people who'd shared their hopes and fears. A friendship, of sorts. In her dreams they had a future, but then dreams were the notions you turned to when reality let you down, and Remy had been through her share of disappointments.

She'd been worried about making the drive out here, worried that she wouldn't be able to find her way back to the Kings' house among the sparsely marked farm roads and miles of dormant fields.

Fortunately, those proved to be useless worries. The sight of the familiar cluster of buildings that comprised the Kings' farm brought her a surprising feeling of release . . . as if she'd just come home after a long time away. Or maybe it was relief that the drive had been smooth and uneventful. Not even a trace of the strange weariness or tingling that usually warned of a coming seizure.

As she turned onto the unpaved road leading to the Kings' farm, she recalled Arlene's admonitions. "Go on the record," her boss had said. Bottom line, Remy had to let Adam know she was writing a story about his family. No squirming around the topic, the way she'd done in the Reading Terminal Market.

Even Sadie's statements wouldn't be printable without Adam's permission, and she could forget about quoting anything Simon had told her. Right now Adam was the key to her story, and Remy was convinced that soliciting his cooperation was similar to a diplomatic mission. It couldn't be rushed or minimized.

She would have to take it slow and easy, like the horse and carriage in front of her car. She would have to wait for Adam to open up, the way you waited for a bud to unfurl in the spring.

Although the concept of patience was not something she wanted to explain to the *Post*'s editor in chief. At this morning's editorial meeting, Arlene had been insistent that she head out to Lancaster County immediately. She had even excused Remy from her office tasks for the rest of the day.

"I thought I made it clear that you have an assignment," the older woman had said, her beady eyes stern. "What did you not understand about that?" When Remy had tried to explain that she thought she was supposed to research the story on her own time, Arlene had shooed her toward the door.

"Go. Research. Interview. Write. Remember the four Ws? Who, what, when, where."

Passing the stand of bare beech trees, she pulled up beside a horseless carriage, cut the engine, and climbed out of the car. A cold wind rustled the hillside and licked at her hair as she considered the simple white house, its two blue-curtained windows on the top story peering down at her like a long-lost friend. Should she go to the mudroom door, or knock on the front door, which the family rarely used?

The question was answered for her when the door to the mudroom flew open and Mary stepped out, her white apron pinned neat as could be, a dish towel in her hands.

"Remy?" She smiled a welcome. "I thought I heard a car, and the milk truck has already come and gone. But what happened to your long white car?"

"That was just a hired car. These are my wheels . . . my car."

"And you've driven all this way just to visit us?" She cocked her head to one side, a gesture of concern. "Are you feeling better? No more seizures?"

"Not since the last time I was here. I'm okay to drive, and I promised Sadie I would come visit. Plus I need to talk with Adam." Remy pulled her coat close, her fingers squeezing a wide button. Despite Mary's welcoming smile, awkwardness niggled at her. "Are they home?"

"Not right now." Mary shook her head as she folded the towel in her hands. "Sadie is at the hotel—her job in town. And Adam is in Paradise, taking Susie to the clinic."

"Oh." Remy fought disappointment; she had hoped Sadie and Adam would be available. "Would it be all right if I wait for them? It's important."

Mary's hazel eyes seemed to absorb the situation. "I don't expect them back for a few hours, but of course you can wait."

A few hours . . . Not wanting to disrupt Mary's day, Remy considered driving back into Halfway to kill time at the Olde Tea Shop. It would certainly help to avoid the awkwardness of spending hours with a stranger. "I can come back," she said. "I don't want to get in your way."

Mary laughed. "You wouldn't be a bother. But let me warn you, I might put you to work."

"I'd love to help." She welcomed a chance to get to know Mary a little better. Besides, after Adam gave her permission to run with the story, every smell, sound, and sight of this house would help add texture to her piece.

"Kumm, before you catch cold."

"Thanks." Remy stepped into the mudroom, encountering the wide eyes of the two children peering out from the open kitchen door.

"We were just throwing together a stew for dinner," Mary said.

"Hello," Remy said cheerfully. "Are you helping your big sister today?"

Both children nodded, their round, dark eyes studying her curiously as she stepped into the warm glow of the kitchen, where smells of browning meat, garlic, and onions mingled.

"Smells delicious."

"Sam has been a very big help." Mary tousled his dark hair as she moved past him, toward the sink.

"I peeled the potatoes," Sam reported. "Every last one. But not Katie. Katie plays with her dolly all day long."

Not yet two years old, Katie resembled a doll in her tiny gown, apron, and white kapp. Although her hair was pulled back, translucent strands of baby hair feathered over her forehead.

"She's still little," Remy told Sam, leaning down so that she was face-to-face with him. "Give her a few months and she'll be helping you out."

As if on cue, Kate scampered over to the daybed, retrieved a cloth doll, and tucked it under her arm.

"Does your doll have a name?" Remy asked.

The little girl blinked up at her through wisps of downy golden hair.

"Katie doesn't talk yet," Sam said. "She's a baby."

"But she's learning," Mary said from the counter as she scraped a mound of chopped carrots into the stew pot.

Remy straightened. "What can I do to help?"

"The stew will simmer for a few hours," Mary said as she rinsed items in the sink. "Gabe and Jonah are out working in the barn. Simon, too. I was just going to get him in to watch the little ones, but if you don't mind, I'll start the laundry while you go through a few books with them." She dried her hands on a towel, adding, "Katie usually dozes off this time of day."

"Katie takes naps," Sam said. "She's still a baby."

"I can read to them," Remy said, picking up a worn copy of *Pat the Bunny*. "In fact, I have a gift for you out in the car. A big bag of books, if that's okay." She had struggled to think of a family gift that would be appropriate, and when she'd learned that reading was a popular hobby of the Amish, she picked up some of her favorites at a downtown bookstore.

"New books! Well, this is an exciting morning, isn't it, Sam?"

He shoved his hands in his pants pockets, skeptical, until Remy returned with two bulky bags.

"Don't forget to say thank you," Mary told the little boy.

"Denki," he said with a curt nod.

"Have you ever read *Hop on Pop*?" Remy asked as she held up three Dr. Suess books.

Sam nodded, breaking into a grin that revealed two missing teeth in front. "Can we read it now?"

"Of course, but there are some other good ones here." Remy dug through the bag, searching for *Mother Goose Fairy Tales*.

"I'll just be out on the porch." Mary nodded, her smile a mixture of approval and amusement as she headed out.

As soon as Remy sat on the daybed, the children nestled on either side of her, their doughy faces soft and attentive. She opened the stiff book and immediately the cartoon illustrations captured the children's interest. Katie pressed against her for a better look, and Sam's dark eyes opened wide in expectation. When she smoothed back the page and began to read, Remy's voice was a bit scratchy from emotion at the unfamiliar feeling of being needed. As Sam giggled over the rhymes, sweet tenderness covered the three of them like a warm blanket.

She cleared her throat and continued, hoping to remember this moment for a long, long time.

TWENTY-FIVE

*T*here was nothing like a good session with the laundry to free up the mind. While Mary's hands scrubbed and fed clothes through the wringer, she allowed her thoughts to wander to her future with Five, to the days when she would be washing his trousers, along with tiny pants and dresses for countless little ones.

She wondered if their first child would be a girl or a boy. And what would they name it? Would Five want to call their first boy John Beiler, after himself and countless other relatives? She wouldn't mind another John Beiler, but it might be fun to go with something more original like Kevin, or Caleb, or Gideon.

Dropping a wet, clean gown into a bucket, she realized what a folly this was, naming children when she wasn't even married to her beau yet. And each day that Adam stayed in his bachelor shell was a day longer that she would be obliged to stay here to manage Mamm's duties.

Oh, dear God, there has to be a way through this, she prayed as she threaded another dress through the wringer. *A way for Five and me to marry without abandoning my family . . .*

"Mary?" the Englisher girl called from the kitchen, interrupting her prayer.

A good and kind girl, that Remy, though Mary was worried about Remy's motives for driving out from the big city today. "Did they sit still for you?" Mary asked.

Remy paused in the doorway, hugging her arms to her chest. "They're great listeners. I went through the book three times, and before I finished they both dozed off."

"Even Sam?" Lately her youngest brother had begun to resist afternoon naps. "Sounds like you have a gift for storytelling," Mary said, working a pair of pants out of the wringer.

Remy moved closer, eyeing the washing machine curiously. "I was wondering what the noise was out here. You have an automatic washing machine? I didn't think electricity was allowed."

"It's powered by gas, and it's almost automatic." Mary didn't mind explaining the machine that Mamm had so appreciated. "We have to feed clothes through the wringer, but it's a wonderful help."

"With laundry for eleven, I bet it is." Remy glanced from the moving rollers to the basket of damp clothes. "Do you want help with these? I might as well make myself useful. Where is the dryer?"

Mary laughed as she crossed the porch to the door. "The dryer is a clothesline beside the vegetable garden." When she peered outside, the sky had an opaque wash, like a bucket of milk. She didn't trust it. "But since it looks like rain, we'll have to hang the clothes inside."

"I don't think they predicted rain." Remy pulled a small, slender rectangle from the pocket of her jeans and ran her fingers over the face of it.

"One of those portable telephones?" Mary asked.

"A BlackBerry. I can bring up the forecast on it, and . . . let's see. No rain until tomorrow."

"Ya?" Mary didn't want to offend Remy, but such gadgetry was not a part of the Plain life, and she couldn't place her trust in an object the size of a cookie. "Well, just to be sure, we'll hang the clothes in here." Looping rope through the hooks that were installed in the corner of the ceiling for days like this, she strung a clothesline through the mudroom. "Why don't you hang the clothes while I finish washing?"

"I'm on it." Remy lugged the basket of wet laundry and clothespins to the end of one line. "You know, I was thinking that, since I have my car here, I could go pick the kids up from school."

Mary did not look up as she fed a shirt into the wringer. "That's very kind of you, but it's not necessary. The school isn't far, and the children don't mind walking."

"I just thought it would be fun for them." Remy peeked out around a dress she'd just hung. "Considering the way they enjoyed riding in the limo last time."

"Your kindness is appreciated, but riding around in cars for fun is not how we choose to live." For a second she thought of the three men seated at their table after Remy's visit, Uncle Nate and the bishop and the preacher. Would Remy be upset to learn that they had voiced some disapproval over Şadie and the others riding in the big white car?

"Am I pushing too far?" Remy asked. "I apologize if—"

"No need to be sorry. It's just that there's a reason for living Plain. We hire cars when we have to, but we don't own them. Electricity is forbidden, and yet we have a gas-powered washer and tools. It may seem contradictory, but it's a matter of sticking to a slower pace and keeping worldliness separate from our lives." Mary moved away from the washer and pressed a hand to her lips as she glanced up at Remy. "I don't mean to preach."

Remy shook her head. "It helps me to understand. But when I was here last time, it didn't seem like a problem for the kids to ride in the car."

"Our bishop does not condemn modern things, but we don't want to be a slave to machines. We want to control the technology we use. So we hire cars when we have a distance to travel. Sadie and Gabe travel by scooters, but our order doesn't use bicycles. The bishop says that even bikes can take you too far from home. Too far from the things that matter."

"Too far from family," Remy said as she smoothed the bodice of a dress on the line. "I get that."

Mary lifted a sopping-wet dress from the rinse water. "But Adam and Susie, they could have used your car today."

Remy squinted as she pinned a shirt to the line. "What do you mean?"

"With Susie's doctor some twelve miles away, it's more than an hour each direction."

Remy gaped. "And they didn't hire a car?"

"We have in the past, but it's a manageable trip, and Susie is happy to miss school. Not the student, that one." Mary rose, not wanting to gossip about her sister. It had been a while since she'd had a companion to help her with chores, and she had never worked alongside an English person.

When Remy had decided to wait here, she had anticipated that the girl would bide her time chatting or lazing by the fire until Adam arrived.

As far as Mary was concerned, Adam was the real reason Remy McCallister was here today. She had seen them together by the paddock that cold Sunday afternoon. She had watched from the kitchen window as the two of them talked up close, like a couple. Mary had been sure to turn away from the window as they'd embraced, and she hadn't slipped a word of it to anyone. Not even Five, whom she usually shared everything with. But it was upsetting, seeing Adam take a step back. He needed an Amish wife, not a girlfriend from the fancy world.

Watching from the corner of her eye as Remy shook out a dress, Mary had to admit the girl was a good worker and a cheerful one at that. There was a light in her eyes, a certain glimmer that reminded Mary of her mamm, who used to find joy in everything from cooking to washing to digging in the dirt to thin her vegetable garden. "You do good work, Remy."

"Thanks, but I sense that I'm learning from the master." Remy pointed a clothespin at her. "Honestly, with eleven people, how do you stay on top of all the household chores? Cooking and cleaning and laundry . . ."

"A full day is a good day, and look at what we've accomplished." Mary gestured to the hanging clothes.

"A virtual forest of clothes," Remy said.

"Work is good for the soul, and it's good training for a young girl. After this, I know I'm ready for . . ." Mary stopped herself short of admitting she was ready to start her own family; that was a private matter between Five and her.

"Girl, with training like this you are ready to take on half the state of Pennsylvania. Correction: the entire state."

Mary couldn't help but grin at Remy's joke. Her presence was a pleasant surprise this afternoon. "There's one more load of laundry to do, but with your help it will be finished with time to spare. I was thinking of baking a batch of buttermilk cookies."

"Are you kidding me? Baking is a favorite pastime of mine. Well, it would be if I had someone to bake for."

That struck Mary as sad. No one to care for? "Then today your prayers have been answered. You may bake for eleven people who will surely come home hungry and eager for sweets."

"A captive audience." Remy pressed a hand to her heart. "This is going to be a very good day."

TWENTY-SIX

*L*eaning over a gargantuan mixing bowl, Remy worked at softening butter and sugar with a wooden spoon. Aside from the ticking of the wall clock, the gentle breathing of the sleeping children was the only sound in the King kitchen, and Remy smiled at the true peace and quiet that hovered in the house. This was something she would love to capture for her story.

A portrait of Amish life . . .

That was how she planned to pitch the article when she spoke with Adam. A quaint piece, with a few updates on how the family was recovering from tragedy.

The door closed gently as Mary came in, her cheeks tinged pink from the cold. "Three eggs, fresh from the henhouse. You'll want to add them once the butter and sugar are creamed."

"Just give me one more minute." Remy gritted her teeth and put some muscle into her task. As she stirred, she tried to formulate a question that would not offend Mary. "You know, I met Adam a year ago, just after your parents died."

"A dark time," Mary said as she placed a bottle of vanilla on the counter.

"So much has changed for him in the past year. How do you think he's dealing with it? His return home from a very different world, and taking on the responsibilities of running the farm."

"It can't be an easy position Adam has landed in, suddenly head of our family." Mary cracked an egg into the bowl, then stood back as Remy stirred. "But it will be much easier when he has a wife. I'll be relieved when he finally asks Annie Stoltzfus to marry him."

The words slowed Remy's heartbeat to a sickening pace. Adam was going to get married? Married to a girl named Annie . . . Remy couldn't deny the disappointment that pressed on her at the thought of Adam being in love with someone else. The spark between them, the connection—had she imagined it?

Remy pursed her lips, stirring viciously for a second. "I didn't know Adam had a girlfriend."

"Actually, there are a few Amish girls interested in my brother right now." Mary frowned, her fingers nervously checking the pins on her apron. "The thing is, Adam needs to marry an Amish woman. The bishop, the congregation, and most of Halfway are waiting on him to do the right thing, and soon. If he's to take care of our family, he needs a wife. An Amish wife, of course."

"Of course." Remy nearly choked on the words as Mary's description of her brother's situation loomed in her mind, a portrait of Adam. This was a twenty-four-year-old man enmeshed in another world, committed to his family, sworn to follow a lifestyle completely alien to hers. They lived in two separate worlds, with little in common.

And she had come here as a journalist with the goal of writing a story that would help the King family. She hadn't come here to stalk Adam King, and the sooner she separated her feelings from this story, the better off she'd be.

"Hold on while I add the last two eggs," Mary said, interrupting Remy's thoughts. "The way you're stirring, you'll whip it into a froth."

Remy stopped stirring and stepped back from the bowl, as if it had stung her.

"You're a good worker, Remy. I'm always glad to have help in the kitchen," Mary said as she cracked another egg.

Remy was glad to change the subject. "It's been so long since I had a reason to bake, but I've always liked it. I used to make things with my mother. I was only seven when she died, but I remember baking cookies. My job was to sprinkle in the chocolate chips. And we used to make little balls of dough on the bowl of the spoon. Cookie drops, I called them."

"The smells and sights of a kitchen are good for a thousand memories." Mary began to measure a teaspoon of baking powder. "Our mamm always had us helping in the kitchen. She had special recipes for certain occasions, like pecan rolls for Christmas morning or rhubarb pie in the spring. No-bake oatmeal turtles for a funeral. And everyone likes the traditional wedding rolls."

"And you're carrying on her traditions." Remy tried to focus on the positive. If she focused on the article, maybe the queasy feeling about Adam would fade. She waited as Mary measured baking soda into the bowl, then made eye contact. "So what occasion are buttermilk cookies for?"

Mary touched a finger to her chin. "Let's see. That would be those days when you've got a few cups of buttermilk that the children won't drink. I'll add the sour milk." She patted the lid of an airtight container the size of a bucket. "You add eight cups of flour."

"Eight cups. Are you kidding?"

"We have a dozen mouths to feed," Mary reminded her.

"I know, but eight cups?" As Remy dipped the plastic measuring cup into the bin and leveled it off with a knife, she was struck by the tradition of cooking in this room where the clean linoleum floor had been worn thin by countless footsteps and the old wooden table behind her was scarred from years of use. It was loaded with family history, something that did not exist in the McCallister family.

There was a legacy here that could not be extinguished by death, even the deaths of two parents.

Remy measured the third cup, choosing her words carefully. "Just thinking about our moms. My mother died of heart failure, but there's still a mystery surrounding your parents. Do you ever wonder what happened to them? Are you curious about what went on that night on the roadside?"

"It's not something I think about." Mary poured a cup of buttermilk into the bowl. "Worrying through the details won't bring Mamm and Dat back."

"What about justice for the person who hurt them?"

"There is no justice on earth." Mary shook her head. "Only God can mete out judgment and punishment. For the man who killed them, I pray for peace. I pray that he might one day know God's love." Mary stepped up to the bowl and began to stir, her jaw set, a stern look in her eyes.

The air in the kitchen had changed. Looking behind her at the daybed, Remy was grateful that the children were still asleep.

"Can I ask, do you have any idea who the killer was?" Remy asked quietly. "Do you think it's someone your parents knew?"

"I can't fathom that we might know a human being capable of such evil." Mary's eyes held a dark expression as she stared down into the giant bowl and worked the dough. "My parents had no enemies, but I do know one thing for sure deep down in my heart. It was not Simon who killed them. Those rumors of my little brother gone mad were ridiculous."

"He was just a kid." Remy shook her head. "Why would anyone even think that?"

"Something about the gun in the buggy. Our dat had taken Simon shooting that day, target practice, so it got people to thinking, as he knew how to handle a gun." Mary capped off the buttermilk. "But anyone who would say something like that doesn't know our Simon. He's a good boy. You should see the way he takes care of the horses, how he minds the chickens."

"I've met Simon. He seems like a good kid."

"Only eight years old when it happened, and after the torment he went through, he still suffers at night." Mary stopped stirring and rapped the spoon on the bowl's edge. "No child should have to endure such pain, and Simon, he would never harm another person. Not our Simon."

TWENTY–SEVEN

"Look at that!" Susie pointed to a car parked near the house as Adam turned the gray carriage down the lane. "We have a visitor. More people to share the good news with." The delight that lit her face was typical of Susie. "Sunflower Susie," Mamm used to call her.

"That's true," Adam said as he slowed the horse. Sister Susie had a knack for finding the potential for fun in everything. An endearing quality, though sometimes he felt that it was his duty to keep her tethered to the earth.

"I'm so very happy about the test results. I've been feeling fine, but it's wonderful good to hear Dr. Trueherz say it."

"Good news, indeed, and I know you worked hard to stick to your diet, Susie girl. We're all proud of you."

Her face lifted to the pale winter sun, much like a sunflower in July. "I'm so happy, and I can't wait to share it with everyone."

Adam smiled as his attention strayed momentarily to the car. Did it belong to Sadie's Englisher boyfriend, the one she'd been hiding all these weeks? A weekday afternoon wasn't really appropriate courtship time, but he supposed it would be good for him to meet the guy. Better the devil you know than the devil you don't.

"I'll help you unhitch Thunder," Susie offered when he halted the carriage beside the car. "That way we can go in together with a burst of good news!"

"Sounds like a plan." As they worked together on the quick task, it struck him that fourteen-year-old Susie had been forced to grow up over the past year. Granted, the whole family had been challenged in new ways, but for Susie that meant an end to Mamm's tender loving care for her condition. Susie was coming along, but for Adam the responsibility of taking her for her checkups with Dr. Trueherz reminded him of the parental role he'd taken on. It reminded him of the cloud of loss that still hung over the farm every day, the absence of Mamm and Dat.

While Susie took Thunder to the pasture, he hung the harness up in the tack room. When he emerged from the barn, his sister waved at him, running toward the house.

"I'll race you there!" she shouted.

Adam picked up his step, breaking into a jog. The sight of Susie, hearty and healthy, her cheeks tinged pink from running in the cold, eased his heart. Mamm and Dat would have been proud of her. In moments like this, that cloud of sorrow lifted.

She bounded in through the mud porch, turning back to tease him. "I win, but you didn't try very hard, I could tell."

"I'll take you next time," he said as the warm air and sweet aroma of freshly baked cookies welcomed them into the kitchen. Katie and Sam knelt on benches, trying to spoon cookie dough onto trays, with the help of Mary and another woman seated between the kids, holding the spoon for Katie.

Brilliant colors glowed in the lamplight: the orange copper of her hair, the turquoise and blue stripes of her sweater.

Remy McCallister.

He paused, wondering for a moment if he'd wished her here.

Then Susie let out a shout with the good news that Dr. Trueherz was thrilled with her numbers, and suddenly it was like Christmas morning. As Susie and Mary chatted, Adam nodded to Remy, who nodded back. He couldn't stop smiling, but then this was a happy moment for his sister so he figured that was all right.

Hearing the stir of excitement, Gabe, Jonah, and Simon came in from the barn to share in the news. The room brimmed over with the sounds of bright conversation and Susie's favorite clapping game, the smells of buttery dough baking in the oven, and the warmth from the potbellied stove.

Such a joyous scene that Adam stood by the doorway for a time and watched it unfold, wishing he could ignore the one thing wrong with this picture. Remy, who always managed to fill a room with light and laughter, did not belong here. She lived a fancy life, a world she would return to soon, leaving this happy scene to fade in their memories.

Why had she come here?

Back in the city market she'd made some excuse about buying a quilt, but plenty of customers purchased quilts through the family business without stepping foot in the house or even in the town of Halfway.

Part of him wanted to believe she had come to see him. That she recognized the undercurrent that swirled between them and had to act on it in some way. He liked the theory that she'd followed him here because she couldn't get enough of him, couldn't get him off her mind, which was sort of the way he felt about her. But then, it was a little arrogant to think that his personal magnetism had drawn her here. That line of thinking would lead him toward hochmut, the sin of pride.

He folded his arms, watching Remy carry Katie to the sink to help her wash dough from her hands. The children were taking to her like bees to honey. All the more reason to send her off, quickly, before she broke their little hearts.

He grabbed a towel, crossed to the sink and tended to wiping Katie's hands as Remy lowered her to the stool. "I can finish that for you. Don't want to keep you here if you want to hit the road before dark," he said.

It wasn't a warm reception, and he did not intend it to be.

But Remy didn't pick up on his brusque tone. One eyebrow rose as she shifted to the other foot, her hips swaying in the process. An innocent move, though it reminded him that he was a man. "Oh, I'm not leaving yet," she said. "Mary invited me to stay for dinner, and since it smells so good, I can't resist."

"You're staying for dinner?" Adam asked. "Aren't you worried about the storm headed this way?"

"They're not predicting any precipitation until tomorrow morning." She tapped her pocket. "I keep checking my BlackBerry, and the forecast hasn't changed."

Adam sat down on the bench beside Katie, resigned to a few hours of torture. "I'd be careful if I were you. These back roads can get pretty icy."

"Relax. I'll be ahead of the bad weather, and that stew smells amazing."

"And Remy needs to talk with you," Mary added. "That's why she came all this way."

"That, and Sadie," Remy said, wiping Katie's nose and helping her down to the floor.

"Talk? Now's as good a time as any." He held out one hand, gesturing for her to begin.

She laughed. "Not now. I was thinking of a more private conversation. Besides, Susie's news is very exciting, and I wouldn't want to walk out on the celebration." She sank down onto the bench beside him, lowering her voice. "But I was wondering about this 'condition' everyone keeps talking about. What does Susie have?"

"It's a metabolic disorder that's common among the Old Order Amish." Adam rubbed his chin, the sweet spot where his soul patch used to be. "Glutaric aciduria type one, they call it. Her body has trouble processing amino acids. So when the amino acids build up in the body, they can be toxic, especially to the brain. But a lot of the times, the condition weakens the body and the baby dies from a cold or measles. Something simple."

Remy's eyes opened wide as she glanced at Susie. "Sounds serious."

"It can be. We had two siblings who died from it, both when they were toddlers. David came right after me, but I remember little Deborah, who was born between Mary and Sadie. She seemed just fine as a baby, but died before she turned two from the flu. Mamm was heartbroken for the babies she lost."

"I can't imagine how hard that must have been."

"Now, they can screen newborns. That's how Susie was diagnosed."

"And the expense . . . without health insurance, it must be astronomical."

"We're very fortunate to have Dr. Trueherz. He's working on a research grant, so most of Susie's medical care is free, as long as we travel to his clinic."

Adam watched her soak it all in. Granted, it was a lot to absorb—down to the very name of the disorder. But Remy seemed unfazed.

"And Susie is beating it?"

"It's being controlled by diet. She takes riboflavin supplements and follows a very strict diet that avoids amino acids."

Eyes bright, Remy smacked the knees of her jeans. "Good for her. She deserves a little celebration, right?"

"You don't know Susie." Adam raked back his hair. "For her, every day is a celebration. It's all one big party."

"Excuse me?"

Adam felt a slight sting on his upper arm, then realized Remy had snapped her finger against him. "Hey . . ." he growled. "We're a nonviolent society."

"Don't dis your sis. You need to appreciate her exuberance."

"I didn't dis anyone." He rubbed his arm, thinking that he didn't need her approval but wanting it nonetheless.

As the door opened and the schoolkids barreled in with greetings for Remy and gasps of delight over Susie's good news, he mulled over his own twisted feelings. He wanted Remy to leave, but at the same time he wished she would sit back down beside him. That was the thing about Remy that both attracted and frustrated him.

His feelings for her defied logic.

TWENTY-EIGHT

*A*s day gave way to evening, Remy felt a stab of guilt. An entire afternoon had passed, and she still hadn't talked to Adam about permission for the article. Here in the kitchen, Simon and Mary had no idea she was observing them for her piece, and although that made her feel a little dishonest, she kept telling herself she would be vindicated when she straightened things out with Adam.

Which she would do . . . right after dinner.

Right now he was busy in the barn with the rest of the family, who had filed outside for the afternoon milking. Although the sudden exodus had drained the kitchen of noise, the warm, cozy atmosphere prevailed. The aroma of fresh-baked cookies gave way to the smells of onions, meat, and vegetables cooking down to a savory stew, along with two loaves of bread Mary had somehow slid into the oven during the earlier commotion.

Her current task was to help Simon with his schoolwork. Adam had explained that the boy was being kept at home for the next few weeks, until the threat of "nosy journalists" faded.

That had twisted the knife in Remy's guilty heart.

While Simon leaned over his paper, inscribing neat columns of the "nine" times table, Remy noticed that night had fallen beyond the kitchen window. The end of the day had come too suddenly, with sunset occurring early this time of year. What had happened to her plan to tell Adam everything the moment she saw him?

Her timing had been off. First, Adam had been gone. Then the children had dozed off leaning against her, sandwiching her between sleeping angels. Mary's honesty had spoken to her heart, and then Susie's joyous news had educated her on an entirely different facet of King family life.

Arlene's voice crowed in her head: "Excuses, excuses."

Every time she came in contact with this family, she abandoned her journalistic ambitions in exchange for the possibility of friendship. God help her, she was falling for this family.

Her forearms propped on the table, she turned back to Simon, who put his pencil down and handed over the paper with a proud grin.

"All done."

"Good job. Now, you've got geography. A unit on the fifty states, right?"

"He's to learn the fifty states, and draw a map of one of them," Mary said.

"I can help you with that." Remy reached for his elementary primer to locate the map section in the back. "I still remember my states, but you're on your own with drawing the map. Everything I draw looks like a sick lamb."

"That's okay. I already chose my state. Florida." While she tried to locate a map, he began to draw, his lips puckered in concentration.

"Florida might be a tough one," Remy said. "Personally, I always liked Colorado or Wyoming. Simple rectangles."

"I can do Florida. It looks like a small gun."

Remy's mouth dropped open at his comment.

Stirring a pot on the stove, Mary didn't seem to hear.

Remy stared at Florida on the map. "You're right. The shape does resemble a gun."

"A handgun," Simon said with a quiet confidence that was chilling. "That's what the bear had. A real gun in his hand, and a picture of one on his head."

"What?" Remy's heartbeat accelerated at the thought of Simon sharing details from the crime scene. Was he being truthful, or just imagining things? "You said the bear had a picture of a gun on his head?" A tattoo? "How did you see it with all his hair?"

"Bears don't have hair." He stopped drawing as he lifted his eyes to her. "Don't you know they have fur?"

"Simon?" Pausing over the open oven, Mary glanced over at him. "You know, I thought we agreed to stop talking about the bear. Remember the difference between reality and a made-up story?"

"I know," he said with a sigh.

Mary turned to Remy. "He's got a great imagination. Most children do." She proceeded to remove the bread from the oven, the metal racks clanging as they slid along their rails.

"But I did see him." Simon's voice was a murmur, as if he spoke only to reassure himself. "The top of his head was shiny like an apple. And there was a mark like a gun there."

A mark like a gun . . . Remy struggled to make sense of it. She longed to ask him more questions, but she could see that Mary did not approve of the topic.

Taking a deep breath to slow her racing pulse, Remy leaned closer to take a look at his drawing. "That's a very good map of Florida."

Over at the counter, Mary began to pummel the contents of a pot with a potato masher. She wouldn't hear their conversation.

"Simon . . . did you tell anyone about the map on the bear's head?"

"It wasn't a map." He frowned at her. "It was . . ." He waggled his fingers toward the top of his golden head. "Sort of a shape on his head. A red blob."

"On the bear's head," she confirmed.

He pressed his fists to his lips, nodding.

"And did you tell anyone about it?" Fear flickered in his eyes as he shook his head.

Of course he didn't. The incident had rendered him silent for months. And after that, he'd been told not to talk about bears.

"It's okay," Remy said, opening a canister of crayons. "It's okay to talk about things as you remember them."

From his frown, he didn't seem convinced.

"What color should the state of Florida be?" she asked.

He chose a green crayon.

"You know, they call it the Sunshine State."

He didn't respond, though he grasped the green crayon and began to color. Remy sat with him until it was time for dinner, but the moment was over. He had shut down, withdrawn once again.

Her heart ached for the young boy, who had been told to keep silent when he seemed to be bursting with pain. This was something she would have to take up with Adam.

When Sadie walked through the door just before dinner, Remy strode across the kitchen to give her friend a hug.

"You are the last person I expected to see here tonight," Sadie said as she threw her arms around Remy. "And in this freezing rain . . ."

Remy felt the moisture on Sadie's cape. "Oh, you're soaked. You need to warm up."

They went to the corner by the potbellied stove, and Sadie slipped off her wet cape with a shiver. "And me on a scooter. It felt like my own personal cloud followed me all the way home." She lifted the hem of her skirt, revealing blue jeans rolled up to her knees. "These would be a lot more practical in weather like this, but of course, I can't be going around the house dressed like that."

Remy sunk her hands into the pockets of her jeans with a nod of understanding. "I didn't know you had to work today. This will be a short visit, but I'm hoping to come back, if Adam allows it."

"Adam is not the boss of me." Sadie waved a hand dismissively. "I'm in my rumspringa, remember?"

"Of course I remember." In the light of the gas lamp, her damp hair pressed to her face, Sadie looked girlish, like a child trying to look older in her mother's clothes. Remy felt a stab of regret that Sadie had lost her mother before she could be guided to true adulthood.

"Oh, Remy, I can't believe you came to visit." Sadie looked over her shoulder to be sure no one was listening. "I don't say this very often, but I think Adam was right about you. Remember what he said when he met you on that train? You really are an Englisher angel."

Remy bit her lower lip. *Oh, no, I'm just the opposite. Angels don't engage in deceit and lies.*

"Sadie, there's something you should know." Remy paused, wishing there were an easier way to explain this. "I should have told you before this, but I need to explain why I came here in the first place. It started when—"

"No need." Sadie cut her off, squeezing her hand. "You don't have to explain, Remy. I know why you're here."

Remy's throat constricted. Was it possible? Had Sadie known all along that she had traveled to Lancaster County for a story?

"God brought you to us," Sadie said, a light in her amber eyes. "He brought you here, that I know. And I'm sure He has some wonderful things in store for all of us."

In the wake of such confidence and faith, Remy remained silent, though the guilt that fell over her shoulders consumed her throughout the meal. As the family bent their heads to silently thank God for the bountiful food on their dinner table, Remy's eyes strayed to the lovely scene: the soft light of the gas lamp shadowing the starched white of the girls' prayer kapps, the velvety silence of the house around them.

A place of peace. She was beginning to understand Adam's need to protect his family.

Tonight Remy remained a quiet observer. Adam commended Susie for keeping to her diet all these months. Mary told everyone what a wonderful help Remy had been with the daily chores. Leah and Ruthie expressed thanks for the books Remy had brought them, and Sam gave them a summary of the book *Hop on Pop* in a fascinating combination of four-year-old diction and Pennsylvania Dutch.

Despite the warm, festive atmosphere, Remy could not let herself engage in the exchange at the family table. She had a bad feeling about the conversation that loomed ahead. If her gut instinct was an accurate gauge, then Adam would be grateful for an excuse to sever all ties between her and his family once he learned she was a journalist. And with that in mind, she knew she needed to broach the topic of Simon first, while he was still somewhat receptive.

"Will you help us with the dishes, Remy?" Ruthie asked as she began clearing plates. "It's a lot more fun when you do it with us."

"I'd like to, but—"

"She needs to get on the road," Adam interrupted. "The weather has taken a turn for the worse."

"He's right," Remy admitted. The last time she'd checked her BlackBerry the forecast had changed, though it was too late to do anything about it.

"Maybe Remy should stay until the morning," Mary suggested.

"Can she?" Sadie brightened as she tucked the bread basket in the crook of one arm. "It's cold and nasty out there."

"She needs to go." Adam's tone broached no argument, and the girls continued clearing the table.

"Right." Feeling like a condemned prisoner, Remy placed two plates on the kitchen counter, then turned to Adam.

Her moment of truth.

"But before I go, we need to talk."

"Right," he echoed, his eyes dark as coal. "Come. We'll use the front room."

TWENTY-NINE

*T*he wooden chair felt hard, almost skeletal, under Remy as she tried to formulate a way to win Adam over. Her mind went back to her story pitch, about how her article would be written with integrity, revealing the high moral values of his family. It had sounded good, rehearsing it in her car on the way here.

But now, the pitch would have to wait.

Her story was low priority compared to the welfare of a nine-year-old boy.

"Okay . . ." Adam sat by the chessboard that Jonah and Gabe had just abandoned, the guys leaving the room so that he and Remy could have some semblance of privacy. "What's on your mind?"

A dozen thoughts burdened her mind, but Remy gripped the arms of the wooden chair, as if the old, worn wood might lend her some courage, and started with her number one priority. "Before dinner, when I was helping Simon with his homework, he began to talk about the night your parents were killed. I'm not sure, but

I think he revealed some things about the killer that you may not have heard yet."

Adam winced, his hand on his chin. "I suppose he ran the bear story by you?"

"More than that. He mentioned some details about how the bear looked. He's describing the killer, I guess."

Adam let out a long, slow breath. "Probably. We've talked to a therapist about this. It's a sort of transference, but we're dealing with it. I understand your concern, but it's all in hand."

"Is it?" She didn't want to anger him, but she couldn't forget the glimmer of fear in Simon's eyes or the way he spoke under his breath, as if the topic were forbidden. "At the risk of making you really mad at me, I have to tell you I'm worried about him. He needs professional help."

"You're pushing into an area where you are definitely not welcome. Please, just back off."

"But I can't. Simon needs an advocate."

"Are you kidding me? He's got an entire community supporting him."

"Good intentions aside, the Amish community might not be able to provide the help he needs. Now that he's not in shock anymore, he needs to talk about what happened that night. Is he seeing a therapist now?"

"I can't believe you're asking me these questions."

"Because, when you think of what he went through, I'll bet he's still suffering from post-traumatic stress syndrome."

Head in hand, he groaned.

"Is it a matter of money? I mean . . . I know health care without insurance is ghastly expensive, but—"

"That's what you've come all this way to tell me, that my brother needs professional help? What are you, a spy from social services?"

"No, nothing like that."

"A child psychologist?"

She swallowed over the knot in her throat. "Of course not."

"But you drop in here, spend an afternoon with my family, and then tell me my brother needs to see a doctor for his post-traumatic stress?"

"Adam . . . slow down. I'm trying to help."

"We don't need your kind of help." He let out a frustrated sigh, then sat back in the chair and tipped his face to the ceiling, as if the answers were inscribed there. "You're missing something important here, Remy. When Simon was scared silent, friends and family rallied around him. He was surrounded with love, and prayer. We counted on God's love to heal him. And now, not even a year later, even an outsider like you would have to admit that it's happening."

"But he's still suffering."

In the ensuing pause, she registered the ticking of the wall clock and the dull murmur of female voices out in the kitchen. Comforting sounds, though they belied the turmoil roiling in this room.

"You're probing at a wound, a deep family wound." When he turned to her, his expression was so cold and distant, he seemed a stranger. "Leave it be, Remy."

"I'm sorry. But if Simon is starting to remember details from that night, you need to take him to the officers investigating the case."

"Sheriff Hallinan questioned Simon, and what good did that do? Now he's afraid of anyone in a uniform."

"He'll get over that, Adam, if someone works with him. What he won't overcome is the shame over his grief and the message that he can't talk about what happened. The poor boy was silent for months. Months. And now he's found his voice. Simon opened up to me, Adam, and I think he's crying for help. Help him work through the terrible details of that night—the things he's remembering now. Those are things the police need to know about, especially if the investigation is ongoing. It might help them find the killer."

"We cooperated with the police when it all happened. We won't stand in the way of their investigation, but it's not our duty to bring new evidence forth."

"Not your duty? He's your little brother!"

"The Amish don't seek justice for a crime. It's not up to men to judge and render punishment on other men. It says in the Bible, 'Judge not, lest ye be judged.'"

Frustrated, Remy leaned back in the chair and squeezed the armrests tight. Why was he resisting all of her suggestions? "Even if you don't want the man punished, don't you want him off the streets so that he can't hurt anyone else?"

"That's not up to me," Adam said calmly. "It's a matter of following the Ordnung."

Remy spoke in a measured tone, not wanting anyone in the kitchen to overhear. "So you'd sit back, while your brother's life may be in jeopardy from this killer, because of the church rules?"

"Simon's life isn't in jeopardy," he said quickly. "He's surrounded by family and friends at all times. He's staying home from school right now as an extra precaution, that's all."

"I thought you of all people would understand. You lived on the outside—"

"But I'm Amish now. I took a vow to obey God and follow the rules of the Ordnung for the rest of my life. So your thinking about me is wrong, Remy. I'm not English, and I'm not straddling two worlds. I'm not going to bend the rules."

"Even if it means finding the man who murdered your parents?"

A look of desolation darkened his eyes as he shook his head.

"We both know English, but we're not speaking the same language. I think you'd better go now."

He was right.

Although it crushed Remy to admit it, they belonged to two very separate worlds. Two planets spinning in different universes.

As she stood, it struck her as incredibly sad that two people with so much personal chemistry could never be together. That and the fact that she wouldn't have a chance to help Simon.

Her eyes misted, but she held her head high as she straightened her sweater and walked away from him. By the time she reached the kitchen, tears blurred her vision.

"Remy?" Sadie called. "Are you okay?"

She wanted to answer—Sadie deserved a proper good-bye. Indeed, the entire family did. But she couldn't speak over the knot of emotion throbbing in her throat.

"Remy?"

Their faces were a blur of concern and surprise as she rushed past and plunged into the darkness of the mudroom and fumbled into her stiff, cold boots. Where was her coat? She grabbed it from a hook on the wall as Sadie's voice startled her.

"What happened in there?"

"I can't talk." Remy's voice was raw, shaky. "I have to go. Thank you for everything."

"Remy, please don't go . . ."

Unable to face Sadie, she pushed through the door and hunkered down under the collar of her leather coat. Expecting to be assaulted by sheets of icy rain, she was greeted instead by tiny flecks of snow. Like confetti, it glimmered in the air and dusted the ground.

Her heart sank.

This was a problem.

Despite the beauty of the farm, its buildings and fields blanketed in a thin layer of white, Remy worried about driving in hazardous snow. Suddenly, the turmoil of her dispatch with Adam faded to the task at hand. How was she going to get home in this?

She swiped at her eyes and took a deep breath.

The sweet, clean air bolstered her spirits. She could do it. She had driven through three inches once at a ski resort in New York, and she'd managed just fine. She could do it . . . but she would have to take it slow.

As if to underline the hazard, her boots slipped over a patch of frozen ground and she waved her hands in the air to regain her balance.

Take it nice and slow.

The blanket of ice and snow over her car only validated Adam's warning about the weather. She started the engine, put the defroster on full blast, and searched for a scraper. No go. She'd have to make do.

Leaning against the side of the car, she began to chisel at the frozen windshield with a credit card. There was only a light dusting of snow. No big deal, she thought.

"Chance of precipitation, zero percent," she muttered as her bare fingers began to ache from the cold. "And I was stupid enough to believe the satellite forecast." Adam had to think she was a total fool.

Glancing up at the house, she scraped faster. She didn't want Adam to think that she was stalling. Would they realize that she couldn't drive with a frozen windshield? She supposed that glass on their buggies frosted over at times. Maybe. Probably. She didn't care, as long as she could get out of here, fast.

The ice gave way to the warm air from the dash, and a fan-shaped patch melted away completely. Remy scraped at the edges, clearing enough space to see straight ahead for now.

She was good to go.

The blast of warm air inside the car was nauseating now, but it eased the pain in her frozen hands as she held them in front of the blower for a minute. Molten warmth. She sighed, then pulled herself together. She buckled up, hit the wipers, and put the car in gear; at last, she was rolling down the bumpy driveway.

She held tight to the steering wheel as the car wheels began to spin in the dipping driveway. The tires slipped on the little hill, the rear end fishtailing slightly as she gave it some gas. But she managed to get traction and the car climbed the slight rise, rocking as she passed the cluster of beech trees.

It would be better once she reached the road. Smooth sailing, she told herself as she peered through the little porthole she'd cleared on the windshield. Small flakes clung to the glass until the wipers swept them away. Her timing was good, with the snow just starting. In a minute she would be on the paved road, and once she passed through Halfway she would be traveling on the highway, ahead of the storm before there was any real accumulation.

The lane ended, and Remy's tight chest relaxed when she saw the shiny black pavement.

No snow to contend with on the roadway, and no traffic in sight.

She was home free.

Relieved, she turned onto the paved road and pressed the accelerator.

The rear of the car wiggled, like an irate beast behind her.

And what was that whirring sound?

A second later she was terrified by the realization that the noise was the skidding of her rear tires as the car began to fishtail. The shiny dark roadway was covered in ice—deadly black ice—and the crisp white fields whirled past her line of vision as her car spun around.

Her heartbeat raced as panic roared in her head. "Oh, no! Please God!"

Frantic, she tried to grip the steering wheel, to stop the skid, but the car twirled on its own crazy path. The breath was stolen from her body as the cold winter world flashed by her with dizzying speed.

Everything was out of control.

THIRTY

*W*hat had he done?

Head in hands, Adam sat alone in the gloom, the prison of his own making.

She was trying to help, trying to protect Simon—and wasn't that what he wanted, too? They wanted the same thing, and yet he pitted himself against her, widening the gap, preying upon their cultural differences to drive her away.

Off into the wet, icy night.

Although it felt wrong to act like such an ogre, he couldn't let her stay and thread her way into their family. She was already too close, already something of a problem for him with the bishop.

With a deep breath he straightened, his gaze falling on the chessboard where the pieces had been left, a game in progress. Jonah was the chess master here, always the winner in this house. His strategy was to stay one or two moves ahead of his opponent, always thinking ahead.

A fine defensive strategy, Adam thought. A tactic he should

have utilized with Remy McCallister, who seemed to render him vulnerable at every turn. Just when he felt ready for her next move, she came at him with a new attack.

He dragged himself out of the chair and realized he was parched, as if the heated debate with Remy had burned a path clear down his throat.

Needing water, he made his way into the kitchen, leery of the reception there. Mary helped Susie and Ruthie with quilting squares. Simon had his homework, Leah's face was tipped toward an open book, and Sadie was writing, working on a circle letter. Even with all the activity they were uncharacteristically silent as Adam filled a glass at the sink and gulped greedily.

When he turned away from the sink, he saw them watching from the long table. His five oldest sisters had paused in their tasks to stare up at him. From the end of the table, Simon colored the edges of a map, his eyes flickering up at Adam. Curiosity and disapproval blew through the room like a gale wind. He was better off getting out of here before someone gave voice to it.

He quickly turned back to the sink and placed the glass on the counter. If he grabbed a coat and flashlight, he could slip out to the barn and help Jonah and Gabe check on the animals.

He lunged into the mudroom and—

"What did you say to her?" Mary asked from behind him.

Leave it to Mary to reel him in. He should have moved more swiftly. "It was a long conversation," he called from the sheltered porch as he grabbed a coat. "As I'm sure you heard."

"We didn't hear enough of it," Sadie said.

"But it looked like you made her cry." That was Ruthie's voice. "Did you make her cry, Adam?"

"Can we talk about this later?" he called.

Footsteps sounded behind him, and Mary stood in the doorway, her figure silhouetted against the kitchen light. "Adam King, don't think you can escape and leave us wondering and worried about that girl," she said. "Kumm. Explain."

He hung his coat back on the peg and traipsed into the kitchen to face the jury of sisters.

"Why did you drive Remy away after she was incredibly kind to us?" Leah asked. "Did you see the many books she brought us?"

"That was very generous of her," Adam said, leaning against the sink. "But it's not right for her to stop in here and turn everything upside down. Why did she come here in the first place? I don't know."

"She came here because she's my friend." Sadie jiggled the pen in her hands, her lips puckered in a frown. "She's my friend, and she has a good heart."

"Even if her heart is in the right place, she doesn't belong here."

"Because she's not Plain People?" Sadie asked.

"She doesn't understand what it's like to be Plain. Her value system is completely different." Adam rubbed his chin, wondering why he felt as if he had to defend himself to his own sisters. "I didn't intend to hurt her, but I had to defend our family, our faith."

Sadie folded her arms across her chest. "That and you don't want the bishop to know that I've got friendships with Englishers."

"Which you'd better be wary of, or measures will be taken to keep you and all the rumspringa youth in line." The bishop's warning about the path that led away from God echoed in his mind.

Anger flamed in Sadie's eyes, but instead of firing back she looked down at her letter, quiet for the moment.

A small relief for Adam, who was in no mood to take on another battle. At the moment he felt drained of patience and energy.

"Let's stick to the problem." As usual, Mary was the voice of wisdom. "Not to criticize you, brother Adam, but are you sure it's right to drive her off with the weather spitting mad out there?" She pointed to the window. "Do you hear that?"

The kitchen went silent but for the ticking clock and the patter of ice crystals on the windows and roof.

An ice storm.

Adam cocked his head, peering through the window. More ice than snow, and that was probably not a good thing. Minuscule chips of frozen precipitation filled the air.

A call beckoned him. This was dangerous weather, and Remy was alone.

"Terrible weather for travel," Mary said.

"It's getting worse." Sadie went to the window. "And I barely made it home from work myself."

"What if she gets stuck on the road?" Concern filled Ruthie's voice.

"She can't have gotten far," Adam said, turning toward the door. Panic tightened, a fist in his chest, but he fought to stay calm. "I'll go and stop her."

Mary pushed out of her chair and clambered out to the mud-room. "I'll hitch up Thunder while you find a coat and hat."

He plunged into the darkness of the porch, feeling for the hooks on the walls. "There's no time, and it's bound to be too slippery for a carriage. Get his halter and I'll ride bareback."

Without a cloak of her own she dashed out into the night, her skirts swirling as she ran to the barn. Pushing back the feeling of alarm, Adam grabbed a coat and hat and raced out behind her.

Within minutes they had Adam's horse ready to ride, but Jonah warned him to take caution.

"Everything is covered in ice," Jonah said. "I just slipped when I went to check the stables."

"I'll be careful."

"Take this." Gabe handed him an LED lamp, one of the flash-lights they wore on headbands for morning milking.

"Good thinking." Adam tugged his hat on securely, pulled the headlamp on over it, then jumped onto Thunder's back and headed off into the blistering storm.

Although there was a wide spot in the driveway where Remy's car had been parked, the vehicle's tracks were already covered in a thin sheet of snow. How long ago had she pulled out of here? And how far had she traveled? Even though she was in a car, she wouldn't be moving too fast. He could pray for her safe journey, but this was not a night for long passage by car or horse.

He had to find her.

Despite the lack of wind, the falling ice crystals were relentless, a wall of pelting needles. Still, he had confidence in his mount, knowing that most horses could cope well in cold weather. "Easy, there," he called to the horse, if only to soothe his own panic. The frozen ground would be solid underfoot, but he worried that the horse might slip in a patch of ice, which was impossible to see on the snow-dusted earth.

Tamping down the alarm that still sounded in his head, he guided Thunder past the barren beech trees. The horse's footing seemed solid and sure as they climbed the gentle rise. Jonah had gotten the farrier to outfit the horses with winter shoes, complete with antislip road nails, but nothing could be sure to grip on sheer ice.

When they reached the paved road, Adam sensed trouble.

"Whoa." He held the horse back and slid to the ground. A coating of slush, like an inch of pudding, covered the asphalt road. And underneath?

His boots slid as he tested the way. Just as he'd thought, there was slush on top of ice. Nearly impassable.

"Let's stick to the shoulder," he told the horse, leading him to the side of the roadbed. "Just stay out of the ditch."

Knowing Thunder could manage the terrain as long as they stayed off smooth ice, Adam hitched himself atop the horse and picked up the pace. In a half mile, he didn't see a single vehicle. It was a wasteland out here.

Concern gripped him as they headed toward town.

Where was Remy now?

He'd been wrong to send her out in this. It seemed that he expended so much energy trying to get her away from his family and out of his thoughts. But he'd been wrong to turn her out in this foul weather. He saw that now.

"Oh, Lord," he breathed, his heart thudding in desperation. "Please, keep her safe."

They crested a hill and he saw it—the lump of a vehicle jutting from a ditch at the side of the road. One of the wheels was off the ground and still moving slowly, and the roadway was a scramble of tire tracks in the snow.

Was it Remy? Whoever it was needed help.

He urged his horse forward, his eyes on the car. It had slid off to the right side of the road, and now, with the passenger side pressed into the ditch, it would be near impossible to pry open that door.

When they were parallel to the wreck, he halted his horse and left the horse to wait on the shoulder as he slogged across the ice to the disabled car.

"Remy?"

No answer in the falling snow.

"Remy? Are you okay?" he shouted as he approached.

In the sickening silence, he listened intently and prayed.

Then, the driver's door opened, and the beam of his flashlight illuminated her tearstained face.

"Adam?" She sniffed. "I feel so . . . so stupid."

"Don't. It wasn't your fault." He bent down beside the car. "Are you okay? Any bumps or bleeding?"

"No . . . I don't think so."

As she swiped at her eyes, he stared into the dark car. His

heartbeat quickened at the sight of her face, illuminated by her cell phone. Her lower lip trembled, but there were no injuries that he could see.

"There was ice on the road. . . ." She sniffed. "I didn't realize until it was too late and . . ." The dashboard was covered by the disheveled gray fabric of the air bags. Now sagging, they had done their job.

Her eyes were round and glassy with tears, and as one tracked down her cheek he allowed himself to brush it away with the tip of a finger.

"The important thing is that you're safe," he said.

"Don't. You're going to kill me with kindness, after I've been a total idiot. I should have listened to you about the weather, and now . . ." Her voice broke. "I wrecked my car and I can't get cell service. And even if I could, I wouldn't be able to tell a tow truck how to find me."

"No trucks will be heading out here in this storm, but don't worry. We'll help you find one tomorrow, after the snow stops. For now, let's get you back to the warm house."

"I can't. Sadie told me you got in trouble when I stayed last time."

"That's not entirely true. . . ." But he was intrigued to know that Sadie cared about what the church leaders thought.

"You can put me out in the barn. I'll sleep in the hayloft."

"The barn?" All the pent-up anxiety over her safety drained in a laugh at the thought of Remy holed up in a pile of hay. "Don't be silly. You're coming home with me."

As if suddenly weary, she leaned back in the seat and closed her eyes. "I'm so sorry, Adam. I keep causing you trouble."

She spoke the truth. She probably had no idea how much trouble she had brought into his home and heart. But this was not the time.

"Look. You need a safe place to stay. We have plenty of room. Let's get you out of here." He reached across her to remove the keys from the ignition, then remained close, his face inches from hers. "Are you sure you're all right?"

She nodded.

"Okay. Let's see how you are on your feet. Careful getting out. You might be in shock, and it's really slippery out here."

Of course she knew about the ice, having skidded off the road, but he knew shock could do strange things to people.

He stepped back from the door and extended a hand. She swung her feet around and accepted his help. A good thing, as she wobbled when she stood up.

Relief washed over him as he held tight to her, steadying her. The car might be a wreck, but she had been spared. That was all that mattered.

She stared at their hands, then looked up at him. "No gloves?"

"I left in a hurry."

"Oh." She turned to close the car door, but the force sent her legs skittering out from under her.

In an instant he was behind her, catching her slender body, which seemed light as she collapsed in his arms.

"I'm not doing too well." She held on to his shoulder as if clinging to a cliff edge. "It's not a seizure or anything, I just—"

"You're probably in shock. It happens in accidents like these."

"Yes." Her face was inches from his, so close he saw a snowflake catch in one of her eyelashes.

With Remy in his arms, safe and soft, he didn't feel the cold, but suddenly he became acutely aware of the details of this moment, the thick white flakes falling in her hair, the silken sound of her breathing in the stillness, the glimmer of trust in her green eyes.

"I would carry you to my horse, but I'm not sure how solid my footing would be on the road."

"Oh. Right. I think I can walk." She slid from his arms, a soft, light, perfumed dream.

After she retrieved her purse and locked the car, they slogged toward Thunder, who didn't seem to mind the cold at all. Remy slipped again, reaching for him as she went down. He managed to catch her, and slid an arm around her waist for support.

"Pretend you're skating," he said.

Lips pursed in determination, she slid a foot forward, then clutched him again. "Skating was never my thing." But she took another sliding step, and he loved her for trying.

"That's your horse?" she asked. When he nodded, she observed, "He doesn't have a saddle."

"I told you, I tore out of there. Have you ever ridden?"

"Here's one area where I won't give you trouble," she said. "Lucky for you, Herb was a big believer in riding lessons. Horse camp, dressage, the whole deal. I've even ridden bareback."

"That will help."

He wove his fingers together to give her a boost, and was impressed at the way she mounted the horse with ease. He swung up behind her. But when he reached around her shoulders for the reins, the smell of her hair so near his face took him by surprise, traces of honeysuckle and mint in a winter storm. To be inhaling the scents of an Englisher woman, to have her delicate bones pressing against him, the heat of her body melding with his . . .

This was unlike anything he'd experienced since his return home.

Sweet torture.

For a moment he considered going on foot. Feet pounding the frozen earth . . . that would calm his heightened senses, but it would slow them down. And he didn't want to risk exposing Remy to the cold after the trauma of the car accident.

He squeezed the horse's sides with his calves, and Thunder

moved forward. The motion sent Remy leaning back against him, awakening thoughts and sensations that had faded long ago. The touch of a woman, her smell and softness . . .

Clenching his jaw, he urged his horse on through the snow and pushed toward home.

THIRTY-ONE

*T*hrough the layers of shock and cold and rejection, Remy was struck by the irony of the situation. Sitting in front of Adam on the huge draft horse, she allowed herself to melt back into the warmth of the one man she would never be allowed to love. She knew that from their argument back at the house. From the way he'd hammered at the separate worlds thing, the message was hardly subtle.

Nothing would ever transpire between them.

She shifted her head, fitting into the cradle of his arms. Such a perfect fit, though it would never happen. That was sad. Tragic.

And now she'd wrecked her car.

Her eyes stung as they misted over. To add insult to injury, a fat snowflake flew at her face and caught in the lashes of her left eye. She gave it a rub, wincing at the picture of what her life had become.

A ruined car. A failure at work. An absent father.

If she had died in that crash, who would have cared? A handful of people.

And since Arlene had given her permission to take some time off to get her story, she might not have been missed for days or even weeks.

And she had thought the fact that Adam King hated her was tragic? The real tragedy was her life ... or the lack of one.

Here lies Remy McCallister, a woman who really didn't matter.

That was the thought that had consumed her as the world went spinning beyond her car. I'm going to die, and I haven't done anything with my life yet.

And she'd asked God for help.

And she had survived, intact. Was that God's answer? Was this her second chance at life, to do it right this time?

Were her thoughts scrambled?

Probably.

It was difficult to process the tangible information coming at her right now. The warmth of his body curling around her shoulders like a winter cloak. The gentle motion of the horse beneath them, rocking her to a daze, lulling her to a fantasy that the strong, warm man behind her actually cared for her.

No, don't go there.

For now she had to hold on to the relief of being safe. A double bonus to have been saved by Adam, though she could never admit that to anyone because it was insane to fall in love with an Amish man when you were a millionaire's daughter from the city.

She closed her eyes and breathed deeply, trying to inhale the scent of him, a way to memorize the moment. He smelled of wood smoke and soap.

"Easy," he called. "Almost there."

Was he talking to the horse, or to her?

She didn't want to return to the house. She didn't want to go back to reality, back to her empty life.

To stay on this magnificent creature, cocooned in the crook of Adam's body with leaves of snow dancing around them—that was the picture of bliss.

But maybe, just maybe, her life could begin again when her feet touched the ground. A do-over, like in schoolyard kickball. A second chance.

Although Remy had thought she would never see the inside of the King home again, most of the family seemed to be waiting there to welcome her, relief warming their eyes.

"You're safe!" Sadie threw her arms around Remy as she stepped into the mudroom. "We were so worried."

Remy hugged her tight, touched to know they were concerned about her. "I smashed my car. It's a mess."

"But you're okay?" Sadie leaned back to look at her.

"I'm fine."

"She needs to sit down," Adam said from behind her. "She might be in shock, and she's cold and wet."

"Soaked to the bone." Sadie rubbed Remy's shoulder. "I can feel it. Your jacket, is it ruined?"

"I think it will dry."

"Get those wet things off, and we'll warm you up." Mary stood in the doorway, hands on her hips as she summoned her into the kitchen.

With a mixture of relief and weariness, Remy turned to the outside door, but Adam was gone. "Where did he go?"

"Thunder needs to be put away, but he'll be back. Quick, now. Out of those wet things."

Remy shed her jacket and boots and stepped into the warm kitchen, where Leah and Susie, Mary, Ruthie, and Simon waited anxiously.

"There's snow in your hair," Ruthie observed, her eyes bright. "It's been coming down like crazy."

Remy ran a hand through her hair and droplets fell. "Look at me, dripping on your clean floor."

"Don't worry." Leah handed her a clean towel, then leaned down to swipe at the floor with a rag.

"Jonah said we might not make it to school tomorrow," Susie reported. "That's why Ruthie and Simon got to stay up extra late."

"And I wanted to see Remy," Ruthie said.

"Me too." Simon seemed happy to include himself.

"We're all so very relieved, Remy. The children couldn't sleep one wink until they knew you were safe," Mary said. "Now that you've seen her, it's time for bed."

"But if we don't have school, why can't we stay up longer?" Susie asked.

Mary shooed them toward the stairs. "The cows still need milking before sunrise."

"The cows don't get a snow day," Simon said.

That brought laughter from the girls.

"That was funny, Simon," Ruthie said, patting his back as they headed up the stairs.

While Remy changed into a borrowed nightgown and toweled off her wet hair, Mary warmed milk on the stove.

When they convened on the daybed in the kitchen, near the warm glow of the potbellied stove, Remy's body was weighed down by weariness. "I feel like someone put me through that wringer on your washing machine."

Sadie adjusted the quilt on Remy's shoulders. "No wonder. You had a rough night."

"Drink some milk, and then it's off to bed with you," Mary said in a tone as warm as a mother's embrace. Funny, Mary was younger than Remy, and yet she was so capable and caring.

"I can't believe I wrecked my car."

"What happened to it?" Sadie asked.

"It went off the side of the road. It's still there, stuck in a ditch, but I can't drive it. The air bags popped out." Remy sipped the warm milk, not wanting to recount that terrible moment when she lost control. The skidding tires. The impact. The crash of metal against earth.

She shuddered. "I'm thankful to Adam for rescuing me. I . . . I don't think I got a chance to thank him."

"You'll have your chance in the morning." Mary patted her knee. "Now, finish up your milk. You will stay with us as long as need be."

Remy swallowed, hugging the warm mug. "Adam is not going to like that."

"Don't let my brother's ways offend you." Mary sat back, smoothing the apron pinned to her dress. "His role in this family is an important one. On most matters I wouldn't dream of arguing with him, but sometimes he pushes us all down a difficult road."

Remy thought of the cold, detached way he'd asked her to leave . . . and then the exquisite gentleness he'd displayed when he'd helped her from the car. What had she called it? Killing her with kindness. "He's a man of contradictions."

"That he is," Mary said, "but his heart is in the right place." She rose and tucked her chair under the table. "You get some rest. If you need anything, just ask Sadie."

"You're in the girls' room, just like last time," Sadie said, taking the empty mug from Remy.

Upstairs, Sadie led the way to the familiar room with its dusky rose walls and six beds, three of which were occupied by Ruthie and the twins, already fast asleep under their quilts. This was the room she had slept in more than two weeks ago, though it seemed to be an older, cherished memory, like the locket she'd had since childhood, the heart-shaped charm holding a tiny picture of her mother's smiling face.

Sitting on the edge of a bed, Remy yawned. If it weren't for the overwhelming weariness, she would have stayed awake to savor the safe, peaceful feeling of being in a room full of sleeping girls, their hair splayed over pillows, their chests rising and falling in the rhythm of sleep.

"This reminds me of summer camp." Keeping her voice to a husky whisper, Remy turned down the quilt and slid into bed. "I always loved sleeping in the cabin with my friends." The air in the room was cool, but it was cozy under the covers.

"Sweet dreams," Sadie said, shutting off the gas lamp.

As the light faded and the room's rosy hues gave way to velvet darkness, Remy found comfort in the deep quiet broken only by the stirring of breath. Real peace abided here. Secure in that comfort, she let go of her worries and found her way to a blessed sleep.

THIRTY-TWO

S now.

It covered everything as far as Remy could see. The barn and outbuildings, fence posts and fields, tree branches and troughs. Every hill and valley was made white, smooth, pristine. Dancing flurries filled the air, adding magic to the scene, as if someone had shaken a snow globe of a Tyrolean village in the Alps.

The white covering brought its own illumination to the purple light of dawn, making it easier for Remy to watch from the bedroom window as Adam and Gabe, flashlights on their heads, guided the cows in for milking.

Milking time. She had to get out and help.

Turning back to the room, she was amazed at how quietly the other girls had slipped out without waking her. It was actually the moo of a cow that had pulled her from sleep. That and the fact that she had probably gotten to bed before nine P.M. and slept straight through.

She crossed the room, taking a moment to bounce on her bed

and take it all in. Amazing how your disposition improved with a good night's sleep. She straightened the pillow and smoothed the quilt, then hurried downstairs.

The kitchen was empty, though the coffeepot on the stove was still warm. A quick search revealed her clothes hanging on a chair by the potbellied stove. Still damp. Whatever.

She pulled her leather jacket on over the nightgown, stepped into a pair of muck boots on the porch, and headed out to the cow-shed, the section of the barn with stalls for milking. Although she hadn't had success with milking last time, she'd learned that there were plenty of things she could do, from cleaning the cows' teats to toting pails of milk to the larger vats.

The large barn door was still slightly open, and Remy slipped into the welcome warmth as well as the earthy smells of hay and animal. Cows were tied to the posts, and Remy could make out the forms of people seated beside each creature, milking by hand.

"Good morning!" Ruthie called as she lugged a silver vat down the aisle. She wore a bright blue bonnet that covered her ears and tied like a gift package under her chin. "Come for another milking lesson?"

"I think I'll stick to the manual labor," Remy said. "How about that snow? Isn't it gorgeous?"

"No school today!" one of the girls chimed in from behind a cow. "Adam said we'll turn into Popsicles if we try to walk in this weather."

"No school!" Ruthie clasped her hands under her chin. "That makes it a very special day!"

"I have half a mind to hitch Jigsaw up to the old sleigh." Jonah was milking the cow to Remy's right. "Do you think it would work, Adam?"

"Depends on how well packed the snow is." Adam's voice came from up the aisle. "If this keeps up, we can give it a try. It's really coming down and from the way the air feels, the look of that sky, I don't see it letting up anytime soon. You're probably stuck here for the day, Remy."

"Oh." Just like that, he was giving up on getting her out of here? Not that she minded so much. It was nice to be welcome, and today he didn't seem at all upset about the prospect of her staying on.

Still, if Adam couldn't help her find a way out by noon, she would find a towing service to retrieve her and her car. "That's okay. But it might stop, right?"

Jonah turned to her, his eyes dark with the serenity of a person who accepted things as they were. "That's not likely."

Adam's head poked out from under one of the cows. "Remy?" He stood up for a better look. "That's some getup you're wearing there."

"Do ya think?" Remy swirled the skirt of the nightgown around her knees. "My clothes are still drying."

Sadie peeked out from under a cow and gave a little laugh. "You may be on to something. I want to do the morning milking in my nightgown."

"You didn't have to come out here." Adam's voice sounded kind today, without a trace of the disapproval she'd faced the night before. "Especially after the accident. You should probably take it easy."

"But I want to help," Remy insisted as Ruthie handed her a pair of work gloves. More than that, she wanted to be a part of the easy banter that passed as they kept to their tasks.

"Don't let Mary see," Gabe said. "She gets upset when I get mud on my trousers. But a nightgown?"

"There's no mud." Jonah stood and moved out of the stall, three-legged stool in one arm, bucket in the other. "Everything is frozen solid." He handed Remy the pail of milk. "If you'll take this, I'll move on to milk Elma."

"Got it." Remy took the bucket, though it weighed down her left arm considerably.

"I'll show you where to pour that." Ruthie picked up a bucket from Sadie's stall and led the way down the aisle toward the back of the cowshed.

As they worked, Ruthie explained how the big vat was hooked up to a refrigeration unit that kept the milk cool until the driver, a Mennonite man who had worked for their family for years, came and carted it off in a big truck.

"Most of it goes to our uncle Nate's farm, where it gets turned into cheese," Ruthie explained.

Remy glanced back down the aisle, where Gabe was moving some of the cows out the wide barn door. "And you have to milk them twice a day, every day?"

"Every day." Ruthie rolled her eyes. "Even on Sundays."

"And snow days."

"But Adam says it's going to get easier. We're getting milking machines, like the ones at Uncle Nate's farm. You just hook up the hoses and it does all the work, easy as pie."

"Really? With a machine like that, maybe even I could milk one of your cows." As Remy poured milk from a bucket into the larger vat, some of the liquid splattered onto the hem of her nightgown.

"Oops!" Ruthie's eyes went wide. "There goes Mary's nightgown."

Remy stepped back from the vat and flapped the damp fabric in the air. "That's what I get for going out to the barn in a nightgown."

"Don't worry. Mary will understand." Ruthie picked up the empty bucket in one hand and assessed Remy with narrowed eyes. "Mary is just your size. I think she'll loan you a dress you can wear while you're out and about in the snow."

"That would be perfect."

"You'd better go back to the house," Ruthie advised with grave authority. "You can't sit at the breakfast table in a wet nightgown."

"You are so right." The girl was wise beyond her years, Remy thought as she hitched up her nightgown, ducked out of the barn, and ran through the snowstorm, rubber boots flopping all the way back to the house.

Breakfast was sausage and granola cereal and a scrambled egg casserole everyone called Hidden Eggs that smelled of melted butter. Wearing a deep purple dress that Mary generously loaned her, Remy sat at Adam's right hand, but not before she noticed a new face at the far end of the table.

"Remy, I don't think you've met our grandmother, Nell King." From Adam's relaxed demeanor, Remy sensed genuine affection for his grandmother as he made the introduction.

Remy gave a respectful nod. "I think we met at the market, but not officially."

"Ya, I remember." The older woman nodded, the hint of a smile on her lips.

"She lives in the Doddy house." Sadie placed a pitcher on the table. "It's the little cottage down the lane, just past the vegetable garden." She said something to her grandmother in Pennsylvania Dutch and took the seat beside her.

The older woman's dark eyes, magnified by her spectacles, held a bit of amusement as she responded in kind. Remy suspected that their grandmother didn't miss much.

"I couldn't open my door this morning. The snow was this high. . . ." Nell King lifted a hand above her head.

"Oh, Mammi!" Susie's eyes were bright with amusement as she took a seat. "Did you dig a tunnel to us?"

"Jonah came to my aid. Jonah and his horse."

"The horses like the snow." Jonah stepped in from the door of the porch. "The ice can be a problem, of course, but they can gain steady footing in the snow, and they've got a thick coat to protect them from the cold."

"The only thing is . . ." Simon held up one finger, capturing everyone's attention. "You must make sure the horse's legs are dry at the end of the day. They can get very sick from wet legs. Their legs get chapped and cracked, like our lips."

Adam nodded in approval. "Someone has been paying attention."

From the encouragement given to Simon, it was clear everyone in the family was pleased with his progress. To think that he hadn't been able to speak more than a word or two just a year ago—it was a wonder that he'd come so far.

Once everyone was seated, with Katie in the high chair, the meal progressed like the others Remy had attended.

There was a moment of quiet as each person said a silent prayer of thanks. This time when Remy bowed her head, she felt words come from her heart. *Thank you, dear God. Thank you for saving me from injury on that road last night. And thanks for sticking me with this noisy, big family. They're like . . . the family I always wanted.*

Every word was true . . . true and startling as the white snow falling over the countryside. Putting aside the way she had landed here, it was a treat to be staying with the Kings. A dream fulfilled.

In this short time Remy had gleaned a sense of their personalities and how they fit together to comprise a cohesive family. She learned that Simon loved working with the horses, especially his favorite, a shy mare named Shadow. In getting to know the family, she observed that Leah seemed happiest when lost in a book while her twin, Susie, avoided books like the plague. Sadie longed to escape the dairy farm for the changing world, while Gabe seemed angry about the possibility of changing even the way the family farmed. Already Remy knew she could rely on Ruthie, the family soothsayer, for the blunt truth, and Mary for genuine support.

Just don't get too attached, she told herself as she lifted her head to find Adam watching her.

Could he read her thoughts and prayers? His piercing dark eyes seemed to have that power over her.

She was grateful for the diversion when he passed her the platter of eggs. As far as attachment went, it was too late. She already cared, way too much, for Adam and his family.

Platters were passed, and plans were made.

"I just can't take my eyes off that window." Susie absently passed the bread Nell had baked. "Did you ever see anything so beautiful as snow?"

"It's truly a blessing." Mary put a dollop of egg casserole on Katie's tray and blew on it. "I love the feeling of being cozy and warm and surrounded by snow. And we're so fortunate to have a full storeroom. Potatoes and canned produce and some dried meats."

"And it's still snowing down," Simon said. "Like God is sifting flour."

Amid the smiles, Remy marveled at how the Kings took it all in stride. Instead of complaining about extra chores or frigid temperatures, they were enjoying the snow.

Nell reached for the apple butter. "My mother used to say that the angels were having a pillow fight."

"There are some extra snow chores to divvy up," Adam said. "We need to dig a path to the Doddy house, and one to the barn. Either today or tomorrow we'll need to ride the fences. We can't have animals getting loose or stranded out in the snowdrifts. And there's wood to be chopped."

Mary poured granola into a bowl and placed it on the tray in front of Katie's high chair. "It's the perfect day to do extra baking, and since the girls are all here, we might do some quilting so Remy can see how we do it."

Remy nodded as she broke off a crust of bread. "I would love that."

"Can we build a snowman?" Simon asked.

Sam giggled. "And a snow boy!"

"There's plenty of snow for that, right in front of the Doddy house." A smile appeared on their grandmother's wrinkled face. "Enough to build a family of snowmen. Snow boys, too."

"We'll take care of that snow, Mammi." Gabe spread apple butter on a slice of bread. "Jonah and I will start shoveling, right after breakfast."

"Me too." Simon's amber eyes were bright. "As soon as I check on the horses."

Remy smiled. That was Simon, always thinking of the horses first. When she returned to the city, she would miss his sweetness, the genuine quality with which he approached everything.

But return she must. As breakfast wound down, she thought of the BlackBerry in her coat pocket. Before its battery drained, she needed to get on the phone and find a towing service. Her snow day would soon be drawing to a close.

Immersed in chores, the Kings were only slightly amused by Remy as she paced through the house in search of a signal for her cell phone. It took a while, but when she donned her coat and borrowed boots, she found a hot spot in front of the house, just up the lane by the cluster of snow-covered trees.

Although her cell phone was beeping from low battery, she managed to get through to a towing service in Lancaster.

"Are you in a safe place, ma'am?"

Remy looked back at the house, the lights of the kerosene lamps providing a cozy glow against the white roof and lawn. "Yes, I'm safe."

"Then stay where you are. My guys can't make it out that far today."

"Why not?"

"Have you seen the forecast?" Annoyance seeped into the woman's voice. "Record snowfall . . . blizzard . . . freezing temperatures?"

"Oh." Actually, Remy hadn't seen the forecast, as a tow truck had been her first priority.

"Some of the main roads are already closed out where you are. Call me back in a few days, when it starts to clear, and we'll fix you right up," the woman promised.

"A few days?" Remy stared out at the curtain of snow. "Won't they have trucks out clearing this?"

The woman laughed.

As soon as she hung up, Remy called the office and left a voice mail for Yasmina saying that she was snowbound in Lancaster County, but everything was okay. As she asked her friend to let the boss and her father know she was safe, the beeping persisted. The battery was draining, and there were no outlets on the farm to recharge it. She thought about trying to save the battery, but decided to put through one last call to Herb.

As the ring tone sounded, her phone jingled and the screen went black. Dead.

Blizzard warnings . . . Road closures . . .

Adam had been right, again.

She turned to the house and gave herself a shake, amused as fat white clumps shuddered from her hair and shoulders. Snow crunched under the rubber boots as she descended the lane, smiling amid the shower of endless flakes.

The good news: She was safe here. The Kings were warm and welcoming. She would be close to Adam.

The bad news: She would be close to Adam. That one was a double-edged sword.

There was also the concern that she might have another seizure without her medication. She would try and get sleep and hope for the best.

And she would have to abandon her article. There was no way she could write a story about the Kings now that she had embraced their family and been accepted in return. She had passed through the wall of professionalism and could no longer write an objective story. And part of her didn't really care anymore.

Outside the porch, Remy stomped her feet and gave a shake to get the snow off before pulling open the door.

Inside, Sadie hummed as she swept a pile of dried leaves and dirt into a dustpan. "Everything okay?"

Remy slid her phone into the pocket of her leather jacket and zipped it away. "It looks like I'm staying for a few days."

"Yes!" Sadie's arms shot into the air, broom waving as she did a little happy dance.

Remy pressed a hand to her chest in feigned shock. "You are too much!"

"I know, I know. But I was beginning to feel trapped, thinking I wouldn't be able to get away to work or to see Frank. I have another life out there, and sometimes it's hard to be sister Sadie, slogging away at the laundry and mopping floors. But having you here is going to make being snowbound bearable."

"Denki," Remy said. "But I need to ask, does your cell phone work here? Mine is out of battery."

"I—oops." Sadie pressed a hand to her mouth. "I left mine at the hotel. It was on the cord, charging up, and when I left in the storm, I was so rattled, I forgot it."

"Oh. I'm sure it's safe," Remy said.

Sadie nodded. "But I wish I had it with me. How will I reach Frank?"

"Forget about Frank, at least for now." Remy put a hand on her shoulder. "From what I hear, no one is going anywhere for the next few days. That's a whopper blizzard out there!"

"A whopper?" Sadie leaned her broom against the wall. "Then I thank God Adam found you last night. This is God's blessing."

Hugging her friend, Remy realized that Sadie was right.

God was showering them with a blessing. She only hoped that Adam saw it the same way.

THIRTY-THREE

A soft sound woke her.

Remy stirred, savoring the contrast between the cool air around her face and the cozy glow in the burrow beneath the quilt.

Smoothing her fingertips over the finely sewn patches of the quilt, she remembered where she was, a dawning realization that lightened her heart.

The day had passed quickly, full of activity and conversation and hearty, delicious foods. She'd helped sweep the house and hang laundry before bundling up in borrowed clothes to help the little ones build snowmen—an effort that might be buried at this point by the new snow that had fallen steadily through the day and evening. In the afternoon the girls had baked buttery pretzels, then quickly cleared the table so that they could get some quilting done before supper.

She yawned. What time was it?

From the darkness outside the windows she could see it was still night, though the hour or so of sleep had taken the edge off the exhaustion of a day spent in physical labor.

There was that shuffle in the hall again, the sound of light footsteps.

Curious, she propped herself up and glanced over at the other sleeping girls. No one else seemed disturbed. Heavy sleepers, Mary had said.

Remy slid out of bed, her bare feet curling as they touched the cold floor. Snow outside the window cast an odd blue sheen over the darkness, hardly enough to light her way.

"Wait! Don't go down there!" The hissing voice came from the hall, where she made out the form of a small person pacing nervously.

"Simon?" She squinted, but it was too dark to make out his features.

"Please, Dat, don't go down there! He's very angry!"

Suddenly a circle of light appeared down the hall. A lantern. The tall figure carrying it was dressed in a long nightshirt and britches.

"Adam?"

He nodded as he joined Remy. "Sorry if he woke you." Adam's voice was husky with sleep, as if he had just been awakened.

In the light cast by the lantern she was able to see Simon's face as he paced, his eyes glassy and frantic. His hands gestured stiffly as he sounded warnings, some indecipherable to Remy.

The boy looked haunted, terrified.

"Simon, what's wrong, sweetie?" She went over to him, planting herself in his path, but he sidestepped her, continuing to rant.

"Simon suffers night terrors. The doctors think he'll outgrow them, but for now . . ."

"Dat, please!" the boy wailed, his voice racked by sobs. "Please don't leave—!"

"Oh, Simon . . ." Remy went to the boy and rubbed his back between the shoulder blades. "Honey, can you wake up?"

This time, instead of avoiding Remy he spun toward her, grabbed her by the wrists, and stared into her face. "Don't go down there. I'm telling you, he has a gun!"

Terror burned in his round eyes.

Remy's pulse raced wildly, but she fought for control. She had some experience with night terrors, but then it was different when you were on the other side.

"Simon, it's going to be okay." She stared directly into his eyes, though they seemed vacant. "Everything's all right. Can you hear me?"

He turned away from her and lunged toward the far wall. "I'm just so afraid for Dat!"

"Hold this." Adam handed the lantern to Remy, then approached the boy, sliding an arm over his shoulders. "It's okay, buddy."

"No! No, Dat!" Simon turned and slapped at the wall. "No!"

"You're going to hurt yourself." Adam squatted down in front of him, hands on the boy's shoulders, and pulled him close. "Do you want to get warm? Should we warm you up?"

With a sob, Simon collapsed against his older brother.

"Downstairs." Adam took the boy in his arms and rose to his full height. "It usually helps to get him out of it if we make a fire in the potbellied stove."

Without hesitation she gathered the skirt of the nightgown in one hand, lifted the lantern with the other, and led the way down the stairs.

They worked together with barely a word passed between them. While Adam added wood to the stove, Remy tended to Simon, who lay shivering on the daybed.

The poor boy's body was racked with tremors. She quickly unfolded a quilt and wrapped it around him. His little face was still puckered with tension, his lips mumbling indecipherable warnings.

"Oh, Simon, it's hard on you." Remy settled beside him, stroking his hair. "I know it's hard, sweetie."

When Remy was ten, she, too, had paced the halls at night with a wild look in her eyes. Not that she remembered details from those nocturnal ramblings, but she'd had a capable nanny who was well versed in child behavior and knew that night terrors were a normal part of growth for some children.

It had been years since she'd seen her nanny Fatima, a softhearted, buxom woman who had no qualms about speaking her mind to Herb when it came to defending Remy.

Adam closed the grate on the stove and took a seat in a chair opposite the daybed. "Thank you." His eyes flicked over to Simon, whose chest now rose and fell in deep breaths. "He's been suffering these terrors for the past few months."

"How often?"

"A few times a week. Sometimes every night."

"And they usually happen around an hour after he goes to sleep?"

Adam nodded. "Sounds like you know a thing or two about night terrors."

"Been there, done that. Although in my case, I was the patient. My nanny put up with these episodes nearly every night for a while."

"Your nanny? You really are a princess, aren't you?"

"No . . . Fatima made it clear, I was not royalty." She closed her eyes and smiled at the thought of Fatima, with her wide girth, chocolate brown skin, and jangling bracelets, telling Remy that she was "no princess, and this is no castle, so you'll be picking up after yourself today."

"Still, I'm very grateful for the things that she taught me. I still love Fatima. She was there for me when I needed a mother, and she made me part of her family. Sometimes, when my father was away, we would go to visit with her family—there were baptisms and communions—and that was so much fun." Fatima's relatives had been the only family Remy knew for a few years, and they weren't legally related. Fatima used to say, "We are all part of God's big family."

She stroked the boy's back, running her hand over the crevice between his two shoulder blades. "He's fast asleep now."

"Warming him up always brings him out of the terror. I suppose it's soothing."

"That makes sense. For me, Fatima said she had to turn all the lights on in the house. Apparently the bright light snapped me back to reality."

"So how did you get cured of your night terrors?"

"Fatima says they went away on their own. A few months before I turned twelve, they just faded."

"That's what we're hoping for with Simon. The doctor said most kids grow out of them. There's a chance that they've been brought on by stress over Mamm and Dat's deaths. Lately he seems to be reliving the night of the murders, and that part tears me up."

"It must be really hard on you. Although I know it's a form of sleepwalking, it's really scary to witness." Simon's rants in the hall upstairs had turned her inside out for a few tense moments.

"It's terrifying, all right." Adam sank forward until his chin rested on his fists. "Sometimes it takes me right back to last year. The grief at losing our parents, and the fear that Simon was lost to us, too." He rolled his head to the side to face her. "Sorry. I don't mean to burden you with—"

"It's no burden." She smoothed back Simon's hair, covering his perfect shell ear with her palm for one second. "If you haven't noticed, I've grown attached to your family. We argued the other night because I worry about Simon."

"I realize that now."

"And I'd like to know what happened that night. Maybe it's irrational, but if I piece the details of the puzzle together in my mind, I feel like I'll be better equipped to help Simon."

"Sometimes I feel the same way. But with every detail I learn, it makes things worse. It's an ugly picture of that night that forms in my mind."

So Remy wasn't the only one who had tried to picture the crime scene—as if, by working through the difficult pieces, she would reach a catharsis.

"I suppose my biggest question involves the police investigation. How could they just drop everything with a killer on the loose?"

Adam rubbed his eyes and straightened. "The investigation is still ongoing. I've known Hank Hallinan all my life, and he's not one to let the ball drop, even if the media makes it look that way. He and his deputies followed every lead. They talked up everyone in Halfway, trying to find out who would want to hurt our parents. In the end, they had only a boot print in the mud. A man's boot. A big foot, like size ten or eleven." Adam shook his head. "It's not much to go on."

"Still . . . there had to be something else, some other evidence to pursue." Remy had seen many crime shows in which perpetrators were found through computer scans of fingerprints, hair, or skin samples left at the scene. It seemed to her there had to be other leads to be investigated.

"Simon was the only witness, and he was scared into silence."

But now he's remembering things . . . a bald head, something about a tattoo or birthmark shaped like Florida. It was vital to notify the sheriff about Simon's newfound memories as soon as the snow cleared, but for now, Remy didn't broach the topic, knowing it would only reignite their previous argument.

Adam rubbed his chin, his dark eyes full of rue. "The gunman used a .32-caliber handgun. An automatic. The police did find shell casings at the scene."

"But they didn't find the gun." Remy knew that if they found a suspect with a weapon, a crime lab could match the gun to the bullets used. At least that was a possibility down the road.

"Apparently Dat was shot on the lane, almost behind the buggy. Mamm was sitting in the front of the buggy, Simon huddled under her legs but . . . you probably read about that."

"I did." The thought of Simon hiding beneath his dead mother made Remy shiver despite the warmth from the stove. "So . . . there were no fingerprints, and the weapon was never found. Though some people speculated that Simon had used the family gun."

"A rifle."

She shook her head. "People can be so vicious."

"That, and they just wanted answers. You can't blame them for that."

"Actually, I could." Remy adjusted the quilt over Simon, thinking that someone needed to look out for this kid. "He was traumatized, scared silent. And people had the nerve to accuse him of something so . . . so heinous?"

Adam took a deep breath, his gaze on the glowing stove. "I can't worry about what the outside world thinks. And fortunately, Simon was protected from most of the rumors."

"Was there anything that didn't make it into the news reports? Anything unusual at the crime scene?"

"No." He frowned down at the floor, then lifted his gaze. "Actually, yes, though they weren't sure it was part of the crime scene at first. But when the sheriff and his deputies were searching the nearby fields, they found the carcass of a ring-necked pheasant. A fresh kill, apparently. They found that the bullet in the pheasant matched the gun that shot my parents."

"Really? Do you use a .32-caliber weapon to shoot a pheasant?"

"No. Never. Hunters use shotguns. The pheasant was found on King land, and no one ever hunts here. Dat saw the farm as a sanctuary for animals, a safe haven for living things. We eat meat and dairy, but no animal is slaughtered on King land."

"I'd say that's a telling piece of evidence." Although she wasn't sure exactly what it might prove.

"It really rattled Jonah and me. It was like a symbol of broken peace."

Remy nodded. Although she had no idea what a ring-necked pheasant looked like, the symbolism was upsetting.

"So . . . the police have no official suspects? No more leads to follow?"

"I'm not a part of the investigation." Adam shifted in the chair. "Remember, Plain folk cooperate with law enforcement, but we don't seek revenge or justice."

"Between you and me, do you think the police are right about it being a random crime? A hate crime perpetrated by someone passing through?"

His hands lifted in a gesture of surrender. "I don't know what would make someone kill, and I don't want to know. The bishop has told us not to dwell on the murders. I try not to, but a part of me dies every time I think of how I must have disappointed my parents."

"But you came back," she pointed out. "You liquidated years of your life. You gave up a successful carpentry business to come home and take care of your family."

"Ya, but I didn't get back in time." His eyes burned black with despair. "My parents never knew their oldest son would return to the Plain life."

"You're beating yourself up," Remy said. "You couldn't have known...no one could have predicted what happened to your parents."

"But if I'd been here, maybe it wouldn't have happened at all. When they were late coming home, I could have ridden out to find them—"

"Adam, don't do this," she interrupted. "You couldn't save them. If I've learned anything these past few days, it's that God's will is unexplainable. We need to accept the things He hands down, even if it hurts."

He squinted at her as if trying to decipher a code. "That is what the Amish believe. How do you know that?"

"I've been talking with Mary and Sadie. And I listen."

"You are a good listener." He leaned toward her, the room suddenly warm and intimate around them. "I remember a train ride when I talked and talked, and you listened."

She thought of their first encounter on that train. So many obstacles had been encountered since that day, and here they were, both wiser from the experience. "After we met on the train, after I learned the details of what happened to your parents, I was overwhelmed. There I was, feeling sorry for myself for returning home a failure, while your circumstances were a thousand times worse."

"You can't really compare lives that way."

"But sometimes we need a dose of reality to jolt us out of self-absorption." She turned away from the sleeping boy so that she faced Adam. "Maybe I shouldn't tell you. It might sound weird and obsessive, but I became consumed with your story for a while. I read everything I could find about it, as if I could vicariously help you wade through the heartbreak."

"That was kind of you." His brown eyes captured hers. They were knee to knee, face-to-face; she wondered what it would take for him to kiss her.

Just a few inches closer, she thought, wishing that he could read her heart.

"But you did help, more than you know. Did you know you were the only person I could really talk to in the past year?"

She swallowed, her heart beating strong for him. "Really?"

"Ya. I thought you were an angel. Sent from God."

She smiled up at him. "And now what do you think?"

"You're no angel." His lips spread in a grin as he took her hands in his. "You, Remy McCallister, are a real woman. Flesh and bones." His touch warmed her, and cradled in his large, strong hands her own hands felt tiny and delicate.

"You're a real woman, and I thank God for bringing you to me."

A tiny gasp escaped her throat as he tilted his face toward her and their mouths came together. The kiss was wide and white as the snowy fields beyond the window. Huge and expansive, the kiss opened up her world like a camera lens clicking open.

He still smelled of wood smoke and soap, a scent becoming familiar to Remy as she squeezed his big hands, wanting even more. How she longed to rise and press against him, their bodies aligned in that perfect fit of man and woman.

But even as she wanted more, she became aware of Simon snoring softly behind them. They were not alone. And they were in the wide-open kitchen of his house.

No, this would only be a taste.

But as their lips separated and Remy waited for her heartbeat to slow, she was struck by how simple it could be: two people, falling in love, wanting each other, dazzled by the first taste.

Love was truly a beautiful thing.

And this was only the beginning.

THIRTY-FOUR

*A*dam leaned back in the chair, trying to put a safe space between them before his heart, mind, and body raced too far ahead of good sense.

Such a kiss.

He'd never known a kiss that could turn a person inside out even as it healed. That kiss—like manna for the hungry, sweet spring water on a thirsty tongue—it was amazing.

He took a deep breath, trying to recover, and she turned away shyly, tending to Simon, who was still fast asleep. He expected his heartbeat to slow, but his pulse only quickened as his mind raced ahead. The sight of her leaning over Simon, soothing the child, was suddenly a picture of all their tomorrows. He saw her tending a baby—their child—with all the instinct and love of a mother.

He closed his eyes to clear his head, but the images came at him quick as the white lines down the center of a road.

Remy stretched out beside him in their marriage bed, her long curls gleaming over her supple ivory skin.

Remy astride a horse, her skirts flapping as she galloped ahead.

Remy with child, her small hands rubbing her round belly.

Remy seated at his right hand, passing a platter around their dinner table.

He could see her here, living on this farm as his wife.

He leaned back in the chair, counting the familiar points of the dark kitchen. The potbellied stove. The window facing the paddocks. The cabinets that were built by his grandfather.

His palm pressed the ancient grain of the oak table, where countless meals and meetings had taken place. This old slab of wood had supported the elbows of his family members through laughter and tears, joy and grief. He could see Mamm sitting in her spot at Dat's right hand, showing Mary how to even out her stitches on a quilt. Dat sat there, at the head of the table, the first one to start talking every morning at breakfast.

Adam had inherited Dat's place at the head of the table. Was there any way on God's good earth that Remy could find a place beside him?

He reached for hope. The fact that Remy kept coming back was no accident; God was at work in his life.

"So . . ." She turned back to him, her lips still swollen from their kiss. "Sadie says you're the man to talk to about becoming Amish, since you're baptized and everything."

"What do you mean? That you're curious?"

"More than curious. I've been feeling at odds with God . . . sort of drifting. Honestly, I haven't been a member of a church since I was a little kid, but I'm searching now."

"A seeker?"

"That was what Sadie called me, and I sort of like the sound of that."

"Well, sorry to disappoint you, but most seekers do not become Amish."

"Oh. Why not?"

He smiled. "Too much work?"

"I'm not afraid of work."

He'd seen that. "In the end, I don't think they're willing to give up their personal freedoms to follow the Ordnung."

"That sounds like more of a challenge, but I don't scare easily."

He smiled at the way Remy wiggled bits of light into the dark cracks. They talked for a while about the Amish faith. Remy already knew some history. She had learned about their beginnings in Europe and their belief in adult baptism, but she had some questions about the structure of their Order.

Adam tried to answer her questions. "If you're interested you should talk to the bishop sometime, or Preacher Dave. They could answer your questions better."

"Would you come with me?" she asked.

"Ya, sure. Just as long as you know that joining the Amish, getting baptized, isn't something to take lightly. It's the biggest decision of a person's life. And you haven't even been around Amish much. A few weeks with one family is nothing."

"We'll see," she said, hiding a yawn.

"It's late." Adam rose. "We'd better get some sleep."

Remy took the lantern from the table. "I'll take the light. That one's a bit too much for me to carry."

"I got him." With ease Adam lifted his little brother into his arms and headed up the stairs. Simon's bare feet dangled, but he burrowed his head against Adam's chest.

Following the glow of Remy's lantern, Adam felt that sense of rightness once again. If he followed her up the stairs every night with a child in his arms, that would be a good life. A very good life.

Over the next few days snow fell continually, piling on layers of powder that made every nook and cranny on the farm seem clean and new. God's hand over everything.

Adam felt cleansed, too, washed white as snow by the grace of the Father. Something about Remy chipped away at his bad temper, warming his heart with the light in those moss green eyes. And if the milk truck couldn't get through, there was no way a city girl like Remy would be able to drive these country roads. Who could argue with God's hand through a blizzard? For now, Remy belonged here, and he no longer felt guilty about the joy he felt in her company.

Now, in search of Gabe, Adam moved through the shoveled lane of snow between the house and barn. A few yards from the barn he spotted Gabe and Simon in the paddock. Simon was walking Shadow, his favorite horse, in the area of mashed-down snow, while Gabe sat on a hard ridge of snow by the fence, giving him a few pointers.

Adam reached up onto a snowbank, gathered a mound of fresh snow, and packed it between his gloved hands.

The perfect snowball.

He launched it at Gabe—and struck! A patch of white snow clung to his black pants, just above the knee.

"Hey!" Gabe swiped at the spot, his narrowed eyes searching the perimeters before they landed on Adam. "You!"

Simon held back a grin as he kept his horse steady. "Don't hit Shadow!"

"Don't worry, my aim isn't that bad." Adam ran one glove over the packed bank of snow. "We need you at the house, Gabe. Mammi wants to go over the costs for bathroom renovations and adding to the herd."

Gabe waved him off. "I've got no head for numbers. And you know how I feel about those changes."

Striding toward the paddock, Adam knew his brother didn't want changes to the farm procedures or the house. Gabe said it was all in the name of loyalty to Dat, who believed that milking the cows by hand helped to maintain their way of life, with its slower pace and simpler ways.

And Adam respected his father's decisions, but he also knew that Dat would want the farm to survive. That meant some modernization in the cowshed. Their current methods of milking did not allow them to sell fluid milk, and that limited their earning power and profits. Based on the numbers Adam had gone over with his grandmother, expansion of their cow herd with the addition of milking machines could triple their profit, which was now marginal at times.

Add to that the fact that a machine could milk a cow in five minutes, while the process took fifteen to twenty minutes by hand. Adam was convinced that this would be better for the entire family.

"Come on, Gabe. We need your help with this. You know the cow herd best." He also needed Gabe on board, and he believed that if his brother heard the details, he would see the logic in making the changes permitted in their district.

"Gabe?" Adam rounded the snow bank and faced the paddock, just as a white missile shot toward him. "Ach!" At the last minute he spun, and the snowball hit him squarely in the back.

"Oh, come on." Gabe faced him, hands on his hips. "That couldn't have hurt."

"No, but you wounded my pride. Are you coming?"

"Ya, sure." Gabe started toward the shoveled lane. "Just as soon as I give you this." He lunged for a pile of snow and paddled frantically, sending snow spraying toward Adam.

"Denki, brother!" Adam raced away, circling behind Simon before he ducked behind the cover of the snow bank. "Kumm, before

Mammi loses patience. And no fair smuggling snowballs into the house."

As Adam headed toward the house, the sound of laughter floated toward him, muted by trees and snow flurries. On the other side of the bare trees the women and children stood in clusters on the frozen pond, their dark shapes recognizable against the brilliant white snowscape.

Mary skated slowly beside Samuel, who took small heavy steps on the ice. Sadie chased after Leah, while Susie and Ruthie practiced pulling each other along.

Sadie tripped and went down, her body sliding a few feet. Her laughter resounded through the trees as she stood up and dusted herself off.

And then there was Remy, skating carefully on the bumpy ice. Her arms were spread wide for balance, reminding him of a fledgling bird testing its wings.

From a distance, you would never know she wasn't Amish. In her borrowed clothes, her coat, dress, bonnet, and boots, she looked every inch an Amish beauty.

But being Amish was more than a manner of dress.

For Adam, it was about an inner light. Faith. Love. Resilience. But at its core, it was a flame of steadfast peace . . . something he saw now every time he looked at her.

When had it happened? When had her scattered energy given way to the solid glow of Amish peace?

He couldn't say. But at some point over the past few days she had changed, a gradual shift, a subtle transformation.

It only steeled his conviction to move ahead with changes on the farm.

Gabe would come to see the light; change could be such a good thing.

THIRTY-FIVE

"Just rock the needle, Remy." Mary's lips were pressed into a straight line of concern as she watched Remy work the small needle through the fabric spread out on the kitchen table. "I think you're working too hard. I can tell by the way you're biting your lower lip."

Remy's fingers paused as she blew a breath out through billowed cheeks. "Reading my tension, are you? I'm just trying to keep up. You guys have stitched five or six lines for my one."

"It's not about speed," Sadie said. "There's no prize for the person who finishes first."

"I know, but I don't want to be so obviously bad at this."

"Because you're learning?" Mary's brows rose. "Give yourself a chance, and find the patience in your heart. This is not one of those things you can rush along like a fast car in the Englisher world. It takes time, and that's a good thing."

Moving her needle at a slower pace, Remy realized she hadn't even thought of her real life—"the Englisher world," as Mary had just reminded her—for days. How many days had it been since she arrived Wednesday night? Counting back, she realized this was day four—Saturday. Four days and she had fallen into the patterns of the King household with an ease that surprised her.

Earlier in the week, she had been waiting to play a round of checkers with Leah and Sadie when Ruthie remarked about Remy's hair.

"It's so thick and wild, like a horse's tail," Ruthie observed.

Remy had answered with a wobbly smile. "Thanks . . . I guess."

When Ruthie asked if she might comb it, Remy consented, and the younger girl had parted Remy's hair down the center and twisted it back from her face at the temples in the way that the Lancaster County Amish girls wore their hair.

"You're going to need to borrow a bonnet when you go out." With skilled fingers, Ruthie pinned her hair at the back of her head. "It's far too cold to be out there long without something on your head."

"I'd appreciate that. Do I get to wear one of the white bonnets underneath?"

"You mean a prayer kapp?" Ruthie twisted around to face Remy. "It will bring you closer to God when you pray. He'll hear your prayers."

The notion had charmed Remy as she imagined prayers floating from the crisp white organdy bonnets, straight to heaven. "Would I be allowed to wear one? I don't want to step on anyone's toes."

"There's no rule against fancy folk wearing it," Leah chimed in, jumping two of Sadie's checkers.

"Oops!" Sadie squinted at the board. "I didn't see that coming." She told Ruthie where to find an extra kapp, and within minutes Ruthie was pinning it onto Remy's red hair.

Dressed in the prayer kapp, the vivid purple dress, and a white apron, Remy felt a strong sense of belonging here on the Kings' farm. She fit in. And when she occasionally caught her reflection in a shiny window, she wondered at the new Remy, a woman so unlike the shell of a person who'd arrived here last Wednesday.

She had begun to awaken before dawn, in time to help with the milking. She and Mary had worked out an efficient assembly line so that they could make eighteen peanut butter and jelly sandwiches in a snap. She had figured out that evening was the best time to wash up in the house's only tub on the mud porch. And every night, she had lain awake in bed to listen for Simon, who inevitably padded down the wood floor of the hall, lost in his subconscious need to escape from the killer who had taken his parents' lives.

As head of the household, Adam was a fine supervisor, and he had helped her move toward tasks that utilized her strengths, much as any corporate manager might do. He had asked her to come along to help him check the fences, and she had cherished the time spent alone with him. She had also enjoyed riding a horse in the snow, using muscles she forgot she owned. One day he had surprised everyone by enlisting help in moving the sewing room downstairs. They cleared out the room that would become an upstairs bathroom, just as soon as the snow cleared long enough to get plumbers and fixtures onto the property. Remy believed in him as a leader, and that wasn't just because he'd chosen her to ride the fences.

Of course, she still shoveled the muck with Sadie, who had taught her all the words to "Amazing Grace." When Simon learned that she used to ride, he took her under his wing and taught her how to groom horses, a task she'd always been spared during her riding years, when all those things had been taken care of for her. She jumped into recipes with Mary, dried the dishes after every meal, and helped make beds in the morning. In the evenings she enjoyed reading to the little ones, playing games with Simon, Ruthie, and Susie, and discussing aspects of zoology and astronomy with Leah.

And then there was the quilting . . . a challenging skill for Remy.

Just when she thought she was getting the hang of it, she would pull her stitches too tight or run them crooked. But whenever she became discouraged, Mary or Sadie would show her a new trick that helped.

And no matter how uneven her stitches, Remy wouldn't dream of leaving the quilting table.

Quilting spoke to that part of her that longed to have a home, the only child, who was stranded when her mother died.

Quilting made her feel like part of the King sisterhood, part of the family.

Now, as she pushed her needle through the square of aquamarine fabric at the corner of the Diamond in the Square quilt, she thought about the finished product. One day, someone would tuck this quilt around them for warmth, and their fingers would graze the stitches she had added.

Her eyes misted over at the thought of being part of something bigger than herself. Part of a real family.

"When do you think this quilt will be finished?" Remy asked as she poked her needle into the turquoise cloth along the line Mary had marked for her.

"You want to be finished already?" Mary clucked her tongue. "Rushing, always rushing, when the joy isn't in the finished quilt. It's in the stitching."

"What's that proverb?" Sadie worked on a swath of purple along the border. "Life is not about surviving the storm. It's about enjoying the rain."

"Remy, hold on, you're poking again." Mary touched her wrist. "Rock the needle."

"Rock it. I am *so* going to rock it." Remy clasped the needle in her fingers and wiggled it the way Mary had, being careful to catch the layers of fabric and backing. "I'm rocking the stitch. Rocking the rain."

The girls laughed.

"It's called rocking the needle," Ruthie said.

"Whatever. Just call me Rockin' Remy."

"Saturday night, and me in my nightcap." Sadie plunked a white cotton cap on her head and sat on the end of her bed. "This is not my usual Saturday routine."

Yawning, Remy turned down the quilt of her bed. "After everything we did today, I would think you'd fall into bed. Or do you want to squeeze in one more hour mucking the stables?"

"Saturday night is the time you meet your beau when you're in rumspringa," Susie explained as she hung a gown on a hook. "Every Saturday Sadie goes to meet her Englisher boyfriend, and sometimes they sing very loud songs in restaurants." She leaped across the cold floor as if she were landing on stones across a river, then pounced on her bed. "But don't tell Adam."

Remy nodded, having covered this territory before with the younger girls. They seemed alternately intrigued and horrified that Sadie was interested in a boy from the outside.

"No one is going anywhere in this snow." Ruthie pulled the quilt up to her chin and squirmed under the covers. "I'm happy for the snow, even if it did cancel school."

"And my job at the hotel. And Saturday." Sadie turned toward the window of the long, narrow bedroom. "I wonder what Frank is doing now. Having a good time out in Lancaster, I suppose."

"You don't know that." Remy sat up in bed, hugging her knees. "Honestly? I think Saturday night is overrated. And I'm happy to be snowed in with you guys."

Snowed in for four days with no weather break in sight. It had stopped snowing a few times, but the freezing temperatures remained. And Adam had explained that the county and state did not have the machinery to clear these farm roads.

There was no telling when she would be able to make it home safely, which was more than fine by Remy.

Sadie got up to turn off the light, but paused beside the gas lamp.

Leah lowered her book. "Do you have to turn it off now? Just let me finish this chapter."

"Fine, but don't forget to say your prayers. You, too, Susie."

"I always say my prayers." Innocence chimed in Susie's voice, a clear, solid faith. "Talking to God makes me end each day with a smile."

Talking to God . . .

How long had it been since Remy had allowed herself an open conversation with God? She sighed as she grabbed the pillow and nestled in. Oh, there'd been some prayer, like the plea for help the other night when her car was spinning out of control. But that was sort of a selfish thing. Like a baby who simply wants her needs answered.

Since her mother's death, God had seemed out of reach, as if He lived in the magnificent stone and glass churches, where she just didn't have time to visit. So many times, when she felt lost and alone, when she was so desperate for a home, she had driven back to the old house in Philadelphia, just to sit outside and try to recapture memories.

She had been a lost soul, lonely and wounded inside. She had pushed herself to stop looking for a real connection and accept her loneliness, her disenfranchisement, as a part of growing up.

She was trying to survive the storm, without a thought of enjoying the rain, as Sadie had so wisely said.

And then . . . then she met Adam, and his tragic circumstances and loving family cracked open a world she didn't know existed, a world where she saw evidence of a benevolent creator every single day.

In the procession of children and adults headed out to the barn for morning milking.

In the hands that kneaded dough to feed a family of eleven.

In Sadie's creamy smooth voice and Simon's gentle touch on a horse's withers.

In heads bent over a colorful quilt in progress.

Here, God surrounded her in whimsical snowflakes. His bold hand painted snow-covered rooftops, meadows, and hills, and his gentle love had begun to heal her heart.

So gently . . . she didn't even realize it was happening until now.

Her eyes misted and her heart twisted in her chest at the realization that God was in her life now.

And now that she had found Him, she made a solemn promise to herself that she would never let Him go.

THIRTY-SIX

*R*emy rolled over in bed and stared out at the purple sky of another snowy night. Something had awakened her. Simon?

She was listening carefully for sounds of his footsteps when a bright round beam of light hit the girls' bedroom window.

She sank down and pulled the covers to her chin.

Was it a sign from God?

The light illuminated ice forms at the edges of the window. Then, it moved to the side and dropped off.

Aliens?

Really, who would be outside the farmhouse in the middle of a snowstorm?

"Hey, you guys?" she whispered. "Did anybody see that?"

The only sounds were the silky breathing of deep sleep.

Remy climbed out of bed and edged toward the dark window. Now the light was off to the left side of the house, emanating from a spot on the lawn, a dark figure. A man.

Who could it be?

Her thoughts went to the worst-case scenario—to Simon, and his raw memories of the man who had taken the lives of Esther and Levi.

Stung by fear, she pushed away from the window and flew out the bedroom door. As soon as she turned left, she saw Mary standing at the hall window. A lantern sat on the floor beside her as she tugged on the window sash.

"There was a light at our window. . . ." Remy pressed a hand to her chest; she could feel her heart beating rapidly. "And a man outside. Do you know who it is?"

"It's Five. My beau." Mary could barely restrain her lopsided grin as she opened the window and blew at the ridge of snow that lined the sill. "Where are you?" Shielding her eyes from the beam of light, she peered out. "How did you ever get here?"

"A fella hikes miles through snow and ice and that's the welcome you have for him?"

"Did the cold affect your thinking? Because you went to the wrong window and nearly woke up half the house."

"Such a warm welcome, and me with my fingers turned to icicles. Maybe it wasn't just the wrong window I went to, but the wrong house . . ."

Mary covered her mouth to suppress a giggle. "That may be, but now that you're here you might as well put your horse in the barn. Meet us at the kitchen door and we'll get the stove going." Mary started to close the window, then paused to add: "And bring in some wood on the way."

Remy blinked as Mary closed the window. "How did he get here?"

"Oh, he'd climb many a mountain to get here. No snow or ice will keep him from coming round courtship night. Come on."

Mary grabbed the lantern and floated down the stairs ahead of Remy.

From the landing, Remy noticed light spilling from the kitchen. The lamp near the daybed was lit, and Adam was sprawled there, dozing with a book open on his lap.

"Adam?" Remy called, surprised to see from the wall clock that it wasn't even nine-thirty yet.

He opened one eye, his chest rising slowly. "I'm awake."

"Don't tell me. You figured you'd be one step ahead and have the potbellied stove going when Simon got down here tonight."

"Something like that." He shifted, darting a look toward Mary, who was busy at the stove. "What are you two doing up?"

"Mary's boyfriend is here."

"Ah, Five. That's right, it's Saturday. You could set a clock by that man."

Remy realized she was wearing a nightgown with socks—hardly charming. She sat down on a kitchen chair to minimize her fashion blunder. Mary wore her dress and apron, and her prayer kapp properly covered her restrained hair. Remy suspected that Mary had been expecting her beau.

The sound of pounding feet came from the mud porch, and Mary bounded out, fussing over the arrival of the frozen man.

Remy curled the sleeve of her flannel nightgown around one pinky. "Can I ask you something?"

Adam closed his book on the bookmark with a nod.

"You don't mind that Mary's boyfriend shows up late at night with a flashlight?"

Adam laughed. "That's the way we do it. Saturday night is date night. The fellow usually waits until the parents are asleep, then comes to the house and wakes his girl." He nodded toward the porch. "They'll visit till early in the morning. Some Sunday mornings you hear the clatter of hooves out on the road. That's the young men returning home."

"Really?" Remy was surprised that parents didn't give their teens curfews. Of course, Mary and Five were different, already in their twenties. "If Saturday is date night, why didn't Sadie ask her boyfriend to meet her here? She seemed disappointed that she wouldn't be able to see him."

"First, there's no way he could have made the trip, even from Halfway, if that's where he lives. Five's parents have a farm a few miles away. There's also the fact that he's an Englisher, and she'll probably never bring him here. It's too uncomfortable, with him not knowing the ways of Plain People."

"Am I uncomfortable to be around?"

"Not usually." He rose and leaned close to her. "But you were a little difficult in the beginning. Pushy and stubborn." He touched the tip of her nose, but ducked back as she swiped at him.

"I was not! Coming from the king of stubborn, you should know."

Just then a tall, lanky man appeared in the doorway, his blond hair slightly damp from the snow. Mary followed him in, brushing at his black felt hat.

"Adam . . ." Five nodded. "If I'd known you'd still be up, I would have waited another hour or so."

"Look what the wind blew in!" Adam clapped the young man on the back, knocking some snow to the floor. "Nice to see you, but I'm sorry you can't stay. Wouldn't want to wake the sleeping children in the house."

"Adam . . ." Mary put her hands on her hips. "You're not my keeper."

"He's just trying to be funny. Trying and failing," Five said with a grin.

"This is our friend Remy," Mary said, introducing them.

Shaking his hand, Remy could see why Mary had fallen for him, with his quick wit and crystalline blue eyes.

"I'm heating cocoa on the stove." Mary placed Five's coat and hat on a chair near the potbellied stove. "Why don't you go in and get things going in the fireplace? We can play Parcheesi, or Scrabble. Though Remy here has a wonderful vocabulary. She always wins."

"Then maybe we should play checkers." Five grinned, then ducked toward the porch. "Almost forgot—the wood."

Soon Adam and Five had flames crackling in the fireplace. Mary placed a blanket on the floor and they sat together picnic-style, sipping cocoa, joking, and playing Scrabble, despite Five's protests that Remy knew too many words. Five entertained them with the tale of his adventure getting here, joking that the snow was higher than his horse's withers, and that, at one point, he had to dig a tunnel so that they could pass through high drifts of snow.

"All for a Saturday night out," Adam said. "Sounds to me like too much work."

"Or are you just thinking that you should have had the same idea, Adam?" Mary picked tiles out of the box. "Maybe you could have dug a tunnel to Annie's house."

While Remy pretended to rearrange her tiles, she watched Adam for his reaction, looking for a hint of how he felt about this Amish girl named Annie. Although Mary had mentioned her before, Remy had completely forgotten about her, and now she felt a stab of jealousy over the possibility that he might love someone else.

By way of response, Adam mumbled something about needing vowels and plunked his tiles into the box to "scrabble."

While Mary took her turn, Remy tried to reel in her feelings. Yes, she was attracted to Adam. In getting to know him over the past few days she had observed that he had a heart of gold, good and kind, so genuine compared to any of the guys she'd ever dated.

But Mary had made it sound like he had a girlfriend, and he had not disputed it. A negative voice niggled at her conscience.

He's taken. He's Amish. You are not. End of story.

As the game went on, she snuck a glance at Adam, who was stretched out on one side, his head propped on one hand. She kept telling herself that she had fallen in love with his family. That was the crux of the matter. So if Adam wanted to marry this Annie person, it didn't mean that she couldn't still come visit everyone occasionally.

The more she told herself it was fine, the more it was not. Yes, she adored this family, but her moments spent playing friend or sister to the Kings paled in comparison to the role she had begun to play with Adam. When they worked side by side, they complemented each other so beautifully. Like yin and yang, salt and pepper, fork and spoon.

It scared her to think of the snow clearing. Would she simply pick up and drive away from this intrinsic sense of rightness she had found? She wanted to think that Adam wouldn't let her go. She wanted to hope that rules might be broken so that they could be together. . . . But without an idea of how this could all end happily, she pushed it to the back of her mind, a problem to be solved some other time.

"High score goes to Adam." Mary's brows rose as she tallied on the pad of paper. "You seemed to lose steam at the end, Remy."

"And how about my score?" Five leaned close to Mary, placing a hand on her shoulder. "I don't think I had any steam to lose. I never reached a boil."

A tender smile crossed Mary's face. "I don't think it's your game."

Remy turned away from them, wanting to afford the couple some space.

"I'm going to get some more wood," Adam said from behind

her. The resignation in his voice matched Remy's mood. It hurt to give Adam up, even if she had never truly had him.

While Remy picked up the Scrabble pieces, Mary and Five moved to the couch and started to set up the Password game. The couple spoke quietly in Pennsylvania Dutch, and though Remy respected their privacy she secretly longed to learn the language so that she could share quiet words with Adam in the first language he'd ever learned. Glancing up at the red embers in the fireplace, she realized she had it bad. Did every thought have to be about Adam?

"Okay." Adam's voice registered some surprise as he moved past Remy to the fire. "Looks like we've lost the other team."

Up on the sofa, the couple had dozed off, Mary's head nestled against Five's shoulder.

Adam moved the grate back and hoisted a log over the ashen red embers. As he worked the fire with a poker, Remy swallowed back a feeling of awkwardness. The softly lit room was closing around them, intimate and quiet.

They needed a safe topic . . . something that would not inflame either of them.

"I've noticed that Leah is a total bookworm," Remy said. "And she seems disappointed that this is her last year of school."

"Ya, Leah is quite the student." He sat back on his haunches, waiting for the log to catch. "The schoolhouse teaches up to eighth grade. After that, children work at home, a more practical education."

"But Leah is a scholar. Eighth grade barely scratches the surface for someone with her intellect. Isn't there a high school nearby?"

"That's not how it works in the Amish community." He closed the grate and sat on the quilt beside her, his elbows resting casually on his knees. "A high school education won't help you here. It's time for Leah to pick up some skills that will prepare her for real life. She needs to learn how to cook and sew and run a house."

"I know, but it's a shame that she can't pursue the things she loves. Her God-given talents."

"Here with her family, she can learn the things that really matter. Life skills. Humility. And an appreciation for God's creations." Commitment gleamed in his dark eyes. "It's my job to make sure she becomes a good Amish woman."

In another time and place Remy would have argued for higher education, but the Kings did just fine without high school. Jonah was the farming expert here. Gabe understood the Holsteins' habits and needs. Mary could feed a family of twelve almost single-handedly. Even Simon, at just nine, was becoming a horse whisperer, capable of grooming and managing the eight horses in the stable.

Besides, Remy recognized the responsibilities that weighed Adam down. This was his family. Young lives relied on him.

"Although I don't agree with all the rules of the Amish, I have to admit that I'm absolutely in love with the strong sense of family."

"Ya?" He swung his feet around so that they were both facing the fire, now dancing with flames. "Absolutely in love? Is that more or less than totally in love?"

She smacked his knee, attempting playfulness, though the physical interaction seemed to startle them both.

"I'm serious now. Your family is wonderful, and Sadie says most Amish families work together this way. No one complains about their chores and when we're sitting together at the table or working together in the barn, there's such a sense of . . . cohesiveness, I guess."

He nodded. "That was something I missed in the years I was away."

"It's a wonderful feeling. I wish I had even one sister or brother, someone to watch out for and get my back, a friend for life." She stretched out on her side, propped up on one elbow. The warmth of the fire, the security of having Adam close, the sleeping house around them . . . it all conspired to relax her.

"And you know what else I love, love, love?" she said. "How the Amish home is the center of everyone's lives. Every person in your family knows they belong here. This home—it promises warmth and love and security. Despite my father's material success, he never gave me a home like this, at least, not after Mom died. And all the money in the world doesn't match the wonderful home you have here." She sighed. "It doesn't even come close."

THIRTY-SEVEN

She was beautiful.

The long lashes of her eyes fluttering closed. The play of firelight on the contours of her face. The curve of her neck as she stretched out completely on the quilt and dozed off.

How natural it would feel to place his palm on her shoulder. He imagined raking back her hair, its silken copper gliding through his fingers. How he would delight in pressing his lips to hers for a small taste.

That was stone-cold crazy.

He knew that. Yet as he stretched out behind her—within inches of her slender body—he imagined leaning closer, closing the space, pressing his body to hers.

This had to be wrong. Was it temptation?

He closed his eyes and tried to think of a Bible passage to illuminate this moment, but the only thing that came to mind was Genesis 24:67: ". . . and he married Rebekah . . ."

Rebecca . . . When he'd learned that Rebecca was Remy's real name, he had looked it up in the Bible index, and there was that passage, like a message from God. "So she became his wife, and he loved her. . . ." Why wasn't her name something Englisher, like Heather or Muffy?

He took a deep breath, trying to breathe some sense into his tangled thoughts. The smell of wood smoke and the semisweet scent of lantern oil sobered him. From some of her recent questions, hope had begun to beat in his chest like a wild bird.

Hope that she might want to stay.

If that were true, theirs would be a twisting, bumpy road. The bishop was not in the habit of baptizing outsiders to the faith. The district's reluctance to accept outsiders was based on experience. Seekers came and went, and Adam had never known anyone from the outside to stay. Although Englishers sometimes enjoyed "simplifying" their lives, most did not understand the daily workload and religious commitment of being Amish. People got nervous when they learned that baptism meant they would be Amish forever.

There were many obstacles to their future together. Huge mountains in their way. But the problems scattered like dust in the wind whenever she was near.

Creaking floorboards overhead interrupted his thoughts, alerting him that someone was coming.

He sat up on the quilt in time to see movement on the staircase.

Down came Simon, his eyes round and glassy, his hands splayed at his shoulders, as if in surrender.

"He is coming!" he cried. "He is coming after us, Mamm!"

Adam met him at the bottom of the stairs, but the boy stared beyond him, as if the devil lurked over Adam's shoulder. "Oh, I have to hide!"

"Who is coming? Who is it?" Adam followed his brother over to the outstretched quilt, where Remy was sitting up, rubbing her eyes.

From the sofa, Five called softly to the boy. "Hello, Simon. What's wrong?"

Simon paced in a wide circle, his agitation mounting. "What if he finds me? I'm sorry, Mamm, but I must hide."

Then, to Adam's amazement, his little brother dove toward Mary.

Mary let out a yelp as he pushed his way under her knees. "Simon . . . oh, liewe . . ." She pulled her gown aside, but he burrowed deeper under the dark cloth.

"He's coming!" Simon wailed. "I can't let him see me!"

"But you're safe here," Mary told him. "No one is going to hurt you."

Simon's shrill cry was barely muffled by Mary's skirts. "I can't let him see me. If he finds me, he will shoot me dead, too!"

The noise brought Sadie hurrying down the stairs. "Is he okay?"

"He'll be fine." Adam held up his arms for her to stop. "But the memory is very sharp for him."

Remy knelt on the floor by the sofa, where Simon still crouched, huddled under Mary's knees with only his head poking out on the other side.

"Simon, what did the man look like? Did you recognize him?"

"No. He wasn't a bear, but I don't know who he was."

"But you saw his shiny head, right? His bald head?"

"Because I was up in the buggy, when he . . . when he came back the second time. He pushed Mamm, and I stayed very still, the way she told me to. But after he left, I peeked out. His hat must have been knocked off, because his bald head was shiny. A balding head with a red mark on it. I will never forget it. The shape reminded me of a gun. But now I know my states. It's like the state of Florida. Ms. Emma taught us geography in school, and I like Florida because they have warm weather and palm trees there."

The room was silent as no one wanted to cut him off. Such a long string of words, maybe the most Simon had spoken since the murders. And loaded with information.

"A red mark, like a map of Florida on his head." Sadie winced as she crossed her arms over her nightgown.

"Was there anything else?" Remy asked. "Anything else that you saw? Do you remember what kind of clothes he was wearing?"

"Dark stuff. And he was big and round like a bear." Simon crawled out from under Mary's legs, but hugged her dress close. "And his pants. The man had something fancy on his pants. A stripe down the side. A black stripe."

"A cop?" Remy guessed.

"There, there." Mary patted her brother's back as the room grew silent.

No one wanted to believe it could be a police officer. Adam had always trusted the police, but now he recalled Simon's fear of cops after the incident. Was it just because the police came soon after the murders, or was a cop involved in the killing?

Simon popped up onto the couch and Mary rocked him in her arms, whispering endearments in Pennsylvania Dutch. In moments like this, she reminded Adam of their mamm.

Remy straightened and crossed the room to join Sadie and him. "Do you think the killer was a cop?"

"A bald cop," Sadie corrected.

"Good thing Sheriff Hallinan has a full head of hair." Adam watched his brother as he spoke, relieved to see Simon calming down. "I've always liked Hank."

"And his deputies?" Curiosity lit Remy's green eyes.

Sadie shrugged. "One is a woman, and she's not bald."

Adam ran through their faces in his mind. "The other deputy

is a young man just back from Iraq. Blaine Collins. He's got a buzz cut, but plenty of hair."

"So at least it's not someone from the Halfway police." Remy seemed to cling to every detail. "But there are probably county and state police who patrol this area, right?"

"Right." Adam frowned. "But it's not our place to stand here and play crime solvers. It's late. Let's get some sleep."

As Adam went to douse the fire, Mary pointed out that Five would need to stay, too. Normally on a Saturday night a beau was permitted to stay until the early hours of morning, when he would return home. But with the heavy snowfall outside, it was best for Five to stay till sunrise.

"I would send him to the Doddy house, but I don't want to disturb Mammi." Adam raked back his hair. "There's the daybed in the kitchen. Or he can bunk in the boys' room upstairs."

Mary's smile brought genuine delight to her eyes, and Adam wanted to kick himself for not insisting she marry her beau last fall. His sister was obviously in love with Five, and they would make a good couple, but Mary was afraid to leave the family right now.

"Let's get you up to bed again." Adam lifted Simon into his arms, touched when the arms and legs of his precious cargo flopped down in total release. With a prayer that God would watch over this family always, he headed up the stairs.

Light spilled onto the desk, buttery light that illuminated the plans he'd been sketching. Once the snow cleared, it wouldn't take long to transform the upstairs sewing room into a bathroom.

Once the snow cleared . . .

It would be any day now. He and Jonah had discussed the state of the roads, in anticipation of the milk truck getting through. Maybe Wednesday or Thursday. Although it would be a while until they could travel by carriage, the sleigh would work on local roads, once the snow was packed down.

From the rocker in the corner, Simon lowered his book. "Can I see?" He hopped out of the chair and leaned close.

"It's for the upstairs bathroom. I already measured it, so now the floor plan will give us an idea of exactly how much wood and flooring we need." Simon nodded and returned to his book.

Adam sketched in the shower stall, glad for the relative quiet. It was a typical Monday evening, if you didn't count Remy in the kitchen or the four-foot snow drifts outside their window. Over on the sofa, Gabriel read an old edition of *The Budget,* while Leah turned the page of her book. Jonah sat at the portable table mulling over a huge jigsaw puzzle. Out on the mud porch, Mary was supervising baths for the little ones. Occasional conversation drifted in from the kitchen, where the rest of the girls were baking a birthday cake for Sadie.

Turning eighteen on Wednesday. The prospect of his sister as an adult was daunting, especially knowing the way she'd been leaning lately.

Trust God, he told himself. Sadie had to find her own way to Him, much as it pained Adam.

Picking up the kitchen conversation, he listened as the girls explained something for Remy.

"When you want to be baptized, you tell the bishop and then start going for classes," Ruthie said. "Eight or nine classes."

"But it's really serious," Susie said gravely. "They keep asking you if you're serious, and you have to say 'I am a seeker desiring to be part of this church of God.'"

"Do you have to be born Amish to join the church?"

His pencil froze at Remy's question.

"You don't have to be Amish," Sadie explained. "But I don't think I've ever known our bishop to baptize an Englisher."

"Really? You'd think more people would join."

"Lots of Frank's friends tell me they would love to streamline their lives and become Amish. Put their stress behind them. But most people don't do much more than talk about it. When they try to change, they usually miss the freedom and nice things that Englishers have. I think the freedom they're looking for, that's something that happens on the inside. You can't escape from life just by putting on a prayer kapp and giving up your car."

Words of wisdom from his sister Sadie. At least she understood the bigger picture.

Not that Remy hadn't gotten a taste of Amish life.

Nearly a week had passed since that first day when she came barreling into the cowshed wearing a nightgown and boots, eager to help. Since then Remy had always appeared fully dressed for morning milking, with her bubbly desire to help and learn.

She was one of the hardest-working Englishers he had ever met.

When the roads cleared, she would return to the city. And after that?

Trust in God, he reminded himself as he sketched the tub area. *Trust in God.*

THIRTY-EIGHT

"Look there. You can see the frog." Simon pointed to the triangle in the center of Shadow's hoof, pockets of V-shaped ridges that Remy had just cleaned. "When you see the frog, you know it's clean."

"I see the frog, but I don't hear him. Oh, wait. *Ribbet. Ribbet.*" Remy looked up at the giggling Simon. "Made you laugh. Can we put his hoof down now?" She was amazed that he got these horses to lift their hooves and keep them up, but the boy did it. He was a capable stable master, even at the age of nine.

"Yes, but you have to pick out each hoof, every day. Or it can hurt them."

"Got it." Simon's lessons on horse care were always filled with his thoughtfulness and concern for the horses. "Next hoof."

Simon held Shadow's other rear hoof so that Remy could pick mud and stones from the hollows. "How's Shadow doing with the other horses?"

"Better. I think she's making friends with Thunder."

"Isn't Thunder the lead horse? I thought Thunder was kind of mean."

"He's strict. But the other day I saw the two of them together in the paddock. They stood very close, head to head, and Thunder was nuzzling Shadow's mane." He brushed off the hoof with his glove and let the horse set it down. "Do you know what that means?"

"They're getting to know each other?"

He nodded, pleasure gleaming in his eyes. "They're friends now."

"That's terrific. And now that Shadow's in with the leader, the other horses will think she's way cool, right?"

He pulled off the gloves and moved to the horse's side to stroke its withers. "Things are going to be better for Shadow. Dat would be happy to know that."

"Maybe he knows. Maybe he can see us from heaven."

"I don't know, but that would be nice."

"I wanted to ask you . . . you know, the last few nights when you've had those night terrors, you talked about a man. In your mind, it's a man who did those terrible things. A man who killed your parents, not a bear."

Simon's lips curved. "Maybe I said that because it *was* a man."

"Not a bear?"

Simon squeezed his eyes shut. "I used to see a bear. I wasn't lying."

She shook her head. "Nobody's saying you were."

"But now I think it was a man in a puffy coat. A dark shape, all round and furry, like a bear."

"That makes sense."

"And after I kept talking about the bear, I believed it. You see, if a bear kills people, you can't get mad, because he's a bear. He kills for his food. It's called instinct."

Remy swallowed hard, touched by his logic. "That's right."

"But people aren't supposed to kill. It's not their instinct."

"And you convinced yourself it was a bear, because you just can't imagine why a person would do something so wrong."

When he nodded, tears dropped from his eyes.

"Oh, Simon, that makes a lot of sense." She closed her arms around him and hugged him close. "I understand what you were thinking, and you're right. People are not supposed to kill people."

A shout from the door broke the tender quiet of the moment. "Simon?" Adam called through the stables. "Are you there?"

"Over here." Remy rubbed the center of Simon's back briskly. "You are a very brave boy. Really. You're my hero."

"No." He stepped out of her arms and swiped at his eyes with his sleeve. "God is what makes you brave." Sniffing, he pressed one hand to his chest. "It's the little bit of God's strength inside you."

"I need you to saddle up Thunder." Adam's open coat flew behind him as he jogged down the aisle.

"What's wrong?" Simon was immediately alert.

"One of the cows didn't come in for the milking—Clementine. I'm going to ride out and see if I can find her."

Simon grabbed the tools they'd been using and headed down the aisle. "I'll get him ready. Is Gabe going with you?"

"He and Jonah are needed for the milking. I'll be fine."

Remy patted Shadow, then stepped back. "I'm going with you."

He shook his head. "It's going to be—"

"There isn't time to argue about it. I'm a skilled equestrian, and two sets of eyes are better than one."

He hitched back his hat and frowned. "Fine. But get yourself a bonnet and gloves. The sun's going down soon, and the temperature is dropping already."

It was a different land they crossed this time. As a clear periwinkle sky began to close overhead, the red ball of sun shot mad swirls of color along the horizon.

Brilliant pink angel-hair clouds swept across a deep purple background in a composition that brought tears to Remy's eyes. This land, these sparkling white hills and fields of pristine snow. God's breathtaking creation had always been here at her fingertips, and she'd had no idea.

"It's beautiful." She shot a glance at Adam, a lean cowboy in black, his broad-brimmed fedora tipped against the setting sun.

"It is. In the years I was away, I kept telling myself that I was exaggerating the impact of this place on me. But it is God's magnificent earth, and it does a man good to live close to it."

In that moment Remy felt such a swell of love for this man that she had to turn away, afraid he would see everything revealed on her face.

"It stopped snowing," she said, stating the obvious. This was the first time she'd seen the sun in more than a week, and it seemed to shine light on new possibilities even as it began to melt the snow that had bound them together all these days.

They rode in a splendid silence for a while. Urging her horse along, Remy considered the history of this land. How many generations had ridden the property's perimeters, searching for lost cows or breaks in the fences?

When they reached the back end of the property, there was still no sign of the missing Clementine, but Remy spotted lights beyond a distant slope.

"What's that little building over there?" She pointed to a rectangular building. Golden light gleamed from two windows, like two eyes in the twilight.

"The Muellers live there."

"Are we on their property?"

"They used to own all this property until Dat bought them out. He worked out a deal so that they could stay in their house and rent back from us."

"They're not farmers anymore?"

"I don't think they ever were. They're not Amish. Gina is Mammi's age, and she keeps to herself. Her son, Chris, does different jobs in Halfway. You might have seen him at the Halfway farmers market. He manages the market for Joseph Zook."

"Big guy, scruffy beard, but sort of meek?"

"That sounds like Chris."

As they headed around the east side of the farm's acreage, Adam removed a high-powered flashlight from his saddlebag. Its beam cast an eerie light over the sloping drifts. Darkness was closing in, and Remy worried about the missing animal. Where was she?

When the pond was in sight, Remy thought she heard a mewling sound. "Is that coming from back at the barn?" she asked.

Adam swung the beam of the light around. "Over there."

A dark spot moved in the snow, then it let out a moo. "Clementine."

They rode over to the stranded cow. Remy held the flashlight while Adam climbed off his horse and tried to figure out the problem.

"She's caught in the wire of the fence." With clippers from his bag, Adam started cutting wire and bending it back, away from the animal.

"How did she get herself tangled up in that?"

"They do it all the time. You'd be amazed. They find the holes in the fence. They fall in ditches. Not the most graceful creature on God's earth, are you, Clementine?"

Remy smiled. "Hey, give a poor cow a break. Everything's covered with snow out here."

In minutes Clementine was free and trotting toward the barn.

"See you back at the house, Clem," Adam called after her, and they laughed together.

"I'm glad she's safe," Remy said as Adam mounted Thunder.

Astride his horse, Adam reached over and squeezed Remy's hand. Through two pairs of gloves, she felt his warmth and held on for dear life.

There, under the diamond dots of winter stars, Remy knew she loved this man. Maybe that would be her burden to bear. Maybe it would be her secret to cherish in the cold, lonely nights ahead.

Still . . . he was here now, and she was learning to live in the moment.

"Let's go home," he said, and she urged her horse forward, toward the home of her heart.

THIRTY-NINE

Near noon on Thursday, a rumbling noise sent Mary and Remy hurrying to the front window.

"The milk truck." Mary held her hands aloft, her fingers still covered in flour. "Thank the Lord. The roads are clearing."

With a mixture of excitement and dread, Remy kept stirring the giant bowl of melted butter, cinnamon, and sugar in her arms as she watched the driver pull his rig over by the cowshed.

The roads were clearing.

The arrival of the milk truck meant that yesterday's and this morning's batches could go to the dairy. There would be no more waste. There would be renewed income for the family. That was the good news.

But the fact was that the roads clearing up would bring this dreamlike interlude to a sickening halt. Remy's insides churned at the thought of her inevitable departure. But then she took a deep breath and reminded herself that she had learned how to live for the moment, how to be in the moment, and she wasn't going to let worries about the future damage the current day.

But that night, something collapsed inside her when Adam announced that he'd be taking some of the family to the Friday farmers market in the morning.

"Everything is still covered with snow, but we can make the trip to Halfway in the sleigh."

That created a buzz of conversation over who would go along, what they'd bring to sell, and how cold the open sled would be.

Drinking her milk, hiding her face in the tall cup, Remy knew she would go to the market. She would see what she could learn about the condition of roads leading into Philadelphia.

If she tried, she could probably find a place to recharge her cell phone while they were at the market. She could call Herb to arrange a tow and a ride back to the city.

But before she made a move to leave, she would make sure the sheriff heard about Simon's recent recollections about the murders of Esther and Levi King. That might tick Adam off, but she could not leave here in good conscience without supporting Simon in that way.

On Friday morning as the sleigh crested over the rise in the road, the sight of Remy's abandoned car drew a flurry of interest.

"It looks sad and very lonely," Ruthie remarked as they approached the ditched auto, now just a listing fender covered by a massive lump of snow.

Remy glanced to the backseat of the sleigh, where Ruthie, Sadie, Leah, and Susie sat, all heads turned toward the stranded car.

From his seat in the front between Remy and Adam, Simon twisted around to watch as they passed the car, then sat back down. "It will be okay, I think." He patted Remy's arm. "Don't worry."

She forced herself to smile. How could she explain that her worry wasn't for her car or any of the facets of her life in the city, which now seemed flat and bland compared to the warm, animated days and peaceful nights with the Kings? She had grown attached to this loving family. She had fallen for the man sitting beside her, guiding the sleigh. Yes, she had fallen, big-time, and she didn't know what to do about it.

Still, the tingle of fresh, cold air and the merriment of a sled gliding into the town of Halfway on hard-packed snow lifted everyone's spirits—including Remy's. Since the parking lot at Zook's barn had been cleared, making it impossible for the sleigh to maneuver on wet pavement, they parked across the street in a field, alongside two similar vehicles.

While Adam and Simon unhitched the horse, Sadie and Remy supervised unloading their wares from the sleigh. They had brought a few colorful quilts, as well as half a dozen large plastic bins of baked goods produced during the snow days. There were loaves of fresh bread, cupcakes, and a huge variety of cookies—whoopie pies and peanut-butter, ranger, pinwheel, and flower-shaped spritz cookies, all delicious. Remy felt a personal joy in the baking she'd helped with. She couldn't help but smile as she strode into the Zook barn with an armload of plastic cookie bins.

Arms full, they filed into the marketplace, past the tables stacked with honey, lavender, jams, and shoofly pies. The market seemed warm and familiar to Remy, and she laughed at the twist of events. Who would have imagined that she would now be here in Amish attire, selling items, just weeks after her initial visit?

"Are you afraid to come here now?" Sadie asked as they set up their table. "The last time you were here, it all ended with your seizure."

"That seems like years ago . . . but it was just weeks." Remy set out the spritz cookies, perfect pointed flowers made from a cookie press. "You know, when I first realized I was snowbound, I worried about missing my medication. But I haven't felt this good in years. I think the hard work, regular meals, and sleep were good for me. I feel like a different person."

The vendor beside them was from a bird-watching organization, and Leah was immediately drawn to their books and calendars. The couple on duty introduced themselves as Nora and Jerry, and Leah immediately engaged them with a list of birds she had spotted in her own backyard.

"We see so many migratory birds on our farm." Leah flipped through one of their books, pausing to admire the vivid color photos on a poster. "One year, we had some red-winged blackbirds nesting in our fields."

"*Phoeniceus.*" Jerry flipped through a book. "They're in here somewhere."

"Dat wouldn't let anyone go near them until the nests were empty. He thought it was important to protect the birds."

"Sounds like your father was a very good man," Nora said with a smile.

"Oh, ya, he was."

When Susie called Leah over to help with a sale, Remy secretly purchased a small pair of binoculars designed for bird-watching, and swept them into her purse, an odd accessory to be holding now that she was wearing a borrowed forest green Amish dress and black apron. Still, she was glad to have cash with her, as the binoculars gave her an idea. She would purchase a small gift for each member of the family, a small token of her appreciation to pass on before she left.

As she slid behind the Kings' table to help with cookie sales, she began to think of gifts for the others. Susie would love some of those fleece-lined slippers; she was always hopping around to warm her feet in the house. Those heart-shaped cake pans would suit Mary, and for Adam . . .

Adam would be tough. Something special, but not embarrassingly sentimental.

She was mulling it over, packaging cookies in wax paper bags, when Adam and Simon finally made their way to the table. From the way Simon clung to Adam's coat, his face nearly buried against his brother, Remy sensed trouble.

"They want to take my picture!" Simon exclaimed, looking behind him.

"We ran into some more reporters." Adam's mood had soured, and no wonder. "They backed off for the moment, but I don't trust that they'll do the right thing for long." He shot a look over his shoulder. "I think I'm going to have to take Simon home."

"But I want to stay and help." Simon burrowed into his brother, his eyes pleading. "Please, let me stay with you."

It tore at Remy to see him that way.

"I know a way to escape all this." Sadie glanced over her shoulder, then nodded toward the lavender lady's table. "There's a staircase behind the wall over there. It leads to a hayloft where we can hide out for a while."

Adam put a hand on Simon's shoulder, considering. "Do you want to go to the loft?"

Simon looked up at Adam. "Will you come with me?"

"I need to stay here and supervise, but Sadie and Remy can keep you company."

"Okay."

Feeling protective of the boy, Remy took Simon's hand and scanned the crowd for media types. "What did these reporters look like?"

"Another television news crew. The woman's face was thick with paint. A thin lady with dark hair. I think her name was Mai Tonka. The cameraman, I didn't meet him, but he's lugging a big black camera."

"We'll keep Simon safe," Sadie promised. Then she led the way past the popcorn stand and around the corner.

The stairs were blocked by a chain with a sign in the middle that warned: NOT AN EXIT. STAFF ONLY. Simon ducked under the chain, but Sadie unhooked it for Remy and herself.

"I've been coming up here for years," Sadie confided to Remy. "It's been my hiding place when I need a few minutes to myself. I listen to my iPod, escape through the music."

"It's coming in handy now," Remy said, taking a look around.

The loft was tidy, swept clean. Not a strand of hay remained, although plastic milk crates were stacked in one corner, and a few hand-painted signs—advertising fresh summer produce, watermelons, juicy tomatoes, and no Sunday sales—leaned against the wall.

"But I wanted to work at the market." Disappointment weighed Simon's voice as he went to the edge of the loft and stared down at the maze of tables.

"Most people don't ever get the chance to see the whole market this way," Remy said, hoping to distract him. "Look at that. This is a bird's-eye view."

Simon's brows rose. "Like we're birds flying over it?"

"Exactly."

Sadie joined them, her gaze sweeping the panorama below. "It would be fun to be a bird, circling above everyone."

The three of them dropped to the floor of the loft, close enough to see below without being seen.

"Oh, and I have these." Remy removed the small binoculars from her shoulder bag. "I bought them as a gift for Leah, but she won't mind if we use them for a bit."

Simon held them up to his eyes and scanned the barn. "It makes you very close. I can see the writing on all the signs. Alfie Yoder is here, and he has snow on his boots. And Susie is packing cupcakes into a box. A very good sale."

As he spoke, Remy searched for the reporters, squinting every time she saw any couple walking together.

"Nancy is here today, but she doesn't have much on her table," Sadie observed.

"I see her." Remy liked Halfway's stalwart mayor. "And I recognize the lavender lady. She brought her little baby with her last time, too."

"Good memory," Sadie said. "Simon, why don't you put those glasses down and botch with me."

Remy suspected she was trying to distract him by playing one of the popular clapping games.

"Okay. You can use these." Simon handed Remy the binoculars and turned to face his sister.

As Sadie hummed "Pop Goes the Weasel" the two began clapping each other's hands, then alternately striking each other's legs.

With the help of the spyglasses, Remy got a closer view of passersby, but didn't see the reporters.

Had they left after Adam turned them down? Maybe he'd gotten angry enough to scare them off.

She leaned closer to the edge, looking at the people passing directly underneath. The lavender lady wore a rainbow print beret today as she paced to rock the baby strapped to her chest. A heavyset man in a blue uniform greeted her as he shifted from one foot to the other. Remy recognized the guard as Chris Mueller, the Kings' neighbor.

Chris looked different from up here. The top of his head was bald, which she hadn't realized before, but then he'd been wearing a hat.

She blinked. What was that mark on his head . . . nearly hidden by the tuft of hair combed over it?

She adjusted the focus on the glasses and sucked in a gasp.

A red birthmark . . . and it was shaped like the state of Florida.

FORTY

*T*he epiphany zapped her with all the ferocity of an electrical shock.

Chris Mueller was the killer . . . He had to be.

A balding head with its distinctively shaped birthmark. The uniform pants of a police officer. His burly build, like a bear.

He was the one.

And he stood just a few yards from them.

Remy rose and stepped back so abruptly the binoculars fell to the floor of the loft.

"What's wrong?" Sadie stopped clapping, attuned to Remy's panic.

"I . . . I have to go downstairs." Remy tripped over her words, trying to downplay the internal alarm that was beating a tattoo in her ears. She didn't want to scare Simon.

"Why?" Sadie frowned. "Are you okay?"

"Fine." Big lie, but she had to focus on Simon's safety right now. Granted, Mueller wouldn't act here, but if he detected the smallest hint that someone was on to him, he would surely slip away. She moved toward the stairs, then paused for one more glance below.

Priorities. She had to get word to the police . . . or a higher authority, if Mueller was part of the police.

Remy wasn't sure whom to trust. But Adam would know.

With a hand pressed to her chest, she peered down toward the Kings' table. Adam was engrossed in conversation with an older couple, the woman bedecked in cheetah print and baubles. An apparent quilt sale.

A sale she would have to interrupt.

"Stay here." Despite the concern on Sadie's face there was no time to explain now. "I need to do something, right away. But I'll be back. Just stay here."

The skirt of her dark green dress swirled around her legs as she spun and charged down the stairs, stopping short of the chain. Her fingers felt numb as she fumbled to unhook it and replace it.

Then she hurried into the marketplace, full-out running. She whipped around the corner and nearly ran head-on into Chris Mueller.

"Whoa." He stepped aside, nimble for his size.

"Oh . . . sorry." Remy felt sweat prickle the back of her neck, beneath her prayer kapp.

"You're in quite a hurry."

For an Amish girl. She knew that was what he was thinking, that the Amish didn't take to rushing around, but it didn't seem right to say the words.

Beady eyes glimmered in his meaty face as he stared at her.

Her pulse thundered under his scrutiny until she read the confusion there.

He doesn't recognize me. He's never seen me in Amish clothes and he can't place me.

"I was just trying to . . . to catch someone," she blurted out. A lame explanation. "Trying to catch up with my brother."

"Okay, then." His eyes didn't release her, but he was gesturing for her to move on. "Go."

Her hands balled into fists as she held herself back from running. Instead she strode quickly around the corner vendor to the Kings' table—where Adam now stood, blocking the table from a woman who was trying to show him something on an open pad of paper and a man with a hefty TV camera propped on his shoulder.

The news crew . . .

She froze. Approaching Adam right now was out of the question. The reporter would smell a story.

Remy turned down a different aisle, forced herself to think. Who could she turn to?

Faces of vendors, Amish and Englisher, loomed around her until one came into focus.

Nancy Briggs, the town mayor, was folding cartons at her muesli bar stand. Nancy would understand.

Remy hurried over. "Nancy, I need your help."

The older woman didn't look up from her work. "I'm telling you, snow makes people hungry. It's the hoarding mentality."

"It's not about that. I need Nancy the mayor."

Deep creases appeared in grooves at the edges of Nancy's eyes as she looked up. "Do I know you?"

"I'm Remy McCallister. We met before the big snow—only I wasn't dressed in Amish clothes then."

"You're the poor girl who collapsed here a few weeks back. What can I do you for, dearie?"

"I've been staying with the Kings through the snowstorm and . . . and Simon King has begun to remember things from last year, details from the night his parents were killed."

"You're not kidding?" Nancy pressed a flattened carton against the top of the table. "Let me have the facts."

With a look over her shoulder to be sure Chris Mueller was out of sight, Remy explained how she'd pieced together the details, how Simon's recollections added up to a profile that fit the Kings' neighbor. "I'm sure about this, and I'm afraid for Simon. This man is walking around, in a position of power—"

"We've got to talk to Hank about this."

"The sheriff?" Remy bit her lip. "I was worried about that. Does Chris Mueller work for him? Isn't he a deputy?"

"Chris? No. I know he likes to wear the hat and the gold badge and all, but he's just a hired security guard for events like these. Hank has two very capable deputies. Pristine records, both of them. And if they can't figure it out, they've got access to county and state resources. There's the crime lab where evidence is being stored . . . the whole ball of wax."

"Then I need to talk to Hank. Simon needs to talk to him. But we have to be discreet. I'm afraid of what Mueller might do if he knows we suspect him."

"Just take a deep breath and relax a minute while I close up shop. Chris isn't going anywhere unless he gets wind of trouble."

"I hope you're right." Remy pressed a hand to her chest and turned to glance up at the loft. If she squinted against the lights, she could make out the tops of two heads there—Simon and Sadie waiting safely.

"You know, Remy, I'm a bit flabbergasted that you've managed to piece this puzzle together in so little time while the rest of us have been banging our heads against a wall for the past year. I've known Hank Hallinan for years, and he's good people. He's been here round the clock since the snow started. Roped off Main Street so that people wouldn't walk in the way of snow removal equipment during the storm. What I'm saying is, Hank is about as good as it gets in the law enforcement community. How did you leapfrog ahead of him on this case?"

"I suppose the time was right." A line from the Bible came to mind, the one Adam had shown her about there being a time and a season for everything. "A time to scatter stones and a time to gather them." Remy believed the time had cóme to gather the pebbles strewn along the path to justice.

"I've been snowed in with the Kings. I was there to see Simon suffer some flashbacks of a sort, episodes that brought him back to the night it all happened." Remy took another breath in an attempt to steady her nerves. "In the meantime, I was searching for some answers. My father is Herb McCallister of the *Post,* and originally I came here to pursue the real story behind the murders."

"I see. It does sound like fortuitous timing all around. Hold on while I pack up. I'm taking you to Hank. We can pile into my Jeep."

"But your merchandise—the market just opened."

"I didn't run for mayor to sit on my duff and sell snack bars while someone needs help. I'm going to stay on this thing until we see some results. We're going to see this thing through. I made a pledge to this town, and I won't back down till this killer is off the streets."

FORTY-ONE

*A*dam had wasted twenty minutes arguing with the reporter, Mai Tonka, to leave his family alone.

And now this.

His stomach knotted painfully as he stood at the side of the quilt table, talking with Remy and Nancy.

Was Remy right? Could Chris Mueller, the Englisher neighbor down the road, have killed his parents?

It made him sick to think about it. He found it hard to believe anything bad about Chris, but when Remy lined up the facts, it made sense. Remy had logic on her side, and Nancy Briggs had the authority of age and the law.

Adam rubbed his chin, still not sure. "It's hard for me to believe. Chris and his mother, Gina, are our friends. Gina sold her land to my parents, and Chris is always making jokes about buying it back from us."

"Maybe there's something behind the jokes." With arms folded across her chest, Nancy Briggs was a force to be reckoned with.

"Maybe Chris resents losing the land to your family, or maybe this is all a mistake. But we've got to get this information to Hank, and I think he'll want to talk with Simon."

Would the bishop approve of Adam taking Simon to the sheriff?

When Adam had returned home last year, the bishop had advised him to steer clear of the police investigation. He was to answer questions, cooperate, then let it go. The Amish made a point of living separate and apart from the Englishers. They strove to live in this world, but not of it.

But in the process of remaining neutral, the Amish were not supposed to break the law or defy law enforcement. Even if the district leaders were here to consult, Adam doubted that any of them would have crossed the mayor and sheriff of Halfway.

He would cooperate. He hated to put Simon through questioning again, but the boy would need to reveal the truth.

Adam was glad when Nancy insisted that the female deputy call the sheriff in from the field. From his seat on the sofa in the sheriff's office, he nodded as Hank entered with his jacket still on, snow dripping on his boots.

"Hey, there. It's not too often I get visitors in my office." Hank hooked his jacket onto the coat tree, where Simon and Adam's black hats were hung. "Give me a minute here, and I'll be ready to talk with ya."

"How's it going out there, Hank?" Nancy asked from the wooden chair by the window.

"So far, so good. Aside from a few people missing oil deliveries, seems like everyone made it through the storm just fine." He wheeled his chair out from behind his desk and moved closer to the couch where Remy, Simon, and Adam sat waiting.

"Thanks for coming in, Hank," Nancy began. "When I heard what we had here, I knew you'd want to handle it yourself. Seems Simon here has been remembering some details from last year . . ." She glanced down at Adam's brother, who seemed okay so far. "Some of the particulars that might help you home in on the person who killed Esther and Levi."

"Is that right." Hank wheeled his chair closer, his broad face kind as he leaned on his knees, getting on Simon's level. "What do you have to say, young man? Some of it's coming back to you?"

Simon nodded.

"He remembers seeing a man that night," Adam said, turning to his brother. "Tell him what you saw ... . looking down from the buggy."

Simon's amber eyes seemed to draw strength from Adam as he spoke. "After he shot Mamm, he came back over and poked at her. When she didn't move, I think he gave up. He was leaving when I peeked out at him. Looking down from the buggy, I saw the top of his head." He patted his own head. "It was shiny bald, and there was a red mark on it. A mark shaped like . . . like a map of Florida."

"Is that right?" Hank kept his tone casual. "So you're learning your states in school?"

"All fifty."

Adam was encouraged by Hank's demeanor and Simon's response. So far Hank's line of questioning wasn't upsetting Simon.

"And you saw what he was wearing, right?" Remy prodded.

"A puffy black coat. And pants with a stripe." Simon pointed to Hank's long legs. "Like yours."

"Wow." Hank sat back in his chair. "A man in a uniform."

Simon nodded.

"Sheriff, we were going to come to you with this information, but then today at the market I started making some connections."

Hank turned to Remy, squinting at her. "I'm sorry. I thought you were one of the Kings, but I don't think we've met before."

"This is Remy McCallister, from Philadelphia," Nancy said.

Hank nodded at her. "Ms. McCallister."

"Call me Remy. I've been staying with the Kings and . . . well, anyway, we were sort of collecting all this information and then today—this." She gestured to Nancy, who handed him a cell phone.

"I took this photo from the loft in Zook's barn," Nancy explained.

The sheriff squinted at the image on the phone. "You got a good shot, Nancy. Who is this?"

"Chris Mueller." Nancy winced and swallowed hard.

Adam could see this was hard for her. Nancy was friendly with Chris Mueller's mother, Gina, but she had always been good to Adam's mother, too. The two women had shared recipes and gardening tips. Nancy was the one who told the Kings about Dr. Trueherz's clinic after two of Adam's siblings had died so young.

Hank took a deep breath, then handed the phone to Adam. "Okay by you if Simon takes a look at this?"

The image was the top of a man's head, a red mark prominent on his bald pate. "Sure." Adam handed the phone to his brother.

"Oh, no." Simon stared, his face puckered in horror. "That's what it looked like. The man who shot Mamm." Suddenly his eyes filled with tears. "He shot her, and then he came back and pushed her again. He killed her."

Slipping his arm around his little brother, Adam held him close.

"That was a terrible thing he did, something no boy should have to see." Hank took the phone from Simon and patted his knee. "You're a brave boy. Now all these things you're telling me, it's all the truth, right?"

"It's true." Swiping at his tears, Simon nodded. "A lie is a bad thing. You must always tell the truth."

"That's right, young man." Hank rose and stood there for a moment, scratching one side of his white mustache. "If you don't mind waiting for a few minutes, I'll have Alice run a quick background check on Mueller."

Nancy waved him off. "I'm here for the long haul. But, Simon, you're looking a little pale. I've got just the thing, in here somewhere." Flipping open her satchel on the floor, she began digging.

When Hank turned to the sofa, Adam said, "We can wait." They had plenty of time. Not even lunchtime yet and already Adam had wrangled a camera crew and snuck his brother out of the market without raising suspicion from a suspected killer. A very odd day, but it seemed like progress had been made. No one could bring his parents back, but it would be good to have their killer in a place where he could kill no more.

On the couch beside him, Remy was talking softly to Simon, pressing a tissue into his hand. She had pushed this investigation along. It seemed she was always pushing in some way. Pushing him to be mindful of his brothers and sisters, pushing him to say what was on his mind . . .

Pushing him to love.

He turned to see her playing gently with Simon. Her eyes, the color of an alfalfa field after a spring rain, shifted to his for a moment and he felt the bond between them. It was always there now, an invisible tether. They were like a team of horses, pulling together. Each one careful to stay in line with the other.

Simon's tears began to dry when he had to choose between chocolate or strawberry granola on a stick from Nancy's bag. He was unwrapping the snack when Hank returned.

"Alice is working on that for us." Hank took his seat again. "She's also going to call Judge Fletcher. We need a warrant to check out Mueller's place, and I figure now's as good a time as any. We'll see what the judge says."

"What would you hope to find there?" Remy asked.

Hank rubbed the back of his neck. "Well, as I remember the evidence collected at the scene, there was a man's boot print and a couple of bullets. A boot that matches might place him at the scene, but the ballistics . . ." He nodded. "If we find a gun that matches the bullets from the crime scene, I'd say we have our man. I hope that's not too graphic for you."

"It's fine," Remy said. "I just don't want this guy to walk."

Nancy pointed at the air. "If he's guilty."

"Of course," Remy agreed.

Hank rubbed his jaw thoughtfully. "This is not the first time Chris Mueller has been brought up in this investigation. He was a person of interest for a while last year, when a witness reported seeing him at Jeb's Hardware arguing with Levi King."

"Arguing with Dat?" Adam shook his head, unable to imagine his father arguing with an Englisher. "Over what?"

"Something about wildlife. Bird hunting? We checked it out, but at the time it didn't seem to amount to much. The altercation occurred weeks before the murders."

"But that's not the first time Chris has mouthed off to someone." Nancy shifted, burying her hands in the pockets of her fleece vest. "He has a problem with booze. That doesn't make him a killer, but it's made him surly from time to time. I know Gina has had her issues with him."

"I've always found Chris to be respectful," Hank said, "but I have had to ask him to leave the bar of the Mockingbird Inn a few times."

"And do you remember that phase he went through when he kept taking on new get-rich-quick schemes?" Nancy asked Hank. "Nothing panned out for him, but he had big plans. He was going to sell Amish things on eBay. And then there was something about starting a pheasant-hunting preserve." She shook her head. "I can barely believe it. To think that boy might have killed my good friends. . . ."

"I know what you mean." Adam tried to picture Chris as a kid, but could only remember Chris's mother keeping him home, afraid of the giant horses on the surrounding farms.

"It may be hard to believe about Chris, but someone killed Esther and Levi," Hank said. "And it's my job to put that person behind bars."

Hank was called out of the room. When he returned, he went to the rack for his hat. "I'm going to have to cut out for a while. You're welcome to stay, come back later, whatever suits."

Nancy rose and grabbed her satchel. "Anything we can do to help?"

"Just keep a lid on this for now. Our check on Chris Mueller came back with half a dozen arrests in Pittsburgh, where he went to college. Mostly barroom brawls, drunk and disorderly. But based on that and the information you gave us, Judge Fleming called in a search warrant."

Hank put on his hat and grabbed his coat. "Good thing the wife let me take the Snow Monster today. I'm taking a ride out to the Mueller place."

FORTY-TWO

*W*arming her hands around a mug of tea, Remy settled back onto the yellow gingham love seat in Nancy Briggs's sunroom and tried to relax.

After the sheriff had left the station, Nancy had pointed out that the police station was no place to pass the time and offered her home as a place to wait. As they didn't want to bring Simon back to the farmers market with Chris Mueller there, Adam had suggested they all share a pizza for lunch.

"Great idea," Nancy had said. "I'm famished!"

Just three blocks from the police station and city hall, Nancy's house was a modest Colonial tucked behind a white picket fence. Melting snow dripped onto the edges of the wide wood porch as Nancy led the way through the front door.

"Shoes off here. You can hang your hats and coats on the hooks there. We'll eat in the red room," Nancy had instructed.

The red dining room overlooked a snow-covered birdbath that

resembled a big white sugarplum. Simon set out place mats and napkins while Remy poured glasses of water and milk for Simon.

"Your kitchen is amazing. It's awfully big for one person," she told Nancy as she navigated the large room with two granite islands, a double-wide refrigerator, and an industrial-size range.

"That's because it's my factory and test kitchen, too." Nancy slapped a hand on the smooth granite counter. "This is where the muesli bars are made."

Simon had been thrilled to have "a real pizza, hot in a box," as he said, and Remy had agreed that a bubbling hot pizza really hit the spot on a cold winter day.

Now, with lunch finished, Nancy was showing Simon her "trade secrets" as he watched her mix a batch of lemon poppy bars in the kitchen. Adam had grinned at the sight of his brother and Nancy wearing paper caps over their hair, but he seemed just as relieved as Remy to have some time alone in the sunroom.

So much had happened this morning; Remy's head was still spinning.

"I'm trying not to count my chickens before they hatch," she told Adam, who sat beside her on the love seat.

"Speaking in proverbs now?" He shot her a grin. "You're really getting into the Plain way of life."

She shrugged. "I've enjoyed it." She had loved every minute, each and every day, from waking to the family milking under a purple sky to playing games by the fire to nestling under a quilt at night, tired to the bone. So wonderful . . . but right now so many things were drawing to a close, and the idea that she'd had a hand in solving the murders of Levi and Esther King was sheer exhilaration.

"I can't stop thinking about Chris Mueller, and what it might mean for Simon if Chris is convicted. It will help Simon to know the killer isn't lurking. I think it will bring Simon closure."

Remy leaned forward to place her mug beside the magazines fanned out on the coffee table, then added: "*If* Chris is found guilty. That's my problem, pushing ahead to the next thing. The sheriff isn't even back from searching the Muellers' house, and in my mind I'm lunging ahead."

"I've been meaning to talk to you about that." Adam picked up a magazine from the table, one that showed a Northwest timber cottage on the edge of a blue lake. "You do push a lot."

"I like to think I have a healthy curiosity."

"And you like to get your way."

Remy turned to him, hands on her hips. "Are you saying I'm a spoiled brat?" She knew it was probably true, but she liked drawing Adam into the verbal fray.

"I never said that, though it may be true."

She leaned toward him until his smooth jaw was just inches from her face. His eyes held that brown shadow, which she'd come to recognize as a mixture of intrigue and attraction.

Those smoky eyes . . . she could stare into them forever.

"There are a lot of things you don't say, Adam. You're a little stingy with words at times—maybe that's a cultural thing. But I think I've gotten pretty good at reading your body language."

"Ya?" He tossed the magazine away and folded his arms across his chest. "What am I thinking now?"

Cocking an eyebrow, she tugged on the white string of her prayer kapp. "You're thinking of how much you enjoy teasing me."

"You got me." He let his hands drop to his lap. "You're good."

"Denki."

"So . . ." He took a breath and closed his hand over hers.

A tiny gasp escaped her throat at the electrifying contact.

"What am I thinking now?" he asked.

"I would read your mind if . . ." She closed her eyes.

If my pulse would stop racing.

If I weren't so blinded by emotion whenever you touch me.

She opened her eyes and, squeezing his hand, pressed her cheek to his shoulder. How wonderful it felt to lean on Adam, to feel his warmth and solid support.

"Remy ..." That gentle voice, the low baritone she'd often heard soothing Simon late at night, rumbled in her ear. "You know the roads are clearing."

"Yes." Without lifting her head, she slid closer so that her face was pressed to his chest. Her nose pressed into the fabric of his shirt, picking up his familiar smells of soap and wood smoke, pleasant odors. Adam's scent. His arm came around her, holding her in place, safe and secure.

"And that means we're getting to that awkward moment where I'm supposed to let you go. . . ."

"I know." She bit her lower lip. She didn't want to leave. This felt like her home now, here with Adam and his family in Halfway.

"But there's a problem. Somewhere along the way, I fell in love with you," he whispered.

I fell in love with you. . . .

Whispered or shouted, the words couldn't have been more thrilling if he had written them in the sky with stars.

She lifted her head so that she could meet his eyes. The vulnerability she saw there made her reach for both his hands.

"And now I can't let you go," he said. "Since you arrived, you've lit up our home with laughter and joy. All these days . . . I noticed how much you adore my family, how you shine in the glow of their love."

So he had noticed.

All those times when she had thought he was preoccupied, when he seemed to be mulling over plans or talking business with Jonah, Adam had been in tune with Remy. He'd been watching her, really seeing the woman she'd become.

"I don't want to put too much pressure on you, Remy, but I want to be with you always, and it's not such a simple matter, with you being Englisher." Her heart pounded in her chest as she anticipated the question that smoldered in his dark eyes. "Are you serious about talking to the bishop about becoming a baptized member?"

Unable to speak over the knot of emotion in her throat, she nodded.

His chest swelled with a huge breath of relief. "I had hoped . . . crazy hope . . . but now, maybe not so crazy."

"Not crazy at all," she said, blinking back tears.

"Are you willing to make that promise? Would you give up the city, give up a life of ease and—"

"In a heartbeat. I know I have a lot to learn. I know your family well, but I still need to meet the other families in your congregation. I realize it's a huge commitment, but my heart is in it, Adam. I feel like I've found a home here."

He smiled. "Then I hope you'll think about being my wife. I want you beside me, always. I can't imagine life without you." He lifted her hands to his lips and pressed a kiss on her knuckles.

The sweet gesture unraveled her composure. Remy sniffed, overcome with emotion.

He loved her, and she had fallen in love with him, fallen so hard that she could barely remember life before Adam.

In fact, her entire life before Lancaster County now seemed a dull, gray blur, like a decaying movie filmed in black and white. The past was a bleak contrast to the brilliant hues of her life here, as colorful as the green, purple, or blue gowns worn by Amish women here.

"You're crying." He frowned. "I didn't mean to make you cry."

She sniffed. "Tears of joy."

"Joy, as in . . . yes?"

"Yes, a thousand times yes. I love you, Adam, and I want to be by your side, always and forever."

He folded her into his arms, and Remy closed her eyes and gave herself up to his kiss. How she loved him.

On the small of her back his hands pulled her closer, as if beckoning her to his world. Willingly, she leaned against him, feeling the soft contours of her body meet his very male muscle and bone. Despite their differences, Amish and English, she knew they were meant to be together.

For Remy, it would be the promise of a lifetime, vowing to live Amish and be Adam's wife forever. An ominous step, but not scary at all. Locked in Adam's arms, Remy knew it was the right choice for her.

A lifetime of loving Adam would not be enough . . . but it was a start.

A wonderful start.

The ringing phone interrupted their kisses. Adam's arms released her, and Remy slid away reluctantly, fingertips pressed to her lips, as if to hold on to the passion.

"I'm glad we don't have telephones to interrupt in Amish homes," Adam said, a smile playing at his mouth.

Remy sighed, squeezing his hand. "No. You have ten siblings instead."

He laughed. "Plenty of interruptions there." Taking her hand, he rose and gave her a tug. "Kumm. Let's tell Simon."

Inside the kitchen, Nancy was pacing, a cordless phone pressed to her ear. Simon sat on a bar stool, pressing glistening moist granola mix into a shallow pan.

"We're done with the mixing," he reported. "Now it must sit and harden."

"Good job." Adam touched his brother's shoulder as he began to talk about how much their family loved Remy.

Wonder played on Simon's face as Adam outlined their plans. "You will marry . . . and Remy will live with us always?"

Adam nodded. "After she's baptized, in the fall. What do you think of that?"

A grin ruffled his lips. "I think it will be a very good fall."

"Okay, Hank." Nancy's voice was clear as she turned back toward them. "I'll let Adam know. Thank you much."

"I finished!" Simon pointed the spatula at the tray.

"Good work, Simon," Nancy said as she ended the connection. "How about you take that pan down those stairs there. You'll see a big silver door down there. Pull it open and you can tuck that away on an empty shelf."

Simon hopped down from the stool and walked off with the tray.

"That was Hank," Nancy reported. "Says he just got back from the Mueller place, and knew you were waiting here to get word."

"What did he find?" Remy asked eagerly.

Nancy pulled off her paper hat and carried the big mixing bowl to the sink. "Hank searched the house and he thinks he may have found the evidence that makes the case." She paused to run some water in the bowl, as if to be sure she had their attention. "Under the bed there was a steel box with a handgun—a thirty-two-caliber automatic, like the weapon that killed Levi and Esther."

"Wow. It really was him." Adam let out a sigh. "Thank the Lord Gott. I really didn't think we'd ever see this day."

Remy sank down onto a stool, feeling as if an enormous weight had been lifted. Of course, there would be further investigation and charges. The wheels of justice might turn slowly with a trial and sentencing, but in her heart she now knew Chris Mueller was the killer, and it felt so good to know he would be out of circulation soon.

Out of Halfway.

Far from the King family.

"Hank is running all the evidence into the state forensics lab to match ballistics and whatnot. He's got the county prosecutor in the loop, and they're ready to go."

"Hank thinks Mueller is the man?" Adam asked.

"Oh, yeah. He's at the farmers market, picking up Chris for questioning right now. We may not have enough to hold Chris in custody at this point, but my guess is, when confronted by the sheriff, Mueller will break down. I wouldn't be surprised if he confessed to killing Esther and Levi before the day is over."

Raking a hand through his hair, Adam let out a deep breath. "Then it's almost over. They'll get this man off the streets."

Nancy nodded. "Yup. And as your friend and mayor, I am much relieved to put this one to bed. Maybe now your family can start healing. Maybe we all can."

Gripping the granite counter, Adam took a deep breath. "Thank you, Nancy. Thanks for pushing this forward."

Nancy waved him off. "Oh, Remy here was the one who connected the dots." She winked at Remy. "This one has good investigative skills. It's no wonder your boss sent you here on assignment. Which reminds me—mind like a sieve—what newspaper did you say you work for?"

Remy's jaw dropped as the energy in the kitchen drained.

Did Nancy really say those words . . . those poisonous words. She felt Adam go stiff beside her, felt the bitter fallout coming.

"What did you say?" His voice indicated they were lingering on a dangerous edge.

"I wanted to know what newspaper Remy writes for."

He wheeled on her, his dark eyes piercing. "You're a writer." A statement . . . he had already worked beyond disbelief.

"I can explain about that—"

"A newspaper reporter." His voice held the grit of disdain. "There is no excuse in the world that could cover a lie like that."

Nancy winced. "It looks like I just stepped in it." She backed away from the granite counter. "Let me go check on Simon. I'll leave you two to sort this out. Did you hear me? Fix this. After what you two accomplished today, you can certainly work this out." She went to the cellar door and paused behind Adam to mouth: "Sorry."

Remy shrugged. It wasn't Nancy's fault. This was a mess of her own design.

"Listen, Adam . . ." When she turned to him he was stone cold, a stranger critiquing her flaws. "It's not the way it sounds."

"You're not a reporter?"

"Technically, I am . . . I was, but—"

"Who do you work for?"

"The *Post*. My father owns the paper, but I'm not writing a story anymore."

He folded his arms defensively. "I've been a fool. Everyone warned me to stay away from the Englisher, but I didn't listen."

"Adam, don't freak out about it. I'm not writing the story, okay? Besides, I'd never write anything hurtful about you or anyone in the family. I love your family. You know that."

"Ya? Then tell me, Remy, why did you drive out here in the first place? What was that . . . that business proposition you kept choking on? You were writing a story from the beginning, but you were afraid to tell me."

"I . . ." At a loss, she pressed a hand to her chest, then tugged on one string of her prayer kapp. "Okay, at first I came out here for a story. Way back in the beginning I was hoping to do a story on the unsolved murders, a follow-up on how your family is doing now. But I wasn't going to publish anything without your permission. And as I got to know you and your family, everything changed. I fell in love with you."

"That's right . . . you fell in love with the Amish." The edge in his voice frightened her. "So much that you wanted to join us."

"But that part was genuine," she insisted. "It *is* genuine. I fell in love with you, Adam. With you and your family and with God. My old life, a very privileged life, just doesn't hold any appeal for me anymore."

She couldn't go back to Philadelphia now. She knew she belonged here, and Adam knew it, too.

He had just proposed to her. They were going to be married in the fall. . . . Surely he wouldn't toss that all away over a misunderstanding like this.

"I can't trust you, Remy. I thought I could, but . . ." He stood there, his face crossed with pain.

My fault, she thought, biting her lower lip in an attempt to hold back the tears stinging her eyes. *This is all my fault.*

"Adam, I am so sorry about this. Please, forgive me. It was wrong to lie, but it was long ago."

Before I knew you.

Before I loved you.

He shook his head, his dark eyes glittering. "I have to protect my family. It's my responsibility to keep them safe from . . . from people like you."

"Remy! Adam! There is a very big icebox downstairs. So big, you can walk inside!" Simon bounded over, his arms outstretched, his fists full of shiny cellophane-wrapped candies. "And there are so many pans in there already! Do you want to come see?"

"No, thanks." Adam's voice was clipped, restrained.

Remy tried to answer but couldn't form words over the swell of tears in her throat. She shook her head, a hot tear coursing down her face as she realized it had all come tumbling down around her.

There would be no forgiveness.

Simon looked from his brother to her, a panic filling his eyes. "What happened?" He burrowed into Adam's side, pressing his face to his brother's jacket.

"We need to go." Adam placed a hand on Simon's shoulder and gave a slight squeeze.

Simon lifted his head, as if to check that the tempest had cleared. "Okay." He reached across the table and took Remy's hand. "Come on, Remy. Time to go."

"Not her."

Simon's face puckered.

"She's staying here." Adam took his brother's hand and tugged him away from the table. "She is never to come round our home again. She will not be invited inside, and you are forbidden to speak her name."

A startled gasp peeled from Remy's throat, and she pressed a hand to her face in an attempt to hold it all together. He was treating her like someone who had turned away from the faith! How could he cut her off so quickly?

Simon's small hands clenched the hem of Adam's jacket. "But Adam, I don't understand. You said you and Remy are going to marry."

"No more." Adam turned away, his broad-shouldered silhouette ominous against the light from the kitchen's broad windows.

Simon took one look at his brother, pivoted, and flew into Remy's arms. Her heart filled with gladness as she dropped to her knees to hug him.

"I don't understand," he mumbled against her neck. "What happened, Remy?"

It all slipped away. One lie, one flaw, and the bottom fell out from under her.

"Kumm! Now!" Adam's gruff voice caused Simon to flinch in her arms.

"You'd better do as he says," she whispered. She squeezed her eyes shut, preferring not to see as Simon was pulled from her arms. If only she could shut her ears to avoid the muffled whimpers that tore at her as he was shuffled away.

PART THREE

No Place Like Home

To everything there is a season,
And a time to every purpose under the heaven:
A time to be born, a time to die;
A time to plant, and a time to pluck up that which is planted;
A time to kill and a time to heal;
A time to break down and a time to build up . . .

—ECCLESIASTES 3:1–3

FORTY-THREE

*T*he workshop door creaked as Simon pushed it open and held the lantern high. "I think you're going to like it," the boy said confidently as he lifted the lantern into the shadows.

The birdhouse that sat on the center of the workbench was a thing of beauty, not for its design or craftsmanship, but for the tender care that had gone into its construction. At nearly three feet tall, the structure had many peaks on the roof, dozens of holes for birds to enter and a wide opening at its center.

For the first time since that terrible moment when he'd turned his back on Remy, Adam smiled.

The idea was born when Adam sat the family down to tell them that the man who killed their parents had been taken to jail. At first, everyone had been quiet. No one would dare celebrate the punishment of another man, even one who had committed a terrible sin.

Finally, Jonah had sighed. "I feel bad for Chris," he said. "And I forgive him."

"We must all forgive Chris Mueller and help his mamm in any way we can," Sadie said firmly.

They talked for thirty minutes about ways to help Gina Mueller. Mary would make a casserole. Sadie would offer to clean her house. Jonah would see if there were any things to be repaired at the Mueller place. Ruthie thought Gina might want to go for a walk when the snow cleared, since she'd had surgery a few months ago.

Watching them, Adam felt warmed by their goodness, the goodness of God shining in his brothers and sisters. It was a glimmer of hope he sorely needed with his body and mind sick over Remy. Losing her was like losing a family member, and reminders of her were everywhere. It stole his appetite to look at the place where she used to sit at the table. He kept thinking he heard her voice in the barn. At times his eyes searched the white horizon for a sight of her on a horse.

Physically, he felt like one of the cows had kicked him in the belly. Seeing his siblings begin to heal had eased that pain, just a bit. "God willing, this will help us all heal and move on," Adam had told the family that day during their special talk.

"But remember how much Dat liked the birds?" Simon had piped up suddenly.

Adam kept quiet, letting his brother talk.

"We do." Leah patted his hand. "That's why I share my field glasses with you. Whenever I see a new bird and log it in my notebook, I think of Dat."

"We should do something for the birds," Simon said thoughtfully. "I think Dat would have wanted that."

"I've noticed lots of hungry birds pecking in the snow," Mary had said. "Seems they can't get to their seeds. No matter how many crumbs I toss at them, the food disappears in minutes. I say we build a birdhouse."

And from that meeting, the King family gift to the birds was born.

Everyone had to help; Simon insisted on it.

Simon worked with Adam on the design. He wanted points and peaks on the roof so that squirrels wouldn't sit up there. He also asked for small holes leading to small cubbies, so there'd be a place for small birds like sparrows to get away from bossy jays.

Ruthie and Susie were in charge of painting and allowed Katie and Sam to fill in some spots. Jonah and Gabe planted the post that the house would sit on. Leah picked out popular birdseed—black sunflower seeds that the birds found delicious. Adam was the master builder. Sadie and Mary glued on shingles.

Now Simon set the lantern down on the workbench and touched a panel on the small house. "It's dry, all ready to mount. Susie painted the top blue to match the sky, and Ruthie painted her part yellow for the sun. What do you think?" Simon asked. "It's a fine birdhouse, ya?"

Adam tousled Simon's hair. "I think it's a wonderful good home for some happy birds," Adam said.

It would not be the first birdhouse on the farm, but it was certainly the first one everyone had contributed to.

The next day, when the family gathered together in the north field to mount the birdhouse, the mood was light. Sun sparkled on the hills of melting snow. Katie and Sam kept reaching up on the fat post to swing their legs, while Leah gave out handfuls of seed so that everyone could help fill the house. Lifting the house from a cart, Gabe joked that he'd birthed calves that weighed less.

As Jonah and Gabe set the birdhouse onto its post, Adam saw the design of Simon's plan. This was a memorial that they had all contributed to.

Honor thy father, the commandment said.

This was a way to honor Dat. A way for all of Levi and Esther's children to say good-bye.

⊞

"Adam?" Susie's brows rose as she passed the scrapple. "Don't get mad at me. But I miss Remy. There! I said her name."

Oh, why do you want to go and do that? Adam stared down at the table, his appetite ruined.

"That's against the rules," Simon said. "You're not allowed to say her name."

Susie scowled at Simon over her water glass. "I never heard that rule."

"I miss her, too." Mary stabbed at her hash browns with a fork, her head cocked to one side. "It was nice to have someone my age to talk to."

"And she was a wonderful help around the house," Sadie said.

Gabe's cheek twitched, the beginning of a grin. "Not so much in the barn."

"She tried her best, and she didn't mind the dirty work," Sadie defended.

"She was learning how to care for the horses." Remembering, Simon held his biscuit aloft. "I think she understands how they think."

Simon had come so far in the past few months, and they had Remy to thank for a good part of that. All the wonderful things she had done for his family made it that much harder for Adam to free his mind of her.

"Did you ever notice the little lights in her eyes?" Ruthie waggled her fingers near her face. "That's how I always think of her. With a light around her, like a halo. Do you think God sent us an angel?"

"No." The thunderous force of his voice surprised even Adam. Ten faces whipped toward him.

"She's no angel." He mustered all his strength to keep the dark anger in check. "Remy lied to us, remember? And she used that lie to insinuate her way into this family."

"I think it wasn't so much a lie as a misunderstanding." Sadie kept her eyes on his, her hands on her lap. "I mean, she never said she *wasn't* a reporter. And she gave up on the article once she got to know us, right?"

"She lied." Adam would have argued more, but he didn't want to get into it with Sadie. Defiant, spirited Sadie . . . her know-it-all attitude of youth was getting more and more irritating each day.

"Remy lied, and that's a sin. But no one is perfect." Jonah's dark eyes held Adam's gaze as eating ceased, except for Katie chewing on softened apples.

Adam swallowed back the fire in his throat. "I'm trying to protect this family."

"I know that, brother. But where is the forgiveness? When Chris Mueller was sent to jail, we brought pies and casseroles to Gina. Everyone in the community prayed to God for forgiveness, and we forgave Chris Mueller. God says we must."

"Of course." Adam nodded.

"Forgiveness comes from God. It's not up to us to decide who is worthy." Jonah paused, looking down at his plate, then back up at Adam. "Doesn't God's forgiveness apply to Remy, too?"

Jonah's words cut him to the marrow.

Adam shot up from the table, knocking over the jar of apple butter. Mary caught the jar and righted it as he turned and fled to the cooler air of the porch.

Forgive me. . . .

Remy had begged him, but he didn't know how to do it. He had searched the depths of his soul and found no forgiveness there.

Only a sizzling anger, a poisonous mix of guilt and fury and heart-break.

He strode toward the barn, a mixture of melting snow and mud sloshing under his boots.

Jonah's point made sense. His brother was right, of course.

But love defied logic and explanation. To have fallen in love with a woman for this first and only time, and then learn that she was a spy who had come to prey on his most vulnerable family members. . . .

"She tried to stab us in the back," he muttered to his horse as he tightened the saddle.

How could he explain to his family that Remy wasn't the woman they thought she was? She was not the Rebekah of the Bible, the woman Adam thought God meant for him to take for his wife.

"I was wrong about her." He swung onto his horse and urged him down the lane.

Remy was not the answer to his prayers. It was time to man up, take the advice of the wisest men he knew. A gust of wind hit him, and he pressed his hat tighter and rode into the sunrise.

While Preacher Dave waited on a customer in the front of the buggy shop, Adam continued sanding the slab of wood that would become a buggy dashboard.

A good sanding required the whole body, head to toe—and while it could be exhausting, Adam liked to think that the process brought the wood to its finest luster, the way God intended.

He was putting his back into the work, brushing the sand-ing block in the direction of the grain with long, even strokes, when Dave Zook returned. "Let's see the fine job you've done."

He inspected the wood, his palm following the grain. "Very nice. I forgot you were a carpenter. Sorry to be called away, but now we have a moment to talk. What brings you here?"

Adam dusted his hands, the words sticking in his throat. "I came to announce my intention to marry Annie."

Dave blinked. "Annie Stoltzfus?"

"Right."

"That's wonderful news. I'm sure Annie and her family are very pleased."

Adam shifted. "Actually, they don't know yet. I just decided . . . well, I knew it was time to take your advice about getting married."

"Oh."

"Annie's good with children. I know she'll be a responsible mother to Katie and Sam, and once they get to know her better she'll be helpful with Simon and Ruthie, too."

"The little ones do need a mamm, but I've never had someone come to me about getting married this way. You sound like you're bartering for a heifer."

"I'm trying to be practical." Adam linked his thumbs through his suspenders. "Just trying to do right by my family, Dave. Trying to do right by God."

"Do you love Annie?"

"I . . ." Adam was going to say that he loved every living thing on God's earth, but he didn't think Dave would buy that line of logic. "Honestly? I love her like a sister, but that can change, can't it?"

Dave rubbed his forehead. "Anything can change, but that's not why you've come to me. What is this really about, Adam?"

Adam turned away and meandered toward a platform where the fiberglass frame of a buggy sat. "My brother says I've got to find forgiveness for . . . for someone."

"Ahh. That's another story. Who is it that needs to be forgiven?"

"It seems I've got a long list."

"Been saving up awhile, have you?"

Shame burned as Adam dropped his eyes to the workshop floor. "Although I've gone through the motions with Gina Mueller, I still boil inside when I think that her son killed my parents over some moneymaking scheme Dat didn't allow. I'm angry with myself for not coming home years ago and letting my parents know they'd done the right thing, raising me for the Plain life. And I can't forgive Remy McCallister. She's the Englisher girl who—"

"Ya, I saw her big white car. Turns out she was a reporter, ya?"

Adam frowned. Word traveled in the community. "Ya."

"I see. You do have a lot of anger on your plate." Dave stroked his beard as he let out a breath. "I know you've heard talk of *Gelassenheit,* one of the foundations of Amish life."

"It's the opposite of hochmut, right? Instead of pride, we strive for humility."

"Sort of. But gelassenheit is so much more. It's tranquility and grace. Acceptance. Letting go. It's the union of our inner spirit with our outward actions."

Adam rubbed his chin. "Okay. So . . . you're saying I need to let go?"

"Sometimes, you have to put forgiveness into action, and the feelings inside will follow later. Take action, do the right thing, and if your heart is open, the Heavenly Father will find His way in. The way you brought food and support to Gina Mueller. Maybe that day you were still hurt, still reeling from grief, but through your actions you moved toward forgiveness. That's a good thing. The action demonstrated forgiveness."

In his mind, Adam saw the line of gray carriages headed down the lane toward the Mueller home the night Chris was arrested. The group of Amish visitors brought food and comfort to Gina Mueller, aware that she, too, was suffering in the wake of her son's violent act. Ya, it had been a step toward forgiveness, though some bitterness stuck to him, like pine sap in the grooves of the hand.

"Am I confusing you?" Dave asked.

"No, I see the point." He hadn't thought about gelassenheit for years, but now he remembered how, when he was a boy, the preachers warned that you could not earn gelassenheit. Instead, you had to catch it. Adam had always loved the image of catching gelassenheit as if it were a flying fish.

"But what about marrying Annie?" Adam asked as Dave returned to his sanding. The groom needed a letter of good standing from his church leaders called a *Zeugnis*.

"I think you had better talk with her first. If you two want to marry, I have no objections to that. You'll get your zeugnis."

As Adam left Dave Zook's shop, he told himself he was doing the right thing. This would be good for the children. It would make Annie happy, and he would be following the instructions of the church leaders.

It's the right thing to do, he kept telling himself as he slowed Thunder to a trot through the town of Halfway . . . where every Englisher woman he passed looked like Remy.

On Saturday, the traditional courtship night, Adam stood on the mushy grass outside Annie's house, shining a flashlight up to her second-story window.

Wind nipped at the bottom of his jacket as Annie appeared in the window and waved him toward the door.

He was far too old for this. Courtship at his age was ridiculous.

Annie met him at the door, her smile bright as she invited him in.

"I'm so surprised to see you!" she said, though he knew she had been expecting him. Mary had spread the word that he would be coming over.

"Mary sends her best," he said.

Annie pressed her hands to her chest. "She has always been a dear friend. You're lucky to be blessed with such a wonderful sister. Have a seat and I'll cut you some pie as soon as it finishes cooling. I just baked it this evening."

The first half hour was excruciating, with Annie prattling on about who she saw at the singing last week and whether the snow-melt would cause flooding and how the secret to a good sweet potato pie was the cinnamon.

After that, things got a little bit better when she cut him a slice of pie. Sweet potato pie with a creamy texture and buttery crust. He thought her skills as a baker might be some consolation after they were married. They would always eat well.

"You've been awfully quiet," Annie said, taking the chair adjacent to him and leaning casually close on the table. "I feel like I'm doing all the talking."

She was, but Adam didn't mind. He really had nothing to say to her, beyond the big question.

He swallowed a bit of pie and cleared his throat. "Annie. I came tonight because I have something to ask you."

Her cherry lips curled in a smile, encouraging him.

"The thing is, you know there are eleven of us. Mary and Jonah are very responsible and, well, you know Mary's plans. It's a big responsibility, but the children need a woman in the house and . . ."

The sour expression on her face cut him off. "What's wrong?" he asked.

"Adam King, are you asking me to marry you or bringing me in as a housekeeper?"

Both, he thought as he choked on a piece of crust. He grabbed a slug of water and wiped his mouth with the back of his hand.

"I can't believe you would ask me that now, and in that way." Astonishment shone in Annie's blue eyes as she shook her head. "Let me ask you a question, and you must be honest with me. Do you favor me at all?"

He took a sip of water, swallowed hard. Anything to stall.

Her jaw dropped. "You *don't*! Why, I could just turn this pie over in your lap."

"Please don't. It's delicious and . . . really, I didn't mean to offend you."

"Offend me? Here I've been mooning for you all these years, thinking you might one day come around and start courting me, give us a chance to get to know each other."

He put his fork down. "And . . . here I am."

"Asking me to marry you, out of the blue." She sighed. "Two people need time to get to know each other and fall in love. Don't you know anything?"

Apparently he did not. He had never been very good at the gaming part of courtship.

"Not to mention that everyone knows you lost your heart to that Englisher woman who was living here. The one wearing Mary's Amish dresses." She put her hands up. "Don't deny it! Emma Lapp saw her at the market, twice, and you know it must be obvious if the schoolteacher can see what's going on."

"Remy is gone." He winced, just pronouncing her name. "She's living in Philadelphia now."

"But you're still pining away." She took the empty pie plate away and shuffled over to the sink. "I don't understand you, Adam. A few months ago I would have been thrilled to hear this proposal. But now . . ." She shook her head. "It's all verhuddelt. I might have tried courting for a while, but now even that seems awkward."

Adam looked over at her with a new respect. Annie had a

strong sense of who she was and what she wanted. "I appreciate your honesty."

She cocked an eyebrow. "Even though I turned you down?"

"Especially because you turned me down." He smiled. "I don't think we're very well suited for each other, anyway."

"Ya, but you don't have to be so happy about it."

He grabbed his hat from the hook, and she opened the door for him.

"Good night, Adam. Go find your true bride. I'm tired and I've got a lot of singings in my future if I'm ever to meet the man the Heavenly Father intends me to marry."

"Denki, Annie." As the door closed behind him, Adam breathed a deep, cold breath of relief. He still needed to find a mother for the children, but somehow he felt as if he'd narrowly escaped a landslide.

FORTY-FOUR

*R*emy stood at the window of Herb's office, looking out on the city of Philadelphia through a pair of opera glasses she'd found on his shelf. Behind her, Herb was going on about a trade show in Las Vegas that he wanted her to attend, but the details floated by her as she viewed the city through the high-powered binoculars.

Sometimes it's good to change your perspective, she thought. Adjusting the focus, she wondered how Leah's bird-watching was going with the little gift Remy had passed on.

Time hadn't done much to heal her wounds. She wondered if Sadie had returned to her job and her boyfriend at the hotel. Was Susie keeping to her special diet, and what new words was Katie saying? And Simon . . . had his night terrors faded now that Chris Mueller had confessed to the killings? Dear, sensitive Simon. How she missed seeing him. And Ruthie with her penchant for the truth; Gabe, with his passion to do the right thing; and Mary and the little ones and . . .

She missed them, every single one.

In the two weeks since she'd been wrenched from the family, the news services had covered the recent developments in the King murders. Christopher Mueller had pled guilty at arraignment and was currently awaiting sentencing for the crimes. Two or three lines of copy, and the story was over for most people. But Remy knew there was so much more to it: striations of layers, personalities and hopes and dreams.

"What happened?" Sadie had asked her on the phone, alarm etched in her voice. "What happened to you and Adam?"

"It's complicated," Remy had said, unable to face the fact that her lie had been the thing that started this faulty tower tumbling down.

Should she have told Adam earlier? Should she have emphasized that she'd given up on the story? And why did a small detail like that matter so much? Couldn't he see that their love was bigger than all the twists and turns of their lives before they came together?

Voicing any of these doubts on the phone would only have drawn Sadie into the situation, and the last thing Remy wanted was to shape a story that pointed any blame at Adam.

"You know I'll always be your friend," Sadie had promised. "I'll come visit you in Philadelphia."

"You are welcome any time," Remy had assured her, though she imagined that a visit from Sadie would only earn her more disapproval from Adam, who saw Sadie's experimentation in the real world as a measure of his own failure to lead her down the Plain path.

As Herb yammered on the phone behind her, she lifted her heavy hair, twirled it into a twist, and stuck a pencil there to keep it in place. She missed her prayer kapp, missed the connection to God that it symbolized. But she had learned to pray without it. Every day, she prayed for forgiveness.

She'd tossed the topic around with Nancy, who had put Remy up for the night after Adam had made it clear that Remy was not welcome back at the farm. While she had helped Nancy stir up granola recipes, Nancy had offered tea and sympathy.

"The Amish are big on forgiveness," Nancy had said. "He'll forgive you, eventually."

"But he won't forget." Remy knew that. Adam would never let her in his home or heart again.

"Forgiveness is like a three-pronged fork. There's forgiveness from the person you wronged. Forgiveness from God. And then, you've got to forgive yourself."

"I'm not sure I can do that."

"You can, but you have to work on it. Put some spiritual muscle into it."

"I've got no muscle left, spiritual or otherwise." Hot with regret and grief, Remy rested her head on the cool granite counter and burst into tears.

"You got it bad, kid. Reminds me a little of myself, umpteen years ago."

Nancy talked about how she'd almost missed out on spending her life with her Ira, all because of a "ridiculous" misunderstanding. "But we worked it out. Had forty-one wonderful years together. Retired in Halfway because we liked the people here, and started making muesli bars for a kick."

Four years later, her Ira was gone and she could not produce enough bars to keep up with demand.

"Do you miss your husband?" Remy had asked.

"Every day. That man was the love of my life. You never get over someone that special."

Remy understood that now. She had found the love of her life, and it had lasted but a few heartbeats.

Keeping her word to Adam, she had not written about the King family. The fabric of Amish life had become the basis of her story for the *Post*. A story they still had not run, though Arlene and Miles had given it a thumbs-up.

"What are you doing, playing mannequin?" Herb barked, interrupting her thoughts. "I just got off with Menkowitz, who's looking forward to seeing you at the convention in Las Vegas. That's right; Vegas, baby!" Herb laughed. "You are going to love that town, and this convention is a great place to start you as the new face of this enterprise with the Menkowitzes. Our new director of public relations."

"Dad, I keep telling you, I'm not interested in a corporate job." She scanned the glass façade of a high-rise building in Center City, landing on a woman at her desk, working at a computer. A lonely scene.

"Remy, I need you in this venture. It's time to step up and follow in your old man's footsteps."

"Would you listen to me?" She lowered the opera glasses and swung toward him. "I've spent all this time in editorial to work my way up. I've written a piece I'm really proud of, and . . . I don't know, it seems like a start. Did Arlene show it to you?"

He waved off the question. "What do you care about editorial? Any English major can do that job."

"Thanks for the show of support." Turning the opera glasses in her hands, Remy thought of her article and the eye-opening experience she'd had getting the story. Somehow that amounted to more than anything she could ever write. Was that why her daily job seemed lackluster now?

"My point is, your talents are being wasted there, and I need you in PR. Are you going to fester in a dead-end job or reach for the golden ring?"

"You know, I'd better go or I'll be late for the editorial meeting." She turned to leave.

"This is a great opportunity," he barked. "Pure gold! The golden ring."

"Gold is overvalued," she called over her shoulder as she headed for her meeting.

"Does anyone have anything else?" Miles asked in an attempt to wrap up the meeting.

"I do." Remy lifted her hand. "I was wondering when you're going to run my Amish story. It's been copyedited and proofread, and . . ." She noticed Arlene was uncharacteristically staring down at her notes. "What's the schedule?"

Miles's face puckered in concern. "Arlene and I both liked that story, but, unfortunately, it's not a go for us. I'm sorry, Remy."

Disappointment peeled at the edges of her composure. "Do you need some revisions?"

"That's not it." Miles hesitated. "We just—"

"It's out of our hands." Arlene removed her glasses and met Remy's gaze. "We got a veto from above."

"Above?" Remy squinted. "But you're the editor in chief. Who . . . ?"

"Herb McCallister killed it. Wouldn't sign off on it." Arlene's mouth curled with disdain. "Talk to him about it and see if he'll soften. We can't publish it without his okay."

As the meeting broke up Remy remained in her chair, crestfallen. How could Herb do this to her? A power play from her own father.

Beside her, Yasmina squeezed her shoulder encouragingly. "What are you going to do?"

"If I know Herb, he's got some trick up his sleeve." She rose, determined to maintain her composure with her colleagues watching. "I'm going to straighten this out."

She strode down the hall, the carpeting in the executive corridor mushy under her feet. It was all so pompous and fake, the posturing and decoration. Remy yearned for something real—a blade of grass, a chunk of sky.

"He's on the phone," Viola said, but Remy stormed past her desk and pushed into the office.

"Why did you kill my story?"

He turned to her, his mouth still moving, finger to the earpiece of his phone.

"Dad, I asked you a question."

"And I'm on the phone here, can't you see that? Hold on a second."

"No, I'm not holding on. I've been waiting for years, Herb. I keep waiting but you're never really here for me."

He let out a groan. "I'll call you right back," he said, then tossed the earpiece on the desk. "Okay, you got me. Here I am."

"I just want an answer. Why did you nix my story?"

"Because I'm sick of hearing about the Amish. Enough with the Plain People obsession. You've got other things that require your attention now. Namely, the PR job. The convention. Vegas."

"Oh, Dad. If you were worried about an obsession, why didn't you talk to me? What you did was hurtful."

"But it got your attention, right? Am I right?"

"Not in a good way."

"Okay, here's the deal. If you want your story to run, I can do that, but I need something in return. Step up and take the PR job."

She squeezed her eyes shut, unable to believe that her own

father could be so manipulative. Striving for composure, she took a deep breath and focused on the high-rise building across the way.

Those squares of light were like the office she'd peered into earlier.

Desk cubbies full of lonely people and stale, static air.

"It's time to grow some backbone, Remy," Herb prodded.

"You're right," she said. "You're absolutely right. I've been so spineless when it comes to you, Herb." She met her father's moss green eyes. Empty eyes, really.

"Forget the story," she said. "I'm taking it to the *Herald.*"

"You can't do that!" he yelled.

"It's too late. I'm done here. I quit." She turned toward the door.

"Oh, really? Then I *quit* paying for your doorman apartment. How would you like that?"

His jab hurt at first, but then, a moment later, it all became clear. She had no life here. Her apartment and her job had become traps . . . traps that she needed to free herself from.

By cutting her off, Herb was actually liberating her.

"Thank you," she said aloud.

"What?" Herb snapped from behind her.

She paused, wheeled on her father. "Thanks. I've never felt so free. I'll start packing my things."

He sneered. "You can't get off that easy. I know you, Remy. You'll never make it on your own."

Watch me. She walked away, the air around her popping with energy. *Just watch me.*

"And then I walked out . . . just like that." Speaking on her cell phone from an overstuffed chair in a downtown bookstore, Remy gave Dakota the high points of her day.

"Honey, I am so proud of you." Dakota's voice, which sounded grainy as usual, reassured her. "You cut the ties that were strangling you, and that had to be doubly hard with your father being boss man."

"I just couldn't take it anymore. Yeah, Herb's a pain in the neck but he was just the last straw. I realized that nothing was going to make me happy there. I felt like an invisible person."

"How's that?"

"I showed up for work every day, but no one really saw me. And despite all the time I was away in Lancaster County, it didn't seem to matter that I was gone."

"Ouch. Did you always feel that way at the *Post*?"

"Always." But not in Halfway. There, she had mattered.

"So . . . what's next? Do you want to hop on a train and hang here for a few days?"

"Don't be mad." Remy turned toward the window of the big bookstore. It was the middle of the day, but sunlight couldn't reach between the buildings. "But I want to go back to Halfway."

"Why would I be mad at that? And . . . well, what would you do there?"

"For starters, I'd like to meet with one of the ministers from Adam's congregation. Sadie said she would go with me for support."

"You're serious about this Amish thing?" Dakota's voice held the weight of their years of friendship. "Even without Adam?"

Remy sighed. "Even without him. But I need to know more. Meeting with a preacher is a way to start. There's also the matter of getting to know the rest of the Amish community. As you pointed out when we last spoke, I spent nearly two weeks with the Kings, but I don't know much about the rest of the community. I need to see if it's a good fit for me. Maybe I can get a job in one of Halfway's shops."

"I think that's a good plan. Just promise me you won't go getting baptized without letting me know first. Even by snail mail?"

Remy laughed. "Relax. The baptism ceremony isn't until next autumn. We'll talk lots before then."

"Just saying . . . I'm not going to lose you, honey. Share you, yes, but you need to stay in touch." After a pause, Dakota added, "So . . . what if you run into Adam while you're in Halfway?"

"I can always hope for the best. I still think of him all the time."

"Of course you do. You fell in love with that guy, and I know you won't stalk him or anything, but I can tell you haven't given up completely."

"I fell in love with Adam and his whole world," Remy said. "Now I have to see if the attraction is real. I can't make this commitment without being one hundred percent sure of it."

"Then go for it, honey," Dakota said. "Give it all you've got."

The next day, Remy found a toll-free number for Nancy's Nutty Muesli Bars online. As she pressed the button to speak to a real person, she paced through her apartment, wondering if she would miss this place. Funny, but she hadn't given it a second thought when she was snowbound in Halfway. The music on the line ended, and an older woman's voice said: "This is Nancy Briggs. What can I do you for?"

"Nancy, it's Remy McCallister." As Nancy was never one to mince words, Remy cut right to the chase. "You said you needed some help with production, and it looks like I'm in need of a job."

"Let me think about that. I know you're a hard worker. Any experience in the snack food industry?"

"Well, I did help you mix up that batch of muesli. I love to bake, and I would work for cheap. Room and board, until I can prove my worth—"

"We need to pay you a wage, too. I'm not in the habit of bringing in indentured servants. But we'll figure out details when you get here. When can you start?"

Remy laughed. "Tomorrow." The promise of escaping the city lifted a heavy burden from her shoulders. It was a move away from a lonely past and a plunge into the only future she could imagine. A life among the Amish. A life within a community.

Remy was going home.

FORTY-FIVE

"The ground isn't frozen anymore," Gabe remarked as Jonah stabbed the shovel deep into the earth. "I guess spring is really here." At this rate they would be ready to set the fence posts and pour cement this afternoon.

Adam scraped some of the loose dirt away, blinking as the sight of his brother digging brought him back to the grim memory of digging their parents' graves.

He had shared the task with Jonah and some cousins. They had needed pickaxes to break through the frozen crust, and Adam had put his anger into it, beating the earth with all the regret of a wayward son. Even after the first cracks, the frozen parcel of dirt held tight beneath the pick, as if to say the earth was not ready to accept his parents' bodies.

To everything there is a season, and a time to every purpose under the heaven. . . .

Adam had been sure that terrible winter was not his parents' season, not their time to die. They should not have died in an act of useless violence. They should not have died thinking their oldest son had left the Plain life and the faith.

Now he realized his own foolishness at questioning God's order of things. His parents' deaths had been part of God's plan, and although he still missed Mamm and Dat, at least now he could accept that they were gone.

As Adam shoved the blade into the earth, a red, white, and blue FedEx truck bounced down their driveway. Although Adam had spent three years among the English, the sight of the truck, contrasting with the pastoral hills, the windmill, and the barn with its silos, brought a smile to his face. The crossover between two cultures was sometimes a reality check.

"Looks like a special delivery," Jonah said. "Want to go check it out?"

"It'll keep." Why waste time making an unnecessary trip back, especially since he and his brothers were in a routine now, with four holes dug already. The sun was shining, a warm day for March, and the pace of work suited him just fine.

As he grabbed his shovel and followed Jonah down to the next hole, he figured the delivery had to be from Remy. Maybe it was another gift for the children, in which case he wouldn't have to deal with it at all.

But he suspected it involved him. He had heard she'd returned to Halfway in the beginning of March. Living and working with Nancy Briggs.

Remy, here in Halfway. Every time he wondered what that could mean, something flickered in his chest. So much energy had been spent trying to forget her. Now, he imagined he'd have to weave through Halfway, trying to avoid her.

A few hours later he was fetching a tool from the old workshop when Mary called to him.

"Adam? Where are you hiding?"

"By the workbench."

Mary held the flat cardboard envelope toward him. "This came for you. From Remy."

"Denki." Adam took the large envelope. He considered tossing it into the wood shavings on the floor, but something stopped him.

Mary's fingers smoothed down the sides of her apron. "Aren't you going to open it?"

"Later. I've got to get back to the fence."

"She's back, you know."

"So I've heard."

"You know she's talked to the bishop about joining our church."

"She did?" That was quite a step. "How do you know this?"

"Our own sister Sadie went with her, but I didn't hear it from her. Someone brought it up at a quilting bee."

So Sadie had gone along. . . . Not surprising, since Sadie had told him she was sticking by Remy. "After everything we've been through, I can forgive her for a lie," Sadie had told him.

Mary moved closer to the worktable. "Are you planning to see her?"

"If I drive through town with my eyes open, I might see her, ya."

She laughed. "You're so hard on yourself." She fingered the handle of the steel vise. "Hard on her, too."

He kept his eyes on the tool tray. "What's for lunch?"

"Cheeseburger soup, and I get the message. I'll leave you alone."

He left the envelope on the tool bench as he combed through the tools, searching for what? He couldn't recall.

The cardboard was crisp and glossy in his hands as he ripped it open. Inside was a four-page typed story, unpublished, from the looks of it.

Worrying the pages of the article that had destroyed his relationship with Remy, he took it upstairs, to the wood shop's tiny attic where the children liked to play. Recently Leah had taken to schooling Simon here, a practice they both seemed to enjoy, with Leah reading to him and correcting his short compositions. On the small carton they used as a table lay Simon's marble notebook, stubby pencils, and a pair of small binoculars he'd seen the children passing around for bird-watching.

He sat beside the crate, knees to his chin, and dared himself a glance at the first page. "Amish Life: The Light from Within" was the title.

Sort of soft for the details of a double murder.

With clenched jaw, he began to read and quickly realized it was not the investigative story Remy had planned. Instead, it was a humorous essay of love for an Amish family. Remy's details were poignant and amusing, and she captured the flavor of life here among the Plain People.

He choked up when she mentioned "the quiet boy" who found his voice.

Their Simon.

Sometimes he wondered if she had championed the murder investigation for Simon, as a way of helping him find some closure. Other times, he chastised himself for thinking Remy was at all trustworthy. He figured that you could forgive a liar, but it was foolish to think you could trust her.

And what of Remy's investigative story? There wasn't a word about his parents' murders in this piece. Not a single word.

She was dressed Amish, and the hunter green dress brought out the hue of her eyes, bringing to mind a verdant summer pasture. Adam paused in Zook's barn, at the edge of the marketplace, and ducked behind a shed, waiting for his pulse to return to normal.

What was it about Remy that set him off balance every time he saw her? Why did he like so many things about her, from her desire to make people happy to that mischievous look on her face when she smiled? If this attraction wasn't so strong, it would be no problem to walk up to her and straighten things out.

But it was a problem.

The sick feeling wasn't going away; he might as well get this over with, and then future meetings probably wouldn't prove so awkward. He approached the table stacked with boxes of muesli bars and waited until she finished with her group of customers.

"Remy."

She lifted her face, her eyes glimmering. "Adam! It's really good to see you . . . well, I wasn't sure if you'd be speaking to me."

He lifted a granola bar, as if testing its weight. "I heard you were working for Nancy."

"She's been wonderful, putting me up and everything. A real lifesaver."

"Nancy is good people."

"Turns out I've connected with a lot of good people here. I'm going to make Halfway my home, but . . . Preacher Dave said I should talk to you first about joining the congregation."

Adam stared at her. She was serious about this.

"He said I could start visiting Sunday services, as long as it's okay with you."

"Okay with me?"

"I don't want you to feel like I'm stalking you, and I don't want you to be uncomfortable. I respect your privacy and . . . did you read my article?"

"I did. It was very nice." He tossed the bar back into the box. "What happened to your investigative report?"

She looked down at her folded hands. "I didn't have it in me. I thought you knew that when I left? Writing about your family was the reason I came, but it drifted by the wayside once I got to know everyone."

Once you became a part of us, he thought, *like the center patch of a diamond quilt.*

It still hurt him. He was supposed to be forgiving her, but the wound was so fresh.

A customer came by, and he waited as she made the sale.

When they were alone again, he moved to a safer subject. "You know, the children still talk about you."

"Do they?" Her brows rose. "I miss them. I really miss them. But I would never drop in at the farm. I'll give you your—" Her hand flew to cover her mouth as she stared across the market. "There's Simon!"

Adam turned to see his brother frozen, his mouth open in a perfect oval.

"Come on over." Adam gestured for Simon to join them, and the boy began to walk over but quickly accelerated to a run.

"Remy! You're here!" Simon looked up at his older brother for approval.

Adam gave a nod, but Remy was already coming around the table, her arms outstretched.

"You are a sight to behold," Remy gushed, taking the boy into her arms and rocking him in a hug.

A grin lit up Simon's face. "And you're a sight to hold on to."

Adam had to smile. He couldn't dispute Simon's attachment to her.

"Leah's been helping me write a letter to you . . . but now you're here! Can you come back to the farm?"

Remy bit her lower lip. "I don't think that would be a good idea."

"Just for a visit?" Simon begged.

It was the last thing he wanted, and yet Adam knew he had

to say the words. It was part of practicing peace: gelassenheit. He cleared his throat and said: "I want you to know you're welcome in our home."

Remy looked up at him, biting back emotion. "That means a lot to me. I promise you, I won't abuse that privilege."

He nodded. "Good."

"Wonderful good!" Simon lifted his finger. "Wait here while I fetch Ruthie and Sadie. They'll want to see you, too!"

Remy straightened as he scampered off. She leaned against the edge of the table next to Adam as if they did this all the time.

When he turned to her, he lost his thoughts because her face was just inches from him, creamy skin, tawny lips, and those green eyes that he longed to lose himself in.

"So, does that mean you don't hate me anymore?" she asked. The way she squinted tugged at something inside him.

He had it bad.

"I could never hate you."

A broken smile parted her lips. "Well, you had me fooled."

He took a breath, thinking he would spare her the lecture on forgiveness. He thought of Dave's advice. Just act like it's happened, faith into action. "As I said, I've been wrestling with a few issues."

"I know how that is."

"Since we're throwing out the difficult questions, I have to ask you what you're doing here. Why did you come back?"

"That's a tough one." Her eyes suddenly clouded with something he couldn't decipher before she looked away. "In a nutshell, I came back to be part of this community. Back in the city . . ." She shrugged. "I just didn't matter there. But here, I make a difference. I feel closer to God here, and when I'm in Halfway, I feel connected to the people around me. Does that make sense?"

He nodded, recalling his time away from home. The outside world had proven to be alive with activity, but lacking in spirit.

Once again they were interrupted when Simon returned with Ruthie and the twins, who squealed with pleasure to see Remy.

"Sadie wants to see you, too," Ruthie said, holding Remy's hand, "but she had to stay and make the sales."

"We're selling cheese today," Susie reported.

"And I spotted a rare bird with the binoculars you gave me." Leah shifted from foot to foot. "An ash-throated flycatcher."

"That's fantastic! I'll come visit with Sadie on my break. I've missed you so much!" Remy put a hand on Leah's right shoulder. "So what did your rare bird look like? Was he cute?"

Adam pulled himself away from the group. Let them enjoy their reunion. For although he enjoyed being near Remy, the pain was still there.

In fact, he wondered if there had been any healing at all.

That night, just after Katie and Sam were tucked into bed, the house was jolted by the sound of thunder. Upstairs in the new bathroom, Adam was on his knees caulking around the tub when the blast rocked the house.

He propped the caulking gun on a piece of old newspaper and went to check. From downstairs he heard the girls squeal and giggle. Then a wailing sound came from the boys' room.

"Simon?" Adam found his brother staring out the window of the bedroom.

"It's okay, buddy. It's just part of the storm. Remember the science books? When the lightning bolt hits the air, it causes shock waves that echo down to earth."

"I know that." Simon sniffed. "It's not the storm. I need the binoculars. Every night I stand here and look out with the binoculars. But tonight I can't find them."

Adam sat on the bed behind him. "What do you look for?"

"Cars. I think if someone gets stuck on the road, then I will tell you, and you will help them."

"I see." After all that Simon had been through, Adam would have thought the boy would be on the lookout for invaders; but it was just the opposite. He was ready to play the Good Samaritan. Simon had forgiven.

Simon swiped a sleeve over his eyes. "I can't see the road now. And the rain makes it worse."

"I think we need to find your binoculars."

A quick search of the room turned up nothing. The field glasses were most likely in the attic of the wood shop, where Leah did most of the homeschooling with Simon. As Adam dashed through the streaking rain, he realized it was time for Simon to go back to school, now that the media interest had died down and the killer had been apprehended. Simon would be happy to return to the schoolhouse with Teacher Emma.

Adam lifted the lantern inside the dark shop and found his way to the ladder. Right away he could see the small binoculars, placed neatly beside Simon's marble notebook. He propped the lantern on the crate, taking a moment to look through the lessons Simon had written. There were lists of spelling words and short essays about snow and how to care for your horse. Adam could see Leah's help in these. Maybe she would enjoy teaching in their little school-house one day.

When he came upon a letter to Remy in the notebook, Adam paused. Was this just for practice?

Dear Remy,

Leah has been bird-watching, but she lets me use her glasses, too. Sometimes I watch from my window at night. I look for the lights of your car. Most of the snow has melted but it's very muddy. If you get stuck in the mud, you can come stay with us. Adam is still very mad, but someday I think he will forgive and he will like you again.

Your friend,
Simon King

Simon's message hit hard. He closed the book, grabbed the binoculars and lantern, and retreated into the storm. Raindrops pinged against his hat as he sloshed through the mud.

All this time, he'd been walking around in a cloud of anger so dark and dangerous even a child could see it. He had hated himself for holding on to the pain. And now he hated himself for hating himself.

Why couldn't he just let go?

Gelassenheit. Peace. Serenity.

Heavenly Father, please grant me the serenity to let this pain go.

The sky flashed bright, followed by bounding rumbles of thunder.

Heal me, Father. Please, let me catch gelassenheit.

Another lightning strike, and in that split second he saw his life torn in half. The hills were white, the sky split by a jagged line of electricity.

Split down the middle, as if to say, *That was your past, this is your future. . . .*

He removed his hat, letting the rain pelt his head and wash down his skin as he returned to the house, a new man.

FORTY-SIX

The storm raged through the night, periodically tapping her window, then shifting with the wind to rattle the branches of trees behind Nancy's house.

Remy was awake through most of it, her state of mind matching the rolling thunder and bright white lightning. She wouldn't have slept even on the calmest of nights, as her thoughts and emotions had been scratched raw again at the sight of Adam.

What was she doing here?

That was the question he'd asked her, and though she'd answered truthfully she was now beginning to question the wisdom of her plan. Building a life in Halfway, dodging the perimeter of Adam and his family, she would be facing painful reminders of her own sin and failure every single day.

What had she been thinking?

Tonight she had more questions than answers.

Sometime during the night the angriest part of the weather

front passed, and Remy drifted off to sleep until the sound of the ringing phone woke her.

Not even six A.M.

She opened her bedroom door and heard Nancy down in the kitchen.

"Right through the roof? Thank the good Lord you're okay. Did you get any rain inside?"

Recognizing concern in Nancy's voice, Remy padded downstairs and faced the older woman across the wide granite island.

"That's awful, Gina, but you know, things can be replaced. You just sit tight. I'm coming over. No, it's no bother at all, and I have no qualms about alerting the Kings. They'll fix it right up. We all will. You just sit tight." Nancy pressed the button to end the connection, her mouth a slash of concern.

"That didn't sound good."

"That was Gina Mueller. You know, Chris's mother? Talk about adding insult to injury. A huge tree came down in the storm last night. Sounds like it lopped off the corner of her house."

"Scary. No one was hurt?"

"Fortunately, it came down on the side of the house, but she now has branches poking through her kitchen ceiling, as well as rain. I'm going to head over, sit with her for a bit. I'll let the Kings know along the way. It's their property, and I'm sure they'll do the repairs, but Gina is too ashamed to speak to them right now. She's devastated about what her boy did."

Although she'd never met Gina, Remy felt a stab of compassion for the woman. It was a difficult situation all around.

"Do you mind if I come along? I'd like to help."

Nancy sucked on a front tooth. "That'll work. I'll get dressed and meet you in the garage."

Although the rain had stopped, the street glistened and here and there trees and bushes were bent from the force of the storm. On the way to the Muellers' house, they decided it would be best for Nancy to stay with Gina while Remy went to the Kings' house. From the crushed-stone driveway, Remy could only see parts of the crown of the tree on the house's rooftop as she jumped into the driver's seat, put the Jeep in gear, and headed back to the main road.

The turnoff to the King family farm was endearingly familiar, as if reading a favorite book once again. The vehicle bumped as she passed the cluster of beech trees and suddenly she was awash with memories of riding on the sled past these trees. The family of Amish snow people had been over by the front of the house, and she'd stood near Adam, almost kissed him by that paddock gate.

Tamping down memories, she rolled toward the barn, where she assumed the milking was just finishing up. Inside the cowshed some of the kids called her name in glee, but she held her hands up.

"I'm here on a mission. Where's Adam?"

A head rose above one of the cows. Adam.

"I have to talk to you," she said.

His stare was intense as he came to the center aisle. She didn't know how long she could maintain composure under the scrutiny of his piercing eyes.

"You probably didn't expect to see me so soon, but there's been some storm damage. A tree came down and hit Gina Mueller's house." His harsh expression softened as she told him about the older woman's distress and uneasiness about contacting the King family for repairs.

"But we'll help Gina gladly. She can't think we would hold a grudge."

"I think her defenses are down. There's the awful business with Chris, her home is in chaos, and she's not sure where to turn."

"And she had hip surgery this year." He paused, calculating.

"I'm not sure she gets around too well. We'll give her help cleaning up inside, too."

Jonah joined them, concern creasing his forehead. "Gina has been our neighbor for as long as I can remember. We'll take care of her."

"It's an in-between Sunday," Adam said, thinking aloud. "We'll gather some friends and get the tree off her house, start repairs. At the very least we can cover the roof with a tarp until all the repairs are done."

It was decided that Adam would drive over with Remy to assess the damage, while Jonah, Gabe, and Mary got the word out for saws and able-bodied workers. Relief fell over her as she put the Jeep into gear. She had known Adam and his family would do the right thing. These were the people she would want behind her in a crisis.

However, the proximity in Nancy's car reminded her of the high emotion that swirled around them when they were alone together. Although she tried to keep her eyes on the road, she couldn't resist quick glances at Adam sitting tall in the seat, his hat in his lap.

Trying to focus, she pulled onto the road.

A second later she was shocked to find his hand on her shoulder.

"Take it slow. The road is still wet."

She nodded, easing up on the gas and wondering why she was still so crazy for him.

"I'm glad you came to let us know about the tree. I suspect it wasn't so easy for you."

"It wasn't. I wasn't ready to drive down memory lane. Much as I miss everyone, I wasn't ready to test my feelings for you and your family yet. It's still too soon." There. She'd said it.

And he didn't seem surprised.

She eased her white-knuckled grip on the steering wheel, trying to relax. "One of these days, I don't know when, but someday I'll find the strength to move on. For now, it's just the way I feel."

"And you can't control your feelings. You can control your actions . . . but not your feelings."

She was surprised that he understood that part. "Exactly."

"Take a left here."

He pointed and she turned down the drive toward the Mueller house. Before she'd cut the engine, Adam was out of the Jeep. He headed around the house and she followed, coming to the unnatural-looking sight of the downed oak.

A massive tree, it lay in a bed of mud and smashed branches. On its side, it resembled a huge ship. "Noah's ark," she said aloud.

He turned to her. "Have you been reading the Bible?"

"Actually, I have." She thought it would be wise to familiarize herself with the Bible again, as the Sunday church services would be in German, not an easy language for her.

A section of soil had been displaced where the bulk of the heavy trunk had landed. Adam moved past it to touch the bark. Then, as if mounting a horse, he hitched himself up and stood atop the trunk. "I'll bet it's more than a hundred years old."

Remy picked her way through damp grass to examine the disabled roots, dirty tentacles forking madly into the air. Fortunately, the bulk of the tree had missed the house, the crown grazing one corner of the roof, where the storm gutter now dangled.

"How are you and your brothers going to move this?"

"We're going to need help."

"I'm so embarrassed." The woman holed up under a blanket on the corner of the sofa was frail and petite, childlike but for her close-cropped silver curls. Remy supposed she seemed all the more frail because she had not completely recovered from surgery, and needed the aid of a walker to get around.

Nancy had made a pot of coffee, and though she kept trying to downplay the inconvenience of the fallen tree, it was apparent that there were other undercurrents rising to the surface here, things that needed to be addressed.

When Adam sat down across from Gina Mueller, all the air seemed to leave the room.

Gina cradled the warm mug in both hands, her eyes on the cracked wall and protruding tree limb. "I'm absolutely mortified. We've caused your family so much grief. Devastating heartbreak. And you've never shown us anything but kindness."

"You have some of the details wrong, Gina." Adam sat facing her from a wooden dinette chair that they had moved out of the damaged room. "You never did anything to harm us. You were a good friend to my mamm for as long as I can remember. You were there for her when she lost the little ones."

Gina pulled her coffee mug closer to her chest. "I was. That was such a terrible thing."

Adam leaned forward, his dark eyes steady on the older woman. "Mamm enjoyed your friendship. You have done nothing to be ashamed of."

"But my son . . ." Gina's eyes glistened with tears. "What he did is unforgivable."

Nancy handed her a box of tissues, while Adam drew in a breath.

For a second, Remy's mind flashed to the scene of the murders . . . the buggy pulled onto the shoulder of the dark winter road. There was some reassurance in knowing that the man with the gun would not kill again. Still, justice could not bring back Esther and Levi King.

"Gina, you know what the Amish believe about forgiveness." Adam's voice was gentle as he pressed a fist to his chest and closed his eyes. "I can honestly tell you, there is no hatred in my heart for Chris."

"After what he did?" Gina put her mug on the side table and dabbed at her eyes with a tissue. "Killing people for money. I know you heard about his moneymaking scheme. Chris's big ideas about having a hunting preserve on our old land, the back acres your family uses for grazing. He was going to stock it with ring-necked pheasant and charge a fee to the hunters."

"Like Mason's Preserve up north," Nancy said.

Gina nodded. "Only Levi wouldn't allow it."

"Dat wanted our land to be a safe haven for all living things. I can see why he would object to a plan like that."

"Ironically, Chris thought he was doing it all to take care of me. He thought I wanted to buy this land back. He was trying to raise money for it, because of me. As if any of that was important . . ." Gina shook her head. "I am so sorry, Adam. So very sorry."

Adam kneeled beside Gina and took her hands. "I know your heart is heavy. Only the Lord God can ease that pain." He drew in a breath, waiting until she met his gaze. "But I can remove that tree and fix your roof. And you can keep working at your physical therapy until you're strong again." He squeezed Gina's hands. "And right now, you can help Nancy start another pot of coffee because any minute now, there's going to be a league of men outside working on that tree."

"Oh, my goodness!" Gina squeezed his hands hard. "You're a good man, Adam. I wish your mother were here to see what a fine young man you've turned out to be."

Straightening, Adam stood tall, a smile warming his face.

A genuine smile, amid all this heartache.

Remy blinked as she realized there'd been some shift deep inside him. Like shifting sands that begin to build over time and one day . . . suddenly there is an island in the stream.

Outside the cold nip in the air was fading, the wind dying as Adam circled the fallen tree, as if measuring.

"What happened in there?" Remy asked, following him.

"It's part of a process, something I've been praying for." His eyes swept over her, warming her. "Have you heard of gelassenheit?"

She squinted as the sun shot out from behind a cloud. "Can't say that I have."

"It's at the core of the Anabaptist faith, and there's no single word to describe it. It means peace, or tranquility. To be calm or surrender inside. A silence of the soul."

"It sounds like a beautiful thing."

"It is." He turned to face her and extended a hand.

Her pulse raced as she reached out to him, their palms touching with a jolt of their own electricity. And then suddenly, he was pulling her close.

His dark eyes shone with a new intensity, the smooth hum of peace, the light of love.

"Remy . . . I was wrong to push you away. I tried to punish you, and ended up hurting a lot of people in the process. Myself included."

She gasped as the planet stopped moving, then turned again, this time on a slightly different axis. The air around them seemed to snap with renewal.

"My heart was broken." She bit her lower lip, trying to control the swell of emotion. "I didn't know where to turn, what to do. I just knew that I had to get back here to Halfway and try to salvage something from the life you showed me."

"I thank God that you came back." His hands moved to her shoulders, his thumbs gently caressing her neck. "You came home."

When his lips touched hers, the kiss was sweet, then deeper, with a promise of more. She reached up to his shoulders and held on tight as sensations fiercer than last night's winds whipped through her.

He broke off the kiss, lifting his head. "Marry me, Remy. Marry me and share my home and family."

"Oh, Adam . . . I can't imagine a life without you."

He brushed her lips again, then pulled her close. Remy closed her eyes and breathed with him, her senses alive, her spirit reborn.

"I love you, Remy . . . even if you are named after a brandy."

"Call me Rebecca," she said.

He leaned back. "Before I speak to the deacon, I want you to be sure." He brushed a thumb along her jaw line. "There'll be no chance for rumspringa for you."

"Are you kidding me?" She cocked an eyebrow. "I've had a lifetime of rumspringa. I'm ready. I love you, and I want nothing more than to be your wife."

Was that thundering noise the beating of her heart? She closed her eyes and thanked God for this amazing blessing as the pounding sound grew louder. Galloping horses.

"And then there's the matter of my ten siblings needing a mother."

She opened one eye. "Ten? That could be a deal-breaker."

"They're very well behaved," he said with a wink.

"Well, as far as I can see Mary and Jonah are old enough to be on their own, and Sadie and Gabe are well on their way, but I'll be happy to get to know them even better as their sister-in-law."

"Aah, they grow up so quickly."

"The others, you know I just adore them, and I'll try to guide and help them in any way I can."

"You've been a huge help already. You brought light back into our home. Light and laughter."

He pulled her hands to his lips and placed a kiss on her knuckles. "And if ten isn't enough, we can pray God will bless us with a few children of our own."

Her eyes misted at the prospect of having Adam's baby one day. "A big Amish family," she whispered.

"We'll work on that after we're married. For now, I'd better get to work. It sounds like the men are here." He hurried away from the fallen oak, playfully tugging on her hand to follow.

As they moved away from the fat tree trunk, the panorama that emerged on the landscape took her breath away.

Horses galloped over the near slope, their riders clad in black with broad-brimmed hats on their heads like New Age cowboys. A line of gray buggies filed down the lane, their steel wheels wobbling over the rutted road. Someone needed help, and the community had sparked to action.

As lemony sunshine broke through the clouds, Remy thanked God for bringing her to this land and into the arms of this community. Men began buzzing around the huge tree with saws, steadily cutting the fat trunk into manageable timber.

When women began to arrive, Remy jumped into the fray. They moved through the workers, serving water and coffee. On the long tables set up on sawhorses, Mary set out trays of sandwiches. Mammi, Nancy, and Gina sat on one of the benches, enjoying the fresh air and the symphony of hammers and saws.

Remy finished pouring lemonade for an older man who'd been rigging a pulley. Then she glanced to the ladder and watched as Adam swung onto the roof. She wanted to savor the sunshine and the lean, handsome man pounding nails into the rooftop. Today was the beginning of their Amish life together, and she had never known such happiness. She prayed to God that their union would be blessed.

Forever blessed.

ACKNOWLEDGMENTS

While writing this book I became aware of the many groups within a community that lend us support, and I am grateful to everyone who helped on this project.

To my agent, Robin Rue, who got it all started: "It's all good!"

I am grateful to my editor, Junessa Viloria, for her gentle hand in shaping a story, her understanding of the juggling act, and her bright enthusiasm.

I am indebted to Professor Violet Dutcher for her attention to both small details and the big picture of Amish culture. Her personal experiences, her understanding of story composition, and her relationships to people in various Amish communities have been invaluable.

The works of John Hostetler, Donald Kraybill, and Suzanne Woods Fisher provided a wealth of information and insight.

And many thanks to the people in Lancaster County who have inspired my characters and stories and helped verify customs, language, and traditions. Denki.

Read on for an exciting preview of

A

Simple Spring

the next Seasons of Lancaster novel

by Rosalind Lauer

"Oh, send the sunshine down my way. . . ." Sadie King sang the bright song to the green juniper bushes and the chickens and little Sam and Katie and anyone else who wanted to listen on this glorious morning.

All around her on the King family farm, plants and animals were coming alive, blossoming and sprouting green leaves and pushing up strong shoots through the earth. Birdsong filled the air around them, along with the scents of sweet flowers like honeysuckle and wisteria. The sweetness mixed with the sharp smell of the fields, where her brothers had turned manure into the warming soil to make it fertile for more things to grow.

Signs of spring surrounded her, and she poured her joy into the melody that flowed from her heart. God was renewing the farm, breathing life into everything.

Including her.

Sadie was in rumspringa, and her new life included an Englisher boy named Frank Marconi and the wonderful good bounty of music he had shown her. Music outside the Amish community wasn't just used to praise God. There was jazz and rock and roll, music to dance to, folk music, and songs to sing along to. The English had songs to make you sad and songs that made you feel like you were soaring between puffy clouds.

Like "Blossom," the song she was singing this morning as she steered her youngest siblings toward the chicken coop.

"Stay out here, Katie. You can start feeding them." Sadie removed the heavy lid from the seed bucket and grabbed a small handful.

Two-year-old Katie giggled as she tossed feed onto the ground, attracting the flapping hens. "Eat, now! Eat!" she ordered, enjoying this almost as much as the chickens.

"Why do we gather eggs twice a day?" Sam asked as he shooed a handful of hens from the coop. At the age of five, Sam was full of questions.

"If we let the eggs sit for too long, the chickens might hop onto them and break them," Sadie explained as she reached to the hook inside the coop for the pair of leather gloves. "Besides, we want our eggs to be fresh as can be."

Most of the chickens had fled the coop, but as usual cranky Lumpig perched on the edge of a nesting box. Her beady eyes dared anyone to come close.

"She always stays inside." Sam put his pail down, frowning. "Why is she so mean?"

"She's just keeping watch over her little treasures. Aren't you, Lumpig?" Sadie held up her handful of feed for the hen to see, then tossed it out the doorway onto the ground outside the coop. "Skit-skat."

Immediately Lumpig hopped from the nest, flapping her wings and scurrying to her breakfast.

"How do you do that?" Sam asked.

"Just distract her with the feed."

"Can I do the eggs today?"

"That's fine, but mind you're quick about it. Lumpig will be back to guard her eggs again." Sadie reached for the broom. "You do that, and I'll sweep up." As she started to sweep old hay and manure from the corners of the small hut, she launched into a song that made her think of Frank.

"Daydreaming and I'm thinking of you . . ." When their band was choosing music to learn, Frank always wanted songs that Sadie could belt out, songs that allowed her to hold the notes a long time. "Bluesy songs," he called them.

"Look at my heart," she sang, caressing each note with her voice.

Sam worked just fine while she sang; he never minded her music, though one day he noted that she knew a lot of songs. And why did he not hear Sadie's songs at Sunday church?

"Because . . ." Sadie had stammered, not sure how to explain the hundreds and thousands of songs to be learned and enjoyed in the world beyond their Amish faith. "Because they're not in the Ausbund," she had told him.

Sam seemed satisfied with her answer, but it shifted Sadie's thoughts to the Ausbund, a book published over four hundred years ago. There was no music printed in the book, only words, but the melodies had been passed down over generations. Was that the reason music seemed to be part of her very soul?" Even as a little baby, she had been brought by Mamm and Dat to Sunday services, where *vorsingers* led the congregation in song. Over time, the German songs were carved into each person's heart.

Amish songs were very different from music in the Englisher world. Sung without an organ or piano accompanying it, an Amish song was slow and haunting. Sometimes it took more than fifteen minutes just to do three stanzas. Most of the songs in the Ausbund had been written by Anabaptists while they were prisoners in the dungeons of Passau Castle so very long ago, back in the 1500s. Amish songs were the music of her childhood, part of her heritage. Sadie believed they had unlocked the voice inside her and opened the door to her curiosity about music.

All music.

She had met Frank because of music. They both worked at the Halfway Hotel, Sadie as a housekeeper and Frank on the maintenance staff. One day, Frank had heard Sadie singing as she pushed her cleaning cart down the hotel corridor. She'd been singing a popular hymn that teens might do in youth groups. She couldn't remember what exactly, but she did remember how he came tromping down the corridor with a rake in his hand.

With his dark hair that stood up straight from his head and the little triangle of a beard on his chin, Frank had frightened her at first. He was just a bit taller than her, but his shoulders were broad and he reminded her of an angry bull as he stomped toward her. Oh, he'd scared her.

"Is that you singing?" he demanded, leaning the rake over one shoulder. "What's a church girl like you doing with a voice like that?"

She pressed a hand to her mouth. She had already stopped singing.

"What's the matter?" He squinted, studying her. "Are you shy?"

"I . . . I thought you were mad."

"I'll only be mad if you let a voice like that go to waste. Do you do any singing professionally? Choir? Band? The shower?"

She laughed aloud, and that eased things between them. Although Sadie wasn't comfortable talking when she was supposed to be working for her boss, Mr. Decker, she agreed to meet Frank after work. They went across the street to the pizza place, and Frank had bought two slices of cheese pizza, one for each of them to eat while they chatted.

The whole thing still made Sadie's heart race when she recalled how she had gone on her first date with an Englisher, just like that. They had talked and laughed, and before they parted she agreed to sing for him—just one verse of "Silent Night" in the parking lot.

Oh, the courage she'd had that night! And foolishness, too. Dates with strangers in town and performances in dark parking lots were not the sort of activities Amish girls engaged in. Even Amish girls in rumspringa, their "running around" time as a teenager.

But Sadie knew she was no ordinary Amish girl. It wasn't about hochmut or pride. She wasn't proud of the fact that she was different. But there was something driving her from inside, something in her heart, and she believed it was Gott pushing her to use the gift he'd given her—her voice. All good things came from the Lord in heaven, and she was grateful to have music in her heart.

Soon after she met Frank, he brought his friend Red to meet her after work. And a few days later the three of them, along with a girl named Tara, were "hanging out" in Red's garage, making music. Real music! Red had a drum set and a deep voice, thick as molasses. Tara played bass guitar, which Sadie was convinced was music from the belly of the earth. And Frank's fingers danced over his guitar, finding melodies or strumming to make a field of sound that surrounded Sadie's voice, broader and bolder than any field she had ever worked.

The band had been rehearsing at least once a week ever since, and they'd even taken some trips in Frank's van to Philadelphia to perform some songs at clubs. These clubs allowed groups to come up to the microphone and give it a try. "Open mike night," Frank called it. So far Sadie enjoyed performing with her band, but she hated having to sneak away from home to do it. She had never lied about what she was doing—not exactly—but she suspected that their bishop would not approve if he ever found out.

Phew! It made her heart heavy to worry about such things ... especially on such a beautiful spring day. And she had much to look forward to today. After she finished her chores here, she would scooter into Halfway and work a shift at the hotel, cleaning rooms and pushing the big, growling electric vacuum over the rugs. She wasn't sure if Frank was working tonight, but the band would surely be practicing at Red's house in the evening, and that was the part of her day that truly warmed her heart.

She pushed the load of dirty hay into the compost heap. It would make good fertilizer for the vegetable garden.

Having finished with the feed, Katie squatted down with a stick in hand, scratching in the dirt. Katie loved her crayons and was always drawing something.

Sadie and Sam made quick work of putting fresh straw in the henhouse.

"Can I carry the eggs?" Sam asked. He was a good boy, always wanting to take on more grown-up jobs on the farm.

She tested the bucket—not too heavy. "Ya, you can carry it."

As they walked down the lane, little sparrows chirped and jumped in the dense bushes, while a handful of blackbirds soared overhead, heading toward the barns and silos, then circling to the right, down toward the fields and pond.

"Look at those birds, so happy to be flying over God's land," Sadie told the little ones. "Our dat used to take care of them, putting out seed and making sure they had a safe place to live."

"And now he watches them from heaven," Sam said.

Sadie smiled. "Ya." Sometimes, when she was singing, Sadie felt like those birds, gliding on the wave of a breeze. The music could lift her right out of these old sneakers. She couldn't wait for tonight's rehearsal. She was already dressed and ready to leave the farm, with her blue jeans on under her dress, the cuffs rolled up over her knees so no one in the family would notice.

Sam moved the bucket to his other hand and hitched up his straw hat. "Adam's coming."

Sadie raised one hand to shield her eyes from the sun. Ya, Adam was heading this way, moving like a ram with his head lowered. Something was wrong, and Sadie had a feeling it had something to do with her. Now that their oldest brother was the head of the household, they seemed to butt heads often. Although he understood that rumspringa permitted her certain freedoms, he wasn't as generous as Dat had been about letting her make her own choices and mistakes.

Although Sadie adored the small freedoms of rumspringa, she did her best to respect Adam and the church leaders. She had taken on the henhouse chore this morning because she wanted to stay out of the way of her brothers and the visiting men, who were bustling around the farm with the excitement of change. After months of preparation, pouring cement for stanchions and erecting a milking barn, they were expecting the arrival of new milking equipment today. It would be powered by a generator, so they would be following all the rules of the Ordnung, but once it was all set up, what an easy task milking would be! Adam said that there would be hoses with clamps that you hooked onto the cow's teats. Hook it up and it milks the cow, one, two, three! Just like that! Sadie was glad that milking would be easier, though in her mind any amount of time spent milking cows was too much. She didn't mind hard work, but sometimes she felt overwhelmed when chores filled every minute of the day with no time to escape to Frank and her music.

As Adam came down the lane, a straw hat covering his dark hair, she wondered what his chin would look like with a marriage beard. Although Adam and Remy wouldn't be published until the fall, there was no doubt in Sadie's mind that her brother would marry come wedding season. And that was wonderful good. Adam seemed to have a lighter heart since his soon-to-be wife, Remy McCallister, had come along.

When Adam reached them, they were just passing the Doddy house, where their grandmother had lived alone in the years since their doddy had passed away.

"We got the eggs." Sam held up the smaller bucket with authority.

"We got eggs!" Katie repeated, still holding on to her drawing stick.

"Gut. You and Katie take them to Mary. She'll show you how to clean them."

"I know how to do that," Sam said.

"Then go," Adam said. "Ask Mary to prepare a cooler with lunch for Sadie and Susie."

Sadie was already shaking her head as the little ones turned toward the house. "What's wrong? Is Susie sick?" Their sister Susie suffered from glutaric aciduria, a disease that might have killed her if it weren't for the help of their doctor.

"She's fine, but she has an appointment with Dr. Trueherz today." Adam tipped his hat back, his body rigid. At times like this, Sadie could see responsibility sitting heavy on her brother's shoulders. "You know I usually take her, but I have to be here when the milking machines arrive. You need to take her to see the doctor."

Sadie blinked. "All the way to Paradise?" By horse and buggy, the trip would take an hour each way. "That will take the rest of the morning and part of the afternoon, too."

"Ya. We'll handle the rest of your chores here," Adam said.

"What about the hotel? I'm due there by eleven."

"Call Mr. Decker from the phone shanty. Tell him you can't make it today, or that you'll be late."

"Why can't someone else take her?" Sadie's throat grew tight as the prospect of her wonderful day began to slip away. "Why can't you ask Mary? Or Remy? I'll scooter over to Uncle Nate's and see if she can come immediately." Adam's beau, Remy, an Englisher girl, had moved in with their uncle Nate and aunt Betsy when the bishop advised that she needed to live Plain if she was serious about joining the Amish community.

Stepping closer, Adam put his hands on his hips, his tall frame suddenly blocking the sun. "You are to do as you're told and don't ask so many questions."

"But it's not fair when I have a job to do, and—"

"Don't question my decision," he growled.

"What's all this chatter about?" Mammi Nell appeared at the white fence by the Doddy house.

Sadie's breath caught in her throat, and Adam turned to their grandmother, dropping his hands to his side.

"I could hear you from the vegetable garden, cawing like two angry jays." Their grandmother stepped through the gate, her eyes stern behind her spectacles. "What's the matter?"

"Susie needs someone to take her for a checkup," Adam explained. "Jonah, Gabe, and I are tied up with the new equipment that should be here any minute. Nate and his sons are on their way, and Mary and Remy have their hands full preparing lunch for all the men who've come to help out."

Sadie frowned, wishing Adam had explained all that to her instead of just trying to order her around. Still, she hated to miss work . . . as well as band practice.

"And you are supposed to be at your job?" Mammi Nell asked Sadie, who nodded. Creases formed around the older woman's mouth as she mulled it over. "And this is what the two of you are snapping about on this beautiful morning?"

Sadie and Adam both looked at the ground.

"Adam, you are the head of this family now, but sometimes a parent forgets what it's like to be a young person."

Sadie couldn't resist a peek as he lifted his face. Adam had left home when he was eighteen, and only the deaths of their parents had brought him back. Sadie knew that he regretted leaving, but he didn't speak of his adventures in the world.

"Do you remember your own rumspringa?" their grandmother asked him.

His brown eyes were warm with regret beneath the brim of his straw hat. "I do, Mammi."

"Don't forget it. And Sadie, your brother Adam is a good man, and a family must follow the man at the head of the table. You must listen to Adam and try to help." Sunlight flashed on Mammi's glasses as she looked from Sadie to Adam. "Now, the two of you can work this out in peace, ya? If Sadie cannot get out of work at the hotel, maybe you'll find a driver to take you to Dr. Trueherz's clinic. It's too late to hire anyone, but you might try a friend. Maybe Lucy Kraybill or Nancy Briggs. If that doesn't work, I'll take Susie myself."

Sadie's eyes went wide at the thought of her grandmother driving a buggy to Paradise. Although she was moved by Mammi's offer of help and glad to have her grandmother on her side, she worried about the older woman driving an open buggy for nearly thirty miles. With local farmers working their fields, there was much traffic on the roads these days, and Mammi got tired easily.

"The appointment is at ten," Adam said hesitantly, and Sadie sensed that he shared her concern about their grandmother's driving. "But Sadie can go to the phone shanty and see if she can contact someone to drive."

"Gut." Mammi wiped crumbs of soil from her gloves. "You work it out, and don't let me hear angry voices again." She turned toward the garden to go back to her weeding.

"I'll ride my scooter to the phone shanty. I'll try to find a driver," Sadie said as she and Adam headed toward the farmhouse. Once she was out of sight of the house she could stop and try her cell phone, but she usually didn't get a strong signal out here in "the boondocks," as Frank called it.

"You can try. But if you can't find anyone, this is your responsibility, Sadie. I don't want the chore passed on to Mammi."

Sadie bit back an angry answer. She wanted to point out that her brother could have explained the circumstances better, that he could have told her Mary and Remy were busy. Sadie also would have agreed that Mammi wasn't fit to make this trip. But she kept mum. It wouldn't be right to argue. Adam was in charge.

She was glad when he turned off toward the milking barn. "Mind you get Susie there on time," he said before pulling his hat down and striding away.

Oh, how she wished it were proper to speak her mind. She had a few things she would tell brother Adam. Why did he wait until the last minute to tell her that Susie needed a ride to the doctor today?

Her oldest brother had become mean and bossy, so different from Dat. Their dat had believed in letting all living things fulfill their potential. It was one of the reasons that Levi King had turned this farm into a sort of sanctuary for birds and frogs and all of God's creatures. Dat would not have been so critical of Sadie. This wouldn't be happening if Mamm and Dat were here.

But Gott had chosen to take them.

And so Adam was the head of their family now, which made things difficult for Sadie. Here she was, eighteen years old, and still being treated like a young girl who'd just as soon skip through the meadow as take care of the livestock. Sadie was a hard worker, but Adam didn't see that. He didn't see her baking or cleaning or mucking the barn. The only time Adam seemed to notice her was when she was going against Amish ways by heading into town on her own or singing along with her iPod, a device not allowed by the Amish but tolerated as one of the Englisher things teenagers explored in rumspringa.

Rumspringa allowed Sadie a bit of freedom here and there, but it was not the wild time the Englisher people talked about. Amish youth were still expected to follow the Ordnung, the system of rules that had been upheld by their families and brethren over many years. The Ordnung was to be strictly followed, especially by baptized members. Under the Ordnung, there was a rule for every part of your day, from the clothes you wore to the way a farmer plowed his field.

All her life Sadie had followed these rules. They were part of her nature now, and most of the time Sadie loved her life here in Lancaster County. From planting to harvest, from sunrise to sunset, days on the farm were chock-full of work and rich with love and laughter. For all her fun with the band and her music, Sadie was always happy to come home at the end of the day and drop off to sleep in the big room upstairs that she shared with her younger sisters.

She was in a pickle. Though her heart told her to cherish and follow her music, she didn't fully understand the Lord Gott's plan for her. There wasn't really a place for a girl singer in the Amish community, and she wanted to abide by the rules of the Ordnung yet still allow her gift to grow.

It was as if she were trying to capture night and day in a single jar.

And Adam didn't have the first clue about her problem.

Her jaw was still set with resentment as she toed off her sneakers on the screened-in porch, ignoring the clatter of the kitchen where one breakfast shift was finishing. She swung the basket of eggs through the kitchen doorway, nearly mowing down her younger brother Simon, who was about to leave for school.

His eyes were as wide as quarters as he held his lunch cooler against him. "What's the matter, Sadie? You remind me of a charging bull."

Sadie sucked a breath in through her teeth and shook her head. "Never mind." She put the basket of eggs on the counter with a thump that brought a stern look from her older sister, Mary. "You'll understand when you get older."

"Older folk always say that to me, but I don't think so." Simon took his straw hat from a peg on the wall. "I don't think I'll ever understand."

"A wise boy," Jonah said, pressing his own hat to his chest. Twenty-three-year-old Jonah was only a year younger than Adam, but very different, with a quiet manner and a true knack for farming. "And you're probably right, Simon. I don't think we'll ever understand the goings-on in a woman's head."

Simon hid a grin behind the brim of his hat, and Sadie couldn't help but crack a smile. Such a tender heart, their Simon. It was always good to see merriment in his eyes.

"Off with you now, or you'll be late for school," Mary said, shooing Simon out the door. "I reckon Ruthie and Leah are already halfway down the lane."

"But I'm a fast runner. Don't forget, I run with the horses."

"Let's see how fast," Jonah said, stepping out the door behind Simon.

"Good thing they're gone," Sadie said, sorting through the eggs. "Simon is so attached to Adam, I didn't want to say anything in front of those young ears, but Adam is picking on me again. We got into it right in front of the Doddy house, and Mammi was none too happy about it."

Mary let out a breath as she nodded toward the egg basket. "There's a crack on that one. Quarreling with Adam or not, you've got to take it easy with the eggs. Next time take your anger out in the cowshed. Manure doesn't break."

"It's only two that cracked," Sadie said as she gently transferred the eggs. "I'll cook them now. Scrambled or fried?"

"Scramble them, and I'll add them to the sausage casserole. That'll help me stretch it out. Simon and Ruthie had big appetites this morning. They must be having a growth spurt." Mary turned the flame up under the coffee. "And what were you and Adam going round about this fine spring morning?"

Sadie's lips hardened. "What don't we fight about? He made it my chore to take Susie to see Dr. Trueherz, and I don't mind that one bit, but if I go, I'm going to be late for my job at the hotel. And Adam doesn't care one bit."

"Oh, Sadie." Mary glanced up from the stove, her brown eyes heavy with sympathy. "Why is it so hard for you to follow Adam's rules and decisions? He's the head of the household now, and the weight of it all is heavy on his shoulders. You know he doesn't want to argue with you."

"I know that." Sadie felt her spirits sag. She never wanted to cause trouble, but somehow, when she tried to reason with Adam, she always managed to step right into it. "But he could have told me about Susie's appointment earlier in the week. I could have talked to my boss at the hotel."

Mary just nodded. "That's all water under the bridge. What worries me is you and Adam. Storm clouds darken the sky overhead whenever you two speak."

Sadie snickered at the notion of black clouds following Adam and her. "You're right. We're always butting heads, and I don't know what to do about it."

"We'll pray to the Heavenly Father for peace in our house. I know you don't mean to stir the pot, but mind you keep quiet when Adam gives an order. I shouldn't have to tell you that Adam's decisions are more important than your boss at the hotel."

Sadie nodded. This she knew, but she was always juggling so

many things—her music and her chores, her job at the hotel and her English boyfriend—sometimes her sense of order wasn't so clear.

"Now, open that jar of peaches while I get the biscuits before they burn. In a few weeks we'll have fresh cherries and peaches. Spring fruits."

"Spring is my favorite season," Sadie said.

"Because of the fruit?"

"Because of the new life everywhere. Remember how Dat used to get so excited when the birds came back?"

"Back from their winter vacation down south, he used to say." Mary's face glowed with the memory.

Their dat had taught them to respect all God's creatures, and though he'd been gone for more than a year now, Sadie still felt Gott's peace when she worked their farm—the peace their father had opened their eyes to.

Sadie missed her parents, but she was grateful for all they had taught her. If Dat had shown them peace, Mamm had helped Sadie delight in song. Was Sadie the only one who remembered the sweet lullabies Mamm had sung for them when they were babies, with a voice as fresh and smooth as a spring wind?

"Tell me why the stars do shine," she sang as she broke the seal on the peaches.

Without looking up, Mary joined in. "Tell me why the ivy twines. Tell my why the sky's so blue. And I will tell you just why I love you."

If Sadie closed her eyes she could almost hear Mamm's voice chiming in. Mamm had taught her how music could make the most boring chore pass quickly, and they had spent many an hour in this very kitchen singing together.

"Because God made the stars to shine," the sisters sang together.

As she put the peaches on the table, Sadie's eyes combed the mouth-watering breakfast Mary had prepared for this second shift of the day, after the children under fifteen had eaten and headed out to school. Sausage and egg casserole. Biscuits. Peppers and peaches from the pantry.

Sadie felt a sudden swell of tenderness for the older sister who had stepped in to care for their household after Mamm had died. Mary took care of everyone in so many ways, always guided by a calm that kept peace in their home. But come wedding season, Mary would be starting a home with her beau, Five, on the Beilers' farm.

"Sadie?" The song had ended and Mary stood staring, oven mitts on her hands. "What's the matter?"

"Oh, Mary, what will we do without you around here?"

Mary patted her shoulder with the puffy mitt. "I'm not going far. And we know it's all part of the Heavenly Father's plan for me to leave this house. Remy's going to be moving in, and you're a mighty good cook yourself, when you don't get too lost in all your singing."

Lost in her singing . . . lately Sadie had spent so much time in her music, practicing with the band or singing in the barn. Funny, but it was far easier to imagine herself singing on a stage in front of people than cooking up an entire breakfast like this.

And that thought tugged at her conscience as she went to the porch to call the others for breakfast. Here on the farm, work was proper and good. Her faith gave meaning to every sunrise, every blooming violet. And the close bond of family showed her that she belonged here.

Not singing to strangers in the big city.

ROSALIND LAUER grew up in a large family in Maryland and began visiting Lancaster County's Amish community as a child. She attended Wagner College in New York City and worked as an editor for Simon & Schuster and Harlequin Books. She currently lives with her family in Oregon, where she writes in the shade of towering two-hundred-year-old Douglas fir trees.